*Marcella Polain weighs the spoken and unspoken
understandings of a family across generations
against a vast human catastrophe, leaving the
reader with a full heart and a sense of the great
dimensions of suffering and love.*

Brenda Walker

The Edge of the World is a powerful, monumental
story of an Armenian family, spanning one hundred
years, five countries and several generations. A
family fragmented by genocide, exile and
emigration, but which, through extraordinary acts
of courage and compassion, is eventually brought
together again — albeit utterly changed.

A compelling, imaginative and beautifully written
story of a remarkable family.

*... an unforgettable, courageous and moving act of
poetic testimony, which will make an important
contribution to the rewriting of the historic truth of
the Armenian Genocide.*

Marion Campbell

*... a story that is both public and private, epic
and fugitive, concealed and contested, yet
continually renewed.*

Nicholas Jose

Marcella Polain was born in Singapore and immigrated to Perth when she was two years old with her Armenian mother and Irish father. She has a background in theatre and screen writing, and now lectures in the Writing program at Edith Cowan University. Her first poetry collection, *Dumbstruck* (Five Islands Press, 1996), won the Anne Elder Prize; her second, *Each Clear Night* (Five Islands Press, 2000), was short-listed for the West Australian Poetry Prize. She completed her PhD at the University of Western Australia in 2006 and *The Edge of the World*, based on her family's survival of the Armenian Genocide and developed from her thesis, is her first novel.

The Edge of the World

MARCELLA POLAIN

FREMANTLE PRESS

First published 2007 by
FREMANTLE PRESS

Fremantle Press Inc. trading as Fremantle Press
PO Box 158, North Fremantle, Western Australia, 6159
www.fremantlepress.com.au

Consultant Editor Susan Midalia.
Cover Designer Tracey Gibbs.
Cover photograph by Graca Victoria / Stutterstock, image 888249

 A catalogue record for this book is available from the National Library of Australia

ISBN 9781920731274 (paperback)
ISBN 9781760991555 (ebook)

Fremantle Press is supported by the Western Australian State Government through the Department of Cultural Industries, Tourism and Sport.

Fremantle Press respectfully acknowledges the Whadjuk people of the Noongar nation as the traditional owners and custodians of the land where we work in Walyalup.

In loving memory
of my mother,
Lucin Vartevarian Kirk Cromb

Author's note

The narrative in parts one and two is based on oral history received from my mother. The genocide survival narratives are based on stories my mother overheard her own mother tell, and which she then told my brothers and me. However, it has been necessary to both research and fictionalise a great deal in order to write this. The story of the unnamed, contemporary narrator, who is significant largely in part three, is a fictionalised autobiography.

Glossary

chettis — criminals
djinn — ghost
effendi — sir
hai — Armenians
hamam — bath-house
medjidia — cents
tonnir — heater

1

Everywhere I look and sleep

(Perth, present)

Much later, I dreamed I was on a beach with everyone I
love. But this was after everything happened, of course. It
was also after the girl with the yellow hair returned, even
though I thought that, once I had written this, I wouldn't
see her again. It was after the man made entirely of shadow
also returned, darting as usual from the corners of my eyes
into the next room and then the next. And it was after I first
heard the demon run up behind me, growling, as I left the
supermarket and the hair on my neck stood up and I gasped
and swung around, swung my bags of shopping wildly but
no-one was there. It was after my child grew up and I lay
awake, weeping because I already knew how grey Europe
was, like a very old timber door too heavy to open but
behind which you know all manner of things happen. It was
after the letters stopped coming from Elisabeth in France
and from my sister in Sydney. It was after my brother locked
the door of his office one morning and didn't answer the
telephone and eventually the police had to come and break
their way in. And it was after I phoned my sister that same
day and she said, *Well, things will never be quite the same*

now, will they, thanks to you. Idiot. As if somehow I was responsible.

And it was after we last saw one another and she told us our mother had been right all along with her stories and predictions about just what would happen to the world, and the price we'd pay for rolling our eyes. And about how nobody — *not a single country,* she would say, wagging her finger at us — did anything when the Turks held each member of our family by a handful of hair and pressed a sword to their throat, saying they could live if they converted. And, *I know what you think; you think you're so clever with your educations,* the three of us not looking at her, our lips pressed together, embarrassed by the blaze of her.

Burning has a particular smell, and it took me a long time to discover that other families have other smells. They might stink too, but they don't all stink like ours. I think my sister must have always understood these things better than I did. I think this because she was right about me. *Idiot,* she said. No-one but our mother had ever before called me that.

When the police broke in, he was sitting at his desk, his dark eyes round and looking at them. He didn't say a thing.

But it's logical. I too would kill the best Armenians first. The most intelligent and respected, the most courageous, the beautiful. And so, I am none of those things; I am an idiot and a liar. Because how can an idiot recognise truth?

And I am also a liar, of course, because I am Armenian. If all I say happened really did happen, wouldn't you already know? And who is likely to be in possession of the truth: the remains of a people, the bits and pieces left of them, who wander the earth, ablaze with visions of an apocalypse —

past and future — or Turkey's emissaries, respectable men in suits and ties, negotiating a way into the European Union?

I listened to my sister. She knows how to stand, to speak, how to be the centre of attention. It occurred to me that she, too, seems to be, if not ablaze, then smouldering. But I would never say that. She was born here and that is that. She's Australian, whatever it takes. In that way, she has kept her head down. When we have spoken, she has spoken only of the future, of the outline of a life: the names of the cities in which she'll some day live, the names of the children she'll some day have. I have always laughed because I know the future is a trick and I've told her. I never mean to make her weep. Sometimes things happen that you just can't control. This is why I listened but didn't look at her. Her voice was clear, and heavy with some kind of menace. She sounded like our mother.

I can tell you this because I've written the remainder. What I can't tell you is the point at which the story begins. The truth is I have to write this story in this way because there is no beginning. We just like to think there is, that we can hold everything neat and complete in our hands, examine it.

My sister would say if I did something useful with my hands instead of writing things I shouldn't, everything would be different. It's as if she believes that writing can actually make things happen. It isn't like that. The facts are the facts, whether we like them or not. And the fictions are awfully like facts. I would tell her writing is dreaming; it has never really raised the dead. But I would also tell her I think there are some things we're born with and they sit there and sit there, waiting for something, who knows what, and one day that thing arrives and the whole lot just unfolds itself and breathes, a concertina, an intricate fan. It unfolds itself like a creature and stretches, fills its lungs, raises its head and stares back at us with its shining eye.

Each evening, on the television, I find myself watching for blood. It appears: a child's painting, what we imagine blood to be. A woman carves her arm with glass, working as studiously as if she were preparing a menu or an installation. Another woman, in a quick half pirouette toward him and away from her bright sink, stabs her startled husband in his buttery chest. A man breaks open his wife's head with a hammer as she bathes. Her meagre blood sprays one inoffensive trail across his face as a child might from a water pistol.

And then, one evening, a German NATO soldier in Kosovo stammers something like *people were herded in this room, a policeman threw in grenade, finished them with machine gun … so much blood it ran down walls into basement.*

Today I am at my kitchen table, surrounded by a vase and papers and pens and washing. I am holding on to an open book, a book someone has given me. I am looking through the window, beyond the computer where one day I will write and into the almost-dark, at the newly turned earth at the base of the lemon tree and the white chrysanthemum my son laid there. I remember the first time I saw a basement. I am in Vancouver where, even in summer, the air is sharp with cold and the light shifts all day with the rush of clouds. In Vancouver I felt for the first time that I was on the edge of something, standing on its very edge as if land were just a platform after all and I was leaning out over that edge much too far northwest and into the teeth of something huge and inhospitable, feeling its teeth pricking my ears and nape. So, I could understand the need for basements: the central heating control unit, the stack of firewood; shelves lined with tinned and bottled food; the ham radio, a water tank. I am visiting the sister of a close family friend, and her husband, both elderly now, putting faces to their names that have circulated in conversations all my life. The skin of their faces and throats and hands is pale and, when they smile, their cheeks fold into deep soft lines. They are pleased I have come, insist I stay the night. She will enjoy the company, she says, because in the evening, she continues, he will excuse himself and disappear. He has people to talk to in Fiji, South Africa, Argentina, England, New Zealand, Poland. His disappearance is not to be taken personally, and am I quite sure that I understand?

I follow them as they slowly ascend the simple concrete steps to their door, their bodies folded, too, into gentle stoops. Later, she makes tea in an elegant pot and we sit by the large windows that overlook their garden, green and moist and soft with July light. And it is here she points out to me something I am having trouble seeing. *Have you ever noticed*, she says, *how the Negro has a prominent forehead?* I look at her. Behind her own head, wind blows her wet trees about and the slant of the sun catches drops of water on so many leaves that, for a moment, there is light enough for it to be as if jewels are falling. Did I nod? Or is it hers, that encouraging nod, the nod of someone grandmotherly, two

generations ahead, that triggers mine — me both unaccus-
tomed and disbelieving, respectfully nodding back? *Well you
see, then*, she says. *Like monkeys.*

Should I be afraid?

In the Christmas of 1959, my parents found a photographer whose paper and chemicals were so stable that the
colour shots he took remain as reliable as if we were still
standing there, my mother Lucine and I. My child hair
springs from me like angry copper wire. My eyes look deep
into the lens, my gaze direct, if apprehensive. Behind, the
Christmas tree is large and furious with lights. I wear long
white socks and tiny blue, buckled shoes. I could not be
called a beautiful child but there is something intense,
something that flushes me now with a quick embarrassment. I stare into the parent's eye, down the long lens of
history, and spy something there, moving.

The hair on the back of the photographer's neck rises.
The shutter opens. Her cardigan is blue; the pleats in her
skirt are small white knives. *Keep very still,* somebody says.
And she does, knowing already the harshness of light, what
this might mean; knowing the flashes of things in the world
— fireworks, the sun on the water, anger, the edges of
blades.

For decades I see ghosts. They run and run around the
house; they stare in at windows, hold their limbs up to the
glass. They like a game. They know just how much to show,
for just how long, and how quick to run. They are not the
ghosts we meet in books — those elegant, serious figures.
They don't stand tall or turn slowly to meet one's gaze. They

are not sad. These ghosts like to hide; they are nimble and young.

They appear, of course, in unexpected places: in the street, walking away; on a passing bus; exiting a bank or cinema. I have learned the ways of ghosts — that they sunbake, drive cars, enjoy parties more than I do, and that they must have access to surveillance equipment. This can be the only explanation as to how they follow me from house to house, suburb to suburb, beach shack to wheatbelt farm, to interstate cities and other continents. They even follow me into dreams, where they smile and pull up a chair, or watch me pass by, leaning easily in open doorways. They say:

Girl, come closer. And I look up. There are men and women. They seem happy to see me. I slow my step; a smile staggers in my mouth.

Girl, what is it?

Nothing, I say.

What is it you want?

Nothing at all.

They turn to each other. Then a short, fat woman with a mild, round face and pale eyes cocks her head a little, like a dog might and, with a small smile, says: *What is it, grand-daughter, you want from me?*

I try to smile back; my face feels like a fence. *Nothing,* I say. *No thing, not one single thing. No stone, no tree, no blanket, no book. No word, no touch, no house, no song. No fire or light or star or dawn.*

She looks at me.

Turn away, I say. *Be a statue. Be stone. Turn your back, your shawl, your long thick hair, your skirts, your coins, your crucifix. Turn away your arms, your singing arms, your arms once full of bracelets and your bracelets full of song.*

But she looks at me.

Leave me. Leave me be. Be a stone. Be a tree. Be a stitch. Be still.

What does she think? That she can turn up now?

Don't look, I say. *Don't look at me. I will take up threads. I will stitch you up. My needle is sharp. My needle is intent. I'll use skin and hair. My wire hair, your plaited hair. I'll use your shawl, its fine black threads. I'll use your home, your voice, your dreams, your arms. My needle is immense, my needle is obliging. My needle offers no resistance or opinion. My dumb needle does my own bidding. Your eyes and lips like three dumb leaves. I'll sew them up, your own dumb song, the dumb leaves of your face.*

When I look again, she is gone. They are all gone. Hovsanna, grandmother, I've seen you always, everywhere I look and sleep. Now I am older and less afraid. I want only to touch your face. Come back to me.

Someone phoned me. He had heard about the story I was hoping to write and he had a book that might interest me. He had found it in his late father's shed. I drove to his home, an old, sprawling stone house by a river. Frogs and cicadas croaked and whirred in the thickly shaded lilies beneath the trees along the bank. He stepped out onto the wide, cool verandah, and handed it to me. I knew it at once: *The Treatment of the Armenians in the Ottoman Empire*. I had a library copy at home. I smiled and thanked him. *And don't worry,* he grinned, *I don't work for the Turkish secret police.* I looked down at the book, searching for something to say. I felt my mouth move, but no sound came. *Believe me, I've thought about that,* I heard myself say at last, not looking at him. Then we smiled and I thanked him again, and all the way home I could think of nothing else.

And here I am at the table. The book is open at page 70, to a letter written by a Mr Rushdouni about what happened in the city of Van in 1915. I don't even know where Van is but it is something someone has said that has stopped me, something Mr Rushdouni reports that a Mr Proudian's wife says: *Show me at least the bones of my dear one.*

Read me slowly, my paper skin is brown and folded. Open me here, and here. I am dry with years and dust. You are breathing me in. Look — I am all over you. Open yourself here. And here. Open your mouth, your hands, your arms, your eyes. Can you smell me? This is my undoing. I am unravelling my skin, my skin thin as paper. Hold me. I am coming apart. For you. Despite you. I am old between your fingers. What will become of me?

Hovsanna, grandmother, I have seen you always. And now my blood is hot beneath my skin. It takes my anger everywhere it goes, rushes ninety-seven times a minute, carries its cargo to the tips of my fingers, the edge of my ears, the beds of my nails. Cells open in my sleep, divide, divide and multiply. My nails become thick, white, curve. The speed of my blood, the speed of time. I am a sudden forest sprouting, my hairs curl black from my skin. I am evening morning evening, a flushed sky. I am bougainvillea, hibiscus. I am rampant lantana. I am wasp, ambulance, pillar-box red. I am blistered, sunburned, fevered, rashed. I am pandemic; I am volcanic, flood. I am all bridges swept away. I am the tumbling of houses; the floors all slip beneath our feet.

I am Earth split open, Mount Saint Helens, her bare southern face, that great grey scar. I am ash, Krakatoa, a darkness over land. I am a B29, its belly open. I am a plane falling. I am all blood slowing. I am breath and prayer, vapour, space. I am the suffocating chambers of the dead, the Jewelled Lady of Pompeii, fingers curled about her rings, throat packed with dust, mouth forever wide against the avalanche of time.

Slow me, grandmother, my heart, the hurtle of my blood. Give me this: a long cool night, new sheets, crushed ice against my lips; a wide bright bowl glazed blue, its twitching rim of yellow fish. Stand it by my bed, fill it brim full. Let me hear you tear an old white sheet. Fold that soft familiar cloth, let me hear you dip and squeeze it, the soprano trill of water falling. I will imagine fountains, lakes, the rowdy course of water over rocks and into streams, the thundering of rain onto mountains of trees. Let me feel it slide against me, against my skin, my feet slide in the mud as I descend, panting and driven, slipping through a forest like a throat.

Allow me this: beneath this ring of light from the soft bed lamp, meniscus taut and glistening like skin trembling as I shift my weight, this hot, this burning mass of me; that turning, my breath, my bloodied anger, the splitting off of all my cells, will make a mark upon the world, a trail.

And give me this: a day; a beach in the curve of a bay, a

steep cliff at my back; a small, cold stream; a wide blue bowl of fruit. Give me bluster and sun, the broad, gleaming, indifferent sea; time enough to feel my bones long and white against the sand, my quiet unrepentant heart, the patience of my belly.

I return to my Vancouver room. All night, I remember, I struggle to the surface of sleep and run my fingers over my calf to try to find what I know is growing there. In my dream I see it clearly. My leg is pale and undulating as a range of bare dunes and, in the deepening night, it is rising and opening. Each hour finds it more swollen, bulging, and the sore itself deeper and wider. All night my leg aches and finally, at dawn, floundering in the soup of sleep, I recall I once before had such an eruption there — sudden, unexpected — that welled for days and broke and that its breaking filled me with relief and disgust at what can come out of me and what I am able to endure. Its dark scar remains, knotted tight — a spent volcanic core wedged deep into my flesh.

At dawn, beneath the tips of my fingers, my body bewilders me. My leg is no crater or dune. It is smooth and closed, my simple flesh. But for half that day it aches.

If I tell you everything, things I believe and things I don't, if I take you to places that once existed and those that never did and if I make ghosts speak, what then? What will you say if I show you everything? You will say: look what she has done, that woman, look where she has opened, her dissection. She has laid out everything. Look where she lies, that woman, where she lies! Staked herself. Like a pig, like an old dead pig. Steaming and rotten as an old dead pig. Jesu Christos, what a stink, good for nothing, that woman, that pig, good for nothing but bait.

If I enter my own death, will you sit above me — up in that tree there with your gun? Once there were tigers in my country, sleek pale tigers that came down from the mountains every winter, their paws soft and quick in the snow.

The business of desire

(Cilicia, Ottoman Empire, 1890)

On cold nights, when Hovsanna was a girl and before her father disappeared, she and her brothers and sisters would draw closer to the heat of the tonnir and her parents would tell them stories by the flickering yellow light. The stories were of children they had known — or their own parents had known, or their parents in turn — who had ventured into the plains of Anatolia at night and been taken. Sometimes their screams could be heard for miles; other times it happened in silence and in the morning they simply were no longer there. Sometimes one of the children would ask why the dead child had gone out that night. *What does it matter?* Hovsanna's father would reply, waving his hand. *You just remember there are tigers out there, and they will eat you.*

Hovsanna would lie awake at night, listening to her sister's breath beside her. She would press her small body against her sister's even smaller one and shut her eyes tight, trying not to see the creatures come down from the high lands into her village of Hassan Beyli, their paws gentle on the stones and the damp wild grass, their bodies tunnelling through the low ferns, the arced fronds heavy with water, damp forest sweeping against their flanks the way she had seen her mother bathe a limb or a newborn's head, water scattering over and over like light. She would keep still and listen — for what? A growl or the creak of the door? She would say to herself, *I will listen all night. And when I hear it I will leap up and shout. And Papa will wake up. And we will all be safe. We will all be safe. And Papa will be proud of me.* But eventually, her body tired from its watch and warmed by her sister, she would slide into a fitful sleep.

How elemental, this water, this earth, this dark wet clay. The tiger's paws slip a little in the mud. If we could see its tracks, this big one, we would see how its footing is precarious, how it skims across the earth, how everything is finely balanced. How its weight and its intent, its momentum down the hillsides are laid bare. Its muscularity, its pace; those huge pads wider, much wider than the heel of a man's hand; those bowls of mud, those deep impressions into each of which — look — we can place two fists. And here and there, the evidence: the gouge, the track scraped long, suddenly rectangular, as if something unfamiliar has ploughed and bounced into the earth, looking for a place to land. But look ahead. What is unfamiliar about tiger? She disappears from sight, this big one, intimate with hunger, her huge head low and swinging as she steps, her steady loping gait, down the low forest paths that open for her as if stepping back before the cloud of her hot breath and then, as quickly, close behind her as if the hunger that drives her down towards the villages and the sea lives not in her but in the forest and the plains and she, herself, is slipping down its throat.

What is unfamiliar about hunger? Some years later, in the town of Alexandretta, the newborn's head is wet from birth. The blue umbilicus curls back into its mother. The room is full of candles. The mother, Hovsanna, is naked. She is fifteen years old. She is on her hands and knees. She is rocking a little, back and forth; she is rocking and saying *aaaahh*. At the foot of the low bed the grandmother kneels, her husband's mother, balancing her grandchild on a square of linen. She stares into its face. At the side of the bed two other women — aunts, perhaps — drape a blanket across the young mother's back, tip her over onto her side. Then, lifting one foot each, they roll her onto her back. One of them holds up a cup of water to the mother's lips. She is dry, and she drinks. The other tugs the mother's nipple between two fingers and rolls it deftly into a small dark stone. With her other hand she strokes lightly down the breast from throat to its now glistening tip, over and over. The body of the mother, newly made, stiffens. Breasts and belly harden. Between her daughter-in-law's knees, the grandmother makes a crucifix over the pink body of the baby, wraps it closely in its soft linen cloth and lays it across the flexing belly of its mother. The baby turns and turns its open mouth to skin, and its grandmother, her fingers sliding easily inside her daughter-in-law, says, *Push, Hovsanna, push a little my love,* the hot placenta easing out into her hands.

Later she will study it. Now, she takes cloth and water and, kneeling at the foot of this, cleans her daughter-in-law's vulva, carefully works away the blood from the small twist of hair at its head, sluices it from her buttocks and thighs, presses a cool cloth against her clitoris, proud as an egg, swollen as a stone.

Ah, Hovsanna, my grandmother. What is unfamiliar about hunger? Your baby attaches to your breast with a miraculous and frightening strength. You have known such tenacity. You have known what it is to be desired like this, a mouth at work. And who is this baby — Lucia, your first, who would die alone and exhausted, on a roadside, in her own act of giving birth? Your children fall from you in fruitful abundance, or unseemly haste. But what can be expected of such a desirable woman? Who can blame him? He is a lucky man, my grandfather. Ten years your senior, maybe more, already widowed and twice heired, a professional man, successful business man, very tall. Handsome? I imagine so. All the children he planted in you were beautiful. And you — graced by God. That yellow hair, white skin, grey eyes. From where did these come? Such rare things (as you) bring your parents every possibility.

We could say this is 1898 and that, a year earlier, a sister of your father's friend had been told by her cousin's friend's mother, whose husband was skilled in these matters, that Benyamin Vartevarian, having grieved for an appropriate time, and having two young children to think of, was again in the market for a wife.

If architecture is the business of desire, then Benyamin's eye is well trained. He understands line, space, balance, is schooled in scale and economy. And these judgements are no small thing. He knows about possibilities, how wood or stone can be combined, the differences between qualities.

This is a man accustomed to the touch of marble and of parchment. This is a man of imagination who, scanning the view from his window on the journey from Alexandretta to Hassan Beyli, sees not colour but shape. In him he feels stirring not the realisation that the word 'green', when applied to these hillsides, is so broad a term as to be rendered meaningless, but rather a particular excitement at the challenge its elevation could offer a man of vision.

* * *

Architecture, what is that? Hovsanna Kalidjian hears her mother speak quietly across the table to Mrs Arlenian. *Always rush to build, build, build, make plans. This one, that one.*

It is a profession, well paid. The Vartevarian family is known throughout Cilicia. His parents' sorrow in having only one child is your good fortune. No brothers and sisters to split his inheritance. Now he has good business. Mrs Arlenian's fingers are quick at the zucchinis, the point of her knife locates their centre lines, some hidden seam, and eases its way along each length. The glossy fruits fall open, stark beneath her wide brown hands.

Good business, yes, good business. Mrs Kalidjian waves her spoon. *Life is not always just good business.* She holds a zucchini half in her left hand and jabs at its centre with the spoon. Hovsanna, fourteen years old and a woman, watches it disgorge soft white seeds, strips of spongy white flesh.

The time is right, she is grown. And … it is a good offer. You may not have a better one.

Huh! I think that's your daughter you are thinking of, not mine. Just look at them, compare. Her mother flicks the contents of the spoon into a wide shallow bowl. *Are you mad?*

The house of Mrs Arlenian is often noisy with children. Today, it being early afternoon, most of the children at home are girls. In the mornings, Hovsanna and her sisters see Mrs Arlenian's sons when, from next door, they call in to collect Hovsanna's brothers on their way to the local Orthodox school. They are loud and rough together, laughing and running in the street, shoving at each other. Hovsanna sees them over and over, disappearing up the cobbled street in which she lives, going somewhere far away and mysterious, and where — in the way of mysteries — Hovsanna has come to believe lies a key. But a key to what? She overhears her brothers' occasional discussions in the afternoons. She listens carefully, remembers everything, turns their language over and over late at night, reading it as if lifting letter after letter from beneath her pillow — letters that would tell stories if only she could read them.

Today, in this early afternoon, Hovsanna and one of Mrs Arlenian's older daughters, a stout and serious girl named Araxy, wash zucchinis for their mothers in a vast metal tub set at the far end of the kitchen's long wooden table. Hovsanna tries not to listen to their mothers talking. Her face burns hot enough to wish it under water. She and Araxy rub at the films of red clay, rub them into the thin orange water, plunge them under and under until the water is wild with swirls and the clean fruits bob and knock against each other like glossy green boats at the mercy of wind and sea. Then, as if from the other side of the world, Hovsanna sees Araxy lift her face. And she, too, straightens a little. And she sees, as if across lakes and skies and continents, Araxy's small, dark eyes dance and her face split the horizon with a smile like the sun across earth after rain. Then later, lifting the tub between them, they carry it out into the garden. There, in the sun, another sister looks up, her baby brother on her left hip. She hooks her right thumb into the waistband of her skirt. And she sees how Araxy and this strange, pale visitor, this silent, yellow-haired Kalidjian girl from next door, carry the water slowly, their shoulders drawn up, their slim arms stretched. She sees their small, stiff steps and sees that they speak only to synchronise movement and angle, to hurry or slow one another, intent only on arriving at the long furrows between tomatoes and beans, on their burden and its welcome release. She doesn't hear their whispered conversation, her sister say, *Will you become Mrs Vartevarian or Mrs Vartig-var-ian? Mrs Vartig, Vartig, Vartig-var? Because that's what you have to do when you get married, you know, Mrs Pantsdown, Pantsdown, Mrs Pullyourpantsdown.* And she doesn't hear Hovsanna's trembling reply: *Shut up, jealous. No offers yet? Maybe that's because you know too much.*

Much later, Hovsanna's father turns to his wife in their bed. Over her shoulder, the night through their window shivers a little under too many stars.

It is better she is married soon. It is safer. He speaks softly, close to her ear. *Much safer.*

Things have been quiet for a while, haven't they, she whispers, *thanks be to God.*

Thanks be to Him, but it's not God we need to be wary of. He kisses her hair. *You smile at Ali and —*

She draws back and looks at him. *I know, I know, he shits on your carpet, but do you think there will be trouble soon?* He sighs and lies back on the bed. *Soon, not soon, how would I know?*

But what do you think?

Why do you keep bothering me, wife? What do you think?

Hovsanna's mother turns her face to the window and gazes out. *I think … we will be safe. And then I think it will never stop because they hate us so much.*

No, they don't. Our neighbours don't hate us, our Turkish friends don't hate us.

Huh! she replies. *Do you think the Armenians in Sassun didn't have Turkish neighbours, Turkish friends? How many thousands were killed there? Children, too, and women, old people.*

Yes, may God keep their souls, but that was four years ago. And there have been talks since. You know this.

Talks? Yes, I know talks. Armenians talk all the time. Does anyone listen?

Are you listening to me, wife? Hovsanna will marry this man, Vartevarian, because that is my decision.

Yes, I know, she says quietly and, for a long time, she gazes hard into that night of so many stars, but sees nothing move.

Listening to her husband's heavy sleeping breath, she thinks: I am under siege. At night, asleep beside my sleeping husband, I am as close to alone as any of us can be. In my dream tonight as in all my dreams, I enter a room. The first time I entered this room I thought I would meet a staircase, conventionally designed, steep but regular, with a railing to steady my hand and wide steps my feet would grasp. I expected to understand. Instead, here I am again, gazing up into a joke. Who designed this? It twists away from itself and vanishes into … what? The room is full of cordial voices. People have gone before me: I waited in the queue behind them and now I see them disappear above me, their legs climbing strongly. People are waiting politely behind me. I pull at the structure, testing it. It is sturdy. It does not budge; it will take my weight. Indeed, it is already holding a number of people. I have no choice. I have to go. But I don't know where to put my feet, my hands. I am not an ape. I am not strong enough for this. This is like climbing a mountain; this is someone's idea of a challenge. This is not what I came here for. My child is behind me. I am blocking his way. I must show him how to do it. No-one else appears afraid. I know my son will follow me. That's what children do. If I step aside, he will step aside too. Where is everyone going? The structure is like an enormous puzzle, strong timbers nailed and bound together crazily. It is a crazy, leaning, vanishing tower. Near the top, the tower is suddenly made of metal — huge cogs, anvils, hubs, anchors welded together, their surfaces slick and treacherous from use. They offer me nothing to hold; I am clinging for my life. My son is at my heel. Someone is smiling, someone who has gone ahead of me and who waits on a white mezzanine. I know that everyone who comes to this must leap. I know, now, there is no going back. I know this is the only way to our destination.

*　*　*

Do you believe me when I tell you that once, in this region — in all the lands west of the Caspian Sea — were one hundred thousand tigers? An estimate, yes, but what does it matter now if there were a few more or less, or even if they were there at all, when for decades they have vanished?

Tigers are tigers; everyone knows what they are. And tiger will tear us apart and leave. And, then, when we are soft, she will return and, piece by piece, devour us. Will she swallow even our bones? Or will she, full and satisfied, leave them to be cracked by dogs, picked clean by birds, buried by wind and sand?

This place, which I cannot name — because I am a liar, because there never was a tiger the colour of snow and desert sand, because, after all, this story never happened — is in the regions of the Caucasus and Anatolia, between the Sea of Marmara and the Caspian Sea and is, in its vast east and on its western fringe, deep green and wet, dotted with lakes and rivers, and cradled north-east by the long arm of the Caucasus Mountains. The Syrian and Iraqi deserts lie south and, to their east, forested peaks slow to the long dry hills of northern Iran.

I have never been there. At least, not in my waking life. But for days I have been thinking about nothing but tigers. And, in that time, I have been dreaming about litters. In my dreams the babies, blind and hairless — fearless, too, or stupid in the half-formed way of beasts — have been crawling to their deaths, dropping from the platform upon which they were born. And, standing at their precipice, I have been trying to block their way, holding up my arms against them, yelling. Yelling for them to go back, yelling for someone to help. But there are so many of them. So many, and my arms are so small that they slip through, fall past me, and I hear the thud, thud, thud of them.

In this time, too, we have buried our cat, sleek and long as a young panther, beneath the lemon tree where my son has placed the white chrysanthemum. Are we sure he is dead? How can we know this when his throat is still warm? But night is falling, and where would we keep him until morning? So we lay him, supple and warm, in the hole. It is the middle of May and, since Mothers' Day, we have drained the large glass vase of its foggy water and refilled it several times, the way I've seen my mother do. This is how we keep things alive as long as we can. The chrysanthemums with their bitter smell, their stringy stalks, their odd, fluffy heads. Beneath my fingers I can feel the fraying edges of the cover of that book. My palms are damp; beneath them I feel the kiss of the open pages like lips. I am holding on tight to its stiff, warped cover. Beyond the window, dusk is falling.

In Perth, where I live, on the edge of the world, winter is approaching. But in November 1897 in this other place, this place of tigers and snow and stories and sand, at the approach of winter on the western slopes of the Anatolian plains, the villagers closed their summer houses and drove their goats down into the valleys. In the town of Hassan

Beyli, families simply moved deeper indoors, burned their fires brighter, piled up their wood, laid down more carpets for their feet. But it was in another town, Alexandretta, roughly one hundred miles south-west, where the Mediterranean Sea became the calm blue Gulf of Iskanderoun, that Benyamin, sitting in his office, had first contemplated the journey to Hassan Beyli.

The problem, Benyamin thought, is one of light. He stared at the thick white paper, the few new lines he had drawn. They told him nothing, offered no solution. How to open the space, to fill it with light? How to marry interior to exterior world?

Do you remember Sancta Sofia? he asked himself.

Of course, replied his partner, without looking up.

Had he spoken aloud? He glanced over at his friend. Nerses Yarjanian was messy. There was discarded paper on his desk and Benyamin could see from across the room how his fingers were already smudged by the leads. A good architect, true. But Benyamin didn't like mess.

What of it? Nerses asked, catching Benyamin's eye. Benyamin looked down at his lines.

I was just thinking about the way it floats.

The dome.

Yes.

Is that what you want?

Yes. No. Something like it.

Hmm, said Nerses. *I didn't realise we were being paid to build a house for God.*

Hah. Benyamin tried to smile. *Don't worry. When God*

comes to our door, I'll send Him to you.

Benyamin drew the lead across the paper in an arc. And then another, until they filled the top left section of the parchment. That was the sense he wanted, he thought, a building that hung in the air like cloud. Impossible. He pushed his chair back. It scraped loudly on the tiled floor. He crossed the room and leaned against the frame of the window, looking out. Between the building and the street, a modest courtyard garden, neat, orderly. Here and there, in small dedicated spaces between paving stones, tiny plants grew although, so close to winter, they were fewer now, the last of them stubborn in the geometric shapes of sun. What are they, he wondered. His wife would have known. Herbs of some kind, he ventured. Against the vast wash of dusky pink stones, their bright green leaves, their occasional white or yellow head were like sprays of strangely coloured inks. In the courtyard's centre, a small fountain made of the same pinkish stone. The sunlight caught the water in it, made its edges thick and silver. Even from here, if he closed his eyes and listened past the rustle and scratch of his partner's fingers, Benyamin could hear the endless sound of it, running.

So, he said, without turning. *Do you think it's a good idea? What? The maid?*

Yes.

Nerses had hoped they wouldn't have to talk about this again. *The man is in love with a memory. What could he possibly say to him?* He leaned back in his chair and sighed. The timber creaked. He looked at Benyamin, the length and bulk of him leaning heavily on one leg, that hip braced and the other knee bent and pulled slightly towards him, as a horse might stand dozing in the sun. His head was tipped back against the window's frame, chin raised, throat exposed, eyes closed. He could be asleep.

Will it stop you spending your days at the window? He thought he heard Benyamin snort in reply.

It's a long journey, Benyamin said.

Yes, but the best fruit, my friend, said Nerses, smiling, *is always at the top of the tree.*

As you know, I've already had the best fruit.

Nerses looked down, studied his hands, and thought. He cleared his throat.

Of course, may she rest in peace. But we are men and men become hungry. He heard a sharpness in his voice that he hoped Benyamin didn't hear. He steadied himself. *It's the way of God,* he said, gently.

Nerses glanced up. Benyamin didn't reply; he didn't move. The light from the courtyard dissolved the edges of him. Nerses looked down again at his hands. He saw they were smudged and he thought he should wash.

Later, clean in his bed, lying close beside his wife, Nerses gasps. His eyes fly open. Close by, the goat screams and screams. The tiger closes its jaws. The goat's throat is breached. It cannot breathe. Goat froths saliva and blood into tiger's mouth, hears tiger pant. It watches the fog of tiger breath drift in clouds across the stars. His wife stirs. From somewhere in his house, he hears one of his children cry.

Benyamin Vartevarian is not a superstitious man. Five years in Paris has taken care of that. He is a man of reason. His French is competent enough — being most at home with diagrams, he enjoys the challenge of its script, its intoxicating turns of alphabet, its peculiar demands of syntax. But, most of all, he has taken from Paris its permission. He has said this, once or twice perhaps, to close friends: *In Paris, I was given permission.*

If they had wondered what he meant by this they never asked him, for he would have said it with such conviction, the strength of which (they may have thought) only one who has been to Paris can have. If they had asked him, if they had laughed at him and asked him to explain himself, he could not have done so. For he was certain that in Armenian he could find no easy equivalent. That being Armenian meant a different kind of living, where permission was something narrowly and carefully sought and received. And that, even if he had tried, he could never have made them see it.

And so, on his journey to the house of the Kalidjians, on the road from Alexandretta to Hassan Beyli, he gazes from his carriage window. And it occurs to him that, while it is always difficult to be Armenian, it was perhaps more so when one has been elsewhere — when one has sat in rooms lined with books on every wall, floor to ceiling, every leather spine raised with the evocative letters of French — and when one has been the only Armenian there. When one's professor has peered over his spectacles and asked quietly, *Benyamin, why don't you stay in France? Why go back? Can you be certain of your safety, your freedom?* When one has been some place where, in the evening, one has walked the public thoroughfare with a cluster of friends, male and female, making jokes. Or stood alone with a woman, in the dark beneath trees, and exchanged stories and kisses. If he had tried to tell them, they would have wanted to know all about the woman and the kisses, and even more than that. And he would have found himself telling things that had happened and things that hadn't happened. And, afterwards, after they had all returned home, after they had all kissed their mothers goodnight and climbed into their beds, some beside their wives, others — like Benyamin — alone, he would have turned his face into his pillow and wept.

No, it is better, he thinks, on the road to Hassan Beyli, the feet of the green hillsides everywhere about him ragged with rain, it is better not to try. Sometimes it is better not to speak everything.

There are men in Paris with whom he still communicates, writing back and forth, practising their language, reading aloud their replies, pushing the language forward in his mouth. No women, of course (there are certain things impossible even to an Armenian man, travelled or not) but some fellow-students, that one favourite professor. These missives, always carefully inscribed on thick parchment, found at once the long spaces between Benyamin's first and second fingers — left hand and right. In these same spaces he would run the edge of a favourite coat or the length of a woman's loosened hair. And in that way, with that parchment held firmly there, he would raise it to his nose, where, in the long inspiration that followed he could be, for a moment, elsewhere, transported into someone else's language, their laughter, their mouth.

It was to one such correspondent that Benyamin wrote as he sat in that carriage to Hassan Beyli, remembering Paris.

Mon cher ami, Philippe,

I trust this will find you well. It was most pleasing to receive your welcome letter, which I have taken with me on the journey I am currently undertaking to the family of a young woman of marriageable age.

The journey is tedious, and I hope that God will make the meeting worth the endurance and that, at its conclusion, the company is better than the expedition. If her family and I are in agreement, it may all take place quite soon. Being without a wife is awkward — the business, the children. They miss their mother, of course.

This is a good family, recommended by my uncle (who will meet me there) and I have heard she is unusually pretty — blond, I believe, which is always a welcome distraction, my friend, don't you agree? It is especially so here, I can assure you. And grey-eyed too, it seems, although I find that difficult to believe. Even in Paris I don't recall seeing that.

Matrimonial business is done at length and so I expect to be here for some days before returning to Alexandretta. The countryside here is quite different from that of the coast, with many more of the smaller type of village and low hills populated by herds of goats and their keepers, the small and scowling among my countrymen with their even smaller, blank-faced boys — although not as bad or as numerous as the provinces further east. As I have told you in the past, those are people of whom I am not fond, people with whom

I simply have nothing in common. I make no apology for it; we speak the same language, that is all, although I know this remains difficult for you to understand. The land itself is attractive enough, in a rugged and uncivilised manner. It occurs to me just how much could be done here in the way of improvement, of making beautiful, and this of course interests me. However, I cannot imagine there being either the money or the enthusiasm in these districts for such things.

I shall write again with news of the completed negotiations. Please send my best to your family.

* * *

Benyamin is brought to a halt at last in Hassan Beyli's civic square. It is of modest scale, and calm at this time. The last light of evening glows on the church stones, slants across this open space in the day's final orange moments. Benyamin steps into this and, as he does so, several men move towards him across the square. And from the rear of the church strides Father Sarian, with his smiling face and his hands outstretched. Someone's son is sent to inform the Kalidjians and Benyamin's uncle. Someone else takes Benyamin's baggage from his hands, and he is taken up by the small and beaming crowd to the door of Father Sarian's sitting room, where he is given the comfortable chair by the window beside which is placed a covered tray of sweet cakes and coffee. From here, Benyamin can watch night fall while, in the doorways of this house, children's faces appear. One child climbs upon her father's knee, curls in among his black robes. And others, older boys, step forward with a bow of their heads, to be introduced, saying, *Mr Vartevarian, it is an honour and a pleasure to meet you.*

Mon cher Philippe,

How to begin to tell you of that which has occurred? It is as if I have moved into another world, as if the journey east (a simple enough thing, God knows) has given me so much to ponder that I fear I will never be the same. Yes, I do fear, for — it seems — life has altered unexpectedly and irrevocably. Allow me to impart these events, for I very much crave your response. If, as I expect, you tell me I am a fool, I will believe you and will heed any advice.

My arrival here, in the evening of last Tuesday, seemed to be happily anticipated. So many strangers met me as I disembarked that, at first, I was disconcerted. But I tell you they were exceedingly civil and the local priest, Mr Sarian, and his family very welcoming. I was glad of the chair by the window in their house and of the coffee to put to my trembling lips, for the sight of this honourable man cradling his small child and of his sons, one after the other, coming forward to greet me with such respect, and his smiling wife and daughters bringing more cups when my uncle and his friend arrived — this was, in one moment, all too much, and my heart was greatly moved. So much was the conversation that I was able to turn my gaze at this moment to the window, to stare out as though suddenly deeply interested in the darkening town. One would think I may have had enough of views from windows (as, indeed, was so) but, if such thoughts passed through the minds of those present, they gave no indication, and so I was permitted the moment to recover. I saw, in that room, that which I had foreseen for myself, that which all men foresee, and that which I feared forever lost. I confess, Philippe, I cannot recall the last time I cradled my child on my knees, and this knowledge struck me like a fist.

After an appropriate time, during which I refreshed myself, my uncle Bedros Danielian and his friend Ashot and I, having thanked Mr and Mrs Sarian for their kindness, strolled the short distance to Bedros's home. It was quite a beautiful night, still and clear, quite early, yet already our breaths fogged the air as we walked. It was invigorating to be out but, as we neared, I felt a sudden nervousness. Not, as you may think, because of any threat. Things are quiet here; in Cilicia we seem, in the main, to be spared the frequent attacks that occur in the more outlying regions but, of course, one needs to be careful. No, we passed many houses, the light of their lamps shedding yellow into the streets, and I remembered the last time I had taken such a walk. That time I was full of eager anticipation, but this night I saw nothing other than my dead wife's face in every lamp and every shadow, and it suddenly occurred to me that this girl would not have that face. I can hear you, my friend. How very foolish, you say, and of course you are right. How can such a thing not have been obvious? Am I a stupid man? Bear with me, Philippe, for I must ask you: if I marry this girl will I always wish her to be someone else?

It was in such a state that I arrived at the house of Mr Kalidjian. After such an unexpected evening as I had already experienced, I felt I could not possibly know what would next come to pass. Dear Bedros, Ashot and I were most cordially greeted. Mr Kalidjian is a successful merchant, and a man who looks successful: not as tall as I am, but of considerable build, very broad across the shoulder. In other circumstances he could be quite imposing — intimidating, perhaps. Also in our company were his brother and cousin, and these two gentlemen were so much like him that, at certain turns of their heads, one suddenly felt one was intoxicated and seeing more than double. It may be, by the close of this letter, you come to believe, indeed, I was intoxicated, that I must have been in order for my ramblings to make sense, that they are not simply the confused, maudlin perspectives of a foolish drunkard. That it could be so! I wish, with all my heart, I had awakened so ill the following morning that I could not rely upon any recollection of sense or feeling.

When the six of us finally bade one another good night it was very late — well into the morning — and my uncle and I took our leave of Ashot at his gate and made our way home, mainly in silence. Late the next morning, over coffee, I asked Bedros what the girl was like and whether it was true that she has grey eyes. *Would you marry her if she didn't?* he asked. *I suppose I would*, I replied after some thought, *if you recommend it. Aaah, well*, he smiled, *would I have called you all this way? Yes*, I said, *for the pleasure of my company. You cheeky boy*, he laughed, *you drove your poor father crazy, God give him rest.* And then we were quiet for a while.

I must explain how things are done here, for this will be foreign to you, I imagine. It is not the Armenian way to hurry or to watch clocks. Doors are always open and people call upon one another without invitation, and often at length. When the sun rises, it is morning; when it is overhead it is the middle of the day; and when it sets it is evening. Surely, there is nothing more simple in the world than this. In every village, church bells indicate time, and time is given to us, yes, for the prosperity of man, but also for the worship of God. Today is a glorious gift to man from God, and tomorrow is another until God chooses. Do you understand my meaning?

So it was that, even later in that next morning, one of the Kalidjian boys arrived — a slender, smooth-skinned boy, very unlike his father in appearance, but seemingly possessed of a similarly jovial disposition, for he so beamed at us from the doorway that even Ashot (who, as far as I am able to tell, is not one to comment on or even notice these things) remarked on the happiness in that face. And, so invited, we made our way back to the Kalidjian home to partake of lunch. It was, I know, a promising sign, but it was difficult for me to be filled with anything other than an odd blending of curiosity and sorrow. My dear, astute uncle must have caught this time the mood on my face — or, perhaps, in my voice, or lack of it, for I spoke as little as needed on that short walk. All at once, he was no longer at my side, and I turned to see him stopped on the path, his hands on his hips, head cocked to one side, his dark eyes narrowed and fixed upon me. As I approached him, his lips stretched into a thin smile and he rested a hand on my shoulder as I came to a halt before him.

My dear nephew, he said, *remember we can turn back now. Your aunt will be preparing food for the children. Two more will be of no consequence. I could then make the short journey myself and simply explain you are unwell, indisposed. It is still a short time since your bereavement. It can all be done easily, most gracefully, and no-one will think any less of you, be assured of that.*

Oh, Philippe, I confess my eyes moistened for the kindness of this dear man. How lucky I am to have him! I was grateful for his words, but I knew them to be only partially true. Indeed, it is not so difficult for me — my home is far — but would be somewhat more so for him, at least for a while. There was a voice in me crying, *Yes, take me home, Uncle. I have made a mistake in this which I am too proud to admit.* Yet, I heard myself saying: *no, Uncle, let us continue. It is for the best. They expect us.* And, once we had started out again, side by side, I added, *It is also true, Uncle, that I have never seen a grey-eyed Armenian woman.* And the most peculiar thing, Philippe, was that I truly meant that which I had said — all of it.

I imagine you are wondering where this is leading, this revelation of my intimate and irrational workings. Momentarily, I feel an embarrassment before you. Shall I even send these confessions? What must you think of me, moving into such negotiations with so fragile a conviction? Remember, my friend, the world I inhabit is not the same world I shared with you. Here, the heart is saved for other things. A man loves his mountains, the snow and rain, his country's dusty tracks, its summer gardens full of fruits and herbs, his God and his church, his parents, his home and sons. This is plenty, is it not? How much can a man's heart hold? Sometimes he grows to love his wife. There are many ways to love. Must a bull love his cows for his herd to prosper? Think on this, and not too harshly of us.

My uncle and I sat with Mr Kalidjian for some time, discussing our concerns about business and politics and Mr Kalidjian recounted to me the most recent events in the eastern districts, some of which had filtered west with visitors from the region, but many of which I had not before heard. Numerous, small-scale events of the type to which we have all become accustomed; stories, one after the other, of the taking away of distinguished men, family men, who never return. Apparently, one witness, returning from the town of Ourfa, still tells of hearing such a man scream from within the police cells for a whole day and night, and a police band setting up outside the walls early the following morning and playing for three days more until he became silent. I know not what to make of these tales, Philippe. As you know, trouble has long been our companion. But, in remote areas such as these there is a lack of civilised company and intellectual stimulation, and a tendency, perhaps, to embroider the truth. I did not share these thoughts with my hosts, of course. They are decent enough men. I only silently thanked God I would soon be delivered home.

During our discussions, Mrs Kalidjian — whom I recognised from our meeting of the previous day — entered the room, carrying a covered tray and accompanied by a girl I had not seen before. I knew at once, of course, who she was, for not only were her wisps of hair around her headkerchief uncommonly fair, but her father looked upon me with such meaning that my conversation faltered. Mrs Kalidjian laid the tray beside me and then, with slow, practised movements, her daughter came forward and, without once looking up at me, poured our coffee. I did not look upon her directly, of course. I watched the cups — which were at first beneath and then held by her hands — so that always on the edge of my sight lay her face, her intent mouth, her lowered eyes. I waited for one moment's glance, for one moment's curiosity, but she handed each of us our coffee and left us without — as far as I was able to see — a moment's tremor and without raising her eyes nor looking even once into the face of her father.

Your daughter is a most modest girl, nodded Bedros. *You have raised her well.* Mr Kalidjian smiled. *Indeed*, I agreed. *Is it likely, sir, I may have the chance to meet her again?* I blush to recall my boldness, Philippe. Mr Kalidjian's head tilted slightly to one side, as a dog's head might when it hears something odd, and he said, *Possibly*. And then, *Why do you ask? Are you not sure?* I cleared my throat. *Your daughter's modesty is as well known, sir, as is, indeed, her beauty. Across our country word has come to me of her, of her good family, her fair hair, her unusual eyes. In my travels I have seen many European women with eyes of various shades, and occasionally an Armenian or Turkish woman with greenish, or even blue eyes, as I'm sure you must have done, for you, too, sir, are a man of the world, I believe. But, until this day, God has not granted me the honour of seeing an Armenian woman with eyes the colour of which some say He has given your daughter. I should very much like to see such eyes, sir.*

I think I may have held my breath, such was the silence that hung about us when I stilled my idiotic tongue. Both men seemed rigid, and I felt my colour rising and a slight trembling in my chest, as if my heart could not believe what it was I had just done or set in motion. Then Mr Kalidjian leaned back a little in his chair, one hand still tight around its arm, and the other meditatively tugging his moustache. Beyond him, my uncle remained motionless, his round eyes fixed on me. *Am I to understand that the very modesty which you say draws you to my house is the same modesty of which you now complain?* I saw my uncle's mouth begin to open, and I said — rather too quickly I fear, for I could hear my voice strange and somewhat breathless — *Sir, forgive me if I have caused you or your family unintended offence. I am a father, too, of a daughter and a son, and although my children are still babies, I understand the feelings of a father for a daughter, and the value to a father of that daughter's reputation. A daughter's life without it is worthless, God knows. You are rightly proud and protective of it. And I, sir, am still a young man with much yet to learn and, perhaps, too much curiosity.*

What possessed me? What devil was in me, Philippe? Was I, in fact, acting in some hope of failure? I heard Bedros's loud intake of breath and saw him lean back in his chair. *Yes,* he said, still looking sternly at me. *My nephew may be a father and a successful man, but still in so many ways he is a boy.*

You may think that, at such a delicate juncture, Bedros's words would seem to me to be only that which they were intended to be, and nothing more. But, indeed, I am the boy my uncle said I am, for what passed through me was as much the flame of indignation as the recognition of salvation. My heart burned to be so belittled at my age and in my position, and by someone so uneducated and unworldly. I wanted to leap to my feet! Despite my love for and appreciation of him, it was all I could do to stop myself from turning upon him, from snarling like some wild beast. How far are men from beasts, yet how close, Philippe! How far am I from these men, both of whom I respect, but momentarily despised?

I felt certain that my feelings must have been plain upon my face which, at that point, was still lowered and — I hoped — unmoving, in deference to Mr Kalidjian, awaiting his response. So it was, I imagine, that this gentleman was unable to see the evidence of those feelings in my eyes and upon my mouth, and that was why he said, after a significant pause, *Youth may be forgiven. That we were all fortunate enough to suffer its affliction.* Thus, he loudly called in Hovsanna, so that when she stood obediently before me, her cheeks flushed crimson, and raised her eyes to my face as her father commanded, I felt quite ill with shame.

It is done, my friend. I am again to marry. My children will again have a mother, and I will have more sons — if God in His grace chooses, for she is very slight. As she turned from me to leave the room, Philippe, her waist appeared no wider than the space around which I can place my hands.

* * *

I imagine it this way: when my grandmother, Hovsanna, raises her hand to her face, it is only to shade her eyes from the brightness of the sun. It is close to the middle of the day, and everywhere there are people. Perhaps it is that she has never seen such industry, or that she is unsteady from the journey, or that, stepping out from the carriage into the day, she is, simply, momentarily blind.

There to meet her, or rather to meet her father, are two of her betrothed's older first cousins. They are seated directly opposite the station, across the square, in the shade of a tobacconist's awning. On the small, circular table are two glasses, two cups, a long-handled pewter coffee pot, a jug of fragrant rosewater. One of them, the one on the left as Hovsanna and her father face the square, is perhaps the only person who sees Hovsanna step down onto the earth, hesitate a moment and raise her hand to her face. In her other hand she clutches a brightly coloured woven bag. About her head and shoulders, the fine silk embroidery along the edge of her shawl flashes as she shifts her head in the sun.

Across the square, men and donkeys drag their carts, boxes and sacks of goods. Other men stroll, chatting animatedly, with wives and children in tow and, everywhere, traders open their shop fronts into the immense light. Their crates and buckets of fruit and flowers spill out onto the paving stones. Their bolts of cloth and baskets of tightly skeined wool, racks of carved wooden pipes, tins of tobacco, bottles of oil. This is what they may have seen, Hovsanna and the older first cousin, as they peer in one another's direction — although it is unlikely Hovsanna notices this man, notices anything in that moment beyond voices and movement and light.

And what did these first cousins think? What comment

passed between them as they approached? Did they take the opportunity to gaze at the girl before they drew close enough to be seen? Indeed, did they notice her at all?

* * *

Dear Mr and Mrs Kalidjian,

I write on behalf of your daughter, my wife, to reassure you that she is well and settled into married life.

My own family has been most kind, and made her very welcome. My own children, now also hers, have been very sweet. The little girl likes to help my mother and wife to cook, and it gives them pleasure to see her happy. The boy likes nothing better than accompanying me to my office, which he is sometimes able to do, and where he draws at length with chalks while I see to my clients and plans.

My wife seems to enjoy the bustle of this town. Merchants sell goods brought in by boat from areas as far as Italy and Spain. As I have seen these places, I am sometimes able to tell my wife about them.

Perhaps, at some time in the future, you might wish to undertake a visit. If it were possible to do so, you would be most welcome. Please do not worry about your daughter. She has proved to be a sensible woman and is much too busy to be unhappy.

Hovsanna moves closer to her husband's shoulder. She watches the careful dip of nib in ink, its moment of stillness over the well, its half-turn and roll against the well's edge. She sees the particular incline of his head and the flexing of his intricate wrist and she gazes with old longing at this miraculous sixth digit from which flows the precise magic of rows and rows of language. From behind his shoulder, her sight runs across its long rhythms, as it would run over hills, seeking familiar landmarks and coming to rest upon a clue.

Who is it that you're writing to? My father?

Mmm.

What are you telling him?

That you are happy. I have invited them to visit. Now please, move away. I cannot write while you are standing there.

Outside, the evening is long and cool. Hovsanna mends her husband's trousers, working the pale, torn threads together, her oiled needle slipping back and forth under the intensity of her gaze. Beside her, Benyamin's mother sits, her wooden needles click, click clicking, the skein of rusty coloured wool appearing from the dark folds of her lap.

Do you think they will come, your parents?

God willing.

Will it not be too long a journey?

They are both well.

And their other children?

Well, too. I think.

Are there many yet unmarried?

Yes.

It must be difficult then, for your mother to get away.

Yes.

It is always difficult for a woman to get away.

Yes.

Perhaps your father or brother might come.

Yes.

In those first weeks, so many things were strange to Hovsanna that, although people were polite and welcoming, she felt as if — when she had finally slept in the dark night before her wedding — she had not yet woken, and that everything that had occurred since bore the edge of dream. Each day convinced her even further, for each day she caught, at least once, in the timbre of a voice or a bell, in the angle or colour of light, in the shape of a stone or in a stranger's glance, something so heightened that the glance or stone or bell could not simply be itself.

It was as if she had done what she had always imagined, what she had heard, or overheard rather, in conversations between men and schoolboys, and entered a book, a world full of meanings she could feel and see but could not read. And each night, when she lay still beside him and allowed the day's final event — and its most strange — she wondered if tomorrow, when she woke, she would at last be back in her father's house, in her wide white room, with her little sisters asleep on either side and the smell of coffee and the baby's squeals winding up the stairs to her.

It was on one such occasion, while her husband was again lifting her nightdress, that Hovsanna began to wonder if other people would ever stop looking at her. They were respectful enough, never gazing for too long and often averting their eyes as soon as she noticed them. But it was the frequency that was beginning to trouble her. Was there something wrong with her? Did they know something she did not? What was it they were trying to tell her? Were they watching to see if she would realise she was still sleeping?

Or, she suddenly thought, was it that she carried with her all day long that which was happening now? That, despite her careful washing and dressing, she carried a scent or a sign upon her that betrayed her?

She knew by now what her duty was, and by now, too, she was accustomed to it, even if she had been silly at first. It had been — well, a surprise. But he was right — she had learned quickly. It seemed to her there was nothing much to it. It was clear enough: they each had their role and, quite plainly, she had the simpler. Surely any fool could manage it. It was, at those times when they retired, only her husband's enthusiasm she struggled to understand, his urgency and humourless concentration. And, she gathered, something like pleasure — although she wasn't sure about that, for sometimes in those last few energetic moments when he cried out, it was almost a cry of someone lost or afraid. And he was often so exhausted then that he lay weak and trembling and struggling for breath, like someone in shock, and she felt concerned for him, listening, as she must, to his heart banging within the broad chest pressed against her ear. Eventually, he would raise himself from her, as he did now and, resting on his side or on one elbow, kiss and stroke her hair. Later, when he sleeps, she will get up and wash herself and rebraid her hair before creeping back to bed. But now she looked up at him looking down at her, and smiled at him, not knowing what to say. *You are a beautiful woman,* he murmured, and kissed her lightly on the forehead before he turned away to sleep.

Once, with her head tucked under his arm as it must be on these occasions, he being so much taller than she, and her face turned away slightly, she could see both the rising moon and the rise and fall of his flank, palely illuminated. And it was at this time that she began to laugh. Or perhaps it is truer to say that this was when she felt the first stirrings of something she was afraid could be laughter. Somehow she knew this, that whatever it was for him was no laughing matter, and she certainly didn't want to laugh. But laughter is a most contrary beast, not easily discouraged and given to revealing itself at the worst possible moments. So, the more sternly she tried to banish it, the more determinedly it grew in her so that, when she reached out, as she sometimes did, to hold onto the bedclothes while he finished what he was doing, throwing his head back and crying out again as if to God, she felt her body begin to shake. And there was nothing she could do about it.

It took him a few moments but, all at once, he was off her and looking worriedly into her face and saying, between pants, *What is it?* and *What's the matter?* And Hovsanna, her hand pressed to her mouth, was nodding. *Are you sick?* he said. *What's wrong? Shall I bring my mother?* And she, shaking her head, turns away from him, pulls the bedclothes over her head, opens her mouth and laughs out loud, louder than she can ever remember laughing. She laughs and laughs until she hurts, and then clutches her belly, gasping, *Ow, ow,* between the subsiding spasms of her laughter.

Benyamin is all the while just as he was when he last spoke — on his knees beside her, his white nightshirt twisted about his hips. When Hovsanna, her back still to him, is finally quiet and his involuntary smile has slipped away, he waits as if transfixed for her to turn back to him, to explain. But she is looking at the moon. If it has changed at all in those minutes, she thinks, it is perhaps just a little brighter, a little higher.

So it was, for some days, that Benyamin lay as still beside his wife as she lay with him until, at last, his mother, sitting beside Hovsanna on the roof garden in the evening, told her that in the absence of Hovsanna's own mother, Hovsanna should consider her husband's mother as her own.

If there is anything difficult in your married life, any questions you may have, perhaps I could help you. We are both women, after all.

Hovsanna nodded.

And my son seems … not himself these last days. A husband, especially a new one, needs his wife, you understand.

Hovsanna glanced up momentarily from her needlework. Her husband's mother's needles clicked steadily, the concentration on her face undisturbed.

I, too, she said, *was once a new wife.*

Hovsanna nodded again, her eyes intent on the thin brass needle, the evening cool on her cheeks.

But my husband, God give him rest, and I were both new. For you — well, it must be different for you. I have told my son he must be patient. He must remember his first marriage. Men have memories like cheesecloth and hearts like glass. Be kind to him. He will come back to you.

Hovsanna's needle carefully separated the weave in the hem of her husband's trousers, drawing together the required threads into one stitch and the next. She quietly cleared her throat.

Mrs Vartevarian, she said. *Why do they cry out?*

The older woman paused a moment, laid her needles side by side in her lap and picked up the skein from between her knees, unravelling another yard of wool with a long, slow arc of her arm. Then, clamping the skein in her skirts, she picked up her needles again, eventually saying, *Everyone receives something from this. It is pleasure to them and, through their pleasure, God gives children to us. And we all want children.*

Hovsanna guided her needle into the next stitch and then the next.

Yes, she said, at last. And then, *Must they cry out to have children?*

No. Sometimes they cry out, sometimes they don't. But they must have the pleasure. Women, too, can sometimes cry out.

Oh. Must women cry out before children can be made?

No. It is not essential. Some women cry out, others never do.

What makes women cry out?

Mrs Vartevarian stilled her hands and looked at the girl. Hovsanna's glance flickered up to the older woman's face and away again. Even in the now failing light, Mrs Vartevarian could see the sudden sweat and colour on her face as she gazed intently at her work.

Is there nothing … you enjoy … in it?

Staring resolutely into the torn threads, Hovsanna searched for the right answer.

If there is, you tell him, Mrs Vartevarian continued. *Otherwise it might take him a long time to realise it for himself. My son is a clever boy but he is also a man, and men, well … When I was new, I was frightened, and I cried, and my poor husband, who was also new, was at a loss.* She laughed. *Nothing he said or did could convince me. He spoke to his father. I spoke to my mother. It took weeks. My father became so angry. He was afraid they'd send me back. He spoke to the priest, oh dear … it seemed like everybody knew.*

But they didn't … send you back.

Oh, no. My husband was very good. For a while we … had an arrangement. He showed me how to … help him.

Help him?

Yes. There are different ways a man can have pleasure.

Oh? What ways?

Ways. And then one day there was a pitcher of wine in our room. The priest gave it to him, I think, although I never asked. And, well, then it wasn't so bad.

I've never had wine. Did it make you cry out?

Oh, no, laughed Mrs Vartevarian. *It was giving birth that did that.*

And Hovsanna laughed, too — although, if someone had asked her why, she could not have answered them.

* * *

It couldn't be said that Benyamin Vartevarian resented his wife's illiteracy. After all, he was a rational man and accustomed to the rigours of business. He understood many things, including value for money, and he could see the shrewdness in it. Men, himself included, worked hard for their money, and financial investments must be carefully made, must have some chance of bearing fruit. What point is there, he agreed, in watering an ornamental tree?

No, he did not resent it. If a man threatens his family's prosperity, what kind of man is he? Indeed, it occurred to him that the arrangement was both a convenient and sensible one. His mother and grandmothers and their mothers and grandmothers were trained well in any number of essential domestic pursuits. Without them, what would become of their husbands and children? No, he thought, not for me those other kinds of women. They were often pretty, yes, those Westerners, in their ghostly and exotic way, but their boldness had frightened him as often as their intellect aroused. What kind of wives would such studious women make? Can one eat and wear ideas?

But, because Benyamin was also an honest man, he knew, too, that while what he felt might not be resentment, there may sometimes have been a certain irritation, an unfair, yes, but nonetheless, inescapable disappointment. On the most happy of occasions — after a particularly successful business deal, or a wedding, or a convivial evening spent in the company of men — he would sometimes speak in a certain way about books he had once read, drawings he had once seen, or the architecture of a city he once walked through and with whom, and the colour of the light.

The first time he confided in her in this way was during the first year of their marriage. She was smiling at him and he thought how lovely she looked, her body full and rounded with child. They were sitting together in the garden and she was looking directly at him and smiling as if she were really happy and, although part of him knew this had something to do with his leaving her alone in bed, not wanting to hurt the child, he couldn't help thinking that maybe she also liked him more. And he realised, too, that despite the regular visits he made to a woman in town, a woman he had begun to visit after his first wife died and who, for a little more, would do things he wouldn't dream of asking of Hovsanna, he liked being there on the garden chair beside her. He took her hand.

Did I tell you, he said, *the first time I went to Vienna with Philippe, it was snowing? Vienna can be so cold, Hovsanna, everything freezes, everything is white. Philippe took me in his carriage to the home of a man called Charles Mackintosh. I had never heard of him. I was just glad to be out in Vienna. It's such a beautiful city, such a snowy city. I was relieved to be away from university and grey, rainy Paris, where it hardly ever snows, and pleased to be with my friend, the professor. I felt honoured, I suppose, that he would want to keep company with me — a man like him, so learned. I didn't tell him, though, that I'd never heard of this man, Mackintosh, but he probably guessed. I was afraid he already thought me uncouth. My French was not good, I knew nothing about Europe. Still, I suppose he thought me worth some effort. So we went. It was like a dream, Hovsanna. In this house, everything was light and beautiful. Beautiful in a way I'd never before seen. It was as if the brightness of the world outside had entered Mackintosh's mind and he had made the same world inside. It was so still in their house, so silent. But everywhere there was detail. Clean curves in form and ornament. White curved lines carved into gleaming white surfaces. Hovsanna,* and he turned to her, his voice dropping, *even the carpets were white.* He looked at Hovsanna and she looked back at him, her eyes quite round. *I have never seen anything else like it. And I have never felt such*

*arousal in my soul as I felt there — in my soul and in my body,
too. My heart pounded and I trembled when I looked on it. It
was as if I was in Heaven. It was as if... as if, may God forgive
me, I had entered something holy, yet something that gave me
such intense physical pleasure that I can only liken it to —* had
he heard her gasp? — *well, to what you give me.* He looked
at her. *Are you shocked?* Her face betrayed nothing. If a
sound had slipped from her, there was now no evidence. She
squeezed his hand and said, *Never mind, my love. Only a fool
would make a white carpet.*

* * *

Business had slowed, of course. The war meant money and
attention were diverted and — as always in war — while
there were new opportunities for profit, few were prepared
to invest in building. Benyamin wasn't too concerned:
everyone said it wasn't going to last long, whichever way it
went; he had reserves and he knew that, when it was over,
there would be a chance to make a lot of money, in Europe
at least, if not here. A war meant buildings need to be recon-
structed, facilities restored, whoever won. Germany and
France, like his own country, would be short of men and so
his skills would be in demand. He was pleased with himself
for keeping up his contacts in Paris and the thought of being
able to return at last to the cafes, the libraries, the buildings
of his university, made something move in his chest. When
Hovsanna spoke fearfully of the future he reassured her with
promises of profit and travel, but he could see by the way
she stared at him and then turned away that she was

unconvinced. So many children, taking them out of school and into a country where only he spoke the language? She didn't think so. He knew she was a sensible woman and that, when the time came, they would both reluctantly agree that it was much better for him to go to Paris alone.

At first, Benyamin would sometimes leave Nerses in the afternoon and take the longer route home so that he could spend a little time beside the sea. He didn't swim. He had tried one summer on a chilly French beach where he had holidayed briefly at the home of a friend and where he had, on his last night there and after a dinner at which everyone consumed too much wine, made his first quick, whispering love to the mistress of the house in his room after her light tapping on the door roused him from his almost-sleep, during which she had said things he had neither before nor since heard a woman say and he had said she was beautiful even though she was not. At that beach in those few days with his friend he eventually found he could splash about well enough in the sea but his arms and legs were long and difficult to control. As he walked the circuitous way home in the early days of the war, it was the scent of the ocean he enjoyed, the serenity of it in the bay, its shape pressing along the shore, the stony coast curving away and back for as far as he could imagine. One way west, that long stretch of the rolling Mediterranean against the dusty Anatolian plains and then north to face Greece and become the Aegean, dotted by so many islands, until it narrows at the Straits of the Dardanelles before opening again, like a bag cut from flat blue fabric, into the Sea of Marmara and Istanbul (or

Constantinople, as he heard it called in Paris, which confused him at first but the sound of which he soon grew to love, and which he, still now, sometimes spoke quietly, walking alone like this, feeling it roll about in his mouth). And, beyond that city, out through the Dardanelles again, along the rugged Greek coast and away, into Europe, into France and the beach where that first afternoon on his first French vacation he had waded, shivering, into the cold grey ocean and where he had watched his friend leap ahead and dive into the small dull waves that rose and fell suddenly, slapping his own head and shoulders until his ears rang. The other way — behind him, south — he imagined the sea rolled against the sandy beaches and rocky coves and the hulls of fishing boats all the way to Lebanon and Palestine before turning west again to begin its journey along North Africa. And here he was, walking home along the Mediterranean seafront of Alexandretta, his town, caught tight and close in the long arms of coast, pressed up against this blue blue sea, in the middle of the world.

He had always liked the busy port of it, the centuries of trade in tobacco and spices. And now, since this war and the Ottoman support of Germany, the seriousness, the efficiency, the smooth, grey-hulled German ships — fighting and supply — sliding by, day and night, in this shipping lane. Ahead and to his right, the pale grey rocks of cove and hills, just as they had always been, and the sun dropping slowly behind him, to his left. But, in recent weeks, the mood had changed, and he sometimes found himself turning away, taking the interior roads, passing German and Ottoman enlisted men and officers in their grey and green without raising his head, changing direction to avoid groups of them who, he had noticed, had begun to fall silent and stare with what he knew was hatred. He had seen it at other troubled times, just seven years ago and before — the curses, the spitting. People everywhere were nervous. He, too, had heard the rumours of invasion. Somewhere past that long Anatolian coast, somewhere in the Aegean Sea, between Smyrna and the Dardanelles, enemy warships were massing. What else could it mean?

Nerses had started to come into the office red-eyed and pale. *I can't sleep,* he had replied when Benyamin asked. *All night my wife is talking, crying, getting up, lying down. It's impossible. She has had an omen.*

Benyamin sighed. *An omen,* he growled. *You mean an idea someone put into her head. You know what women are like.*

Yes, I do. And I just need to sleep.

Benyamin tapped his pencil against the edge of his drawing table. Nerses stared at his parchment and listened to the steady rhythm, rolling his own pencil between his fingers. Eventually, he looked up.

Things aren't good, Benyamin.

I know. They want our identity documents.

I know.

The Germans are here, though.

Nerses nodded. *Yes, they are, and so are some Americans.*

Yes, diplomatic staff, teachers, missionaries.

Yes. If things get bad …

Benyamin placed his pencil carefully on his desk, adjusted it. *People will know.*

Yes.

You have heard what is happening in Zeitoun, the torture?

Yes, I've heard. They are using the bastinado on old men, prominent men.

Yes. And they're —

Nerses shook his head. *The Germans won't like that.*

No, they won't.

They won't allow it.

No, they won't.

They're Christians.

They're Christians, echoed Benyamin, *and they're Europeans.*

Nerses's chest rose and fell, rose and fell. From nearby — perhaps from the bakery on the corner where he often bought loaves warm and soft from the tonnir on his short walk home for lunch — came the sound of two dogs barking. He inhaled. *You have heard, I suppose, the rumours from Istanbul?*

Benyamin studied his desk, followed the grain of its timber, the mesmerising rise and fall of it. *Rumours?* He lifted his right hand and ran two trembling fingers along its edge, along the knot and swell of a dark line.

My cousin, he heard Nerses say, *has heard from the uncle of a friend that the British are waiting, out there, in the sea.* Nerses lifted his chin in the direction of the bay. *People say they're going to invade.*

Yes, I've heard.

Nerses frowned at his hands. *People say it would be better for us.*

People say a lot of things. Benyamin heard his tone, sharper than he intended. *But Nerses, you must never say them. Never,* he continued gently, trying to smile. *Really,* he said, looking at his friend. *We are Armenians, yes, but we are citizens of Turkey, too. It's a war and they* — and he pointed toward the sea — *are our enemy.* Across the room, across their desks, the two men stared at one another. *Please, Nerses; please, my friend,* Benyamin pleaded, *Armenians die for so much less.*

The middle of the day

(Ottoman Turkey, 1915)

When they came, they came in the middle of the day. Can you imagine this? The middle of the day. When they came I was tired, I had just sat at the table and my husband, Benyamin, said, *Never mind, Hovsanna, I will answer it.* Why would they come then; why would they be coming to do that then, when all decent men are at home for a meal with their families? These men who came, are they not decent men? Have they no families? Shame on them. I know who they are. I know their wives and children; I know their mothers and sisters. Why were they here and not with them? Not sitting at their own tables with their own wives, eating the food each wife had prepared for them? What makes them think they can act like this, taking a decent man from his family meal in the middle of an afternoon, an ordinary afternoon like any other, an ordinary meal, not even anything special — melon, salad, cheese, coffee. I was busy. The baby was irritable. And they come and take Benyamin as if he has no business sitting here. His own house. His father's house. And his before him. Shame on them. Shame. I know who they are.

When they came in the middle of the day I had had a bad morning. I was short with my husband when he came in to sit at the table. You know he had been home some days and, apart from one visit to the police station which I had begged him not to make, wept and begged him when he said he would the night before, *Please, if you care for me at all, if you love your children don't go, don't do this, don't walk into this trap, don't be a fool, for the love of God, please listen to me.* Apart from that visit he had done nothing, hardly spoken to me, hardly spoken to any of us. But when I said for the love of God, he shook his head. He shook his head at me and threw his hands in the air and said, *What am I to do? What am I to do? For God's sake, woman, tell me what you want me to do. Shall I leave him? Shall I? Shall I turn my back to him? Shall I go to Nerses' wife and say I am very sorry about your husband, I'm very sorry I couldn't help him, but my wife wouldn't let me? Or will you go to her? Will you, Hovsanna, explain? What will you say? Will you say I am so sorry you haven't your husband, but at least I have mine? He is my friend. My friend. My partner. My colleague. He is a good, hard-working man. And they have simply made a mistake. Shall I walk away? Shall I? Will you be happy, then? Will you be proud of me, then?*

Yes, I said, *yes, I'll be happy. I'll be happy you are here, with us. With us. If you go and they keep you, too, what will we do? What will become of us? Tell me.*

They won't keep me, he said, *why should they? If they want me, they know where I am, where I've been all this time. And what would they want me for?*

For nothing. Nothing. What do you think they want Nerses

for?

I don't know. I will find out. I think they have made a mistake.

You think? You think?

Yes, I think.

Please, don't go. It is madness and I am afraid, Benyamin.

I know. Everyone is afraid.

And then he went into the garden in the middle of the night and everyone else asleep, and dug up the small metal box and brought it to me and told me to sew the coins into our hems if he didn't return. It was after he had left the room, with me still sitting on our bed and weeping, not knowing what else I could say to make him stay, thinking there must be something I could do but not finding it, I had heard the sounds of the spade working outside in the night. I had gone to see, gone to the kitchen window and looked out from the dark of that room into the moonlight. There was enough moon, not too much, not full, but I could make him out quite clearly under the orange trees. I could see his spade lifting, I could see his shoulders and his arms. I watched and watched him; I remembered things. I remembered everything about him, everything I knew. Time is such a strange and stupid thing. It was as if I had only just married him, as if all these years had been a single day. And, at the same time, it was as if I had always known him, as if there had never been anything else. He looked strong in the moonlight; I could see his large hands. I could see his breath, white and full in the air. And then, after a long while, he fell to his knees and leaned deep into the hole he had dug, so that only his lower body was still on the earth and the rest of him had gone. And I felt sad, as if I had already watched him leave me. I went back to our room and I lay on our bed and I felt too sad even to pray.

He came in; I heard his steps reach the doorway, but I didn't turn at once. I waited, but he didn't come close. When I did turn, he was standing there, in the doorway, holding the box in his arms, and he was covered in earth. He looked so dark. His face was wet. His eyes were shining. He was looking at me. I wonder how I looked to him, if my eyes shone in the lamplight, too, if he could see on my face what I had thought, if he knew I had been watching him.

Apart from that night he had said little. Apart from that visit to the police station he had gone nowhere. And he had left us even though I had wept and begged him, even though he had hardly slept, just lying there, and time being pulled again, so the night takes forever, hours seeming to go by in what is really only minutes. When he left I didn't touch him, I didn't turn to see him, I didn't say anything to him. He stood behind me and kissed the top of my head. I thought if I let go of the mortar and pestle I might fall down, so I just kept squashing the tomatoes, squashing them, squashing them. I didn't even cry. My mother-in-law was wiping her eyes and blowing her nose with her handkerchief. *Oh, Jesu Christos*, she said, *Oh, Jesu Christos.*

Later that day, when he came home, I thought he was a ghost. I thought God had sent me a sign, a vision to tell me he was dead, had sent him back to tell me what to do, ordering me now to sew the coins into our hems and flee. When he smiled and spoke I opened my mouth but no sound came out and, when I touched him, it was like touching something you couldn't believe, something impossible. And then they came, days later, in the middle of a meal, him sitting in his chair as he always did, as if they had nowhere else they should be.

He stood up from the table when they entered the room. They had guns — in my house, at my table, with all my children sitting — and me just frozen, a spoon in my hand and stiff with dread. They asked him his name. Asked him his name! *Are you Benyamin Vartevarian?* one said, the one standing behind the one who has lived near us all his life, whose mother and father know us, who himself knows us as well as we know him, who has passed time with my husband, who has greeted me by name a hundred times. *Are you Benyamin Vartevarian?* the furthest one asked, and the other one looking as if his eyes had never before seen my husband's face.

He stood up from the table and said nothing, but he nodded a little, looking straight back at this man. He did not say, *Of course I am* or anything like that, any of the things you think you might say. He just looked straight at him, and then at me as the man said, *You must come with me.* He didn't ask anything, not why or where or for how long. He didn't ask them to sit and eat. He said nothing. He was like a dumb man, a stupid man, as if he was not a man with three languages and a university education, as if he had no tongue at all. He looked at me, his eyes round, round. Round like two plates or a pair of coins. Round as if I knew what round meant. I knew nothing. I said, *Please, we are eating, sit with us, allow us to finish. I have prepared salad and coffee, there is bread still warm, and fresh cheese. Eat, Ahmed, you and your friend. Let us talk a while. How is your mother?*

It was as if nobody heard me. The children were weeping, my husband's mother was crying out, *He was there, he was there; he went to you and you sent him home.*

They were gesturing with their guns as they spoke. There was too much noise. Nobody heard me. He just looked at me with round, round eyes and I nodded and said, *Never mind, I will keep a plate for you, your meal will be here for you when you return.* But he just turned away as if I hadn't spoken. It was as if I had said nothing; it was as if my mouth were a stone, as if his heart were stone, as if we were all just nothing but stones.

There was noise, too much noise — the men with the guns were saying something, chair legs were being scraped over the tiles, people were moving from the table, the children crying. He was walking so slowly towards them. If I hurry I can reach them first. I say to the man who did not speak, a young man, he has a wife and child, a young baby, a boy. I say to him, *Ahmed, you know my husband, you know us. What are you doing, taking him? You have a mother, you have a son. What are you doing? Why are you taking him?*

No-one says anything; no-one answers me. Did I speak? Did I dream? Did it happen at all? Did I stand there still, still as a piece of wood, still as my heart?

He had wrapped white goat's cheese and salad in bread. It lay on his plate half unrolled, one side of it flung open like the wing of a bird. Hovsanna gathered it up and pressed it together carefully, seam down against the bright glaze of the bowl. Alongside was a piece of melon, and in its glistening yellow flesh, she saw, were the clear marks of his teeth.

For a moment, she saw nothing else. When he was reading, his mouth was open a little, his face softer and his eyes quite round, like a baby's. When he wrote, she knew his lips came together so that one might think every letter was the beginning of a kiss. When he laughed, his mouth opened very wide and many times she had laughed, too, thinking he threw back his dark head and grinned a big grin like a horse. When he was angry, his lips almost disappeared from the effort of holding in words. When he slept, his lips swelled with his dreams. And when he had held this gold fruit in his hand, between his thumb, fore and middle finger, he must have left his prints on it. And when he bit, the taste of his mouth, from the inside of his lips, the taste she knew so well, would have been left behind.

She would keep the melon. She covered it with a dampened cloth. When he came home, he would wonder where it had gone. So, she put it safely in the cupboard. But she poured away the coffee from his cup and washed it. She would make more. Benyamin didn't like cold coffee.

All afternoon she waited, and all night too, rising from her chair and later from her bed to comfort children or feed the baby, or rocking slowly by the window, looking out into the dark, imagining — time after time — that some shadow is him appearing out of darkness. When she finally fell into a heavy sleep, she was too soon shaken awake, and saw (though she momentarily thought it was him returned, seeing — not for the first time — his eyes in his mother's) her mother-in-law beside her, holding the long handles of two spades, one in each hand.

When he comes home, she whispered, *he will expect us to have done as he said.* And so, the women took their spades and with Hovsanna leading the way, walked in silence, carefully and slowly, through the night garden to the base of the tree where Hovsanna had watched Benyamin at work and where the earth was still soft from his labours. And they set to work themselves to undo what he had done there and to set in motion the plan he had laid out for them.

The following morning, the boys didn't go to school.

It is better that they go, Benyamin's mother said. *If they stay, what will they do? And people will start to wonder.*

What will they wonder? What will they wonder that they don't already know? Do you think they didn't see him go with those gendarmes? Do you think a man can be taken and no-one know? If the boys go to school what will people think then? That their father can be taken and life can go on as if nothing has happened? No, they will stay. I want them all here. When he returns, I want them here, to see.

And if he doesn't?

Hovsanna shook her head a little as if shaking away sleep.

We mustn't put too many coins in the smaller girls' dresses. Six perhaps. Six is enough. They are heavy.

Hovsanna, how long will you keep them home?

Until he returns, of course.

And if he doesn't return?

Hovsanna's hands were clenched around the skirt she held.

Why do you keep saying that? she hissed. *You know God is just. You know God is merciful. I have kept food for him in the larder. I have kept his sons home from school to greet him. What more do you want?*

What do I want, Benyamin's mother thought. I want my own husband to come, smiling, through this door, to take me in his arms, laughing, and say, *Do not be concerned, my wife, do not be sad; all those years ago when I, too, was taken under guard, all those ten years were just a joke, a silly trick. See? We are returned, all of us. Me, your father, brothers, uncles, and your son. We are all home now. Oh, do not weep, my dearest wife. God changed His mind and sent us home. We did not mean to hurt you.*

And so it was that the day passed, and no-one came — not the priest, nor any of the neighbours. And all during that day the women and the older girls sewed gold coins into the hem of every skirt they owned, and the older boys, Krikor and Zaven, kept the younger children quiet by reading to them or by being horses and riding their masters around the rooms. And another night came, and another, and again Hovsanna slept in the rocking chair, with the baby, Arpy, all night at her breast, and her own bed full of children.

And so it was a week passed until Krikor, so tall like his father, and Maree, already seventeen and, Hovsanna prayed, soon a woman — for they looked forward to finding such a headstrong girl a kind and patient husband — stood in the doorway, hand in hand with their sisters, Lucia, nearly fifteen, and Anaheed, thirteen, the quiet, inseparable ones — *How could they be otherwise with such an older sister?* Benyamin had often said — and the others behind them:

nine year old Dickran and Dickranhoui, twins but as unlike one another as they could be — Dickranhoui loud, born first and bigger, which didn't seem right, seeing she was a girl, but that was God's will; twelve year old Zaven — such a quiet serious boy — with four year old Hovsep, the one who, as a baby, had crawled his way to the top of the stairs and then tumbled all the way down and never cried, and five year old Ara who still sucked her thumb; and Armenhoui, seven, who liked to mother the younger ones and was so much help to Hovsanna, struggling with a two year old Arusiak on her hip. It was Krikor, at nearly nineteen and the oldest boy, whose duty it was to say, *Mother, what are we going to do?*

To flee is a difficult thing — much more difficult when one has many children to comfort, hush or conceal — hungry, tired younger children or anxious, fearful older ones. For an entire day the two women had baked, cooling their sweet cakes away from their customary place on stout metal racks by the window. Instead, they lined them up in rows along the kitchen table where they took longer to cool and where their aroma lingered in the house rather than wafting into the street. Hovsanna did not wish their plan to be known. In the evening prior to that baking day, she had sat beside her son Krikor, and dictated him a letter.

Read it to me, she said, after watching his careful hand, as she had so often watched his father's.

Dearest Father, read Krikor —

Shouldn't it be grandfather? asked Maree.

No, it's from me. He's my father, replied Hovsanna. *Now, shoosh. Continue, Krikor.*

God willing within a few days of you receiving this letter, we will see each other again. Such events have occurred here that should not occur anywhere, but of the type we all know too well. This time, dear Father, it is my husband who is gone, taken away by the gendarmerie more than a week ago. Others, too, have been taken, many others from here, I believe, including — may God forgive them — our priest. We have waited but have heard nothing. All about here grow increasingly nervous. We have secured ourselves as he intended us to do, and soon we will arrive if it should please God, in a safer place, to be with you all.

Krikor will write a letter for his father and we will leave it here, where we now sit, so he will know where we have gone, when he returns. We will also leave the means by which he may join us. Do not fear, Father. All will be well. Pray for us.

Your faithful daughter.

And granddaughter! And granddaughter! cried Maree.

No, Maree, it's from me. You will see them all soon enough, and then you can show him how faithful you are by being quiet and by being good.

Humph, snorted Maree. *You didn't even tell him about the money,* and she spun around.

Hovsanna watched the hem of her dress swinging behind her daughter, swinging a little too slowly and a little too deeply, like time.

The day after baking day, their sweet cakes divided, wrapped carefully in paper and then in clothes, and these packages stacked neatly into trunks and bright bags among combs and handkerchiefs, Bibles and photographs, a clutch of goats' knuckles tied in an apron, each girl's favourite doll, each boy's school book, a small tin flute, and a polished wooden spinning top tucked inside a sock, the family washed and dressed themselves, and tidied the house.

Come away from the door, Maree, Hovsep. Close it.

But the garden, Mama, we could water it, Maree called over her shoulder. Through the doorway she could see strawberries and tomatoes, bright against the leaves, and the yellow trumpet flowers of zucchini. She could see weeds she had left, and a path she had neglected to sweep. *I've left my boots out there!*

Hovsanna shoved the door shut with the handle of her broom.

Shut the door, you silly girl. Do you want all the world to know you're there, shouting like a street urchin?

Who will care for it? And how can I garden without my boots?

God will care for it. He will make it rain; He will shine the sun.

And all the worms will eat the fruit, Dickran whispered up to her ear. *If the soldiers don't get it first.*

Of all the thoughts that passed through Hovsanna's mind that day, it was indeed, like Maree, the garden that bothered her most. She too had seen the reds and yellows. And, from other windows, the eggfruit, oranges, melons and figs; wanted so much to rush out, to fill her apron and tumble this food — brown and green, purple and smooth, rough and soft — into baskets, and send her children with those baskets to their neighbours saying, *We are going for a while. Please tend for us, and help yourselves until we return.* But she did not. Tomorrow, she knew, those neighbours will notice how still and quiet their house is, and some will worry and together they will come and knock and peer through these same windows. And, hearing nothing, they will open the door and wander from room to room. Some will look for bodies or blood or overturned furniture. Others will look for dust. They will see, at length, the letter upon the table. A man will pick it up and read it. Perhaps, she hoped, they might put it back. Or, perhaps, they might wave it about and shout, angry that, after so many years of living alongside one another, father to son and father to son, she could disappear in the night without a word. *What do you expect of her,* someone might say, *coming from the east?*

In those first days of their journey, Hovsanna's mind will turn often to this and later — much later — in Jerusalem, when she had a home but never again a garden. And, in those first days at least, she would say to herself, *When we are all home again, when everyone has recovered their senses, I will give my neighbours a party. And I will give them meat and cakes and we will be glad to see one another.*

In the evening of that day of preparation, Hovsanna took Krikor and slipped quietly across the back garden, down the lane and into the home of Mr Ursa and his kind wife — a *good Turkish friend, a gentleman and a man of position,* Benyamin had said — believing he might be the best person from whom to seek advice.

Mrs Ursa ushered them in. She took Hovsanna's hand. *I have heard, my dear,* she said. *I have heard. Things are bad. Have you received any news at all?*

Hovsanna shook her head. *No,* she whispered. *None. That is why I am here. I must speak with your husband.*

Mr Ursa bowed to Hovsanna and shook Krikor's hand. *We would have called on you, my friends, but … everything is so … difficult. Will you forgive us? I am so pleased you have come.*

My husband always speaks highly of you, effendi, that you are a man of honour, a decent man, a man upon whom one can rely.

Your husband — is my friend.

And so I must ask you to help us — as an honourable man … and my husband's friend.

Mr Ursa nodded. *I believe I understand. Where is it that you want to go?*

East. To my family. To Hassan Beyli.

Not further? Not Syria, or America?

Oh, how is it possible without papers?

Benyamin has no papers?

Of course not. More than two weeks ago, when they visited his office and took Nerses away, they demanded them. They demanded papers of all Armenians.

Mr Ursa rose and crossed to the window. Hovsanna watched his hand rise to pull back the curtain a little. *Even so,* he said.

How could he not? You, yourself, have said things are difficult. How much more so for us?

Mr Ursa closed the curtain carefully. *Of course,* he said,

of course.

I must go to my father and mother. It is where my husband will expect me to be.

And then?

Hovsanna gestured towards the street. *This is our home.*

Mmm, said Mr Ursa, turning again to face her. *How old is your son?*

Hovsanna looked at the floor.

I can arrange for him to be safe elsewhere, and it may be better, the way things are, she heard Mr Ursa say.

She raised her head and gazed at her husband's friend, the darkness around his eyes. She took a slow breath. *I need him. And I need you to help us. You must know Armenians are forbidden to travel. But I think it is the right thing to do. We will be safe there. I know it is what my husband wants, also. Until things quieten.*

Of course, said Mr Ursa, stepping towards her. *Go home. Tell no-one. Wait for me. But please, think about my offer.*

And so it was, perhaps, that in the middle of the night, Mr and Mrs Ursa came. And Hovsanna watched Mr Ursa give Krikor a small folded paper. *This is important. Should you need further assistance when you reach your destination.* And, with each adult carrying a sleeping child or a trunk or bags, the Vartevarians made their silent way across the town to a large waiting carriage, into which fretful children and baggage were stowed and around which curtains were drawn. At last, Hovsanna and Krikor helped her mother-in-law into the carriage and Hovsanna opened Krikor's hand, took the paper from it and kissed his damp palm. Then she closed Krikor's hand inside her own and placed his arm on Mr Ursa's arm. Her mouth quivered. She looked at the startled face of her son.

You are to go with Mr Ursa, she said quietly.

No, Mama, you need me. You said so.

No, I don't, Krikor. Mr Ursa is right. It's not safe. You are big and strong. It's better for everyone if you go ... a different way.

And then Hovsanna held him and her chest heaved, once, twice, and she turned away. Her mother-in-law leaned out of the carriage and kissed each side of Krikor's stricken face and the faces of Mr and Mrs Ursa. And, from the carriage step, Hovsanna placed in Mr Ursa's hand gold coins and closed his resisting fist around them. *Please,* she said. And she was gone, the night swallowing them all in moments, the sounds of bits and reins and hooves ringing in Krikor's ears as he walked, silent and weeping, a few steps behind Mr and Mrs Ursa, as they led him home.

* * *

Benyamin walked out of one country and into another. He walked out of his house, which he thought was in Turkey, without saying a word. His children were crying, his mother was crying, his wife was speaking. He could see she was speaking. To whom was she speaking? He walked out of his house and onto a cart. He travelled along the Turkish roads and into the Turkish town. On either side of him, the gendarmes were still and silent as two hills. Beyond them, everything was just as he remembered it.

This is the land of Peripeteia. This is the land Benyamin entered. *Ah, yes,* he thought. *I have seen this before.* For, at this time, Benyamin, at forty-two years of age, was old enough to have seen any number of things, to have been wise or lucky any number of times. Periodically, he knew, his country became something other than itself. *Aahk,* he would hear other men say, clicking their resignation in the backs of their throats, *we have always lived with such invaders. They have tried to get rid of us for thousands of years. Despite them all, we are still here. How many years have we had to deal with these Ottomans and their hatred of us — because we are conquered, because we are Christian, because we are successful, because our women are pretty, just because we remain? So, here it starts again, the pogroms. You can almost smell it, like a change of season or a storm. But storms and seasons pass and this one, too, will pass.* And he would nod his head with them. But that was before they had come for him, before he had travelled on a cart through such deserted streets. And now he saw its ingenuity, the thoroughness of its disguise.

He stepped from the cart and into the station, the same station he had entered only days before, where his heart had crashed inside his chest and he had spoken as evenly and politely as he could and where he had been coolly, yes, but also courteously received. The same station from which he had then been free to leave, just as he believed he would. And here he was again as if that time were just a dream. The same men were there, in their uniforms, at their desks. He looked closely at everything. He understood materials, he was intimate with angles and surfaces and densities.

Somewhere, he knew, would be the clue. He listened intently. He listened beyond the words to the tones and inflections of the voices. He listened, too, beyond the voices to the sounds of the footfalls on stone and earth, to the acoustics of the steps and the words against the walls. He listened to the creak of gendarmes' chairs as they raised and lowered themselves, the sighs of timber as they leaned on desks. He listened for discrepancy. Because, despite appearances, he knew this was not the same station. It could not be. This was not the same station because this was not the same country. This was not the country in which he was born, nor the one he had left and wept for and returned to and wept for again. In his other country there were no cells. In his true country — the one in which his ancestors had lived and died, made love and sang and argued and prayed for thousands of years — there were no men screaming, all night, all day, night, day, night. In his true country, he was not taken from his cell to the interrogation room and back, walking at first and then crawling and then carried, and gendarmes did not call him traitor and infidel and cur and son of a whore. They did not use pliers and hammers and demand he confess. They did not say, *You are our enemy; you are helping our enemy; you Armenians have always been the enemy. You grow rich on us; you think you're important; you are nothing; we will squash you.* In his true country he never felt such thirst or hunger. Never before had he been forced to drink his own waste. In his true country he had never pleaded first for his life and then for his death. And so, some time later — a month, perhaps, or was it three? — when he limped from the cell, limped out of the station and into the day, walked as best he could the soft green slope behind it and obediently knelt in the grass, he thought, *Yes, this still looks like my country but I know it is not.* And he saw the gun, and thought about that, too. *Thanks be to God,* he thought. *At last.* And he smiled a little and thought, *There must, after all, be a God,* because this is what he had prayed for each day since he left the true land of his birth: to be out, once again, in a field in the sun, and to leave this country, this land that looks like Turkey but is not, that looks like his homeland, the ancient Mesopotamia, this place the French had sometimes oddly referred to as Asia Minor and which had puzzled him, having never even considered Asia. And now he could leave it, this counterfeit country, and go back to his family and his true home. Any moment now, any moment, may it please God, his soul would fly, and he would be shown what it was he had known all along, but had sometimes been driven to doubt. Because they were good, these Turks. He had always known that. They were thorough and determined, and he had almost believed them. He had almost believed what they had said about him, that he was worth nothing more than this humiliation and then the next, and that he, like all his people, was finished. And then he had heard it.

One night, returning Benyamin to the cell he shared with a handful of other Armenians and two Greeks, a gendarme had paused as he locked the door. *This is a new Turkey,* he smiled, *everything is different now.* And Benyamin was struck with a sudden satisfaction. He knew then that he had been right all along, that somehow the land and the buildings had been changed, swapped for others that looked just the same.

It was a massive piece of work, an undertaking on a scale beyond his comprehension. And he realised that all the other times had been mere rehearsals for this. He shook his head. *Brilliant and masterful,* he thought. *Generations in the planning, ultimately swift in its execution.* And he thought of all the plans he, himself, had drawn, all the buildings he had made. And he saw them suddenly for what they were: primitive, naive, unambitious, empty.

How could he know that when he was finally permitted to leave Peripeteia, this counterfeit land, that there would be no other country but the one he had always stood upon? And that it would take him into itself in the most ordinary way, through a watery hole in a town that claimed to be a Turkish town, but was really a fake, a part of Peripeteia, a stage set, like the ones he had seen in Paris, all red velvet and suspended breath, like every other Turkish town?

* * *

They have walked over the rise. They are out of sight, as required. He kneels in the grass. He sees the gun. He thinks, *Thanks be to God. At last.* The man stands behind him.

My dearest Hovsanna,

If I could write to you, this is what I'd say: that you and the children are in my thoughts every hour of every night, that ten, twenty times a night I remember our plan and our last conversations. And that I urge you on — you, my mother, our sons and daughters, my aunts and cousins, sisters and nieces and nephews and friends, all. Urge you on, and on and away. If I could write I would say so much. I would tell you many things; I would say leave, leave this place, go. Run, quickly, quicker than that, run to wherever you can. But, I would also say, we must be careful. We must be discreet. If I could really write to you then someone else could read it. And then nothing, no-one would be safe. So, I will say this: remember. Remember and tell no-one else. Above all, trust no-one, for we no longer know who is our friend and who our enemy. Those who have lived alongside us, who have sat at our table, no longer know us. And yet the hearts of those we have never before met can be filled with such mercy and kindness for us. Do you suppose it has always been so? Or has something, this war perhaps, gone so wrong with the world and made it so? If I could write to you there are things I would tell you and things I would not. I would tell you I spend my days resting and sometimes sleeping a little and then always dreaming. Sometimes I dream of the things I would tell you. And sometimes I dream of the things I would not. Sometimes I can't remember which is which. These lists I have made become fused, confused. Events leap about, leap from one to the other. When that happens, I find it very difficult. Sometimes I weep. I am sorry, my dear. Do you think any less of me?

So much has happened, so much. How many months have passed, Hovsanna, how many lunar cycles, how many seasons of your body, your scent, the tenderness of you? Everything has changed. I watch the moon fill slowly, each night rising fatter, making the middle of the night like day for me so that I cannot travel at all at that time. So I move as quickly as I can early and then find a place to watch out the night. I see easily the outline of objects at some distance, so I know they must also see me. I watch the nights grow darker again, and so I move further, longer, and with a little less fear. I am coming to know the dark, and to know it differently from the way I have known anything else. It has become closer to me than life, much closer. It is closer than love, as close as death. But, it is not death; it is life to me. Now a month is a long time. And to think you carried each of our children for nine of them. I cannot imagine it. How is it possible that a person can come from nowhere. And, being delivered into the world, that they are unlike anyone who has gone before? How is it possible that our children are unlike us, you and me, from whose bodies they are made? A month is now a lifetime to me. How much more, then, is a year? If we weren't to see them for that time, for one year, or for ten, would we recognise them? And, if we did, would they know us? I am afraid. A year is beyond imagining. My body is thin; my face is bearded; my night is day, and day is night. Will you know me when I find you?

I still pray, and I pray you remember our plan, our secret, our secret place. And that you are all together and safe. And that God will guide me. And sometimes, just before sunrise, when the world is coldest and when rocks and grasses are coldest of all, and I am hungry, hungrier than I have ever been, and I lie down somewhere, in some hollow or shrub, it seems I am back in our kitchen, at our table as we were when all of this began. I know this is madness, but we are laughing and the room is bright, and you have kept food for me as you said you would. In the long days since, I have eaten it many times, and felt my coffee cup warm in my hands. I wish I did not know this is madness. If I did not know, perhaps I would be able to stay there, lie down in some hollow and open our door and be back home, in our kitchen, slice open an orange, its fine mist spraying up in the bright light. I can smell it, Hovsanna. Oh, wife. I can smell it. And I can smell you, the lemon scent of your hair when you return from the hamam, the sharp musk beneath your arms at the end of the day, the deeper musk between your legs, the milky scent of your breasts, the sweetness of our baby's skin faint on your hands, your wrists.

When I find you, we will make things as they were. We will forget. We will go home. We will sleep soundly, once more, side by side. No more this exhausted sleep, curled up like a dog. We will not dream, and will not sleep a waking sleep, where everything is like a dream and you can't tell wake from sleep and time after time, hour after hour, day after day, you drop off into a memory and wake again gasping or weeping. And then I lie still and my heart's pounding and I'm fearful that I've cried out and someone will discover me. Not a snake or a bird. Not an eagle like the one that hovered over me, just above me, just my height away from me, thinking I was dead already. But a child or a man or a woman. Yes, a woman out walking in her husband's field. She will call her husband or her son. And when they look at me and I look at them, I won't know whether they are my friend or murderer. Perhaps I will hold my breath and look at them through almost-closed eyes. Perhaps they will see how thin and motionless I am and they will think I am already dead. And perhaps they will walk away. If they speak to me, I will say nothing. I will pretend to be dead. How far away is death, anyway. Death is someone's decision. It can be as simple as a whim. I will keep silent. Some days, I no longer know if I can speak, or what words mean, or how to put them together. If I had some paper and ink, I could no more write this to you than step up to our front door, listen to the children's voices — little Arusiak singing, Krikor and Maree shouting as they play with the little ones, their handful of small white knuckle bones rattling again and again on the stone floor, and Dickran's voice calling 'Baba', the shuffling sound of his slippers as he runs gleefully toward me.

What is it for, paper and ink, paper and leads? There are so many other things to be done. Gardens to be tended, animals to milk and feed, horses to be shod, carpets to be woven, wells to be dug, coins to be minted, cooking pots shaped. Jewels to be set, and skins to dry. So many useful things. What use, in all this, are lines on paper? What use are words? You are lucky, Hovsanna. You cannot read. You are unburdened by its pointlessness, undistracted by its lies. No, I could no more write to you than fly.

There are many things, my wife, I've thought I couldn't do. I thought I couldn't bear the beatings. I thought I couldn't bear the cell. I thought I would die when my hands were broken. I thought I would die when my clothes were removed. I thought I would die from pain, humiliation. I disgusted myself. My body so undisciplined as if it, too, had turned on me. Sometimes I prayed to be allowed to die. I said things to them, things Armenians should never say, things men should never say. I have done things, too, that shame me and of which I cannot speak. At first I prayed, and then I didn't. But what else is there? I ate cockroaches. I drank my urine. I did what they told me. I told them lies. I did what they told me. I accepted everything.

* * *

The man stands behind him. They have walked over the crest of the rise and most of the way down its other slope — a shortish distance, but they are out of sight, as required. Perhaps it is afternoon; perhaps it is morning. Perhaps even night, but this is unlikely as prisoners may escape more easily at night. If a prisoner runs in daylight, he is much easier to shoot. Everyone knows that. At night he could be out of sight in a moment, ill and injured or not. In a moment, he could be crouched in a shadow somewhere, or be just the receding sound of running feet. It is extraordinary how men who could barely walk minutes before have suddenly found the strength to run. And then one has to shoot blindly in the direction of the running feet, making a lot of noise, using too many bullets. Put in the right place, one bullet should be enough. He'd been told that, often. If they weren't dead instantly, they soon would be. So, too many bullets is a public humiliation. If one shoots wildly or is away too long, stalking the crouched prisoner, everyone will know something went wrong. No-one wants to be questioned or put on a charge.

So, if we're ordered to take them out at night, and they run, I'd just leave them, most likely, his friend had said. *What's one more half-dead Armenian?*

But they don't, do they, he'd replied.

Not yet, his friend muttered, at last. *But if it happens, I'm ready. I won't be tricked.*

Don't boast, fool. They'll hear you.

The soldier stands behind him. They have walked over the crest of the rise. They have stopped near the bottom of the western slope. They are out of sight. Let us say it is afternoon. Let us say it is a Wednesday and that, out here, the soldier alone knows this. He had glanced up at the sky when he first left the station, so he also knows it is threatening rain. The prisoner, walking slowly in front of him, hadn't glanced up. He had stopped and closed his eyes against the light. The soldier had nudged him in the back with the muzzle of his gun. So he had begun to walk west, up the rise and down the slope, to a place out of sight. All the while, he had listened to the soldier's footsteps behind him. They were in step with his own, and then they weren't. Near the top of the rise, where it was steepest, he had stumbled and fallen on one knee and then onto his side. And his hands, which were broken and tied together behind him, had hit the earth as he fell, and he cried out. Let us say the soldier had slowed, stopped, waited for him to get up and walk on. *Get up*, said the soldier. And he did. And then, when they were close to the bottom of the hollow on the other side, that he had slid on the stones and fallen twice onto his hands. Then the soldier had said *Stop*. But Benyamin had hesitated and taken one more step, and then another, and then a slower one. And he had thought of just walking on, of not stopping, of walking towards the trees.

Would it be better that way?

Stop, the soldier had said, again. Benyamin had heard the rifle being cocked. He stopped. He thought, *Oh, Christos, at last. Is this what there is?*

So now the soldier stands behind him. *Kneel*, the soldier says. So he does. He hears the soldier step around to stand at his right side. He stares straight ahead. He doesn't want to see this soldier, this man just following orders, this man steeling himself. But he doesn't want to bow his head. He doesn't want to be a coward, he doesn't want to be. He stares ahead into the trees. He cannot help but see the soldier's boot and thigh, the fabric of his trousers. He sees the soldier's thigh is muscular and he hears the soldier's voice is young. He sees the shine of the gun. *Thanks be to God*, he thinks. *At last*. The soldier stands there a long time. Benyamin finds it hard to breathe. A bird flits back and forth between branches. And further on, beyond the screen of trees, ducks chase and call to one another, and waterbirds rise up. He sees their pale legs and their slow white wings as they ascend.

Oh, Jesu, he thinks. *Oh, Jesu, look at me. I have said all my prayers*, and he closes his eyes.

He hears the shot, deafening, and he reels from it. He falls to his left, and he lies there. And then he hears, *I don't want to kill you. Run.* And he opens his eyes and realises he feels nothing. And the soldier is standing over him, pushing at him with the warm end of his rifle. *Run*, he is saying. *Run*.

The city of stone

Deep in the heart of Peripeteia the sky is cut by a city's rooves. These rooves are stone; the city is stone. If there is magic in the world it must be here. For what is it that some call magic if it is not the workings of a greater mind? And what greater mind inhabits the world than the mind of God? If the mind of God is at work in the world, then it is here in the city of stone which, when it was built, Benyamin knew, was built by and belonged to his own ancestors, who lifted each stone from the belly of the earth, and which has not changed although all around may change. The city of stone is rooted in the earth in the centre of this country which still now, as I write, just as then when Benyamin wandered it, is called Turkey, but which remains — now as then — a masterful performance, an indefatigable disguise.

For a moment, Benyamin may well have believed he had entered into the mind of God, as people do when they enter a dream, knowing that the dream is so much bigger than they, that it acts in its ways beyond their understanding and yet in accordance with its own entire and perfect logic. How can people argue with a dream, let alone the mind of God?

Deep in the heart of Peripeteia the rooves are as symmetrical and beautiful as a hundred Turkish slippers curving away from the earth and up to God in the way that slippers do. Benyamin rubs his eyes. There have been nights when, awoken by something — a sound, perhaps, or a struggling to surface from some other terror — he has found himself stranded between two worlds, unsure of where his body is, the nightmare he sought to escape still in tow and real, real as air, as dark. And this is why he rubs his eyes, not understanding what he sees, believing that the lightening sky before him, all cut away by silhouettes of such extraordinary shape, has been brought with him from out of sleep. He rubs his eyes, but it remains. And so he enters it.

* * *

In the city of stone, which was the first city, there lived a man who was the oldest man in all the world. And, because he was the oldest man, he knew everything that had happened in the city of stone. He knew more about the families there than the family members themselves. He knew their births and deaths and their broken hearts. He knew their acts of compassion and betrayal. Accordingly, he was greatly respected.

This man — whose name, like the country, began with the letter P, but whose entire name has now been lost among all the events of the last hundred years which, as we know, was an intricate century — was the person to whom anyone in the city of stone would make their way if in need of advice. For, having experienced so much himself and having listened daily to the confidences of others and witnessed every event in the lives all around him, it was widely accepted that he had wisdom. For wisdom, as we still understand it, usually comes with age. And P was indeed very old. But, despite being very old, older than anyone else had ever been, he appeared as young as you and I.

Although the climate was arid and the terrain was rocky, P lived in the midst of a beautiful garden. Apart from each Sabbath, he passed all his days working the soil, as he had done for as long as any citizen could recall. His many visitors would bring him gifts, often fruit or grain, sometimes an animal freshly slaughtered. For all these gifts he was very grateful, but the most pleasing of gifts was animal manure. For, with just a handful from the stores of manure kept by each of the pilgrims for their own garden, he had built his plot into an oasis. Within his garden grew every kind of fruiting tree: almonds and apricots, oranges and grapefruits, persimmons and dates, lemons and hazelnuts, and green and purple figs. And between his trees grew clusters of other fruits: pumpkins and eggplants and several types of beans, watermelons and rockmelons and honeydew melons, blueberries and strawberries, pendulous tomatoes and other bushes dotted with tomatoes the size of sweets. No matter what the time of year, his garden produced. And all who came to ask advice departed with their basket or hands full of something to eat.

Sometimes there were days when so many people came that the old man was unable to tend his garden at all. He would look up to the sky and pray. *Oh, great and almighty God, how can I alone do all this work?* And sometimes these days came one upon the other so thickly that he wondered if he would ever be free to return to the soil. But, life being what it was in the city of stone, there being, as everywhere, times of calamity and times of calm, in the end all the necessary things were done. And so it was for years and years.

When Benyamin entered the city at dawn, the first man he met was not, of course, this remarkable man. Instead, he met a man leading a donkey. He held out his hand and said to the man, *Something to eat. I am hungry, please,* in the way in which he had become accustomed since he began his wandering across Peripeteia, with his head appropriately bowed, for no-one wishes to look into the face of a beggar. And the man shook his head: *I am sorry, but I have nothing. All I have comes from someone else.* And he walked on. Benyamin thought momentarily about this. He had heard many refusals, suffered many abuses, sometimes even a blow or two — but he understood that. They hit him when he had made himself small, when he was sitting or lying in a doorway or a field. When he stood he was still tall enough to make them think twice — unless the attacker was armed, even if with nothing more than a broom or staff for, properly wielded, these alone can strike down a man. Or unless there were many attackers, in which case size was, in the end, of little consequence, as everyone knew. Yes, he had received many responses. But never before one quite like that.

He looked around him. All about was yellow stone — the buildings' high walls and, everywhere he turned his head, their rooves like a hundred minarets. And, at his feet, the same stone in paths and streets. Already, it was warm in here, as if the stones retained the heat of the sun all night. He could feel it in his back, in the wall behind him. He closed his eyes. It was as if he had reached the centre of the world.

He pondered what he should do. Already he thought this a remarkable place. Perhaps it is here that I will find Hovsanna and the children. Perhaps someone will have heard their names, know where they are. When he opened his eyes it was because he heard the ring of horseshoes over stones, and there, before him, was a man leading a plump bay pony. And, astride the pony, was an equally plump boy.

The boy turned his face to Benyamin and smiled. *How can this be?* he thought. *What is it about children that they may sometimes do these things?* Everywhere he had been, citizens had avoided him. If they were kind, they were kind without meeting his eye. And he had quickly learned never to look at them, their wives or their children. This wasn't hard. Most children seemed to fear him, and he understood that. Tall, filthy, ragged, thin, with wild hair and beard — how could they not recoil from him? He knew about children — and, at this, tears stung his eyes. And all of this in the instant of the plump boy's smile. And then the boy moved past Benyamin. And it was then that Benyamin felt himself lurch forward a little and heard a small, involuntary cry spring from his chest. But the boy and the man, whom Benyamin presumed was the child's father, neither heard nor saw him. And so he watched them walking away, their two straight backs, their pony's easy step, and the strong sweep of its tail — so strong in the quiet of the waking city that he imagined he could hear it. *Shh, shh,* it said. *Shh, shh.*

But how could he be soothed? He had grown thin, he knew that. Thinner than he had ever been, than he'd been born, than a man should ever be. He felt like someone else, weak as a girl. He couldn't remember feeling as small as this, as insubstantial. He had been that plump boy, born too quickly and too soon his mother had said, and angry because of it, *How you would cry then*, she would say to him as he sobbed over some disappointment. *Do you remember, husband?* And his father would smile a little and shake his head. *Leave the boy. He makes a noise and you still put him to the breast. His anger is a gift from God. Without it, how would he have survived?*

Perhaps it was true he was an angry baby. And perhaps, yes, he had need to be. But he didn't remember anger. He remembered tall and strong — and sometimes happy, although he wasn't sure that children recognised happiness. He had seen this in his own children, as if being loved and without a care was the natural state of things. And he had seen, in himself, a part that recalled the bliss of this ignorance and that longed for it, and a part that resented it. He had been that plump boy, he had raised his own plump children, a dozen of them. It wasn't that he didn't know everything was vulnerable. How could he not? Generations of Armenians knew how life balanced on the edge of someone's blade, their holy scimitar. He knew. But he had hope, stupid hope. And now he was here with his body too thin to contain itself, with his stinging eyes as if everything he saw entered his heart directly, as if his skinny, filthy limbs that made him feel like someone else had become the very flesh of his heart, as if the world had turned him inside out the way a pauper may turn out pockets, and he was no longer a man but something unrecognisable and grotesque. The boy had smiled and the smile had entered painfully. He had started and cried out. He had been a fool. What if the boy's father had seen his reaction, had seen such a monster lurch towards his son? Someone soon, he knew, would kill him. It was simply a matter of time. And when it happened he believed he would be glad. If a breeze blew across his face his heart hurt more than he could bear. *At least it is warm here,* he thought, *if I am to die here of hunger or because I am not a man. It is warm. I thank God for that.*

When the plump boy's father led the pony through the gate, his son was still thinking about the sound he heard the beggar make. As the child dismounted, his father looped the reins over a knot, low on the trunk of a tree. The pony dropped its head to nibble the green shoots of wild grass all dappled with light. The boy walked behind his father, as was his custom. Sometimes his father would gesture for him to stand beside him and would drape his arm along his son's shoulders as they walked, in the way the boy had seen him do with other men. But today, as they approached the doors of the house, he watched his father's feet and the black wedge of shadow that appeared and disappeared beneath each of them as he strode.

He frowned. *I should have turned. Why didn't I? Perhaps he was trying to tell me something. Perhaps he is ill, or even dumb. Perhaps someone has already taken out his tongue. Who will help him? Perhaps he will die, and what then? What will happen to me then?* And so he resolved to tell his father and his father's friend, this strange old man he was sometimes expected to call on. When this expectation was visited upon him, it was also understood that it would be the pony rather than his own feet that would take him there, for nothing pleased the boy more than being on horseback. And he knew his father, too, was proud of the bay's gleaming coat and rounded rump. He could see it in his face, the way he stepped back and beamed at them, horse and boy, and could hear it in the slap of his father's hand against the pony's muscular neck. Yes, he would tell these men what had happened, that he had smiled at a beggar because — well, he didn't know why — and the beggar had only stared at him and that had made him feel ashamed, and then — you know how these things are — the beggar was behind him when he heard him make a noise like, like something he should have turned around to, but he didn't because of his shame and because the noise frightened him, too. But he couldn't stop thinking that he should have turned around, that the beggar might be dying on that road and he didn't turn around and he's sorry he didn't. He will tell them because he knows the city is full of beggars these days, his father says, Armenians, Greeks, Assyrians too, and what's to be done? They have nowhere to go and Allah insists we must always be merciful but they dirty the place, even the boy could see that.

When Benyamin saw the party again approach, he looked away. It could be the same pony, he thought, but there are so many bay ponies and he is no horseman to tell one from another at a glance. It could be the same boy but, at a distance, one plump child is like another, surely. It could be them but there were two men this time, one on each side of the beast and the unfamiliar one leaning on a stick, being either older or lame. Only a longer look would decide, and that was out of the question.

It was better, safer, to pretend nothing at all had happened, to make no further connection. He had no desire to be reminded of his foolishness. He listened, though; he listened as if his skin were ears. No matter if it were the same pony, its hoofs struck the stone and the sound leapt from that stone and struck him. He kept his head down. He knew what he was. He was hungry. He held out his hand.

Later, Benyamin will tell Hovsanna how odd it felt to be on that pony. And she would nod and smile a little, but not laugh. She never laughed, never, never, for the rest of her life. But she would smile as she listened to Benyamin's story of the pony because she knew he didn't like horses much and because she could imagine how his legs dangled and his toes dragged along the ground and how he gripped the pommel with both hands and how the leather of the saddle creaked so loudly he thought he was, indeed, no more than a skeleton because, with each of the dumb beast's steps, his hip was swung open in his pelvis — first the left then right, then the left then right.

No-one in the street seemed to notice him. It was still early, but as they wandered further, women poured water into gardens or swept the stones with stiff straw brooms. Children watched or played together, and men unshuttered their shops or sat in the sun. The scent of coffee was thick and delicious and, although people looked up and called out their greetings to the very old man, saying, *Good morning, Pasha, may Allah smile upon you,* and the very old man nodded to this side and that, no-one gave Benyamin a second glance. While on the other side of him, the child's face beamed up at his father, who lay his arm gently along his plump son's shoulders.

When Benyamin entered the house the air was cooler and his skin prickled against it. The room smelled of spice, of cinnamon and cardamom. The room was dim. He stood in the doorway. And then at his feet, he saw a magnificent skin, the head of which faced him. Its golden eyes were fixed and dulled but its jaws were open and, in them, its teeth curved, gleaming. Beyond this, Benyamin saw several vast and tasselled cushions of bright yellow silk and, along the low table, a coverlet of peacock blue, its edge scalloped and embroidered in golden thread. And, upon it, a handsome water jug and an arrangement of tumblers all rimmed in fine gold leaf. Further and further into the room he saw. An enormous green silk carpet glistened. And, beyond that, one in earthy tones. As the very old man walked across the room, his feet left prints the way wind might shift the lay of grain.

Come, said the Pasha, *you must sleep and eat and wash. And then, when you are well, there are things we can discuss. Books, perhaps, or history. Do you know gardens? Where are you from?*

Benyamin looked to the man at the far side of the room. The man stood with his back to Benyamin before a pair of half-open doors and a bright slab of light between them. Benyamin watched as he pushed the doors wider and wider and so he saw how the man disappeared into the brightness and space of his home.

When he awoke it was night and he wondered where he was. A lamp, its wick low, glowed in a far corner. The bed was soft, and the bedding slid against his feet. He sat up. In the light the bedcover glittered as he moved beneath it. It reminded him of a lake at night. One evening, a long time ago, his father had taken him to fish in a lake, and he remembered the sun going down — hanging so long in the west, on the rim of the world, then suddenly it was gone — and how cold the night became. And although they had poles and hooks and bait, his father seemed content to sit. And the moon came up huge and orange and much too slowly, so that it frightened him being out there. And he shuffled closer to his father but said nothing and refused to watch the sky, but watched the water instead. And then the breeze gusted across the lake and into his face. The water's surface folded and stretched and all the pools of quiet starlight flashed at him and he had to close his eyes and turn his head away. His face turned into his father's chest and his father's urgent whisper, *Look, boy, look. The fish are here.* And he opened his eyes and turned back to the lake and saw the flanks of a thousand silver, darting fish. And when his eyes hurt he closed them and when he opened them again they were gone. And they sat together, silent and waiting, with Benyamin's ear against his father's chest and when he awoke he was in his bed and it was morning. And now here he was, waking at night in a bed like a lake full of glittering fish, waking into something he was never sure he hadn't dreamed.

Who had come in while he slept and set the lamp? Benyamin had seen no-one but the very old man, so it must have been him. Benyamin listened. Somewhere, he was sure, he could hear voices. He pushed back the cover and slid his legs out of the bed. He looked down at himself. His hands were clean. He stood. The hems of these trousers sat just below his knees. The cuffs of the tunic sat at his elbows. Ah, yes, he thought, I remember this.

A pair of slippers had been placed by the bed. He slid his right foot into the slipper as far as it would go. His heel hung over the slipper's heel but his toes felt warm. With those right toes he pinned the heel of the left slipper and shoved in his left foot. Then he shuffled out of the bedroom, his careful feet pushing each slipper across the tiled floor. In the Paris winters he had seen children skate like this — beginners rooted to the ice, afraid to lift their feet lest a moment's separation from the surface should dismantle them. Standing around the edge of ponds with friends in bruised and sodden groups, or drifting, rudderless and alone, into the centre of things, feeling the terrifying thinness of the blades and how they act according to forces which the child cannot understand.

In the room of the tiger, Benyamin found his host. He sat alone at the low table, with his back to the hearth, where a fire burned steadily. Beneath and around him, the bright yellow cushions glowed orange in its light. The table was set with an assortment of shallow bowls. The fire glinted in their metals, gold rims and glazes. A number of lamps were set around the perimeter of this vast room and, as Benyamin skated towards the old man, he moved through the diffuse light into a moment of shadow before nearing the table and the hot red light of the fire.

The very old man looked up at him. *Sit,* he said, *eat. You have slept?*

Benyamin hesitated. The fire made a halo about the old man's head. *I thought I heard voices.*

Oh? replied his host. *Perhaps the wind or just an unfamiliar house.* He smiled. And so Benyamin sat opposite, folding his limbs as best he could. And the old man took the bowls of walnuts and cherries in his hands and held them out, and Benyamin selected fruit and ate, slowly and in silence.

When he at last held up his hand and said, *Thank you, I have had enough,* the old man settled deeper in the yellow silk cushions and surveyed him.

I have had others here like you.

Like me? Armenians?

All kinds. Armenians, Greeks, Assyrians. Zealots.

Zealots?

Yes, over the years.

Is there a zealot here now?

Well, of course.

Oh. I thought … Could it have been his voice I heard?

The Pasha laughed. *It is always so pleasing to have an amusing guest.* And, still laughing, he rose to fetch the apricot wine — his most precious, as he said, *for apricots have so short a season.*

Surely, wine has made all manner of things possible: confession, murder, sex. All these, but not these only. It has lessened pain and animosity, fostered schemes, encouraged nostalgia, laughter, sleep. And Benyamin's body hurt. How long had he been hungry, walking, sleeping on the ground? He watched the Pasha return, smiling, his right hand clasping the pitcher's handle, his left cupped about its base. He knew it was April when the soldiers came, and then the summer had come, too. But what month was it now? In this stony place the world was not the world he knew. He watched the old man fill the glass goblets. A drop of the orange-coloured wine splashed onto the table from the pitcher's lip.

What date is it? he asked.

The old man placed the pitcher on the surface between them. *It is the second Wednesday of September. The twelfth, I believe.* And, after a pause, *Is it significant?*

Benyamin watched his host as he raised his glass, sipped delicately and replaced it with a steady hand. *No,* he said, his eyes on the old man's clean white fingers gripping the goblet's stem. *I had simply lost track.*

Mmm, the Pasha nodded. *So many things have altered since. For everyone. When was it you say you left home?*

It was April ... I don't know. April.

April. A lovely time of year. Do you like gardens?

I — I had a garden once.

Excellent. The old man smiled and slapped his knees. *You are a gardener, then.*

Benyamin shook his head. *No. I'm not. I'm — I was an architect.*

Ah. The Pasha studied him. He raised his glass. *A learned man. A planner. And what did you plan?*

Benyamin looked at him. *Homes. Churches. Civic buildings. People came to me. They told me what they wanted.*

And then you did what they asked you.

Of course.

They needed you.

Yes, I suppose they did.

Their ideas could not be made reality without your skill, your ... participation.

No.

But you don't drink?

I — yes, I do. Benyamin reached for his goblet. His fingers trembled.

Good. You see — we are so similar, you and I, my friend. I, too, am a planner. People also come to me and tell me things. And I see to it that things are done. I look after them. You and I, we are ... men of action.

Benyamin swallowed the sweet, thick wine and shook his head. *I —*

Pah! False modesty! exclaimed the Pasha, with a wave of his hand. *The world, you must see, has all kinds of men. Some are needed by others and some are not. We are the men whom others need. Without us, those things that everyone knows must be done, would not be. You must not be ashamed of it. More wine?*

No. Thank you. Benyamin held the cup of his goblet with both hands, his wrists resting on the table's edge. He saw that the firelight illuminated everything: his cuticles and knuckles, the edges of his body against the air of the room. It illuminated the feet of the highly polished table, the sheen of yellow silk cushions, the sharp gold rims of bowls. The Pasha's manicured fingernails flashed. It illuminated the polished tiles on the floor and the pale stripes on the tiger's skin, its longest teeth, the golden marbles of its eyes.

Ah, the Pasha smiled. *You admire her.*

I — yes. Where is it from? The land here … I didn't think it —

Quite right. In … other times, it is most unsuitable. They prefer elsewhere, somewhere greener, mountainous, as you know. But these days … well, one finds them everywhere. Drawn by the easy food, I'm afraid — as you, of course, know. The weak prey. Terrible. The old man stood.

Yes. Benyamin's voice was a hoarse whisper in his throat.

Such beautiful beasts. Majestic. But, well, it's survival. And we all must do that. He stood beside the skin. *Tell me, my friend, have you ever felt a tiger? Come, touch it,* he said. And, with one bare and pointed toe, he stroked it.

That night the wind sprang up and, in his sleep, Benyamin heard it. And, because he knew, as his grandfathers had known, that the wind brings us messages if we are prepared for them, he rose from his bed to listen.

Down, down he went, slowly. Down the stone stairs with both his hands stretched open and flat against the cold stone wall, feeling their way along its curve in the dark. Down, down he feels with the toes of his bare feet, gripping the edge of each new step, sliding one foot down to find the next safe place, his body following. The wind spirals up the tunnel of stairs. More and more voices come to him, calling. They rise and fall, fall and rise across each other, but he can't make out the words. He is cold; he shivers. *Yes, yes,* he cries, but he cannot hear his own voice. *I'm near. I'm coming,* and with one more step he has walked into the day. He blinks. All about him is bright. He is standing in a garden before a small timber house. The sunlight flashes off its shining, angled roof. The red-brown bricks beneath his feet are very warm.

He can see beyond a wire door. There is a short, narrow passage on the other side. He climbs two timber steps and walks slowly across a creaking verandah. He can smell cardamom and coffee. He hears the soft swish of a broom. He pulls the door open quietly and steps inside.

He blinks again. His eyes adjust. At the end of the passage he sees a table with a pretty cloth and two cups and a pewter coffee pot. He sees a vase filled with flowers. He walks slowly to the kitchen door. A woman is sweeping the wooden floor. She has hair like copper wire; she has tied it back. He watches the woman but she doesn't turn. He can't see her face. Somehow, in the room there is music and singing, the like of which he has never heard. She sings, too. He cannot understand a single word. He watches her, and he thinks, *I will just stand here. Eventually, she will see me.*

And so it was, that night, the wind sprang up and, in his sleep, Benyamin heard it. And he opened his eyes quickly, threw back the covers, stood up, recognising the strange intervals of either keening or song, each long vowel enticing. And, taking a lantern, he followed the sound out of his bedroom, down the wide, windy hallway and deep into the back of the house, halting now and then to listen or to recall his path for his safe return until, eventually, he came to a door. And then there he was, stepping down and down the winding stone staircase, lantern in his right hand, his left opened flat against the curve of the wall.

In such inhospitable landscape, the cool dark of caves must have always attracted the most sensible men. Shelter, a safe sleep, protection from the ravages of enemies and sun, and streams of sweet water trickling through miles of stone. When survival anywhere else is most unlikely, it is always caves that offer hope, and to caves that men and women retreat. But the dark. When one has buried oneself so deep that living becomes unending night. It is the night that men and women fight. Because living is a story we tell ourselves. And a good story, like a good life, needs many things: structure, rhythm, imagination, courage. And the passage of the sun, no matter how fierce, marks out our time in the way that paragraphs do. Without it, eventually, the story falters.

How could Benyamin know he brought the sun? When he reached the bottom of the stair, it was the smell that made him raise his lantern on an outstretched arm and peer blindly beneath it. He knew that smell, that sharp animal stink. He listened but no sound came to him now. Then he stepped forward gingerly and then further forward into a space the dimensions of which he couldn't quite read and, placing the lantern on the ground, walked back and sat on the bottom step, knees drawn up and arms folded about them.

There is a moment when one sees in the dark. The moment arrives swiftly yet, while one waits, there is often brief disquiet. Will it happen? Sight and perception are miraculous things, events we don't understand and can't control. People lose sight or speech, go to bed at night and wake weak or rigid. We know this, and so we cultivate faith. We believe the night will be revealed, and we sit in the dark for as long as it takes, even though few among us can explain this revelation.

In the shadows a man crouched, watching Benyamin. Who is this, he thought, who comes in here with light in his hands and nothing else? Too much bone and hair, too little flesh. Does he know where he is? Has he seen us? He is a long thin fish, with a long thin face, the way he stares and sees nothing. He is an overgrown child, his trousers and tunic too short. I want to laugh. I could laugh at him for his hands are empty. He has no food, but no weapon, either. I could laugh at him but he has the lamp. Someone will shift; someone will cough. But it won't be me. Any moment. Any moment and he'll see my face, see all of us. Any moment and he'll say something. And then we'll see. Then everyone will see what kind of foolish man he is. The mad woman must be asleep or dead, or she'd be shaking her fists and singing like a bird. Maybe they are all asleep; maybe I'm the only one alive. I can hear someone breathing. Is it me?

Benyamin stood. His eyes adjusted, he saw now that the room was very large, its stone walls and ceiling concave. The space he stood in was like the centre of bread, where women's fists had punched and folded a hollow of air. He felt tiny and he felt himself sweat. There was something by the wall ahead, a crouched shadow. He couldn't make it out. Dog? Tiger? Had he mistaken the smell? He crept a slow step back, feeling his way up a single stair. Something moved on his right. He felt the shock of fear in his arms and legs. *Jesu*, he prayed. And then it began, the long slow song that had brought him down here. A high voice, a woman's voice, one open vowel and then another, each sliding over notes in directions that stood the hairs of his limbs on end.

Benyamin breathed. Short, sharp breaths. Her voice rose and fell. And then she paused and he heard her gasp as she filled her lungs. And in that gasp he heard other voices, right and left, men's voices, so low and rumbling that, for a moment, he wasn't sure if it was the earth about to open up.

Benyamin picked up his lantern. He moved his legs like someone else's legs, stiff and awkward, towards the sound. He knew he was being watched. The lamplight shifted like a current across the rough hew of the floor. The closer he came, the more the crouched figure's shadow shrank, until the yellow light washed across the old woman's face. Her head was thrown back and her eyes were tightly closed. Her toothless mouth was wide and working, lips closing opening like some aquatic creature, as if a hole was being dug and dug and re-dug in the damp collapsing earth of her face.

When she opened her lips, she opened them on a short dull consonant. And her voice pushed it away, pushed and pushed it far ahead, so far from her that it was lost on the long long vowels of her song, lost in all that came after it: the sight of her face, her eyes shut tight, her cheeks, chin, throat folding back on themselves, worn and brown, around her open mouth. And, inside it, the short ragged stump of her tongue, wagging like the small severed stump of a dog's tail. Wagging endlessly to make the sound of her incomprehensible song.

Benyamin closed his eyes and jerked his face away. But which shame was greater? The shame of what he saw, or that of turning away? He glanced back, hoping. But she was still there. He knew she would be. He knew that. It's just that sometimes one has to make sure of things because, he also knew, we are easily deceived. Even here. Especially here, he had hoped. But there she was, like a baby — toothless, wordless — singing for something no-one could give her.

Hah, thought the man, now I can laugh! The way he hides his face, the way he turns back and forth like a puppet, a child's doll. Now I laugh, but he doesn't hear me. He is tall like someone … I know this man; I know him. He is tall like someone I know.

Benyamin took his lantern and moved away, towards a male voice, a deep breathy shout like a laugh, and then a wordless growl from someone who, even in better times, couldn't sing. And he lifted his lamp and saw before him a pair of eyes, wide open and steady as ever on him. The two men stared. *Nerses,* whispered Benyamin. Nothing flickered in the other man's eyes. *Nerses, it's me, Benyamin. Benyamin Vartevarian.*

Nerses' right hand gripped Benyamin's right, and then his left hand locked Benyamin's left. And so they remained, Nerses huddled low against the wall and Benyamin crouched beside him. *Oh, Nerses,* murmured Benyamin, his eyes wide and shining as he looked across Nerses' face — the shape of the forehead, the nose, chin. Yes, it was him. He could scarcely believe it, but he knew this face, he could see Nerses in the eyes that now brimmed with tears as they, too, searched Benyamin's face for the same confirmation. *Oh, God, dear God,* Benyamin whispered. And then he leaned forward and, closing his eyes, pressed his forehead against his friend's. The room echoed with the old woman's song.

* * *

What is there for us in unending night? Locked in, we cannot get out. No sun, no air; we are pale and ill. Time becomes a sheet we are tangled in. We toss in sleep, cry out. Wakened, we glance about, then roll back into the wet sheet of our fever. We spend too long dreaming. But what do we expect? We retreated here. Unending night, unending dream. A life lived at night is what kind of life? A life lived at night is out of step, a shadow life, where the dreamer never sees the world that other people see. In the unending dream, the dreamer doesn't really live. She pretends she does. But that is unfair. She thinks she does. She carries herself in expected ways. Or he forms his body into its expected shapes so that what people see is recognisable. *Ah!* they say. *There goes the receptionist.* Or, *That man is a milliner.*

To the dreamer, the unending dream looks just like life. She moves in it, through streets and rooms and rough terrain. Characters enter, speak; there is some exchange; he eats, sleeps — perhaps too little or too much. But when he sleeps, his dreams pick up the threads of thoughts and those thoughts reassemble, resume their shapes. And then he wakes from nightmare, gasps; blinks, over and over; thinks, *Dear God, is there no escape?*

How can the dreamer know this life is not a life? Locked in, they can't get out. They are caught somewhere, some other place, some other time. They are tight in a sheet like a corpse. They are caught in a billowing white tent. They are wading out into deep water, the ocean dragging their skirts. Their life is a dream from which they cannot wake.

But I don't understand, the Pasha said. *For what does an architect need a tongue?*

For the first time, they stood face to face, the Pasha at the head of the stone stairs, and Benyamin a few steps below so that each looked directly into the other's gaze. Each held their lantern before them so that the air around them glowed with light. Benyamin felt his body trembling; his mouth opened and shut. He saw that, behind the Pasha, the door back into the house was still open. The cool night breeze smelled of citrus and tobacco. He stared into the Pasha's dark eyes. *These could be anybody's eyes*, he thought. *They could be my friend's or my own. How can I tell anything from them?* In all that brightness Benyamin stared into the planes and curves of the old man's face. Had he never seen the thinness of his skin, the deep parabolas of his cheeks?

You are ill, he stated. *I can see that now.*

An architect speaks in other ways, surely, the Pasha continued in an even tone. *Besides, they were given a choice. It was their choice. It was not I who gave them the choice, but I can see why they made it.*

A choice, Benyamin echoed.

Well, yes. Death or the loss of their tongue.

Benyamin nodded.

Under the circumstances it's easy enough, isn't it? What would you choose?

Benyamin nodded again. *Who gave them this choice?*

What do you mean?

I mean, who did this?

Oh. I don't know. The Pasha glanced over his shoulder at the open door.

Benyamin squinted into the darkness of the house. *Is there someone else here?*

Ah, yes. To see you.

What do they want?

I came to wake you, but you weren't in bed. I looked all over the house for you. And then I remembered.

Remembered?

You mentioned the voices, so …

Yes, and you laughed.

No, not laughed. I am … keeping them safe.

And me, Pasha? What will you do with me?

Do with you?

Will you keep me safe? What will my choices be?

What do you mean? Your choices have nothing to do with me.

Who did this, then?

I don't know. He gestured widely with his arm. *Everyone.*

Everyone?

Everyone. They came, they went.

Why didn't you stop them?

One old man?

You are powerful, Pasha.

No, no, boy. You're mistaken.

I have seen you. You have told me. People seek you out.

Yes, they seek me out to confide in me, to ask advice.

They respect you. They would have listened to you.

Perhaps they do, but I am everyone's father, not their king. I just do what others ask of me.

Is that what a father does?

They come to me with their concerns and I do what I can for them. They want better lives and I try to help them. That is all I do. Just like you, architect. Just like you. Don't forget it. And don't forget where you are standing — in my home, in my clothes, in my country. It is my food in your belly and my sheets in which you sleep.

Benyamin studied the old man, the tight set of his lips, the jut of his chin. He nodded slowly. *Tell me, Pasha,* he said, *is my ... visitor a man?*

The old man nodded.

Alone?

Yes, the old man growled.

Benyamin set the lamp down beside him on the step, against the curved stone wall. It was so much easier to remove the too small clothes than it had been to inhabit them. His big bony hands slipped the tunic up and over his head, loosed the trousers and then picked them up as he stepped sideways, lifting his feet out of them. He shook the garments lightly, feeling even a slight smile pass over his face at the whisper of them. He heard them rustle the way silk does and saw how magnificently they caught all the combined light. Then he folded them together half-heartedly, for he was not a man accustomed to such tasks, and held them out to the Pasha.

The old man did not move at all. Only his eyes were wider, and his expression was now one more of astonishment than of indignation. He still stood with his outstretched arm holding a lantern, and the other close beside his body, hand still clenched in the anger he had felt just moments before. So, it was over the outstretched arm that Benyamin draped the discarded clothing. And it was under this same arm that he passed from the staircase into the darkened house, bowing his head and feeling the silk of his discarded garments brush lightly down his back, just as he had once felt the caress of his wife's hair.

Hovsanna lies in the curl of his arm, her cheek against his chest. She hears the beat of his heart, loud and even in her skull. She hears his voice telling her all of this. He says, *When we finally released one another's hands, he opened mine with his fingers and he held it open and he wrote on my skin, the inside of my forearm, here,* and he holds up his arm in front of her, *and here, my palm. He wrote with his finger, as if his nail were ink. He wrote slowly while I watched. I didn't want to watch, I don't know why. I kept thinking of us at our desks, working, how quick he was. And the sound of water from the courtyard, the flowers growing between the stones. It seemed impossible we were not there. Watching his hand was better than watching his face, I suppose, and he held my wrist with such a terrible grip, I couldn't have pulled away. Even if I closed my eyes I could feel each letter's shape. There was no escape from him.*

After some time, Hovsanna whispered, *And what did he write?*

I can't remember, Benyamin replied, and fell silent. But Benyamin did remember. He remembered everything — how he stepped naked and without a lantern through the door back into the dark house, how the night wind made him shiver, how he stood in the hallway and listened and thought. *Where are they, those who have come for me? They wait in the dark; there are no lights ahead.* And he remembered all his careful steps: away from the door to the stairs and beyond; away from Nerses; past the room in which he had slept and the many others he had never entered; along the halls slowly, cat-like, towards the front of the house, pausing often to watch and listen. He was cold, and there was a corner of his thinking that began to consider what cloth he might gather, to remember what was in the rooms he had once passed through.

At the double doors to the sitting room he paused again. If a visitor was in the house, it was most likely he was awaiting Pasha's return — or his own arrival — in this first room. But visitors are never left in the dark. There would be a fire and food, as there was when Benyamin sat there. How long ago was that? Perhaps the visit was a surprise, and there was no time for a fire. Perhaps he roused the Pasha from his sleep. But, at the very least, the wall lamps would be lit the way they were for him. Was that only earlier this night?

What choice did he have? He knew no other way out but through the front door. He had seen no other entrances beyond the hall's end and the door to the stairs. All the windows were elegantly barred in finely wrought iron, as was the custom. And it was already autumn in this treeless country, and there was something in this room, he knew, that he needed if he was to survive. He gripped a brass door handle, pulled open one door a head's width, and waited. No light, no sound. He held his breath and slid in, sideways, through the gap.

Again he waited. He glanced around and then ahead. Ten good strides and he'd have it. Another twenty and he'd be at the only exit he knew. Perhaps the visitor had gone. Or perhaps there never was another. Perhaps the old man was lying, and it was he, alone, who was responsible for what had gone on here. Perhaps he had almost been tricked, himself. If it wasn't for the old woman's song ...

He began walking. Ten strides is nothing, nothing at all. He was there in an instant. After all, how far had he walked? He bent down. It was heavy. He straightened and it dragged its claws across the floor. It was loud, too loud, the loudest sound he had ever heard. He lifted it quickly, as quickly as he could, and heaved it across his back. Wherever anyone was in the house, they'd have heard it too. Even if it were only the old man. If he were up from the dungeon, he'd be here in a moment. He hitched the skin higher over him and felt its head bang, empty, against the back of his knee. He took three more steps before he saw the other man move.

He stood. Ahead of Benyamin and to the right of him, the man had stood up from where he had been sitting, quite still on the golden cushions, watching Benyamin creep, naked, into the room and snatch up the tiger skin. Even in the dark he had seen this man was very tall, as he had been told to expect. Naked, yes, but in these times such things were not unknown. So he had stood.

For a moment Benyamin froze, long enough to hear the man's voice. Yes, he had moved first, had stood before he began to speak, not the other way around, Benyamin would later recall. And he had been afraid when the man stood, materialising from nothing but dark and air, between him and the door, and had felt that urge in him to run. Then, almost at the same instant, he had heard the man's voice and been confused by what he said. *Mr Vartevarian?* he had enquired, most politely. *We know where your wife is. She is alive. She is waiting to see you.*

Sometimes the easiest thing to do is run. He was so close to escape. A final sprint to the door, a wrench of the handle and he'd be free, outside, in the dark air and disappearing in an instant on swift, silent feet, running, running all night, finding the small dark places to sleep each dawn. And at dusk he'd come out, enter villages, find food. Eat, run, sleep. Warm in his skin. Sleep, eat, run. In this way, he would survive; in this way, he would come home.

He saw the shape of the future. It was pure geometry. The rectangles of doors; the triangle of positions. The man, the door, himself. The distances between. He saw the form of the man: short, squat. He imagined his stride, its length and rate. Even with the skin, he could easily outpace him. It was the perpendicular that threw him. He understood what this meant. That, even allowing for difference in form, even allowing for the advantage of surprise, the man and Benyamin could reach the doorway together. And then what?

He had once killed a goat. He had slit its throat with his father's knife, with his father's hand over his own and his father's strength in it. Killing is difficult. He had learned that, then. The goat had struggled and his father had sweated and grunted and cursed. The goat had squirmed and pissed. Yet he knew it would come down to that. It always does. In the end, just there, by the door or just outside, he would have to kill him.

Mr Vartevarian? Benyamin Vartevarian, architect, of Alexandretta? Husband of Hovsanna Kalidjian? His questions hung. Benyamin thought that everything, in the end, is about geometry, simple equations, inescapable truths: physics, mathematics. The energy he would need to exert on the man's throat would transfer through his hands into him and, through his struggle, elsewhere. The man interrupted him again. *Mr Vartevarian, my name is not important, but I am a friend. There are many of us trying to help. If you could come with me, sir, we could begin our journey.*

Benyamin thought that no force is ever lost, despite appearances. The force exerted through my father's hand, he considered, passed through me into the knife, into the flesh, to make the wound. The goat's heart pounded faster because of the force we used to keep it still, and the pounding heart forced out all that blood into the ground that then helped grow somebody's food. And then we consumed the goat; it became us. It made our hair and nails and teeth. The force in the goat's free hind leg, the force with which it struck over and over at the earth, travelled outward like a current and entered other creatures through their feet as they grazed or their flanks as they slept. Did it leave them again, in a quiver or start, moving itself through the air I now breathe? Things in the world fit so beautifully together. Killing is difficult, yes, because it requires commitment — determination, strength. But force, energy, is the simplest of things. I gather it from the world and it passes through me. Whether I use it to run or to kill makes no difference to the world at all.

I don't understand, he said. *Where do you propose taking me?*

The man took one step towards him. *To Cilicia, effendi. Home.*

Down and down

Oh, husband. Oh, Benyamin, my dear, dear one. I have slipped down the edges of things. I have let down my hair, my blankets and all my silk dresses, all these things you have given me, Benyamin. I have tied them together; I have looped them about themselves. I have stepped easily off the edge of the earth.

Oh, my dear husband, I have held lightly, too lightly to my hair, my dresses, too lightly to the covers on my bed, your bed, the bed we shared and into which our babies fell, bloody and bawling. I have held, but have held too lightly. And the smooth line of my life whizzes up between my too loose fingers.

How quickly I fall. It is better than sleep, this going, this down and down. The air rushes cool as I suddenly drop. I am in the wind's wide sleeve. I rush through her like I am open everywhere, like I am not quite me, a spirit me, a different kind. She rushes through me as if — inside me — I have been emptied.

There was road, my dear; there were stones. Beside the stony road were more stones and sand, all pale. At midday it was blindingly pale. Sometimes the carriage wheel would slip into the sand, I could feel it drift and we were suddenly unstable, on the edge of sliding, and then it would return, find the road with all its stones and we would clatter again. Clatter, clatter, the children in their different clothes, jarring up against each other, the baby asleep and bouncing crazy in my lap. My arms were tired from holding her still. I looked everywhere. I tried to remember the way we had come yesterday. Was he, after all this, playing a final trick, this man you knew — or who, more precisely, says he knew you? Were we being taken elsewhere? How could I be sure? I wasn't sure of anything. It looked the same road, but this country, these stones, this sand. I watched the jerky horizon. I saw blue sky and, far away, some hills I didn't remember. I worried. I thought, *If I remember the way we are going now, maybe when he stops and when we have to run and hide, maybe later, if I really think, I can find our way back.* If you were there, my dear, my Benyamin, you would know instantly. You with your architect's eye, your particular seeing. To you each boulder meets the earth, each depression by the roadside catches light. But to me there was a road and there were stones.

When he came yesterday we all heard his carriage wheels clatter long before he reached us. The gendarmes were a little bewildered, I think. They all looked at each other. I heard them asking, *Who is this man?* I hadn't seen them like that before. *At least*, I thought, *it isn't Kurds.* Kurds ride horses; as we know, they are great horsemen. If it were Kurds, there would be many. Their hooves would be loud on the stony road minutes before; there would be clouds of dust from far away, and many voices. If it were Kurds, the gendarmes would say their names and drop back, leaving us on the road. This is what people say. Once I heard a gendarme wish for Kurds to come, to lessen our numbers more quickly, my dear. But his friend said, *No, they'll take all the pretty ones and we'll be left with hags and babies. Oh, well,* the first man replied, *I am not particular.* And they laughed.

When he came we all kept walking because that's what we do. To stop is to risk something. A beating, a rifle butt, or worse. So, if we can walk, we keep walking. If someone falls down, we don't stop to help her. Someone may take hold of the hands of her children and pull them along, away from their mother, crying the way that children do. But there's no point in stopping. Will my own children thank me if I stop for another and am killed for it? So, when I heard what I heard, the gendarmes saying my name, saying *Vartevarian? Vartevarian?* all along the roadside, one and then the other of them, I thought at first I must be mistaken, I must be dreaming. But it is something you remember, isn't it, your own name? My children, beside me, remembered it too, walking, looking at me. *Walk,* I hissed to them. And they did.

They are obedient children, my dear one, as you know. They are dirty and thin, dirtier and thinner than they have ever been. They are tired, too. Tired, as I am tired. But they don't complain. They did complain, at first. But not now. Now they are good. All the children here are good. My children always do what they're told. I am grateful for that. Other children will cry sometimes, when their mother falls down and another woman pulls them along and they lose sight of that mother. Or when she lets go of their hand and walks on, or puts them down on the road and they can't see her anymore. Then they will cry. And who likes to hear a child cry? No-one. We are very tired. It irritates us. But they don't cry for long. At first it was much noisier. Now, we are accustomed to it. Most of the day, if I listen I hear footsteps on stones, occasional voices, angry or pleading. Usually, though, nobody speaks much. When we women speak to each other, we make sure no-one else can hear us. There is, of course, as you might imagine, always the time in most days when the gendarmes take a maid or a married woman. You can hear them quite clearly, what they say to her and to each other, things I cannot repeat. I close my ears with my hands, everyone does, but we can still hear her crying out or shouting to her own weeping children, if she has some, *It's all right, it's all right.* And, if that maid's or married woman's own mother is here, we can hear that mother shouting too. Shouting, shouting her daughter's name. Shouting, shouting for them to stop, or offering her own self instead. I cover my ears but it's no good. Sometimes I wish they would all just shut their mouths. I have made a promise with my friend. When they come for one of us we will not make any noise. We will go quietly with them and we will smile back at our children as we are jostled to the roadside. And we will look straight at these men and tell them we will do whatever they want us to do, even more if they wish, as long as they take us out of sight. And the other of us must gather her children and ours together and tell them all stories. I have thought of the stories I will tell them, and so has my friend. We have talked about this. My friend has made a beautiful story.

But this day, the day he came, was different. A carriage in the distance. A man leaning out of it saying my name, and the gendarmes calling for me. My mother holding my sleeve. *Say nothing*, she whispered, *for the love of God. It's a trap.* And other women looking at me, women from my village who have known me all my life. Looking at me and each other. And my name, my name. And I knew someone would speak. Someone who knew me would raise her arm and point to me. If not now, then now or now. This breath or this. So I stopped walking. It was so easy. I shook off my mother's fingers from my arm. *Walk on,* I said, looking at her. Her mouth was open. And then some women parted, and we stepped out of the column.

Sometimes, doing something is as easy as ceasing to do something else. I didn't have to speak or raise my hand. I simply had to stop moving, to stand still while everyone around me shuffled on. It was as easy as that. Better that I did it. If it were a trap, better that I identified myself, confessed my own name, than that some other woman, my childhood playmate or my parents' neighbour, gave me up to death. How, then, would they live together, that woman and her husband and children alongside my parents in our village when we all go home? Everyone would remember and things could never be the same.

You are Mrs Vartevarian? Wife of Benyamin Vartevarian, the architect from Alexandretta? he asked. I nodded. *I know your husband, Madam. Come with me.* And he held back the curtain to the open door of the carriage and waited. Two things occurred to me at that moment. Firstly, how wonderful it was to be called my name, to be called Madam, again, and to hear your own name, my husband, spoken to me. I felt for a moment that I could almost have smiled. And then, how dark the inside of the carriage appeared, and I thought that if Hell had a door, it might appear just as does this. But I was tired, my dearest, more tired than ever before.

My mother's fingers were still tight on my sleeve and she was pulling me, pulling me and saying, *Don't go, don't go, are you mad, do you know this man?* And it was true, I didn't, but I said nothing. Instead he spoke to her, *Madam, please believe me. There is room for you, too. Please accompany us. You will be safe. My wife waits for you.* But she wouldn't, my dear, she wouldn't, and she stayed. I couldn't look at her. It was so easy to climb into the carriage. I mean, the man had to help us, hold my arm, then lift up our children to me. His mouth was a thin line. But it is the simplest thing to choose to rest. I could hear her weeping and shouting behind us, *Hovsanna, Hovsanna, my children, my little ones, oh God, oh God, my family,* as we drove away. I couldn't look at her. I smiled at my children. They were looking at me. They, too, were crying. I closed my ears.

Shall I tell you the story I have made? It is not as beautiful as my friend's story. This I know because my friend has told me pieces of her story as we lay together at night, our children between us in the dust. She would whisper small pieces to us, and sometimes I would, too. Sometimes I would think about my story as we walked, but sometimes I was beyond thoughts and stories, beyond sleep and listening to whispers. Sometimes I was too far away, beyond my name, beyond everything. If I were close to her, or to you, my dear, lying beside you in the dust now, this is what I would say:

The girl rests on the long bough. She gathers her skirts and folds them tight about her legs. Her clothing should be sheath not flag; no flap of cloth should signal her. When she springs to the ground, her skirt, like her legs, will simply unfold itself. If she were a bird, her wings would unfold and she would travel out of sight. If she were a brother, she would wear trousers and boots and carry satchels of ink and quills and books. If she were a brother she would read and laugh loudly. She would run with all the other brothers and wrestle them with her hard hands. If she were a brother, she would be as swift and cunning as a tiger. Her legs would be longer and faster than the others; her eyes would be keener, her patience greater. She would have whatever she wanted. They would all step back as she approached them.

On the long stout bough, she lies very still, her eyes fixed on the horizon where the road disappears towards, she has been told, the next village. She tries to imagine the place where they have gone, her brothers and all the other boys, and from where they will come, swinging their satchels at one another, twirling them above their heads, yelling. They will not see her. She will spring down in front of them and her skirt will resume its shape about her. And she will walk near to them. And, as always, not one will speak to her.

She fixes her eyes on the disappearing road. She feels the bough, wide and solid along her legs and belly, against her cheek and chest. She hears her heart beat into it, and listens to the sound of her blood in the tree.

Nearby, the old man turns from his window to his wife. *Well?* she says, without glancing up from the stove. *As usual,* he replies. *If she were my daughter, I'd beat some sense into her,* the old woman mutters. And so, she doesn't hear her husband step from the room into the warm afternoon. He stands outside the door. The day is so bright he blinks at it. In his hands he holds a timber stool he has lifted quietly from the kitchen. *If she were my daughter and I were a fisherman, I would string up a net to catch her when she falls.* For he has seen this girl, this young Kalidjian. Both he and his wife have seen her, day after day. Does her mother know? *And when she falls into my net and twists and flails, my net will tighten around her.* A girl her age should not be climbing a tree, not climbing his tree like a cat. *And then I will come and cut the ropes to my net and lift her up in my net and take her home.* And, holding the stool, he steps away from his house and his wife towards the girl in the tree at the top of his garden by the road from his village to the next. But the girl is watching the road at the horizon. She is listening to her heart in the tree and knows nothing of the man until he speaks.

When I was a girl, my dear, there were tigers in our hills. You will remember how we have talked of this, and of how the approach of winter would send them down, wary, hungry. Everyone knew of them; at night the children were told stories by the fire about tigers taking goats and dogs, and we would huddle beneath our blankets and one of us would ask what we all were imagining: if the tigers had ever eaten people. *Yes, yes,* the adults would say. And, each time,

I would believe them. After all, why would our parents lie? But then I would see it. They would look at each other. Or they would not, staring instead too long into the fire or pouring coffee with a different smile, one like a line that hid their teeth. Later, before we slept, I would sometimes ask my older sisters why our parents or grandparents lie to us. But that would only make them angry, and they would shout or hiss or hit me sometimes, saying, *Our parents don't lie. You are the only liar here. Now shut up, liar. Shut up and sleep.* But I couldn't sleep, not for a very long time.

Benyamin, what stories will we tell our children? Will there be tigers still?

All the way back was road and stones; there was road and sky, and where road meets sky. And I tried, I tried hard to see where we had come. It was the morning. It was the middle of the day. And I was watching for them. I knew they would be walking, a long line. Hundreds and hundreds and hundreds of them. I knew they would see the carriage way in the distance, hear the clatter of the wheels on stones, just as we had done yesterday. I knew they would look, one then two, and that someone would say to my mother, *They return!* And my mother would weep and praise God, and I would say, *See, Mother, we are safe. We have come back to you. Don't weep. This gentleman and his wife, they are good, kind people. They have given us clothes, they have given us food, they begged me to stay with them in their home. Truly this Turk is as he has said, my husband's friend.* I knew what I would say. And, later, when my friend asked me, as she would in the night, why I had returned if this man was good, I knew I would try to explain that, if I had stayed, my mother would have always thought we had died. She would always have believed this man had lied, and that somewhere in Anatolia her grandchildren's bones were being eaten by dogs. And I would say, *Try to understand: how can a daughter do this to a mother?* And I knew that my friend would be angry with me, call me 'fool' and worse, names I cannot repeat. And if you were here, you would curse me, too — beat me, perhaps. All this I knew, and then we came fast around a bend and there they all were in the distance, in the middle of the day, lying down on the road and the sides of the road, as if asleep. How tired they all must be.

The man looks up at the girl in the tree. He sees her hair is yellow, and that she has strange, pale-coloured eyes.

The earth grows dark. Where is my mother? These pale Anatolian plains, this dust, these stones we sleep in, these are dark, darker than they've ever been, darker than anywhere. The sky is so blue. And, once — was it yesterday? — everything on earth was pale, like leaves, a kind of yellow, dry — the palest clay. Once, a long time ago, I saw a pot like that, a pot fired from an oven. I was a girl and, in the field, the oven was like a little house and it glowed like Hades. Against it, the black figure of a man throwing something into it. I held tight to my mother's hand. She bought pots from the man's wife and mother. They smiled at me. Where is my mother? They had no teeth. Later, one of my brothers asked what happened to their teeth and my mother laughed and said they were poor and had eaten stones. They had eaten stones. And on the table at home the pot held apricots, and I remember how beautiful they were against the paleness of the clay. Where is my mother, my sleeping mother? Where are you, my plump mother, my laughing mother, my apricot? From a long distance I could see them lying, a long dark mark upon the earth. All asleep, my lazy ones? Or are you poor and eating stones? And who is it who's eating you? My belly's full, and look at us — our hair, our clean new clothes. All look at us. This Turk is true, a gentleman. You see, believe them when they tell us we will be looked after. All we have to do is walk there. And when we do — when we do, we will have apricots again. See? We walk among you, and from your every wound the birds flap up. We are not dead, Mother, we are not dead. Mother, Mother, where is your body? I walk among you as if you were stones. These stones have eyes. They are cold and still. I could walk on you. Where is your body, Mother? Where is the stone of your head?

The man looks up at the girl in the tree. He sees yellow hair, and strange, pale eyes. He places the stool at the base of the tree trunk. *Hey, you. You, kitten. You, sleepy cat,* he says, smiling. The girl in the tree moves only those eyes. She looks down at the man. She does not know him, though she knows where he lives. She knows because she has seen him before, carrying flapping chickens by their feet. She has seen him in his garden; she has seen him beat his dog with his shoe. The girl listens to her blood beat in the tree. She thinks maybe she once was a tree.

My belly is full, and all the birds flap up as I run between them. Oh, Christos, Christos, here the world has an edge. This is the edge of the world at my feet. Everywhere, the birds flap up; somewhere, something growls. Under their wings, as they leap about, I see pieces of clothing, women's, children's. I see arms and legs, this one, that one.

The man taps the stool with one hand. Still smiling, he says, *Come. Come down, cat, and I will give you milk.* The girl knows she should move; she knows she should speak. It is the polite and proper thing. She knows, too, that she shouldn't be in the tree, and that the man could turn away at any moment, go to her mother, tell her. And she imagines her mother coming, her arms waving. She imagines climbing down from the tree, awkward, her mother pulling at her. She imagines her mother telling her father, and she sees that look from him that makes her insides fall away. She looks at the man. *But,* she thinks, *if this man beats his dog, what more will he do to a cat?*

Oh, my dear one, do not believe what those scholars tell you. They are clever, yes. They read books and write them, also, and I do not. I know that I'm not wise like them. I have never been to school. But, my dear, where are they now? They are not here. They cannot see what I can see. The world truly does have an edge. It is here, where I stand, where I balance. My toes grip its edge. I am holding on, but my feet are tired. I have walked too far. Sometimes, doing something is as easy as ceasing to do something else. I hurt. My toes hurt. I step off.

And the girl gazes down at the man still smiling up at her, his hand tapping the stool the way she had sometimes seen him call his dog, and she hears the loud thump of her blood in the bough of the tree. And she thinks, *When my brothers appear, you will give me away.* And she imagines, then, her brothers running, a band of them and all their friends, over the horizon, running to her. And she thinks, *They will say: why do you speak to our sister like that? Why do you coax her to come to you? And they will surround you and shout at you and move closer to you, pushing you. And my brothers will look up at me and smile. They will see the size of me, see me sit up intently, gathering my limbs beneath me. They will see me size him up — his height, the leap. And then I will spring.*

Just before she springs, the girl flicks her gaze back to the still unchanged horizon. Then her skirt, like her legs, simply unfolds. Her memory unfolds itself, and she understands that she is both a tree and a girl; she is a stone and a fruit and a thread and a ghost. *You must,* she murmurs as she falls that longest fall, *also hear them in the night. My father says they come down from the hills. Don't you sometimes think you hear the squeal of goats? Don't you know there are tigers still?*

I take one step only and I am on my way, falling. This is the easiest thing, my dear. I am falling in the wind's wide sleeve. Ah, Benyamin. The wind is pouring through me like I'm empty.

In the moment she unfolds herself, she glances back down

at the man. His head is tilted a little to one side. He is not smiling. She sees he is staring at the girl's wide mouth. *It is a generous mouth,* he thinks in that moment, *yes, a mouth some man will be fortunate to kiss. Perhaps I had once thought of the taste of warm milk from that tongue. But that was before she opened it. Before I saw her look away and back to me. Before I heard her growl.*

Now, I am on my hands and knees. Night after night, I have dreamed of food. Not of sweets or feasts, but of oranges. One filled the palm of my hand. It was very heavy. I squeezed it gently, and it gave a little beneath my fingers. It gave a little like the faces of my children when I touch them with my finger. I put my nose to its skin and breathed it in. I woke and covered my face with my hands. I could smell it. Once, my children played in a bowl of oranges, a bowl as large as a room. The fruit were splitting open beneath their feet. They were all there, every one. They slipped over on their knees and bottoms, laughing. They sucked the juice from their hands. Their skin shone.

A full belly is everything. You, too, my dear, must know this. Everybody knows this. But you must not just know — you must understand. This morning our children ate breakfast, and, last night, supper. Last night my throat closed up and I wept to see them eating. My throat closed up and I wept for my mother and my sisters and all their children, to think that I had left them, and my dear friend, too, and hers. I thought, *If the gendarmes choose her tonight, what will she do? Who will tell her children stories?* You know many things I do not know. You have been on ships to places. Tell me, while I watched my children eat, was my mother hungry still? Did they choose my friend? Or last night did they prefer her children? How many of my sisters' children ate sand while mine ate meat? What flesh is it that we have eaten, this flesh I left them all behind for? From which animal did it come? Which?

My throat closed. I wept. I spat it out. The taste was strong. My throat closed. I was ashamed. I couldn't swallow it. I ate yogurt, cucumber; I held a slice of yellow melon for a long time in my hand. This morning, I drank coffee, ate a little cheese, a piece of bread, and plucked one fat, purple grape from its bunch. I squeezed it; it split open. With my finger I lifted its seeds from itself, and I placed it, empty, on my tongue. I can't remember anything sweeter.

Now, I have something else between my teeth. I am on all fours, and all four limbs are helping me. I am strong; I am pulling. I am pulling at my mother's sleeve. I am her child. I am pulling. I have her sleeve between my teeth. The birds are squawking, flapping up.

There are dogs fighting. Someone is calling. That man, that Turk? The one who tried to hold me back? I am dragging my mother. My mother is heavy. I am strong. I know it is my mother. I know because I recognise her clothes. I recognise her hands and feet. The rest doesn't matter. It doesn't matter. I will find the rest of her later, come back for it later, when I've carried this part of her away in my teeth.

The Armenian woman

When the carriage pulled up outside the home of Mr Seljuk, the Turkish gentleman, his wife was grinding almonds. The mortar and pestle was her grandmother's, then her mother's, then hers. And she both loved and hated to use it, for somehow it made her aware of her loneliness. She knew one day her own daughter would use it when she was older, married, or when her own hands were too old, or her eyes too blind. Perhaps one of her grandchildren would break the sweets into tiny pieces and place each piece singly into her gummy mouth, as she had done when she was a girl, watching her grandmother grow thinner and drier and quiet, wiping the sticky saliva from her smiling chin. It frightened her a little then, frightened her brothers and sisters, too. They whispered about it between them and, although she worked hard at not allowing her face to change when she was doing it, her mother once said to her, *Remember, that will be you one day* — which, at the time, she felt only as another cruelty. And here she was, each day closer and closer. So accustomed to the mortar and pestle was she now that each piece of it felt like part of her hands, and she ground and tipped the grounds away and tossed another handful in while the rest of her was years away, travelling along a line of sweets strung from before her childhood up ahead beyond her own old age. She lifted the pan of warming honey from the fire, poured some into the heap of meal and stirred it with a heavy wooden spoon. And then she heard her husband speak, softly, as a child might, and she turned and he was at the door with a look she had never seen, like someone has flattened his face a little, enough that only she might notice, knowing his face better than she knows her own. *Mrs Seljuk, please,* he said, as he always called her that. *I need your help.*

The Armenian woman opened her mouth slightly. Mrs Seljuk lifted the spoon, rested its tip between the woman's teeth. And the woman gripped it a little, like a cat might bite lightly on your finger, or a husband your breast. And Mrs Seljuk tilted the spoon, and the soup slid in and, as always, the woman swallowed once. Then Mrs Seljuk waited. The woman opened her mouth again and Mrs Seljuk scanned the woman's eyes as she rested and tilted the spoon once more.

This morning, again, it appeared the woman was looking back. At first, Mrs Seljuk had smiled and spoken to this silent woman, believing she was being watched. But, as the days passed, Mrs Seljuk fell more and more silent. How long can one continue to speak to those who refuse to speak back? And so now she tried to ignore the Armenian's look and her own nagging belief. She lay in her bed at night, after feeding and washing and tucking in her own children and this Armenian's children, too, after the slow and careful feeding of the woman herself, and the gentle washing of her most intimate parts with a bowl of warm water and soft cloths, and the changing of clothes and sheets and the boiling of everything in the laundry. She lay in her bed at night and tried hard to sleep, but her legs ached and swelled. She closed her own eyes and then, always, always the woman's eyes would appear, that look that had almost fooled her in the early days. And she would find herself staring through the ghostly image of the woman's eyes at the dark ceiling, or find herself up and down all night, in and out of the children's rooms, listening to them toss and mumble, bringing them water, reassuring them all when one or other of the Armenian's children would shout or cry. There was something about that silent staring woman and about her children who never met Mrs Seljuk's eye and who made more sounds in their sleep than in their waking that gripped Mrs Seljuk by the throat. She didn't mind the work. What else could she do? Her husband was adamant — and he was right. It was the moral thing. And aren't those who show charity rewarded in Paradise? But, sometimes, she couldn't help feeling that she was being taken for a fool. She didn't know the woman's husband; her own said Mr Vartevarian was a gentleman, although she found that ... well, odd. Armenians, after all, have a different way about them. They try to be Turks but, well, they just cannot. Not really. It wasn't language — they all spoke Turkish, and spoke it well. This woman and her children spoke nothing else. It wasn't that they misbehaved — well, most of them didn't, although one heard the stories, all well substantiated, of their treachery. It was just that very thing really — treachery. They didn't want to be Turks, not really, not in their hearts. They liked being different, clung to it, she thought, insisting on going to church and everything else, no matter what the law said, no matter what the Young Turks told them to do. You could take everything from them to punish them and they simply would not yield. Such a stubborn people. She wondered sometimes if they really wanted to live at all. Besides, any Turk could tell an Armenian as soon as they looked at them. Their faces are, well, a less attractive kind of face, less striking. Still, the silent one would have once been pretty. She had her colouring to thank for that. One of her mothers must have been with a European. But they did that kind of thing, she'd heard. Everybody knew Armenian women would go with anyone, and their men didn't mind as long as they got something for it — a few medjidia or a pair of shoes. Once she'd seen an Armenian man run screaming after his wife and daughter who were being ridden off. They were shouting and struggling, lying on their bellies over the pommels of the saddles of a couple of men in a large group, all on beautiful horses. It was quite a scene while it lasted, but they soon disappeared. She had asked a shopkeeper why the Armenian man was running after them, weeping. *Shame on those Turks,* the shopkeeper had said. *They have robbed him. They didn't pay.*

It was as well the Armenian woman was ill and that Mr Seljuk was busy at his work all day because she had seen the way he had looked at her the first night he brought them home, all filthy, their clothes barely on them. She came in from a bath, wearing some of their oldest daughter's pretty clothes and then, such a look he gave her. And her tears, her rush outside to spit out good food, food Mrs Seljuk had cooked for them all, and the strange way the woman had held things. Mrs Seljuk had given thanks they were out of her house the next morning. And now, this. Well, once pretty or not, she's become even stranger, curling herself up like a cat, staring at me from the moment I walk in until I leave, with her peculiar European eyes. Thank Allah the little Armenians don't have the grace to look at me. Pretty or not, even he can't deny it, that even now that she has filled out a little, now that I keep her dressed, clean up after her, feed her children, keep them all hidden, she remains dumb and strange. Dumb but watching. But stupid? Mad? *Where is your compassion, wife? The woman has been driven mad,* is all Mr Seljuk will say. But I say who is it who's stupid? Who is the one unable to sleep? And who is the one sore from work?

At night I have to lock her door. I think it's best for everyone. She takes off her clothes. She messes in the corner. I come in the morning and she is curled up naked. I clean the room; I wash and dress her. I don't mind, but what in the name of Allah would happen if my husband or my sons opened the door? Or if she wandered out, naked, into the street? What would happen even if she went out clothed? May Allah forbid it. Everyone knows us here, and they would know, as soon as they looked at her, what she is. What would happen then — to all of us? So, I lock it. Often, in the mornings, her children are asleep all over the house — under the table, outside her door. I have to step over them to get to her. Once I found one asleep with the dogs. I say to Mr Seljuk, *What is to become of them? How long will they stay?* But he just looks away. He never properly answers me. He has been strange since he returned them here. He told me what he saw. Terrible. I said, *Are you certain?* because I know terrible things have happened, but still it is hard to believe. He said, *Are you saying I am a liar? No,* I said, *no. But who could have done such a thing?* He shook his head and looked at me. *Who do you think could have done such a thing?* he whispered. *I don't know,* I said. *Perhaps, Kurds?* He just kept looking at me. I didn't know what else to say. *Not Turks?* he whispered. *No,* I said. I was shocked. *Women? Babies? Not Turks. Chettis, perhaps.* He didn't say anything for a long time that evening and neither did I.

* * *

Aleppo, September 1915

Dear Mr Ursa

The Seljuk family send the Ursa family good wishes. I hope your wife is well. Mine is quite well, although she is tired and troubled. And she complains a good deal, as wives do. However, on this occasion the reason for her discontent may become clearer as you read this letter.

Everyone knows what happened in 1909 and I have no doubt you are already well informed of the recent events occurring in the eastern regions, but I can no longer resist the need to write to you of that which I myself have witnessed, in case — in case of what? That you do not, cannot, believe the stories you hear? Or that you, like me, have heard them over the years and believed them with some of the same feeling with which one may hear and believe a child's complaint, understanding that, to the child, this is a most serious matter, feeling a genuine compassion for their grief or indignation at the imparting of their grievance, but also knowing that, in time and with maturity and experience, these grievances, this grief, will become less and less, until perhaps the incidents may disappear forever from memory? Perhaps the child will even laugh about them one day. Or perhaps they will see that whoever aggrieved them did so without true malice, was misguided, agitated, provoked. It is to my shame I say this to you, that I have felt this in some part of me. I have, all these years, wanted so much to believe it is all a horrible mistake, a series of horrible mistakes, unconnected accidents. To have believed otherwise would have meant living with a realisation all these years, living with the truth that men are capable of such calculated barbarity, such appalling unmitigated cruelty, and equally capable of enjoying it. That there exists in this country an intensity and breadth of evil that defies either imagination or belief. But I can deny it no longer, for terrible deeds against the Armenians are more frequent and widespread, and I fear what this means.

Should I apologise to my countrymen and my God for not coming sooner to this enlightenment? For remaining wilfully, stubbornly innocent? Which is worse: a man who foully outrages small children, tortures and mutilates young men and old, strips and publicly humiliates old women, opens the bellies of pregnant women with his bayonet or uses it to commit acts of appalling indecency, denies them food, water, shelter, and then leaves their corpses for dogs to fight over, or a man who hears of these things yet truly believes that these crimes are simply the behaviour of some other men misguided or annoyed, and that the life of this country will, one day quite soon, be restored?

How can things ever be the same? And what is to become of us all? How can we pray, knowing what it is we now know? There are some things even God can't forgive. How can we work, raise our children, teach them to be God-fearing and to be good citizens?

This is what I have seen with my eyes, and continue to see every day and every night. Upon receiving your missive through Mr _____ , I took a carriage and set out upon the route he and I discussed and agreed to be the most likely one upon which Mrs Vartevarian, her remaining children and female relatives might be found. When I set eyes upon the line of people, I was astonished at its length, for it stretched for such a distance. There must have been thousands of poor souls wandering one behind the other in that parched, windswept plain. Thousands of people in a slow and wavering line. Nearing them, the sight became even more pitiful, for as hard as I looked I did not see one able-bodied male. All these wretches were women and children, and no boys or girls older than about nine or ten years. Some pregnant women, some carrying thin weak babies who tugged and tugged at their mothers' flaccid breasts. Some old women hardly able to shuffle along. And old men, too, but very few and all infirm, leaning heavily on sticks, and one I saw blind and being led by others. All these people carrying nothing but themselves — no food, no water, no blankets, without shoes, and most in only thin undergarments.

I asked Mrs Vartevarian that evening why so many were in underclothes or less. I was puzzled. Could they have chosen to walk in that way? She confirmed that everything they had left their homes with — money, food, blankets, even the clothing they were wearing — had been taken from them. I also asked something else that bewildered me. When I reached the column and was seeking an officer to speak to, it was immediately clear how very few gendarmes there were guarding these people. And so I asked Mrs Vartevarian why it was that the women did not overpower the gendarmes. After all, there are thousands of women and a handful of guards. *If we kill them*, she replied, *what do we do then? None of us know where we are. We have no maps, no way of finding food and shelter. What would be achieved by killing them? When we arrive at our destination they have told us we will be cared for in camps, there will be tents and wells and animals. It is just the travelling there that is the torture.* We ate in silence for a long while. I didn't ask any more; I couldn't even look at her, could barely chew. What was there to say that would, in any way, have helped? The truth? As I have explained to you, I wasn't entirely sure what that was. If I told her what I had heard she would have been distraught, demanded that we return that night and retrieve her extended family. And we couldn't have done that, it being much too risky. So, I said nothing. In the morning she was most polite but very concerned for her mother and sisters, that they not be left believing she and her babies had been kidnapped and killed and, therefore, insisted I return her. What else could I do? Is it right to hold a person against their will? Is it right to say what I had been told? She wouldn't have believed me. Why should she? So, I had to take her back.

Mr Ursa, this wasn't supposed to occur. The mother and sisters were supposed to come, too. They were invited. But they were afraid, and who could blame them? The carriage was quite big enough. I had made sure of that in accordance with our plan. All night I had prayed we had been misinformed, you and I and Mr _____. I prayed to God. At that point it still seemed a reasonable thing to do, to pray to God. And now? Where is God in this thing now, in this unholy mess, this country? Do not misunderstand me, please, effendi. I love and serve Turkey; she is our mother. And I love and serve Mustafa Kemal; he is a great man of vision and a true patriot, the Father of this nation and its people. Turkey could not continue in its old ways and be left far, far behind. A new century demands a new way of thinking. I question neither our Motherland nor our Father. I question God and man.

How can I explain this vision to you? It was as if I had seen it all before — as if, I stress. I took the same route but at a different time of day. The light, therefore, was harsher, and the plain seemed even more menacing. Or was this my trepidation? I could not tell, but at last, after what seemed an eternal journey, we came into view of something that resembled the miles and miles of slowly moving people I had seen just the previous evening, but was no more like that line than a goose is like its eggs.

The movement I saw was not the movement of people but of animals. Everywhere along the roadsides dogs and vultures feasted on the bodies of the dead. As soon as I realised what it was we were seeing I told my driver to pull up the carriage, to go no further. I don't remember if anything else at all was said, but poor Mrs Vartevarian climbed down from the carriage and ran. I thought she might run away, into the desert, away from this dreadful sight. I was afraid I would lose her in that wilderness, but I would have understood that, as I would have liked to make that very escape myself. But, no. She ran towards it, in amongst the carnage, calling. Calling what, I couldn't make out, for I was calling after her, imploring her to come back. Her children began to cry out. She was running amongst the bodies, amongst the vultures who flew up a little height on their black wings at her approach, and amongst the packs of dogs which scattered and snarled at her, and at each other. I feared again for her amongst these beasts. I feared for myself, too. I feared, also, that whoever had done this thing would return. Were they still nearby? Were they watching us? She ran, darting, this way, that way, oblivious to my entreaties for her to stop, my calls for her return.

And so, I too ran. I ran after her, in amongst the corpses of women and children. I confess I tried not to look. I looked but tried not to see. But I did see. Women of all ages, girls, little boys and babies, all beheaded. The body of each of them in one place, the head nearby or elsewhere. Who could tell? There were so many. Who would wish to put together such a puzzle? Yet, someone should. Hundreds and hundreds and hundreds of the poor souls. Someone should. It is the least someone should do, but a braver man than me. The bodies were mutilated. Limbs taken off. Bellies opened. The torsos of women and children who had been outraged and left naked and exposed. And everywhere, animals. A dog carrying an arm. Five or six vultures at one neck. All of them gorging themselves on the flesh of the dead. I felt as if I had entered a dream, but not one of my own making. Who would choose this? This was someone else's nightmare. A nightmare so immense it must be that of more than one. I fear, Mr Ursa, it is this nation's nightmare. When will we awaken from it?

Eventually, I took them home. I managed to grasp Mrs Vartevarian, lead her back to the carriage and place her in it. Then I, too, climbed in, never letting go her arm in case she should attempt to leap from me, and I took them back to my home. This is what was always intended, of course, as you know — that they should stay a time while their safe passage is arranged. But my wife did not know, does not know still, as I felt it best to keep her out of the proceedings as far as possible, just in case things went wrong, you understand. My wife is a very hard worker, a good wife. When we returned, she was surprised. I had no choice but to give Mrs Vartevarian to her with little explanation for I could not speak of what we had seen. I did explain further, later that evening, but not fully. There are some things I cannot tell her. I know she will look after Mrs Vartevarian, who will need looking after I'm afraid, for the poor woman remains no longer herself. Indeed, effendi, there is something I feel the need to tell you.

Things have gone awry. I cannot simply say Mrs Vartevarian has gone mad, for she does not rant or run about as one may imagine a mad woman might. She, in fact, does nothing at all. She neither speaks nor makes any move to assist in her own survival. Nor does she seem to recognise anyone or anything around her, and not even her own children's tears move her from her trance. She performs none of the tasks necessary to live. She will allow herself to be moved and to be fed with a spoon, and allow other matters as my wife sees fit. Mrs Seljuk must attend to her in every way, and she does so uncomplainingly, as well as attending to Mrs Vartevarian's children and our own. As to whether Mrs Vartevarian has quite lost her mind, who can say? It is difficult to tell, in such a case, whether a recovery is likely. I am not a physician. The poor woman's children, too, are becoming physically stronger, but they are not as children should be. The little girl will neither speak to me, nor look at me. They scream in the night and my poor wife must get out of her bed to comfort them.

My family finds them sleeping on the cold floor in strange places — behind doors, under the beds, and often outside the door which leads to their mother, and which my wife keeps locked. It is better, we feel, that the children do not see much of their mother while she is unwell. We believe it can only upset them further. Besides, if she were to roam, she would put herself, and possibly us all, in danger. Mrs Seljuk has hinted that Mrs Vartevarian seems unable to retain her customary modesty. I can only suggest that this is a result of her wits being affected by that terrible scene, one that shall never leave me. I can only imagine how deeply it must have distressed her, her mother and sisters and their children being among the slaughtered. Over and over, I see her running amongst it all. I see the scene as if watching myself. I call and call, and I chase her, but she darts and disappears in the desecration. When I spy her at last, I run towards her. She is on her hands and knees. She is straining to crawl backwards on all fours. I see she has something in her mouth that she is dragging and, all about her, feasting vultures call and open their wings.

Something must be done for these people. Although I am not certain who is to blame for this particular atrocity, whether it be gendarmerie or chettis or Kurds, Turkey does not appear interested in helping the persecuted among its citizens. I see that now. We are all aware that witnesses of all kinds, including many respectable Turks and representatives of friendly foreign nations, have been managing, in secret, to send statements out of the country for many years, yet nothing changes, nothing is done. How long can the world hear of this and remain unconvinced?

Like me, you have no doubt heard that, in other countries, leaders and other prominent men have spoken of that which is taking place. I believe these men must be good men, men with strong principles. But what good are their words, Mr Ursa? Will they return Mrs Vartevarian to her right mind? Will they give her back her husband and dead children? Will they reassemble her mother and sisters and their babies, breathe life into them again? Will they return to her remaining children their father, their home and their childish joy? And what of Mrs Vartevarian's disfigured child? Will they return her eye to her face, revoke the scars the whole world sees when it looks at her? I thought this half-blind girl was very young, but was told by Mrs Vartevarian that she is almost of marriageable age. Her size is likely due to deprivations and the wounding she has suffered, but perhaps this has been advantageous for it seems she has been thought much younger and been allowed to stay with her mother, who spoke of her chances of marriage that first night. It appears the girl's virtue, at least, remains. Perhaps it is her ugly face that saved it.

Only the beautiful

Hovsanna's second daughter cannot sleep. All night Anaheed dozes and wakes beneath the open windows, rising to shutter them, for fear that someone may enter, then to open them again when she feels she cannot take another breath in this house. She pulls the heavy timber shutters flush to the building and fastens the latch as quietly as she can, not wanting to wake Arusiak. As it is, her sister wakes frequently enough, crying, wandering about and (if she has managed to fall into sleep) rousing Anaheed to soothe her with embrace and whispers, or to stumble after with a blanket to cover her when elsewhere she curls into another small sleep. Sometimes Annaheed fails to wake when the toddler rises quietly from bed, or she wakes but cannot move herself. And then the child sleeps cold somewhere, and Mr or Mrs Seljuk find her and there is a consternation about 'the Armenian child's' health. Or one of the Seljuk children kick her as they run past, and — despite Anaheed's plea — rush to tell their mother, shouting gleefully as if they've found the last one in a hiding game. Then everyone must speak of it — loudly and at length — of the pity of a child asleep on a floor like a dog. Everyone speaks of it except the Armenian children who will not sleep like other people and, in not being like other people, start it all.

The days are long enough, but the nights are longer. Anaheed sees she is living two lives. In some ways they are the same life, yet they are not. In daylight she is careful to move quietly, to listen closely at all times (even to conversations not intended for her — indeed, especially to these, for she has found much can be learned in this way), to do as she is told without speaking and certainly to never ask questions but, most importantly, never to look anyone in the face.

At night, there is rarely anyone's face to avoid (her sister is yet small enough to be undiscerning) and, if she does encounter someone else, there is always a darkness to step into. Even when Mr or Mrs Seljuk appear carrying a lamp — well, a lamp gives shadows. At night, she knows she must always listen and she knows it is essential that she moves utterly without sound. But, at night, with her sister, she will sometimes speak. The situations often demand it of her. Who else is there?

She would prefer not to; even whispering to anyone makes her afraid, and she is not Arusiak's mother. If she was the mother, may God forbid it, she would not be the kind of mother theirs has become — a shameful mother, a baby, who lies on her back and soils herself and allows someone to feed her. A mother with no husband who does things she shouldn't. She has seen that mother taking off her clothes in that room. Was it not enough that the women lining the streets of the villages they walked through, who jeered and hit them with their hands and with sticks, was it not enough that those women pulled their mother's skirt and blouse from her body, and Anaheed's skirt and blouse from hers and then quarrelled over them? And then, later, the men who came and who that mother shouted at and then stopped shouting. And, after that, the man with the sword who held Anaheed's face tight with his other hand and looked at it and said it was pretty and kissed her mouth hard and told her to do something she didn't understand. And how that mother rushed at him, screaming, and took his sword and how that mother looked at Anaheed when she struck Anaheed's face with it. Because it was better, she said, better she be ugly.

If she became a mother, if God insisted on it, she supposed she would have to endure it, but she would never become that mother. A mother who lives in the house of a Turk and takes off her clothes. What kind of mother is that? She had seen her; she had pressed her eye to the crack in the door and seen her. She had watched her stretch herself and roll. She had seen her lick her hands, over and over with her pale sticky tongue until it made Anaheed turn away. This was no mother, she had thought, seeing that. This was like seeing something I have never seen before. Many things I have seen seem to come from the sun because they burn my eyes. But this, this was no mother.

There are things that come from the stars, good things, beautiful and true, that God sends. There was my doll that Mama made me, and eating the juicy tomatoes I pulled off the bushes in the garden without her seeing, and my white knuckle bones. Good things are shiny and cool when I touch them or they touch me. They feel like water. They feel cool on my eyes as if I am washing. There are also things that come from the sun, things that burn our eyes like flames. They make so much heat I must close my eyes. They make so much screaming, and all the men shouting, *Dance, virgins, dance for us*, at the girls tied together and screaming and burning and screaming, all naked and burning, all red and gold, their long hair sparking, all trying to run and falling over all tied together and black and stinking. When I close my eyes they are still there. And sometimes they are there when my eyes are open. I carry them like pictures. Once I had my own bed and I had a tin box and in the box were pictures I drew at school, Easter pictures of our Lord's crucifixion and Mary weeping at His feet and the Roman soldiers standing around. And of Noah on his ark. The ark is resting on top of Mount Ararat with the flood still all around, and Noah is looking at the dove flying over his head with the olive branch in its beak.

The pictures I carry in my head are not like that. And now this is one of them, she thought, this no-mother who does things wrong, things like this, things even I know she shouldn't. What must God think of them, these wrong things that burn my eyes and make my head so hot? What must God think of her? It must make Him angry that things from the sun burn in our heads, that Satan sends them there like a piece of Hell. He must be angry with me. I have Hell in my head. I pray a lot. I speak to God all day, but nothing changes. I listen hard in case one day He speaks to me. Do you think He is sad about everything that's happened? Do you think one day He will forgive us for it?

Anaheed rose again and unlatched the shutters, sliding the bolt slowly and pushing away first one heavy frame and then the other. They swung out into the darkness. She peered out, turning her head steadily so that her vision swept back and forth across the piece of land between them. She wondered where the others were — Maree and Lucia and Armenhoui and Dickran and Dickranhoui and Zaven and Ara and Hovsep — and how it was that they could be there one day and then not. She knew well enough where Arpy was; she'd seen her mother do it, leaving her like that under that tree. And she wondered whether Krikor was still at the neighbour's house, waiting for them, and whether Baba had found the note on the table and the other note, the one she had left for him, the picture she had drawn of them all together, of herself with her real face, her other face so he wouldn't forget, and folded up beneath her pillow. The night was full of stars, so she could see the trees and garden, its paths, the field with its small goat hut and the luminous walls of the neighbouring houses beyond. She saw nothing move — no goat or bird, no tiger or fox, no horse or man — and, after some minutes, feeling it was safe enough, looked up at all the light.

I know God is there. I know it. I speak to Him but I keep very quiet. Nobody else would ever know. He doesn't need to hear my voice, for God can hear our thoughts. Nobody else would know what I say, especially not these other people here, the ones who live here and walk around and sleep. They have a God and we have a God. The God we have is not the God they have. Our God is the true God and

He says we should pity them. They don't understand they have made a mistake and that the God we have is the only God. I have heard people say He is testing us, our only God. No-mother had said that, too. Other people have said other things. I have heard them, as well. Things they shouldn't say about God. God has not forgotten us. May God forgive them for saying so. He is angry and that is why He is quiet. I will stay quiet. One day He will speak. And I'll be listening. All the others will be running and shouting and crying and moaning, and only I will be listening. And when I hear Him I will tell them. They will listen to me then. When He speaks to me and I speak to them, when I tell them what God tells me to, they will look at my face and I will look at theirs because the words of God will make me beautiful. Only the beautiful are allowed to speak for God. And one day that will be me.

The world adrift

When Benyamin told Hovsanna he couldn't remember what Nerses had written on his palm and on the inside of his arm with his dirty, careful finger, she looked away from him into her own hands, then even more closely at her right forefinger, the one she had always imagined she might write with. She knew better than to press; each understood the need for lies, although she might call them something else because lying, they both knew, is a sin. She looked away because, whatever she called it, seeing it in her husband's face and hearing it in his voice made her ashamed. She thought of all the things she would never tell him and felt her face grow hot and her heart drum in her throat. She looked at her finger now, her skin thickened and dry, a pen without ink — no, not even that, as she once had thought — and then into the white sheet of their bed beneath her. And she opened her palm and slowly smoothed it, stroking tenderly as if it were alive.

Benyamin had swung away, planted his feet on the floor, and now he sat, his forearms resting heavily on his thighs, and gazed beyond his knees into the bare, worn stone. She wouldn't ask again, he knew that; she had gone too far and he knew she knew that, also. If she asked again he would make sure she fully understood. She wasn't stupid but sometimes he would swear she deliberately provoked him. That smile of hers, as if she were humouring him, as if he were a child. The way she blushed, the way her hands shook like a girl and not a grown up woman, as if she thought that, by playing at being fourteen again, they could both pretend nothing had happened. *Jesu*, he breathed, clenching and unclenching his fists.

Home? he had echoed. *Home?* And then, peering harder into the darkness at the man, *My wife, you say,* knowing there are all kinds of tricks and that, even in daylight, he can see a man with a donkey and trick himself, think of the Saviour, stumble his way into one city and believe he must be somewhere else, trick himself into seeing a biblical place, a holy city, see a man and a boy walk together beside him and think of — what? God the Father and the Son? He could dream himself into a stranger's house and wake to find himself dreaming in another. And now, here, in the dark, he is to believe these men — the one behind him, he imagines, breathing at the top of the stairs in the light of two lamps and descending like an angel towards Nerses and the old woman and others whose shapes he saw, shifting and thin, and whose voices he heard murmuring, murmuring like someone asleep, like Hovsanna murmuring into the veil of her hair, like their children restless in their beds, and whose hands and feet he heard dragging over the stone floor, that shuffle he had heard before in rooves full of rats. And to believe in the one before him, standing in the dark as would a thief, a murderer, like that which he used to believe meant criminal, in a time before this, before everyone was criminal, before this country betrayed itself, betrayed its true self — a prison, a masquerade, a magic trick. They think, they think you can take something that doesn't belong to you, take anything you want — fields, homes, churches, people — and do whatever you want with them. They think that by putting themselves inside what they take — field, home, people — they make it their own. They think — he heard a sound come from someone, was that him, he almost laughed — you can build a quadrilateral of minarets around the curves of a cathedral and that makes it a mosque. They think nobody sees what it is they do, what is before their eyes, what is underneath, what it is they really stand on. They think, they really do think, that if they say the sun is moon for long enough, we will all believe them, that I will believe them, that we will all go about as if the night is the day.

And here, a criminal speaks 'wife' and 'home', despite where we stand, despite a dungeon beneath our feet, the earth full of speechlessness, despite the sweat of my forehead against the sweat of my friend's, despite watching his finger move across my skin, the slow certain touch of it, its dermographia, angry and pink. What it raised, what it left behind. How it branded me. Are they correct? Am I, after all, just a beast, moaning? A mute goat? Its lolling tongue? A stump of flesh, only?

Benyamin glanced from the man to the door. He saw the man stretch out his hand, take another step, heard him start to say something that, once again, sounded like the beginning of his name. Then he felt himself lurch, saw his forearm rise, felt against his elbow the quick sharp slip of the man's teeth, heard something give. The man staggered, his hands suddenly to his face, and fell. And between his bloodied fingers he saw Benyamin Vartevarian standing over him, baring his teeth, hissing *Liar*, his eyes, mouth, the pale stripes of the skin he wore luminous in the light the moon could shed.

He knew this language. It came to him the way an ocean might — now closer, now distant. I am a shore, he thought. The world's adrift, continents splaying. I am a current, my pulse, a line of thought. I am a washed shell, I have rolled ashore, landed, become land.

He opened his eyes; the air was white. Through it, a face. Someone peering down at him. And the voices, beyond vision, to his left. Armenian voices, men, subdued. He caught the odd word. Was it he they were trying not to wake? He turned his head a little; it hurt.

When he was a child he sometimes heard his parents speak like that in the room he shared with his brothers, discussing some upset or fever. He remembered his mother's voice and tried to bring her face to mind. When was the last time he had seen her? She carried a wide glass bowl, a gift he had brought her from somewhere ... Italy? He saw the open trunk by his bed in the rolling cabin. Who had said the Mediterranean was calm? In the centre of the trunk, the bowl nestled in his clothing, its inside glistened like a cleaned eggshell. She carried the bowl. She was crossing the room; it was the middle of the day. He could see small leaves shining, the wet white and green of cucumber. When was that? He listened harder, his father's voice not a voice at all but another kind of sound, a murmur, a memory, a sense of something, like excitement or happiness. He strained towards it, but the further he leaned the more indistinct it became until it was the wind, the ship's engines, the growl of waves against the hull, the voices of these men somewhere to his left, the low rumble of wheels in the street. Father, he thought, I'm here. I'm waiting for you, to come back home, to come back to me. I can see my mother smiling; she is crossing the room; she is carrying the gift I gave her, carefully, close to her like it's her burden. I am waiting for you, your steps on the stair, your hands on my cheeks, your kisses goodnight.

So, he's with us, he heard someone say.

Yes, came the reply.

Then there was a cup against Benyamin's lips, so he drank.

When next he opened his eyes it was night; there were other bodies, breathing loudly. He sat up. He had no idea where he was.

He sat still. He felt his heart beat, his chest rise and fall, his blood push through the veins in his arms and his neck. There was something heavy and warm over him; he pulled it closer. It was leathery on one side, thickly haired on the other. He ran his hands over it, seeking its edges, its shape. His hands rustled in it like mice. Someone mumbled something, turned, began to snore. He splayed his fingers in the short thick hair, felt the skin beneath, pushed with the grain, then against, through and back, over and over, along every part, as if he was learning it. He remembered; he remembered what it was. He stared so long into the black of the room that he was able to see. All night he sat there, hearing three men breathe, watching their bodies turn and curl and turn again in the small, windowless space, watching the crack beneath the door for light.

He knew he must have been hit. He could recall nothing but there was no other explanation. And, in that case, he also knew who hit him. He was trying to reach the door and that Turk, that Pasha ... And the other man, the one in the dark, what had he done? Benyamin fingered the fraying edge of bandage around his elbow. Had there been a fight? Again, he examined his hands, feeling his knuckles one by one for bruises. No, he must have injured it when he fell.

He looked up.

So, what you are trying to tell me is that, in the house of a man who helped us reach you, who took you in, in a city in which another man and his son were kind to you, is an underground cave, full of Armenians, and that he keeps them there, with their tongues cut out.

Yes.

Did he cut out their tongues?

Benyamin gave a small shrug. *I don't know. He said not.*

The two men stared at one another.

You understand he has been helping us for some time, the other man said. *Several people, not just you.*

Benyamin nodded slowly. *I saw them. I spoke to them.*

What did they say?

Benyamin shook his head a little and looked away. *They couldn't speak.* He looked again into the man's face. *They had no tongue. Are you listening to me at all? My friend* — He held out his arm. *He wrote on me.*

The man gazed from Benyamin's face to his arm and then back to his face. This man, he thought, this tall, thin, imposing man, half-crucified. He had seen it before, clever men reduced to magic — a single feather, a handful of twigs bound together in a particular way by a scrap of fabric from a loved one's shirt. He leaned closer, patted his knee. *Things have been very bad for you, Mr Vartevarian. I am glad, so very glad we have found you.*

Benyamin turned from this man, with his look of — what? He thought. Intense sympathy? — to the smaller man, leaning into the corner of the room, his arms folded across his chest, his mouth cut and swollen, his unreadable gaze. *Yes,* Benyamin whispered. He looked between them, the man far away and the one close whose eyes, he noticed, had narrowed. *Yes.* He felt his own eyes sting and turned away. *It has been very bad.*

Was there anything else you wished to tell us?

Benyamin shook his head. He closed his fists, opened them, closed them again. Why didn't they hurt him?

Then you are happy to follow our directions later, with the others?

Benyamin nodded. The man stood, gently gripped Benyamin above his injured elbow and Benyamin gathered close the tiger skin with his good arm, lifted it higher on his shoulder and rose carefully, took a step. And then, gazing into the space where the floor meets the wall, cleared his throat. *And my children*, he said, as steadily as he could. *Are they waiting for me, too?*

Of course they are. Of course.

Day night day night day night. I lose count. Beneath me, the roll of wheels until even in my dreams it's all I hear. I go to sleep to it, wake to it, turn and doze again. I fear I have become it. I walk now only when unavoidable. And, when I walk, in darkness, from barn to carriage or cart to building, when I step — slowly, carefully — from one room to another, when it is my turn to carry our pail to empty it into a hole or when I step over the other two men to use that pail, I feel the cold stone, the earth shake beneath me. My legs shake, each step a tremor that makes me ashamed, as if my body has become something else. My feet are wheels and the wheels roll beneath me. Wheels roll over me, over my bones, inside me, inside my bones, inside my head. Day night day night, my bones bounce against the wooden floors of carts. My head is bruised. I hold it in my hands. My head is tender. I cannot touch it. How is it possible that I am still Benyamin Vartevarian? How is it possible I am still a man? It is possible I have become something else. It is possible I will return from wherever it is I've been, that I'll come down, down, down, bouncing all the way from the plains to the sea, to the door of my home on the low flat land near the sea. It is possible I will knock on the door, knock on the door of my own house because I know I am changed, I am no longer myself, and Hovsanna will answer, wiping her hands on her apron, and she will not recognise me. It is possible my children will hide from me as I step back in, slowly, carefully, not knowing what I am, a man, a wheel, a beast, an invention. It is possible I no longer look like myself. It is possible, now, that I will live, and that I will never again sleep at night, but doze and doze all day, as I do, and sit up all night watching, watching through the windows for things, things that betray, watching Hovsanna and my children, watching them, watching them breathe.

Sometimes, he drags sounds from his dreams and into the waking world, and this, existing in the moment between the waking and its knowledge, leaves him as he opens his eyes, leaves him alert, listening, confused. And so he wakes, opens his eyes, remembers the sounds of bells. Where is he?

In Paris there were bells. On Sunday mornings he would wake to them, late, stagger from bed, dress, lurch up the steps into the street, rubbing his eyes, the bells still ringing, his stomach empty and nauseous from so little sleep. In the pews he sat apart. He didn't know anyone; a few of the students he knew still attended, but elsewhere. This church was just two blocks from his basement. He had become accustomed to the same faces every week, and they were polite to one another, nodding courtesies, an occasional mumbled greeting. The priest was the only one who spoke, held Benyamin's hand with his two hands, eventually asked. Benyamin watched the unspoken question pass over his face, and said, *I hope you don't mind.* And, of course, he didn't or, at least, he smiled generously and replied, *Orthodox, Catholic, we know the same true God.* And Benyamin knew they did, of course they did, but he felt the heat in his neck, nonetheless.

Now, he blinks and whispers, *Where are we?* But neither man replies, neither the balding man who lies curled in front of him and into the back of whose head he speaks, nor the stutterer, curled behind, whose breath he feels quick against his shoulder. The three of them like this, close and still, one curving into the other as they might in a bed. And beyond the stutterer, Benyamin remembers, the fourth man, the one who never speaks at all. All of them, un-named, anonymous, it is safer that way. They understand this. If they have to run, make an escape, be caught, there are no names to trade for a cup of water or a merciful death.

Beneath the heavy covers, it is dark. It is always dark; they mostly travel at night, pressed like this. Beneath them all there are cracks in the timbers. Through these cracks and in the gaps between the boards, they watch their slice of the world pass beneath them. They watch dust and stones, horse shit and cobbles. The moonlight slants upon these things so beautifully and Benyamin measures time and direction like this: angles and illumination. And when they stop, Benyamin hears the timbers strain, feels them tilt as the driver steps down from the cart, his boots scuffing the stony ground, a pause and then the crunch beneath them as he walks, stops. He hears the stamp of hooves. Another pause and the heavy sound of a stream of water splashing a short way off, then stopping, starting, stopping. Light like rain. Silence. He shifts his numb feet. The stutterer's finger pokes him once, hard, in the ribs. He gasps. And then he hears them.

Hey, you. Where are you going?

Got some room in that cart?

Footsteps approaching; Benyamin tries to count them.

The voices are young.

The driver's voice is older, edged with something. He says, *Good morning, brothers.*

Is it morning? one says, and they laugh.

Yes, it's morning and I have been travelling all night. My horses and I are very tired. I am going to rest and then buy food when the market opens.

We can wait.

A silence.

What, all seven of you? In this small cart? Eight of us pulled by two weary horses? I'm sorry, brothers.

Another silence; someone coughs and spits. Then another voice.

Where are you going?

To my cousin. He is ill.

We need transport.

I can't give it to you.

We could just take it.

There is a long pause. Benyamin closes his eyes. He tries to imagine himself outside, alongside the driver. He thinks about his body, his limbs; his feet, the arm upon which he has been lying, are numb. Would he fall if he sprang up now? Could he run? He wants to speak. He forms the sentences in his head, hears himself think them very loudly. If he shouts them this way will the bald man, whose head is touching Benyamin's, hear them resonate in his skull? They are so close. Surely it is only a matter of will?

What's that you say? The driver's voice is cold and steady. *You would rob me? A man old enough to be your father? Shame on you. Why aren't you at home, with your families? Shame on*

you all. Roaming like a pack of dogs. You shame your mothers.
You don't know how to behave. And the cart lurches.
Benyamin imagines the angry shouts, stones flying, running
feet chasing. He waits. He hears the wheels grind over the
stones, his pounding heart, the stutterer's rapid breathing.

The evenness of his own breath surprises him. *What can
this be*, he thinks, *except confirmation that I am truly no
longer a man?* And he closes his eyes again and listens to his
slow breathing, his steady heart.

One Saturday, in the bibliotheque, he had come across a
cluster of anatomical texts and, in his loneliness, he had
carried an armful to a desk as far from others as he could
find and scanned the pages for clues. Perhaps, he mused, if
he understood the way his body was constructed, he might
come to understand why he felt the way he did.

It was the plates that took his breath away. And, although
he knew he should not, he followed each careful line with
his fingertip. He read of *une échelle des êtres*, a ladder of
beings, that careful catalogue between stones and men, and
he wondered, feeling as he did back then — estranged,
l'étranger — where it was in the ladder he sat at that
moment, upon which rung. There in the corner, so far from
the world, so far from all things familiar to his hands, to his
mouth, from all things he thought of as soft and warm and
glowing.

And, as he gazed at all the careful work, he thought, *Here
is the possibility. For if the hearts of beasts and men are so alike,
if our bellies contain the same parts and innards, then there is
not so much distance as we think. Rather, here is similarity of*

form, and degrees of colour are merely shades or mixtures, some made paler, some duller, some more rich.

Later, he studied another book, smoothing each page with his hand. He found himself taken by this work by Thomas Willis — *Two Discourses concerning The Soul of Brutes, Which is that of the Vital and Sensitive of Man* — and he studied page after page, reading slowly, deliberately, about the animal spirits: how we breathe them in; how they become us and we become them. *Melancholy*, he read, *is a complicated disorder of the Brain and Heart: For as Melancholick people talk idly, it proceeds from the vice or fault of the Brain, and the inordination of the Animal Spirits dwelling in it; but as they become very sad and fearful, this is deservedly attributed to the Passion of the Heart … Melancholy being a long time protracted, passes oftentimes into Stupidity, or Foolishness, and sometimes also into Madness.*

Ah, yes, he thought, *I see.* And while he did not smile — how could he? — he felt somehow comforted, knowing it was the act of breathing that made him and that *the Distempers happen chiefly to men of a melancholy temperament, with a dark aspect, and a more lean habit of body.* For how can he be held responsible for that? Separateness, he knew (and loneliness too, perhaps — why not?), is the natural way of some animals — tigers, for instance — and somehow, somewhere, such a spirit had entered him, and begun living in his brain and his heart, so close are the ways in which men and beasts are made. Structural rules, yes, these he understood — and he loved them also, their logic, their constancy. Why should it come as a surprise? Why had he not seen it all before? Despite everything, he knew there was order in the world. Order and rules upon which his work depends, without which nothing stands: no house, no church and, it seems, no man or beast. The profundity of it, the interconnection of all things in the world, the simple genius of the Divine mind. His hands shook above the books. His eyes stung. And, despite himself, he sobbed once, sharp and loud, and felt his chest and belly tremble, overcome by the simplicity of inspiration. He did not turn around nor lay his head and arms upon the cool and unforgiving surface of the reading desk, as he would have liked to have done. Instead, ashamed at the sound he had made and of the tremors that beset him, he pressed his weight into his arms and his arms into the desk and held his position as if it were nothing. And when at last he wiped away his mucus and tears with surreptitious hands, all the other readers — should they have been uninterested enough in their own texts and contemplations to abandon them for observation — would have seen nothing more than a steady young man, gaze fixed upon these particular pages as it had been for some time, pass his hands across his face, once, twice, three times and again, as if to banish puzzlement or snatch himself from the border of sleep. They could not have known his thoughts: *How insignificant I am; how foolish that I did not see it. This work I do and the work of God. There are so many types of beasts and yet, like all man-made structures, beasts require the same fundamentals. I am a man,* thought Benyamin, *and man is the cathedral of the world. We are both as close and as far from a cow or a dog as the soaring curves of Sancta Sofia are from a child's mud castle. And yet, God be praised* — through his tears the plates swam like some paintings he had seen in the Bohemian quarter — *how far is that? How far is that?*

* * *

She stared at his nape. How could he not remember? She remembered everything and, if he asked, she would tell him what she could. But that was the difference: he didn't ask. Instead, he turned from her when she asked, like this, so she could stare into the bony curve of his back.

Why don't you look at me?

What?

Look at me. Look. You don't look anymore.

Jesu Christos, what do you mean? I'm here. I'm here. I came back. What more do you want?

Look at me.

Benyamin shook his head, then looked at her sideways. *For what?*

I used to think it was because you didn't want me to see you cry but it isn't that. It's — You — you think — She felt her throat constrict.

What? What?

I don't know, I don't know what you think. I never have.

Listen to the way you speak; you sound like a crazy woman. And no, no you don't. You know nothing about me because you know nothing about anything.

She heard herself speak as if she was far away. *You think you're the only one who came back? I came back. Arusiak came back. Anaheed came back. And Maree and Hovsep eventually came back. It's not just you — we all came back.*

In an instant he had hold of her arm. *You evil sow, what do you mean, you bitch.* He grabbed her face hard in his other hand, leaned in close. *We had twelve children. Twelve. Where is the baby who was sucking your teat? And Maree and Hovsep coming back had nothing to do with you. And Anaheed? You mention Anaheed, after what you did? What kind of* — He was so close she felt his spit on her face. *Where are the others, you whore? Why did you come back and not them? Huh? What kind of mother are you?*

He pushed her away. She scrabbled up the bed, opened her mouth, closed it again.

All you're good for is squeezing them out. He lunged at her, his hands under her nightdress. *You can't get enough of that.*

Don't.

Listen to you — *'don't'. Is that what you said to the gendarmerie and the chettis and the Kurds? 'Don't?'*

Stop it, Benyamin, please. I — She drew her legs up close to her chest, struck at his arms with her fists.

You what? You what? You don't want it now? You don't want your husband? You wanted me to look at you, now I'm looking at you. You're my wife. Tell me what you said to them. Tell me while I'm listening, while I'm looking at you.

She closed her eyes. *Stop, please.*

She could hear his voice catch in his throat. *You didn't say anything, did you. You just did what they told you. You just did what they told you like everybody else. If they told you to suck, you sucked. If they told you to bend over, you did it. Everybody did. You think it's something special, what you did, coming back? It's nothing, what you did, nothing. And while you were doing it, you filthy stinking whore, you lost our children.*

He pushed her away. Her head hit the wall and the sound of it rang. She opened her eyes. He was standing beside the bed, looking at her. His arms were outstretched, palms upturned towards her, like a beggar. *You lost our children,* he sobbed. He said it over and over. And, as he said it, he hit his head with his own fists. *You. Lost. Them.* Over and over.

No light

(Alexandretta, 1917)

When Hovsanna had returned to Cilicia to search for Benyamin and her children, the wind blew in the streets as if nothing had happened. She stood in a doorway and watched it. Not her own doorway, of course. Someone else lived there now, she had been told when she asked. But still, later, she had gone there, asking not for her home but for two chairs, a bed, perhaps some plates. They had shouted curses, and she had stood with her head bowed and her face burning with shame at the things they said. Not her own doorway, not her home, but where she lay down, and there were so many empty houses now, silent and hollow, and she just took one, it didn't matter which, it was after all the same wind that blew lightly off the sea, as always, there and here. So she stood in the doorway that wasn't hers and watched the street where a leaf and a little sand, as fine as dust, occasionally lifted. She didn't look up. She noticed there were sometimes shadows on the ground, as if above her head something stronger pushed the clouds around. But she didn't look up. Then, after a while, she went inside.

In the first weeks she had not slept but circled the small

room — listening at the walls, her hands spread wide against the cold stone as if they might help her pick up sound, watching for a long time at the window, locking and relocking the door — while Anaheed and Arusiak slept in a bundle of clothes on the floor, dead-centre. Her circuits were slow and very quiet, and occasionally she swept back the ash that had spilled onto the hearth, turned embers, added a log. But it was as hard to find wood as it was to find food, and people had their own children to warm, their own mouths to feed. She understood that. Each morning she carried Arusiak to the market corner and held out her hand to the passers-by. *Thank you,* she would say with her head bowed, waiting for the cold press of a coin. *May God keep you,* whether they filled her hand or not. But she knew she could not rely on kindness. So she stopped burning the fire into the night and circled the room, over and over, lit only by the more or less light that entered the window. But it did not matter; she did not need it. By the time she needed to ration wood, she had learned the rhythm of her way and she could close her eyes and be guided only by memory, by her body, by her two feet and hands. Wall, window, wall, door, wall, wall. Around and around. Until Arusiak cried and Hovsanna took the few steps and then lowered herself, heavy with exhaustion, beside her child and into a brief and shivering sleep, the little girl pressed hard against her, feeling the thump of her mother's heart and waking and dreaming and waking and dreaming of all kinds of creatures she could not yet name. Then opening her eyes in the early light, tearful, reaching into her mother's clothes for her soft flat breast, and sucking, sucking her way back to sleep, sucking something she loved into her hungry space.

Each afternoon she left Anaheed crouching behind the door and walked the few more streets to where she used to live, Arusiak dozing against her shoulder, and she stood on the road and looked at the house, the sheets — her sheets — flapping on the washing line, the fruit trees shading the paths along which children who were not her children chased one another. A woman with a basket sometimes bent into the tangle of zucchini vines, moving here and there. Or, sometimes, those children tugged the ripe tomatoes from the bushes leaning wearily at their stakes, and pushed handfuls into their mouths or threw them at her, running towards her, squealing. And, at first, Hovsanna would say to the woman's back or the children's laughter, *God keep you, God keep you all, but have you seen my husband or my children? Have they come home?*

And the woman would move silently from here to there and the children would cry out, *Go away, you whore, you filth, you dog.* The neighbours would step out to stare, also silent, until the children, too, would drift away to other games. And then Hovsanna would shuffle forward carefully when she was sure they had all turned away, one hand pressing Arusiak tight and heavy against her body, and she would drop to her knees. With her free hand, she would scoop the remains of tomato from the stones, tilt back her head and allow the soft red flesh and sand to drip from her fingers down her throat.

As the weeks passed, the children stopped taunting her and, after a while, Hovsanna stopped asking her question. Instead, daily she stood still and silent herself, and remembered the night she had seen Benyamin from their bedroom window, burying the box beneath the orange tree. And she remembered, before that, laughing and laughing — laughing at something she could not remember, no longer remembering how laughter felt, and no longer able to imagine anything that makes laughter possible.

* * *

Inside the house that was once the Vartevarian's house, the woman sobbed into the edge of her headkerchief. *I cannot bear it, I cannot live here with that ghost.*

What ghost? There are no ghosts. Her husband glared at her.

No ghosts? she screeched. *No, not for you, you aren't here when she comes. Day after day, week after week. Even the children won't play outside now in the afternoon.*

He stared from one child to the other around the meal table. *So they play inside.* They ate in silence. The lamps flickered suddenly in a gust of wind. *Close the window,* he said.

And so, one afternoon Hovsanna listened from the road but there were no voices; she watched the windows but they did not move; she looked in the garden but the washing line was bare. She waited and thought and then she walked away. The next afternoon she watched and listened, and the next. The shutters were still untouched, askew. No toys or shoes had appeared on the paths overnight. She knocked and called quietly and no-one answered. That evening she walked back and stood outside. There was no light. She pressed her face up to a window. There was no light. She crept into the garden. She pulled oranges from the tree. There was no light.

There was no light.

When she pushed the rear door it swung open. She walked through the house. There were no chairs or beds or pans or plates. It smelled unfamiliar — some other food, some other bodies. It echoed like a cave. In the bedroom where she had laughed, she found clothes she did not recognise. She sat on the floor, pressed her back into the corner. She piled the clothes over her knees and her head. In the dark tent of it all she breathed. She breathed but its scent reminded her of no-one. She tipped her head back; she opened her mouth. In her lap, Arusiak turned and cried, one hand fumbling for the breast. She did not move; she did not open herself. She had tipped her head back; she had opened her mouth. A sound came out. A sound came out. The child cried louder, her fingers frantic. Even the moon wouldn't enter there. She had never felt so lonely.

* * *

When Araxy opened the door and saw the thin arm, the half-open, black-lined palm, the long hair like a nest about the child's head, her own heart sank. It wasn't that she didn't feel sympathy, or something like it — of course she did. Doesn't everyone? A child like that, going about alone and starving? It was just that she hated being asked. Because being asked meant she had to listen and to hear herself refuse. And she hated hearing that, even if she didn't speak, even if she only heard her silence as she turned away or closed the door. And it meant that, when she had closed the door and returned to her friend, Hovsanna, whose arms were plunging clothes deep into a pail on the table, she would have to rearrange her face so that, should Hovsanna look at her, there would be no trace of what she had done or how she felt about it — sympathy, yes, but an anger also, a resentment. Because they just kept coming, those children, knocking on people's doors day after day, month after month. And, if she gave to everyone who asked, how would she and Hovsanna and Hovsanna's children survive? Surely, anyone could see the impossibility of it? How long could it all go on? And it was all very well, all very well for Hovsanna to have other ideas but Hovsanna had always had everything she wanted — marriage, money, and many children. She'd always been lucky, ever since she was born, ever since they were girls together, growing up as neighbours in Hassan Beyli. That yellow hair and everything. She'd even been able to find her way home, and find a way into that home again. She had always been able to afford to be generous. But not everyone could be so lucky. That's what Hovsanna did not understand, and that's what Araxy needed to teach her. But she hated the way Hovsanna made her feel, the way she looked at her, and that's why she had to always rearrange her face.

In the kitchen, Hovsanna said, *Who was that?*

Oh, a beggar again, Araxy replied without looking at her.   And then, into the silence because anything is better, *I sent her away.*

And Hovsanna dried her hands on her apron, as Araxy

knew she would, took one of the four oranges on the table and hurried towards the door, saying quietly as she passed Araxy, whose lips were pressed together, *It's all right. This is my orange.*

She opened the door. The child was gone. She stepped out to look, could see her slowly walking away, small and thin in a ragged skirt and bare feet. Hovsanna hesitated. She felt the weight of the fruit in her hand. She took a few more steps. She knew that tonight, when they sat at the table to eat, Araxy would say nothing at all to her. She knew that her friend would watch as she peeled and fed Arusiak an orange. And she knew that Araxy would then carefully and silently peel and break her own orange in two and slide one half across the table to Hovsanna, as she always did, her lips still pressed together, and without ever meeting her glance. She raised her arm. *Come back!* The girl kept walking. She was further away now. *Come back!* The girl stopped and turned. Hovsanna held up the orange. The girl started walking towards her. Hovsanna watched her approach. She still held the orange aloft, like a ball. She watched her approach.

The girl grew closer and clearer, her head raised, watching the fruit because she knew she could never be too careful; sometimes people played tricks. She kept her eyes on the fruit. It hung in the air like an orange sun. The thought of it made her insides shake. She kept her eyes on it, held out her hand. The woman said something, made a strange noise like a whisper or a croak. So she held out both her hands. The woman didn't move. She waited but the woman didn't move. Her insides shook. She held out her hands. She looked at the woman for the first time. She looked away from the fruit and at the woman's face. It looked strange; the woman's eyes looked strange. *Please,* said the girl, not certain she had said it. The woman said something that sounded like *Maree.* The girl looked at her face; it was moving oddly. *Maree.* The girl's eyes filled. *Please,* she said, *I'm hungry.* The woman lowered the fruit, stretched it out to her. The girl's cupped fingers touched the woman's right hand but she didn't take it. *Please.*

Maree, said the woman, *it's me.* The girl looked at the fruit. She knew to wait, had learned better than to take anything from someone's hands, had learned how quickly their fingers could close about it, had often enough been struck for less. Hovsanna followed her daughter's eyes, looked at the fruit and her daughter's still-cupped hands; she stretched out the fingers of her free hand and ran them gently across her daughter's wrist. *It's me.*

Please, said Maree, looking at the woman's face all strange and watery like a face that appears in a puddle. She could feel how the inside of her shook and now she felt the outside of her began to shake, too. *Please.*

2

The orange road

(Jerusalem, 1925)

Lucine's feet pound the sand. It lifts, fine and yellow under her small heels in pale drifts like a pulse. The evening is always long, the colour of sky and air always familiar. Her rope turns and turns through it and, as she jumps and jumps, everything becomes redder. Her thin brown limbs and her dress and her long thick plait become redder. The bleached stone walls of the house become redder and the hard yellow ground outside the door where every evening she skips becomes redder, becomes — she imagines — gold, a promise of richness that rises from beneath her nimble feet to meet her, turning her to burnished leaf, her skin to something precious.

Sometimes, at absolutely the precise moment, she will glance, mid-flight, whipping her head to the west on the highest point of her arc, so that she can see the furthest distance. If someone asked she would be unable to say what it is that turns her. She would say nothing, but look as if the question was spoken in a language she doesn't yet understand, as if she had been asked why she skips, or as if she had suddenly come face to face with someone who had never felt thirst.

The road is so long and straight that Hovsanna has to unroll it in front of her as she walks. It is an orange road; it is orange in the six o'clock dawn when she leaves the hill; it is orange in the evening when she returns. For six days, she walks up and down and, each day, each way, her wide black shadow is thrown out long before her. For six days she walks the old city, through the city gate, to the homes in the quarter, the sun already at her back, walking into their streets, their courtyards, across their stones, their lit-up steps.

She walks this way: always towards her shadow as if into herself. And, approaching their doors, and if those doors face west, she sees that fat black self sometimes vanish in the cool shade of other people's homes. Or, sometimes, if their homes face east, her shadow is thrown up huge against their walls, so big she doesn't even notice it, its edges far beyond her field of vision so that the darkness before her is an easy thing, so used is she to seeing it.

Hovsanna peers into her shadow as she waits, a darkness so big that the top of her head edges across the shutters of a first floor window, bigger than a woman could ever be. Beyond that window, she knows, is a bedroom, and in that bedroom a child sleeps. A boy. She knows this. But for us, from here, it is difficult to say, the covers pulled up so close to his head. But she knows this family and the others she cleans for; she knows their children, their glowing skin, their shouts and smiles, their little mounds of soiled clothes.

And, as she cleans, she thinks of her own house, her own children, both here in Palestine and far away, a long time ago. She thinks of their faces, each one of them, she thinks of their names, how they came to be, and the days and nights of their births. It is her most silent work, this remembering. She undertakes it religiously, and with all her strength. And then just before six o'clock, when the Jerusalem sun begins to fall, she walks home, back up the hill.

It is not always so, but this evening this is, again, the road of the slicing weapon. This road rises up through the air. This air, heavy with the weight of afternoon, the scent of heat and oranges. At the top of this road is the house and outside is the girl. She turns and turns her rope, the wooden handles slipping and slipping within her hands. Hovsanna sees the rope, the top of its slicing arc, some quick black movement at her house. She knows it is her child, that thin brown girl. She has seen this child, this game, she knows it. She knows that any moment now her child will see her, drop her rope, come running down the hill. She knows a lot; she knows all this, but she quickens her step, her breath, her heart — she cannot help it — her palms slick; she waits.

Tell me: is it possible to do both? To be much too far away, and to already have arrived?

The road unravels at her feet. Each step makes the road itself, this road home, this Jerusalem road. There is the shop with its crates of fruit, its rough bright lemons, the baskets of pale figs at its door. There are the neighbours' upstairs windows, shuttered and slatted with light. There is a woman slicing eggfruit framed by her window, cut through by the wrought iron of her gate, the knife going quick quick quick against the board.

And Hovsanna waits; she is just too far away. Her steps make the road; her blood pounds. The road reddens with the falling sun. She cannot take her eyes away — that quick black thing cuts the air, cut cut cut. Above her daughter's head.

And, then, there she is, her last child, running. Running to her mother, smiling. Glowing almost orange in the almost orange sun. Sometimes Hovsanna smiles a little, too. Children, she knows, are fleeting. They have wings. You turn away a moment and they're gone.

* * *

My mama's face is round and pale as the ball of the moon. When i see her coming home at last it is seeing the light through our bedroom window; it is turning my head to see the moon shining in. When i turn my head i see her walking slowly up the hill. I run down to meet her, my feet quick quick. Quicker than the world. Sometimes she smiles a little at my quick quick quick. My mama's face is round, is the sun, the moon, not like mine, and when she smiles it changes. Not too much, and i have to be quick, my eyes have to be quick to see it. It is something i could miss if i wasn't looking enough or if i rubbed my eyes to make sure i wasn't seeing the things people can't see, like you sometimes do. My mama's eyes are grey, not like mine. Most people i see have eyes like mine. Some people i see have different coloured eyes, but no-one else has eyes like Mama's. My mama's dress is long and black and very plain like rocks are plain. I have pretty clothes and shoes that someone in the church gives me, but no-one gives my mama clothes. Her hair is long and yellow like light can be. Mine is not light, no light. When i skip i fly up and i know my hair follows me up because i feel it. I sing when i fly up and i see the sky change yellow orange red. I see the change in the walls and stones. I sing and when i sing and sing i listen to my face and think how beautiful it sounds to sing. I listen hard. I have quick ears; i know when to turn my head. I know when to turn my head just once, like this. I have quick feet, even quicker than my ears. Quicker than anything stories can think of; much quicker than my mama. I am running running running. My mama's round ball face is dark in front of the sun. Behind her face is sky, the every evening sky, the nearly six o'clock hot red fire sky. And all the little hair that sticks out from her head, the short bent pieces that have unstuck from her long pale plait, all that little hair is burning, she is edges all on fire burning orange like the sun.

I am hot i am hot i am running skipping singing; i am noisy breathing pounding; i am against my mama's body, her soft and fat plain body. And she kisses me at last, her lips on the top of my no-light hair, her soft white arms around me.

* * *

Sometimes in the night I hear my mama's breathing. She breathes like a storm through her mouth. It is a sigh or the deep song of a man; everything heavy coming out of her. The room is full of that heavy thing, and her breath frightens me almost as much as her weeping.

Sometimes in the night when I am not yet asleep I hear my mama's weeping. I hear everything. My ears are so sharp I can point them at anything. I can pick up faint signals. I can stand on hills and mountains, on Mount Carmel or the Mount of Olives, near the monastery, and listen to everything all over the world, listen to people speak to one another from one country to another, in Haifa and Smyrna and old Constantinople and Bethlehem, listen to them argue or weep or whisper, dropping their voice the way my mama does when she sits in the kitchen, at the long cedar table in the night when i'm not yet asleep, and tells her friend all those loud and heavy things. My book, my paper, my pen are open before me. I am pretending to write and pretending to read; pretending over literature and history. Egypt and England and Russia and France: Cleopatra, Ann Boleyn, Jeanne d'Arc, Miss Havisham. So many people are there before me. Sometimes at night I hear the clack of wooden needles. Sometimes, in school, I think about knitting. Sometimes I try to imagine being locked in a tower, I try to imagine handling a snake, I try to imagine living in my wedding dress, allowing rats to run all over me. Sometimes I try to imagine being a man, wearing a white battle uniform, praying for a bullet or a quick fall of snow. Sometimes, on Saturdays, I like to sit on our roof, to sit in the sun and look out over the hills of Jerusalem, all these books open, their pages so blinding in the light that I can't read them. So I listen. I listen to the signals, to everything that's happened. And I listen for my mama coming home.

Sometimes in the night I wake up suddenly. Is it me or my mama who has cried out? Is it my dream or hers? Is that my heart crashing in my chest? Then she is up, and to me. She touches my arm. *It is nothing. Go back to sleep.* Her hands, her voice, trembling. All the stars and moon filling our pentagonal room. Before we moved here, when Hovsep was still with us, our bedroom was smaller and dim, really just part of a larger room, with one window only and facing south, out towards vast desert. But here we have five windows — five! Whoever heard of a bedroom like this — so large that it must have five windows? So large that, in the afternoon when I enter, home from school, the house cool and silent, it is like entering something huge and glittering, a beautiful church, with sunlight warming everything, touching everything, like it's holy. Hovsep would have loved this room but if he were here it wouldn't be the same. He and Mama would have strung up that blue curtain at one end for Hovsep to sleep behind and the red curtain at the other end for Mama and me to sleep behind. Everything would be different, then.

If my father were here, would he believe in this, a bedroom of glass, a place to sleep so full of light? Did he ever plan such places? Would he have made a room for me to lie in at night where, at least when I first lie down and before my mama turns her face to the wall, I can believe heaven is just outside, and my five windows are as sharp and blinding as the five points of stars?

Sometimes in the night I wake up suddenly. I am alone. I am lost. I am screaming. I have lost her. I have lost all of them.

But still, in the night, I wake up, mama loud in the air. In all that bright light I raise myself up and watch her. She lies on her back and her hands twitch high on her chest, near her throat. Her face moves quickly, frowning, mouth open close open close, and sometimes from her mouth a sound comes, a long sound flying out with a breath, one long expiration, then another and another, as if something awful and longer than a dream, longer than the whole night is flying up from the inside of her chest. And sometimes, in all this light, I can see it in the room and, although I am old enough to know there are no monsters, this is what I see: a snake that rises up out of my mama's mouth, an enormous snake with eyes and wings and hot, loud hissing breath.

There must be more people in the Bible than there are in the world. In every nightly chapter — that's what Mama calls it when she's ready, after dinner and before my bed, *time for our nightly chapter* — there are sons and daughters and their sons and daughters. Sometimes I wonder how there can be so many people. But I also know there used to be more of us. We used to be like them. I know this because i've heard Mamma say so when she talks to her friends, though she has never told me. She must know I listen. Do you think she knows? She must, I think, but she never lets me know. I know lots of things. I know I am Lucine, her eleventh child, and my father's thirteenth. I knew Hovsep and I know Arusiak, although I didn't know Arusiak for a long time. But even when I didn't, I knew about her, like I knew about Maree and Krikor before I met them. I know I once had a sister called Lucia who died and then came back and named me. So, with me, that makes six. And that means there are seven whose names I can't remember, seven without names.

They must have had names. Maybe I have heard them. If I have, I have forgotten them. I'm glad Mama doesn't know i've forgotten them, because I shouldn't have. I shouldn't have listened and I shouldn't have forgotten. If I ask her she might tell me. She might, but she would cry. And she would know I have listened and that I have forgotten, and that, alone, might make her cry. Sometimes when i'm playing outside I come in. Sometimes I play outside with my rope or a friend and sometimes when I play I come in for a drink of water or an orange to eat because i'm hungry because it's hot or it's a long time to wait to eat, so I come in and I am running and then I hear it, I hear her and I can't breathe and I don't know what to do I don't know what to do and I say *don't cry Mama, don't cry,* but she does and I cry too. So I try and try to remember their names because I don't want her to cry, but I can't. I'm not good at it.

Every night, when I read a chapter from the Bible, I wonder if any of the names are the same as the ones I have forgotten. Sometimes the stories are long and strange. Brothers kill each other, or sell each other, or run away. And the parents are sad and they cry. And one sister can have children and the other sister can't and so they swap places and everybody's happy. A father puts his son on a stone to kill him, and then God changes His mind and tells him not to. And other men think a woman in their village is so beautiful they have to kill her, so they do. Sometimes God seems to mind what the people do, and sometimes He doesn't. Sometimes they are punished for their wrongdoings, and sometimes the people are saved from God's punishments.

Take heed, my mama says. *Always be modest and never go*

anywhere alone.

In the end, my teacher says one day, *all things are worked out by God. At the end of our lives or the end of the world, His reasons are revealed when we stand at the finish and look back. But it is impossible, girls, to see those reasons if you are standing anywhere else.*

I wish I could remember the names of my brothers and sisters, all the ones who died, so I could tell my friends *there were once many more of us.* And I could say their names and when they were born and when they died and how. And what they were like: were they scared or clever or funny, what they liked to eat and a good thing they once told me. If my friends ever ask, i'd like to have a story to tell about all of them, the way I could tell them about Hovsep. I could begin it, the whole story, like this: *Once upon a time there was a country. And in that country lived my mother and father and all their children except me. When they lived in that country they had twelve children, and those twelve children were all my brothers and sisters. And these are the names of my brothers and sisters —* And I would tell them a long, long story about what it used to be like, about that country and that home and how, on special days, we would all have custard. There would be sad parts, of course, but it would be a happy story, as well. And I would make it sound so happy, make the country so green and my father so smiling and my brothers so kind and my mother always singing and my sisters so pretty and the garden so big and the food so delicious and the house so full of people to talk to that, after I had finished telling them my story, I would look at their faces and see they were all smiling and their eyes were a bit wet, and they would say, *You must be the luckiest girl in the world, Lucine. I wish I had a family like that.*

Arusiak

(Jerusalem, 1923)

At the compound gates, Hovsanna, Hovsep and their neighbour waited while a man went to inform the bishop. The man then returned and ushered them into the wide cobbled courtyard, securing the gates behind them. In the presbytery, it was a priest who greeted them. Hovsanna bowed her head as he approached and heard her neighbour speak. She glanced at Hovsep; he watched the neighbour. Hovsanna whispered in Turkish, *What does he say?* And Hovsep translated the Armenian.

Thank you, Father, for seeing us. May the Almighty bless your eyes. May your children's children prosper. This is Mrs Vartevarian and her son, Hovsep.

Hovsanna raised her head and looked at the priest. He was young, much younger than her. He said *Please, be seated, Mrs Vartevarian,* and she saw his one arm extended in invitation while the other gripped the arm of his own chair as he sat. She wondered momentarily why the bishop had sent such a young priest. *Now,* he smiled faintly at Hovsep, *what is it?*

I have written a letter to His Grace, the bishop, from my mother.

Hovsanna kept her head bowed, gazing fixedly at her hands, each holding the other. She heard the priest shift a little in his chair.

The letter is about my sister, Arusiak. She is in Beirut, in an orphanage, we — my mother had to leave her there after ... when we fled. She was small and my mother was expecting and —

Yes?

We had to walk a long way and she was very small.

Yes, the priest said, quietly. *And her husband?*

Hovsep was silent, the priest looking at him with a calm face.

What is he saying? Hovsanna asked.

About your, about father. And to the priest, *My father died. He — died.*

Then he is with God and we must rejoice for him, said the priest, and reached out and placed his hand over Hovsanna's. She looked at the hand and held herself very still. It was smooth and cool. *He suffers no more,* he said. She felt her eyes fill. And then the hand was gone and the priest said, *May I see the letter?* And her tears, when they dropped unnoticed by the others, dropped only onto her own flesh.

Your Grace,

It is as a loving servant of God that I come to you through this letter I am dictating to my son, Hovsep. For it is through God's will alone that Hovsep has been spared. He is a very clever boy; his teachers believe he will fulfil his ambition and become a doctor, and I will always be grateful to God for His mercy. I once had many children and a husband and a home but these things could not last. It was

God's will that these be taken from all of us and I do not question Him for I know there is a reason for everything that happens in God's creation, even if — as a woman — I am not good enough or clever enough to see it. It is by God's grace that my daughters Anaheed and Maree have been also spared, though each is damaged and is not quite whole any more. God sent Maree and Hovsep back to me when they were lost for many months. He sent Maree to our door, begging for food, and she did not even know she was at her home. God sent my husband back to me after he was taken and we fled — my mother-in-law, my children and I — and after we endured a long journey to my family's home, where we found some few weeks of respite before the gendarmes came there also and all of us set off on the long march with only what we could carry, and then less and less of that until I did not even have my loved ones any more. I cannot speak of this. I can only say that you, too, must have heard of events through others or, perhaps, you may know of them through your own experience. I do not wish to recount what has befallen us. I cannot, although I can think of nothing else each day I live and each night I sleep. I pray to God to give me strength and I ask Him to care for my little children who are now with Him, and for my husband, and to tell them I will be joining them when it is God's will that I do so, and if it is His will. I know he is a forgiving God, and pray that He will forgive us all our imperfection. For I know God works all kinds of miracles. I know this.

Your Grace, as we were walking through Anatolia, a Turkish gentleman came along the road in a carriage, calling my name. I thought about God then and said to myself,

God has already decided my fate, and I stepped out. And this gentleman took my children — Anaheed and Arusiak, the others all lost — and I to his wife for the evening and she cared for us, and when we returned to the others in the morning, something had happened and there was no-one left there. A long time after that I woke up. I had been very tired. And then God sent Benyamin back to me. He appeared one night, as a ghost might appear, at my bedside. He was saying something. I couldn't quite hear him. It sounded like my name. It was dark. His face was different; it was thinner and older and I wasn't sure who he was. He was speaking from so far away. His voice was like a breeze or an echo, not like a human voice. I stared at him. I couldn't move. I was so cold. My belly was trembling. I couldn't control it. *Go away, Devil,* I thought. I could hear my own voice. *Go away.* I prayed to God to deliver me from this. He seemed to leer at me and, as I looked at him, I saw he had two heads and four arms, and that two of those had long and terrible claws. It was the shadows, of course, from the lamp he had carried. Later, he told me and I understood. It was just shadows. But then I had been asleep. I had been so very tired. It had already been such a long, long journey. And so I didn't know. I could hear my voice. It was saying something. But it wasn't me. It wasn't me speaking. It was someone else. Perhaps it was him. He had bowed his head and I couldn't see his true face. I could only see his creature face with many teeth and yellow glinting eyes, so it might have been. I could hear him, his voice. His shoulders were shaking. He was making some sound. He sounded like a ghost. It was a wailing sound. He didn't sound human, so how was I to know? I lay awake a long time in my bed, shaking. And then I must have slept because when I awoke, it seemed like a dream, a fever dream. That's what Benyamin called it, later, when I told him his ghost had come, and he showed me the tiger skin he had spread on the floor, one he had carried all the way home. Of course, I must have seen that there on the floor and somehow mixed it all up.

And soon we were blessed by God and He gave us another child, Lucine, our last, who was growing inside me before my husband left me to be with God. Your Grace, I am ashamed. I tried everything, everything to keep him with me. I cared for him, washed him, fed him soup from a small spoon. I held him, sang to him. I prayed every minute of each day and night. Everything I did became prayer. I slept on the floor at his feet. Sometimes he spoke to me; sometimes he couldn't speak. Sometimes I wept, but I tried not to let him see. He never liked to see me weep. Sometimes he wept but I looked away, or left the room. I pretended not to hear his weeping. He made me promise these things — that I would survive, that I wouldn't forget him, that I would leave that country and never return. At first, I wouldn't answer him because to answer him would have been to agree that he was going to leave to be with God. But he would become so angry. His eyes would grow wild and they frightened me. So I said what he wanted me to say. I am his wife, after all. Even now, I am his wife. And when he died, I was bound to the promises I had made him. He was my husband and had made me swear before his anger and before the Almighty. It was a long journey east, into Lebanon. We walked and walked, with other Armenians, from other Armenians and to other Armenians, who helped to feed and shelter us. My belly grew huge. I was exhausted with child. Maree and Anaheed were grown and Hovsep was a boy. But Arusiak was a little girl and she cried and grew thin and then stopped crying. I was afraid. I couldn't carry her. I was weak myself with the baby inside me.

Your Grace, there is a Christian orphanage in Beirut. It is run by nuns. I told Arusiak it was a special place for the very best of daughters, where there are warm soft beds and plenty to eat and I took Arusiak there and gave her to a nun and said, *I will soon be back for you*, and I turned around and walked away. I put her hand in the nun's hand and she let me do that. She is an obedient child but I heard her crying and crying, *Mama, Mama*. I closed my ears. I didn't look back.

Your Grace, she was five years old and she was small and tired. That was five years ago. I have no money to return for her. I work six days each week. I send Hovsep and Lucine to school. How can I leave them? Please, Your Grace, I beg you to help me. Might God's Church see a way to bring my child home? I trust in God. For when Lucine was born, wasn't it God who showed me a safe place to crawl into, away from the sun and the eyes of the world, to give birth to her, beneath a house in that busy Beirut street? Who else but God would have guided us to arrive outside the Armenian compound here, in Jerusalem, at the end of our terrible journey at last, Lucine at my breast, to find my eldest son, Krikor, the one I sent away years before, leaning against the compound wall, talking with his friend? We had not seen one another all those years, nor did one even know where the other was or if the other was, indeed, still on this earth. How can that be anything other than the work of God? And so I trust in Him that He will find a way for me to hold my Arusiak again. And I pray that it will be soon for, although I send her little gifts so that she will know I still live and I still love and remember her, it has been five years since I told her I would soon return for her, and those five years are as long as she had already lived when I last saw her. So it is as if she has had two lives — one with me and one without.

* * *

Lucine, my mother, says, *You know, those nuns never gave Arusiak the little presents our mother sent her. A doll she sewed, a length of hair ribbon. I heard our mother say so, weeping, after Arusiak came home. She was a very strange sister. I didn't know who she was and she never liked me. She used to say I was the lucky one but it's not my fault. I was a baby; I couldn't help being born.*

* * *

Lucine, my mother, is folding her handkerchief. *When she was about sixteen,* she says, *Arusiak wanted to go to England to be a nanny for a family called Frye. They liked her. They had a little boy with a huge head. He wasn't well. Our mother didn't want her to go but she knew Arusiak would never forgive her if she didn't allow it. Mama cried; Arusiak screamed and shouted. Then, soon after that, she left.* My mother unfolds her handkerchief and smoothes it flat. *When the war broke out, Arusiak refused to go to America with Mrs Frye and the children. So she stayed behind in England with Mr Frye and he asked her what she wanted to do. She said she wanted to learn to cook, so he sent her to the Cordon Bleu cooking school. He paid for it. And that's how she became a very, very good cook.* My mother refolds her handkerchief, in half and half again. *She always got what she wanted,* my mother sniffs.

Lucine: a small knife, a secret car,
a photograph

Until the age of fourteen, says Lucine, holding up three fingers, *I went to church three times on Sunday.* I gaze at her fingers, her long slim fingers with trimmed curved nails. *I went to Sunday school in the morning and then to the Armenian Protestant church. And I went to the Orthodox church with my mother.*

Sunday was the day my mother didn't work. Sometimes on Sundays, I would hear my mother singing, always the same song. She would sing it only if she thought I wasn't there. I would creep closer to listen. If she heard me she would stop. It was such a mournful song. It made me cry. It was the saddest song I have ever heard.

When I was a girl, she says, *I used to walk to school along the Via Dolorosa, along the road that Christ walked when He carried His cross on His way to His crucifixion. I used to walk that way every day.*

When I was a girl, about twelve or thirteen, I used to walk all over Jerusalem. My mother didn't know because she worked six days a week. One day I was with my friend. We were in a garden, like a park. We were stopped by some boys. They took hold of my friend and tried to cut her, began to cut her leg off. I ran and ran, out of the park and into the street, to get help. 'Help, help,' I said, 'some boys have a knife, they're hurting my friend.' And people ran back with me and the boys saw them coming and ran away.

What happened to your friend? I ask.

They — you know, and she makes a sawing gesture with her hand.

For a moment, I am speechless.

She was all right, says my mother with a little shrug, not looking at me. *But you see what can happen?*

But her leg.

It healed, it healed. It was quite a small knife. But you remember. You must never go to lonely places.

I nod slowly. A small knife. A small knife meant more time, more determination. I try not to see it. The rose beds, the clipped green lawn. They must have held her down, in the middle of a public park, on a sunny day.

But why did they do it? I ask, eventually.

Who knows, says my mother with a toss of her head. *The world is full of all kinds of people. Another time, I was walking down a little street and an Arab was standing in a doorway, watching me as I approached. There was no-one else in the street. He was holding something against his chest, half hidden in the folds of his robe. As I passed him I saw it was a knife. I was very lucky. I was young and silly. I should not have been there. Promise me you will never put yourself in danger.*

And, of course, I did.

* * *

In his fifteenth year, my Australian son with the Armenian face said he needed a story to tell his English class. And so I told him my mother's story.

Once upon a time, I said, there was a lonely Armenian girl. She was dark (like her father) and small (like her mother). She had long slim fingers. In church she sketched with them. After school she would sometimes go to her best friend's house where there were brothers and sisters, and a father, as well, and she would sometimes hear a piano being played. And she would stop and think to herself, *Isn't that beautiful*, and she would imagine her own fingers at the keys, but she knew there was no money for such things. And so, when she went home as the sun was setting, knowing her mother would not be far away, she never mentioned it.

She was good at school; she was top of her class. By the time she was twelve years old she could read, write and speak five languages. Above all else, she loved history and literature. (He raised an eyebrow at me, just as she still does, because he knew then who this is. He, too, loves these things.) She had a light and pretty voice but she only sang in church or when she was alone, and she never sang when her mother was home. She rarely heard her mother sing for she, too, sang only when she believed no-one was there. When she did, her mother's song was the saddest she ever heard. Seventy years later the thought of it will still make her weep.

More than anything else, this girl wanted to finish secondary school. But when she was the same age as you are now, whoever was paying for her education — there was no free education and it could not have been her mother, that she always knew — decided otherwise, and she left school to become a nanny for a wealthy English woman, the wife of a doctor, just as her sister had done.

She fed and dressed the daughters of the wealthy English woman. She lifted each of them into their prams. She pushed the little girl to the School for Handicapped Children, and the baby around the park. She pushed them home and she fed them again and washed them both and prepared them for bed. Every evening the little girl would vomit into her nanny's hair as she was carried upstairs. Once a week the nanny had half a day off, and she caught the bus across the city to visit her mother. Then, in the middle of one week, her mother caught the same bus on its return journey to find her daughter. The wealthy English woman's doctor husband took her to the hospital in his car, and she stayed there. After that, the girl would catch a different bus to visit her mother on her half day off. At night, when she lay down in her little bed under the window of her little first floor room, she would gaze out at the stars with their arms and legs and head of brilliant light and her chest would ache with the feeling that they reminded her of something, something so far away now that she couldn't remember what it was.

One week she didn't catch the bus on her half day off because a boy she had met, an Armenian boy, handsome but secret, drove her in his car to the Dead Sea where they picnicked and laughed. She had never been taught to swim but when she was a baby her oldest sister tried to drown her. At least, that's what Maree used to whisper to her. *And I wish I had succeeded*, Maree would hiss into her ear. So, because she couldn't swim, they waded in that salty water. And, the following week when she went to the hospital she said she had been busy, that she couldn't get away, that it was the children who kept her. And her mother said nothing, but looked at the girl in a way that made her face burn. So she left quickly, and she and the boy drove somewhere else that day and she loved being in the car as it drove and drove in the sun and she could close her eyes and it seemed perhaps anything really was possible.

When the English woman told her that the hospital had phoned and she must go there at once, she didn't wait for the bus but ran and ran all the way. And she saw her mother was very still, and she didn't know what to do. So she ran to her home, to her real home, for Arusiak's photograph and ran all the way back again to place it on her mother's chest, saying, *It's all right, Mama, Arusiak's here now.* And she rested her cheek on her mother's arm and her mother's skin felt strange and cold and she ran from the room, down all the empty corridors, calling, *Please, please,* until she found a telephone and she picked it up and turned the handle the way she had seen people do and she heard a voice and she said, *Please, help me, something is wrong with my mother.* And for the rest of the girl's long life she thought about this and told this story many times to her own daughter. And that daughter listened over and over to the cautionary tale, sometimes with little grace and sometimes with more. But the lump in her throat was always for the girl who listened to the music from the other room and who wanted, more than anything else, to study.

But perhaps it was not this story I told him. Perhaps it was another. Or, perhaps, if I did tell him this, he smiled at me and shrugged, the way boys do, the way Krikor smiled and shrugged at the faces of his silent friends when he saw his mother in Jerusalem as she stepped thin and tired (and with that girl just a baby in her arms) from the carriage at the gate to the Armenian compound. And when they both were sure each was real and she fell upon him, sobbing, *My boy, oh God*, and he upon her. And then he looked up, at the faces of his friends who still had no mothers. The way he must have done when he left her that day with the promise of a swift return. The way he must have done when he next saw her, bending his head to step through her door all those years later, the baby now a dark, thin girl in the corner with her nose in a book. The way he did when he left again, just like my son did. The way boys do. A smile, a small shrug and he left the room.

Hovsep and the commotion of birds

(Jerusalem, 1928)

In the hospital, Hovsep is pale and still. His breathing rattles his chest, and Hovsanna counts his breaths. One, two, three … She knows this illness, the one that took Benyamin, and each day she watches her tall, dark son just as she watched his father. Sometimes he opens his eyes. Sometimes he speaks to her. But most of the time his eyes twitch beneath their lids in fevered sleep and his fingers shift against the stiff white sheets, his remembering loud in his head.

Once, Mother, he thinks loudly, loud enough that she might hear him. Once when I was lost, once when I was lost and walking, I thought I saw a boy catch a bird with his hands. It was early, that time when birds dart about, delirious. I was asleep in long grass, the kind of grass we became lost in, that morning a long time ago when we hid in there — me and Maree and Dickran and Dickranhoui — when we were walking and we didn't want to walk any more with all those people, and you and Father weren't there. We hadn't seen you for a long time. Maree said we hadn't seen you since the gendarmes came. I didn't hear them come that morning because I was asleep. Maree said she heard them banging at the door. I woke because of the screaming and the bang. Maree said a gendarme put a gun in grandfather's mouth when he opened the door. She said there was blood and hair and other things on the walls. Everyone was shouting and crying. Two soldiers dragged great uncle out of the house; he was holding his hands up in front of his face and the soldier was hitting his arms and his back with a gun. You pushed us into grandfather's bedroom and shut the door. I peered through the window. The soldier who wasn't hitting him was tying a rope around great uncle's neck. Great uncle was crying and his hair was messy. He was looking at the soldiers and saying something. The soldier with the gun hit him on the side of the head with it and then great uncle fell over and the soldier pushed him with the gun and great uncle climbed onto the little table there, beneath the tree, the one he and grandfather had played backgammon on the day before. I saw other soldiers push you; you were holding Arusiak, and Anaheed held your dress. The soldiers pushed you and grandmother and our aunties into the garden. Then Maree pulled me down. That was the last time I saw you.

Later, I looked out again. Great uncle was turning very slowly. We were afraid to go outside. We went in to the front room but we couldn't close the door because grandfather was lying there. We slept in grandfather's room. His sheet smelled of him. It was very cold. The next morning the gendarmes came again and they looked in all the rooms, we could hear them, and they found us. They looked and said something to one another and then one of them took

Dickran and Dickranhoui and me outside. He said to the others, *Be quick.* When they came out later, Maree came too. She was shaking. I asked her what happened but she didn't answer me. I looked at her dress. It didn't look right. Then I saw that the hem was torn. I said, *Maree, where's our money?* She didn't say anything. They made us walk to where other people were, but we didn't know any of them. And we didn't know where you were, and the gendarmes wanted everyone to walk and they had the guns and so we walked. We walked out of the town, for hours, along rough tracks until we didn't want to do it any more. So we lagged behind. No-one seemed to think anything of it; there were lots of people and we were just four children. And you weren't there to care what happened to us. And when everyone had gone ahead, we hid in the field alongside the track, in the long grass, and waited. I had to keep quiet for a long time. Maree stroked my head, *Ssshhh.* And then, when everything was silent, just the wind and the occasional distant moan of a cow or goat, I stood up. It was as easy as that. Then they all stood up and looked and there was no-one around and everything was quiet, as if all those people who had just been there had never really been there at all.

We looked around. The others were talking, trying to decide which way we should go. Do we go back, home? With you and Father not there any more? Or do we go on, to another town, and see if we can find you? And then something happened.

Later, I realised it must have been the farmer in his field. He must have been there all the time. He must have been watching the people being marched along the goat track, the one he used to herd his own goats, to take them from pasture to pasture and back home to sleep. These last few days, I've been thinking about him again, wondering if he had children of his own, wondering what I would have done if it were my field and my goat track and I had seen that four children had left all those people and the gendarmes, had been left behind and were standing in my long grass, looking about. I wonder if he ever thinks about us, if he ever wonders what happened after he roared, angry, and we scattered — scattered, each of us, running, not looking back.

I have had all kinds of dreams, Mother. Monster dreams and dreams where I turn around and see him behind us, chasing me, with a hoe or a spade. Or sometimes he's a tiger running towards me, his eyes shining, teeth bared. And dreams, too, where I am him and I am calling them — Maree and Dickran and Dickranhoui. *Come*, I call, *Come. Mother is here. Father is here.* Dreams where I am running through that field of long grass, trying to find them. *Come.* And I am crying because how can I go home if they are not with me? How can I find my way home? Because I am little and I know I should have stayed with them. *Come.* Because if I don't find them they will wander in the long grass forever like me and never find their way out. *Come.* They will die in the long grass, the tiger will get them, and how can I go home and tell you it was my idea, that I stood up, I stood up first and I lost them I lost them all and I should have seen I should have seen the farmer when I stood up because I was little and if I had seen him then I could have told the others and they wouldn't have stood up and I could have sat down and maybe he wouldn't have seen us all. *Come.* But I didn't. I didn't. I didn't. *Come.* How can I?

Later, much later in that other field where I was sleeping, I woke to a loud shrill sound like the calling of a bird. It was early, as I said. The light was pale. I was covered by grass. I had broken the grass stems, pulled them down and bent them over so that they covered me in the night but still I was cold and wet with dew. I opened my eyes and turned my head to look up through the thin grass blanket at the shining sky but, otherwise, I lay tightly curled and completely still, listening. There it was again, the highest call above all the other sounds of birds. So I lifted myself onto my elbows and parted the grass slowly with my hands and slipped my head and shoulders up through the gap I made. The damp stalks shook along my arms and back, and I raised myself further on my arms until I could peer through the drooping heads of the field of wet grass that surrounded me. The sun splashed on them and hurt my eyes.

The boy was standing so still that, at first, I didn't see him. All about him small birds flashed. He held his arms out, together, in front of him, palms upward and open, horizontal. For many minutes he didn't move and I began to doubt myself: was he part of my dream, another lost boy in the grass? Or was he like me? Was he peering into other children's faces, saying, *My name is Hovsep Vartevarian,* asking them, *Have you seen, have you seen?*

About him was a cacophony of birdcall. Tiny birds, each with startling yellow flashes on their wings, darted and swooped, chattering. And, every so often, remaining utterly still, he called back. I couldn't see his face, but I knew it must be him for each time I heard it, the call was more insistent, rising like a human shout, and the birds responded with a ripple of intense sound and flight, circling all about him, calling to each other, calling back until I could no longer tell which creature was calling. And then, suddenly, suddenly a small bird lighted on his palm — his left palm, I think — and he snapped his right hand over its head and he had it, trapped. Then he raised the cage of his hands to his face, placed his lips in the space where thumb met thumb and, with his fingers, pressed the bird into his mouth.

At that moment there was only one important thing — only one and nothing else. I closed my eyes. My name is Hovsep Vartevarian. The most important thing in the world was not to make a sound.

I open my eyes. The ceiling is far away and white. I can feel my mother stroke my head. With each stroke she says, *There ... there ... these are birds skimming across the water.* My hot skin jumps. I want to say, *Leave me, Mother. Leave.* But I can't, I can't. I can't say anything. When she goes away there is no-one. And sometimes I wake and only the white curtain moves.

Sometimes I turn my face away. I feel the cold bed linen on my cheek. *Am I dying?* And she says, *Shoosh, sshh ...*

Sometimes I can't open my eyes but I hear everything — her step when she arrives, the way she slows in the doorway and then walks to me; the nurses, their steps quick and certain, their voices saying everything, as if I'm not here, talking about their boyfriends, laughing; my mother's quiet sobs once they've left, *Dear God, dear God.*

Sometimes she cries and sometimes she doesn't. Sometimes she is there and sometimes she isn't. Sometimes I am home in my own bed behind the blue curtain she made and which we strung from wall to wall at the end of our room when I was twelve. I am pulling back my blue curtain and looking out into the room, past our kitchen and our table and our chairs, to Mother and Lucine's red curtain at the other end of the room. I am in my bed in the cool blue light of the wide blue curtain and I am dreaming, dreaming, trying not to remember. But memory memory memory is. I use my memory for mathematical tables and grammatical rules. I use it to remember my future. In my future, the one I remember, I am a man, a doctor, like the one I sometimes hear. But I make well everyone who comes to me. In my future we live in more than one room, we live in a house, a mansion, and we eat meat and everyone is there. My mother and father sit in the garden in the sun and all their children come to them, smiling. I have a wife. She is young and pretty. She looks like the girl I see on my way to school. And I have children and they are never hungry or lost and I never go away and they never have bad dreams. Sometimes I am little again. Sometimes I can't find my mother. I wake and wake and wake but she's not there. I don't know where I am. I cry and cry but nobody hears me. I vomit and vomit but nothing comes out. I walk down the road and there are dead people there. Then it gets dark so I lie next to one. When I wake up someone else is there trying to reach into the dead man's trousers. He is angry and swearing. I watch him with one eye a bit open. I'm afraid of the man. I'm afraid he might touch me. I lie very still and quiet and he doesn't see me. I hear him walking away. I sit up. I can't see anyone else, just all the dead ones. I wonder what the angry man had put in his pockets: was it food? I wonder if he is going back to his house. I stand up and look down the road again. I can't see him. Maybe I'll see him if I walk that way. So I do.

*   *   *

When Mama returned from visiting Hovsep it was dark. I heard voices. I opened my eyes and saw I was in bed. *Mama? Go back to sleep, Lucine,* I heard Mama say. I sat up and looked at Mama's side of the bed, which was covered and smooth. The light from the lamp on the kitchen table threw the shadows of Mama and Mrs Egoyian across the red curtain, and everything in that little sleeping space around me was red. I heard their whispering. *Mama?* I called again.

I pulled back the red curtain but Hovsep's blue one at the end of the room was still tied aside. Mama walked towards me with her face the same as it always was. She held back the bedclothes for me as I lay down again. *Is Hovsep coming home?*

She said, *Sleep,* the way she always did.

When I woke again she was gone. Mrs Egoyian was sitting in a chair with her eyes shut and her mouth wide open. She looked different when she was asleep. Mama did, too, but Mrs Egoyian looked nicer than when she was awake. Her lips looked bigger. I watched her for a long time and then crawled back into bed.

Later she woke me with a brown egg in a beautiful bowl.

She must have brought the bowl from her house because I had never seen it before. It has so many flowers on it, it was like eating in a garden. The egg was boiled but I ate it anyway. Then I got dressed behind the red curtain while she washed and dried the bowl and spoon and left them on our table. It made the room look pretty.

At her house she left me alone with her children. They stared at me the way they always did when no adult was there. Mr Egoyian came in and said something to me. I looked at him. He had a happy face but I couldn't think of anything to say to him. When he went out, one of the children, the one younger than me, said, *Baba says we have to be kind to you because your brother is going to die and then you and your mother will have no-one,* and her sister hit her. And Mrs Egoyian came in to see what all the crying was about and hit the sister and there was more crying.

When everything was quiet again and Mrs Egoyian was cooking and the children weren't looking at me any more, I went back home and climbed into bed. Nobody came for a while and I must have fallen asleep because then I heard Mrs Egoyian opening the door and calling me. I didn't say anything and pulled the cover over my head. Then her voice said *Lucine, didn't you hear me calling you?* and pushed the cover away. I kept my eyes closed as tightly as I could so she'd think I was asleep and, after a while, I heard her say something quietly and the door clicked shut and everything was silent. I don't know how many days went by like that.

I wore my new white dress and white patent shoes, I was so happy to see him. He was lying in a white bed in a white room, and his black hair was messy, like it is in the mornings when he wakes me for school. I haven't gone to school much since he left. I don't know how many days that is, but seeing him there like that, in bed with messy hair, made me think that maybe everything would be all right, that Mr Egoyian was wrong, that maybe he would just get up tomorrow and say, *Lucine, wake up. We have to go to school, you know. What do you want to grow up to be — dumb?* the way he always did. But then I saw his face was different. It was him but not him. It was like a drawing of him that someone might make, and you could say yes, that's my brother, but only after you look hard and see the bits were the same — his nose, his eyebrows, his chin. The bits were the same but he wasn't the same. He was like a drawing of himself that wasn't very good. And then I knew that maybe he wouldn't get up tomorrow to make me breakfast, that maybe I would have to wait longer than that.

He didn't say anything to me. He didn't say anything to anyone, even though his mouth was open. When he breathed he made a horrible sound, like there was something inside him trying to get out. He opened his eyes once but he didn't look at me. I was afraid of him, of not-him, and I didn't touch him. I just sat on a chair on one side of his bed and Mama sat on the other side, and she held his hand and stroked his head and the wind blew the white curtain about behind her so that sometimes it lifted and so much light came in that she disappeared and it was just me and not-him. And I thought, I wish we were home before all this happened. And I thought of me and the real Hovsep and Mama eating dinner, and the real Hovsep talking about where he is going with his friends and laughing that laugh that looks a bit like the way a horse might laugh. I was happy to see him but when the light came in and Mama disappeared, I felt scared. I don't know why.

* * *

When he arrived at the hospital, the first thing we nurses noticed was how long and slender he was. We didn't say anything when we were treating him but later, in the tea room, one of the girls on that shift with me said something about it. Something about his symmetry. He didn't move much in those days — sleeping most of the time, or staring into the walls and floor, or reading a bit, although that didn't last long. But I noticed that, when he did move, it was with considerable grace, as if he had planned even how to turn each page. And I thought he'd probably be a wonderful dancer. Not that I would have ever flirted with him or anything like that. He was younger than me, for one thing. Still, I wasn't the only one who noticed him.

The day after he arrived, a couple of the girls gave him his sponge bath. His mother was there, of course, but they asked her to leave because — well, you know, he wasn't a child. Afterwards they told me he had the palest, smoothest skin and that the distances between each of his joints — elbow to shoulder to wrist, hip to knee — were long. Everything about him, they smiled, was long. And I scolded them. After all, what if his mother should hear.

Sometimes you think you know what will happen but you're wrong. Sometimes you think people should be all right, but you just don't know their history, what weakness there may be hidden in them. Most of the time you can tell, but sometimes there's just no explaining it.

His mother prayed every day beside his bed. It was a bit inconvenient. She had the priest come in a few times, too. And his sister came once, a skinny little thing with a face like an owl. The way she looked at him. Everybody knew the way it had to go: fourteen days, and if he passed the crisis — well. It's an awful thing to see a person's delirium, to smell it, to hold their arms as they thrash, to see their mouth wide open, eyes bulging, each inspiration a moan. Children and old people are different; they don't put up much of a fight. But he — what was his name? — he fought. And you wanted him to, of course. But they hurt themselves and they hurt us and sometimes you wonder whether it's really worth the trouble.

One night, early on, we came in and his mother was asleep on the end of his bed and him with his knees drawn up. So we brought another bed in and she stayed there. She was a help, of course, but she cried a lot. She was Armenian, so I guess she might have seen one or two things. Even so, she seemed to me to cry too much and I felt sorry for the little girl and I felt like saying to the mother, *Look, it's not as if he's your only child.* It made it hard for the other girls, too, seeing her like that. They didn't want to go in there. But I didn't say anything to her because — well, one doesn't. But sometimes I couldn't bear to see her face.

And then, the day before, to come in and see him standing at the window, standing right on the window ledge, leaning out, holding himself in place just by his fingertips hooked around the edge of the window frame, his arms straining, his body leaning way out into the sun and air. I'd heard about this but never seen it before. The mother was there, asleep of course. And there he was, bony and white in his white gown, the white curtains lifting and falling behind him like wings. *Oh,* said Dana — she was with me. It was the early round. *Oh no, oh God.* She was whispering.

I was carrying something — a file, I think; I didn't say anything. It's important not to. I must have moved a little because some papers fell out and fluttered across the floor. For a moment I didn't know what to do. Everything was so blinding.

* * *

Mother, oh Mother, the day is going to be mild, like a smile. Streaks of cloud break apart like cloth you've torn for bandages, and the streets glow. From here I can see all the way across the city. The wheels of carts are loud and slow. The donkeys are small and uncomplaining. They do their work. People laugh. Can you hear them? I can see them. Their mouths open. They stand about. And walk. They stand about. They are murmuring to one another. Occasionally, they glance up, at the sky.

What do you think it is they see? The sky is just the sky, Mother. And I am just a skinny boy flapping my wings, flap flap, flap flap, filling and falling, filling and falling, flap flap, flap flap, trying to get home.

Nothing is far. I see our street. Nothing is difficult. I

know where I am. I know where I am, but where are you? Down there it's different. The world does not glow. There are shadows and guesses and people who shout. I open my mouth. God, there's something in me. Down there are corners and streets and corners and streets, names you don't know. There is cold and guessing and trying to remember things, hiding and praying and holding out your hand. There is crying and vomiting and crying and shaking. There is hungry and hungry and hungry and walking. There is eating grass and beetles and people who spit and sleeping in doorways and boys who throw stones and their mothers who hit you with sticks. There is sleeping with cattle and sleeping in the woodheap and sores and flies and not really sleeping and there is something inside me and pissing your pants. There's bath and a bed and then gritting your teeth and remembering home, remembering home and you're playing a game, kicking a ball in the street with friends, kicking it all the way down the street every morning before school and laughing and Father's face smiling and you reaching up to kiss me and Father's hand waving to you and you looking up to Father's face and no-one having a father as tall as mine, his big hands, your hands pushing hair from your face, your hands on my face, your face. Then there's taking a shirt, a coat or some shoes and climbing out the window, climbing out the window when the men are asleep or gone for food, climbing out the window quickly and there's running running summer winter and summer again and asking and asking, *Where is Alexandretta?* Until one day, one day there is something you have been trying to remember, something like the house of a friend at the end of your street, one of the friends you used to kick the ball to, something like that but not quite like that looking back at you and you stand still and think and you can't move for thinking, thinking about your teacher and sisters and your father's big hand waving back to you, Mother, and then reaching down and stroking the top of my head and his voice saying something to me, something I didn't really listen to because I didn't know, because I thought it was just an ordinary afternoon and I didn't listen even though I know I should, I know I should listen but how could I know that soldiers could come and ask Father if he was who he is, and not answer your questions but just look at you, silent, their eyes thin and hard, their mouths thin and hard, just looking at you as they move towards us as if they're already holding something, something they have caught, something small and frightened between their teeth because no-one would come to our house with a gun and hit a man like that with such big hands and a man like that would not be afraid, would not look at you that way, Mother, and say nothing either, just look at you that way, open his mouth and no words come out, just a bird, a bird comes out and everyone is noisy and I keep quiet, I just keep quiet because if we are quiet everything will be all right, we will stay together hiding, we will stay together walking, we will walk back along the goat track, away from the long grass, away from farmers and soldiers and boys and their mothers who chase us with sticks and guns and spades, who are running behind us as we run from the window and look back as we run from their shouting to see their teeth snarling.

We will walk back home, the last part of the walking,

watching the house to make sure because I know, I know that sometimes I don't look well enough, sometimes I don't look well enough and everything disappears. Oh, Mother, I can see our house from here. And then there's you, standing there. Your mouth opens. I can see inside it. Nothing comes out. You make a strange sound. There is something inside you. Your tongue is moving. You make a strange sound. Are there feathers in your throat? You. You falling, Mother. You are falling to your knees. You. Saying my name.

* * *

So we had to do it. It wasn't that he resisted. We just couldn't trust him. It was sad, with her on her knees, begging God: *Oh God, oh God, oh Hovsep, my Hovsep,* and him pulling at his restraints. But we had other patients and, besides, there are many sad things in the world. Some of us like to think we can tell what's going to happen when a patient comes in. Once I even won a lovely pair of silk stockings from Dana in a wager. After a few years, you tend to feel quite confident.

It's an awful way to die, though, tied up like that.

3

Inside my bones

(Perth, present)

In the dream, we were all together. The beach was a cove of very fine silver-grey sand. I was watching, a little apart from them. The ocean was just as I wanted it to be: untroubled, blue-green, breathing, steady. The horizon was a haze. Above us the sky shimmered. It was one of those afternoons. The sunlight thickened the ocean's surface until it looked like molten glass. I shielded my eyes and watched my family. I could hear them laughing. Things had never been clearer.

My feet are bare. I'm on the edge of the ocean, standing calf-deep. And then it happens. I lose my grip. Beneath me, the sand falls away and the current grabs my ankles like a hand. I am under. The water is swift and cool. I open my eyes. The water is almost white, opaque. Above me, the surface sparkles, full of bubbles. Is that my breath?

I bob up, easily, unafraid. I am drifting out, fast. I can see them all on the beach, hear their frightened voices calling me. I call back, *I'm all right*, but I know they can't hear me. How quickly I am being taken. I watch my family become small black specks and then disappear. The beach disappears. I do not struggle. I am far, far, out to sea.

A ship appears. I raise my arm. On the deck I see them scurrying about, calling to me. They throw me a lifebuoy. It splashes nearby. It is red. I don't need it. I leave it behind. I smile. I wave. *Tell them I'm all right,* I shout. A man leans over the rails, cups his hands to his mouth and calls, *You'll only last minutes in water that cold.* And I'm past him, the current taking me fast.

For a moment I am worried. I know he is right. The water is cold and very deep. But I am flying, faster than a ship can sail. And then I feel the water change and, there, to my right is a small island. It rushes towards me. I feel my feet suddenly against the sand. I slide up onto the shore. I stand. I am not tired. I walk into the forest along a short wide path which opens before me. In a moment I am in a clearing at the island's centre. In the clearing is a structure. It is small, octagonal, lightly constructed and, as I approach it, I see it is built of bone, an open frame of bone gathered easily together, as a bunch of flowers may be gathered, held loose and upside down, in a hand. When I enter, there's a hush. I stand very still. I stop my breath. I know this is holy. I close my eyes. I know they will grieve. I had no choice. I am home. I am home and I've never felt happier.

And so it was that something appeared in my house, slipped from my dream and took its shape. Something has been given permission, been given its moment. In this house, my house, at some point I must have stepped back. Somehow, I was brought to a standstill and then simply stepped back and aside, made a space and time. I know it has happened but I didn't know it was happening. In this way, a way I am trying to trace for you, something has been given breath and slipped out from me, from my dream, or perhaps from a place where everything waits. It has appeared. Like ink, indelible. Like language, this peculiar tattoo.

It appeared to me on the edge of sight in the way things sometimes do, through the incidental view, the transitory glance across a face or from a car, looking up at just that moment, somehow knowing in our skin to do so, our eyes drawn up from the page or from our waking dream, the night bus window reflecting its interior. Or in the way we sometimes learn through the overhearing of things, some tone of the voice, some hesitation that tells us everything. It took its shape and — in the persistent, playful, inconvenient way of its kind — has presented itself until I acknowledge it. Until, having stepped back and looked up, I nodded and said, *Yes, yes, I know you're here. I know who you are; you are welcome, sit.* Until I believed my own eyes, and was able to risk reputation and to say to someone who knows little of me, *Something has appeared, become embodied, brought its three thousand year old blood, its three thousand year old bones, and is living in my house. Someone I know well, who knows me, who is in me but not, who was in me but now is not, who has slipped out of me in the night, with my breath, slipped out like a gasp or the longest exhalation, slid from me, an unintended thing. And now is someone who likes to play jokes — to appear in a room and disappear and send me calling after him until I stand suddenly still, suddenly step back nodding my slow head.*

My head has become the shape of a road and the road in my head is made of stones. It is a long stony road for the travels of night and memory, all its incidents layered one against the other like anatomical sections, like my body sliced thin, sliced one cell deep. Each section, held up to daylight, is foreign and unreadable. But, slipped back into place, pressed one against the other for decades, centuries, millennium after millennium, it becomes complete. It is slumbering and unremembered.

For months, in my dream, in the long travel of night, I walk the same road, falling. I have torn my muscle and skin, my heart, my knees. I have walked and walked. Alone. Away from myself. And now, at last, others walk it, too. Towards me. From the long road of death. They appear vague at first, their arms outstretched, their eyes too wide. They have arrived. They blink, blink out of the long night and into the August day.

Each morning I dress my kitchen table with a fresh cloth, fill a vase with white Geraldton wax or blue and yellow irises. I buy sweet cardamom seeds for the coffee. I sweep and wash, every day, every day.

I wait for my grandfather.

* * *

Grandfather, I need to know what it is you know. Yes, I have imagined you into being, and I was proud and astonished when I did that, believing myself powerful at last, reading your materialisation like a sign. But I also know what that makes me. Now, again, I am weak and empty, unskilled, fraudulent. Grandfather, I am afraid the world will find me out. Grandfather, come back. I need more, much more.

Much more than just those few glimpses of you. Much more than the flat pages of books. Much more than this tongue can give; much more than the particular Anglicised curve of my mouth. The words I need are somewhere else, need to be lifted from another tongue. It is your tongue I need. I need words from you like soft bread, words placed in my mouth from yours, words made for me through my mother's body, words dampened for me by my mother's milk. I need words broken apart, words wet and disintegrating, fresh and sweet on my tongue.

There is no place here for the well-behaved wafers of the Anglicans, rationed and anonymous, small blank papers on the tongue. A body filled with the unwritten. A life ingesting the unsaid. There is no more time for waiting in line, for polite kneeling or for deference. I need my proof; my mouth is open. I need all the stories you and God can fill me with.

I am at a cafe in Paris or on a sofa in an old house in the wheat belt. (Believe me, Grandfather, these things have happened. I cannot lie to you.) And he says, *What are you, where do you come from?* And he says, *Turkey is wonderful country, transformed by our father, the Father of Turkey, transformed by Kemal.* Or I am at a party in Fremantle and she says, *Do you feel Armenian?* And when, after a long silence, I nod, not looking at her, she says, *How? How is it that you feel Armenian? What is it?* she says. *What is it?*

Grandfather, come back. She asks me and I want to say, Grandfather, I want to say, *Would you ask me that if I spoke with my mother's accent, would you ask if she were standing here, would you ask if I could open my mouth and speak to you in a tongue you do not know, if I could speak and make your question vanish, if I could speak myself, speak for myself, if I could speak you away?*

There are things I could do — gestures I could make, rituals I could perform, words I could string together, one after the other, looping sentences around my wrists like chains. All these things I could do — all these things in my marrow. I feel them move inside my bones.

I want to say, Grandfather, I want to say to her, *Do you know what it is that you do when you ask me that? Only someone who knows nothing would ask me that, only an empty person, someone blessed with a terrifying certainty. Do you know what it is that you shake, who it is you diminish?*

But I don't. I am truly your granddaughter. You would be proud of me. I remain rational. I remain civilised. I answer her. I look to the ground and then away to the left and right. It is a party. I am a guest. It is at night. Things are different at night. Escape is difficult. There are other people with her. They squint at me. I see the light from the pergola slant in on their faces. I realise my face must be a shadow. I realise they probably can't see me well. I shrug and say, *Oh, that is a very complex question.* And I excuse myself to fill my glass but I put it under someone's chair and I leave.

Grandfather, help me. Lay your hands on my hands, your mouth on my mouth. Speak to me, through me. I will be your pipe, your pen and ink. I will be your morse, your cable. I will be your optic fibre. I will be your megaphone.

* * *

They buried him in swampy ground and, as quickly as they

dug it for him, the hole filled. The man is dead, his body wrapped, already cold and growing stiff. There is nowhere to store him and nowhere else in Alexandretta in 1918 to bury an Armenian. The gravediggers sweat, even in the cold, their breath fogging, and dig faster. But the water will not be held, and there is nothing further to be done. They curse under their breath; they try not to look at anyone. They ease Benyamin's body into the hole. They say prayers. The water rises to cover him.

Don't look, someone says. But Hovsanna is wild and her eyes are everywhere. She wails at the water, she wails at the men. Someone holds her. *Sshh,* they say. *Don't look, don't look.* But it is they who don't look. It is her they don't look at. Her eyes, her mouth. The men fill the hole. Everywhere they walk the ground subsides, their feet sink.

If my grandfather had lived, a few months later he would have seen his newly born daughter peering into the world, and she would have seen him. But he didn't and there wasn't even a photograph. Instead, my mother passes the things she heard her mother tell others, her eavesdropping, on to me and I pass them on to my children and so our stories are our photographs and live inside us like our blood.

My mother has one picture of her brother, Krikor, my uncle, my grandmother's oldest son. He is wearing his TransJordan military uniform. When she looks at this photo she says that Krikor's face is like Hovsanna's, but he is very tall and very broad across the shoulders. She says she recalls seeing this brother only twice and she remembers clearly how huge he was, ducking his head to enter the room. My mother has heard her mother say that Benyamin was a big man, and my mother knows that, as she herself doesn't resemble Hovsanna, she must resemble Benyamin. And so, through such comments and observations, we make our pictures of him.

If I were a painter I would paint his face for her, half turned away and glancing back at her over his shoulder as he left the room. But would she recognise him? How can the picture she has of him be the same as mine? If I were the painter, I think we would both feel a little flat — like we did when, as a child, I handed her a bunch of flowers I had picked only to discover, through the look on her face, they were weeds.

It would be better that her life had happened differently, that her surreptitious sketches in church had mattered enough to be the beginning of an artist's life, that someone had said, *These are good, Lucine. You must paint,* and that somehow she had. I wish that, year after year, the walls of our houses as we moved from place to place had grown more and more obscured by what she had to say, by colour and form, by the shape of her life. But sometimes all we can do is remember to breathe, remember to eat, and try to forget everything else. And art does not permit forgetting.

Now that my mother's hair is silver she wears the colours of the sea, water colours, luminous and shimmering. She wears white and aqua, the silver of pewter and the deepest blue. She turns through light like a wave. I have seen people watch her. I watch her. If I were a painter this is how I would depict her. The fabric of her jacket folds into itself like the surface of the sea. She has trained her painterly eye on herself, become a watercolour, her own work of art.

I have in mind three particular photographs.

At the end of the Second World War, my mother in Egypt at her first wedding, in a slim black suit and a wide-brimmed black hat, her sleek black hair bobbed, her legs glistening in silk stockings and breathtakingly crossed. She scrutinises the camera; she is utterly self-contained. Alongside her my father looks like an overgrown boy, his hair waved back, his slightly lopsided smile, his face so happy, as if he can hardly believe his luck.

Thirty years later, my mother at her second wedding, smiling broadly and directly into the camera, her head slightly tipped back. I think she is laughing. It's her nervous laughter and her boyish hair is lightly flecked with grey, her body still and slim beneath an indigo pants suit with a chiffon wrap, the fabric caught moving from her like a breath. Her long fingers hold a gold-tipped cigarette.

In the mid-1980s, at Perth airport, she is completely still. I photograph her in profile. She has turned slightly away from us and is staring at the gleaming linoleum floor. My sister is leaving to live overseas. My mother knows that, in the end, everyone leaves. The knowledge has frozen her. All around her people pass. I open the shutter. She wears clothes the colour of the sky. Beyond the observation window behind her, planes soar. I close the shutter. Those who have passed her appear in this photograph. They are mere traces of colours: red, orange, yellow. They are washed out, like so many ghosts.

Sometimes I forget that, between the second and third of these photographs, my mother visited Istanbul. In the days she was there, she bought nothing but bread and sweets and two intricately worked copper vases. She bought bread because it was real bread, the bread she remembers her own mother making, huge and round and paper thin. She bought sweets because they were pulled from the ovens on circular trays more than a metre wide, and were light and warm, melting on her tongue. She bought the vases, perhaps, because she loves the sheen of copper. There were beautiful carpets of silk and wool. Her second husband eyed them closely, but she forbade him, not wishing to make this country rich. She forbade him, too, to tell anyone she was Armenian. *There had recently been trouble,* she says, *there is always trouble. They had executed some Armenian. I have children waiting for me, I told him. If I go with you, you must promise me.* And, despite frowning and shaking his head, he did.

In the bakery where I bought the sweets were two beautiful women. I saw them a few times, and I looked at them and thought they can't be, but they look Armenian. They were so sad, the way they looked at me, as if they were thinking, 'You are so fortunate.' I didn't know there were still Armenians there. I thought they had all gone or perished, and I didn't want to ask them because, if they were, I might make them nervous and, if they weren't, they might suspect me of being one and call the police. Now I wish I had asked them. They were beautiful women. They looked so sad.

* * *

Recently I met another half-breed. This is what he called himself, and 'wog', too, with a smile. I know what it means to be called these things, and I know why he smiles when he says them, so I smile back. But I seem to have felt the weight of words always. Dick and Dora, Nip and Fluff: their neat clothes, their smiling mouths, their big frozen joy. I see the sunny place where I sat alone in the sun to read them, those light sentences a miracle, a taste that made me insatiable.

This is how a hunger grows: word by word, sentence by sentence, cells divide, divide and multiply. This is how a hunger's learned: overhearing conversation never meant for me — the tones and vocabulary, the syntax and silences. I turned this language over in my ear as if I held it in my hands. How heavy it is.

If I had a grandmother, if we had had Hovsanna with us (as this other half-breed had), maybe I would feel like a real Armenian. Maybe I would have learned the languages, Mum, listening to the two of you speak to one another. Not Armenian, no, that's true. But Turkish. Jesus, even Turkish. Even Turkish, Mum, is something, isn't it?

Perhaps I would have heard her weeping, telling you, Mum (at last, an adult now), her stories of what happened to them all, your brothers and sisters, the ones who should have been my aunts and uncles, who should have brought their own children, my cousins, into the world. Who should have been at our dinner table and graduations, and their children at my children's parties. And all I'd need to do now is write it down unadorned and give it to her, watch her turn it over in her hands, looking for the way in.

Perhaps she would have cared for me the way I've since seen grandmothers do — the way you, now a grandmother, have taught yourself and taught me, too. And perhaps (who knows? God is merciful) I could have even made her laugh. Mum, imagine. Imagine that.

If I were any kind of true Armenian, I would be able to tell this story in the way Armenians do — with the story-teller's slow ease, as if we have all the time in the world. As it is, the best I can offer is the illusion of a story — this fitful, half-formed, half-Armenian thing which I write because in my dreams I flew high as a plane. Over oceans and oceans and forests and deserts, came down low over lake and mountain, came down smiling into villages, into paved streets yellow with lamplight, across the rooves of houses, came down into a summer in Alexandretta, came down through the window into my grandparents' home, as it was once, as I wanted it to be, and into my grandparents' arms. And in the morning, waking alone in my room, I would hold my eyes closed, hold, a moment, my journey in my chest like a small warm stone.

Dark side of the moon

April is when the light in this city changes, becomes gold after the harsh white months of summer. It is when we start to wait for rain and, when I was a child, it was when we waited for the Easter school holidays or dreaded their end. Either way, April was the month in which there was always that moment when I suddenly caught sight of the year stretching out ahead of me like a journey that would take forever.

In my final year of primary school, two things happened. My mother had a dream that she would die when I was nineteen and, she told me, it would then be my responsibility to raise my brother. I wanted to ask my sister if she had been told the same thing but somehow I couldn't. In the event she had misheard the dream and died sooner, my mother continued, she was making provision for us to be sent to her sister in Vancouver. And the second thing, one weekend in April, my brother brought home his Social Studies project book. Even before dinner, he opened it all over the dining room table. Mum was still at work. Her key would turn in the lock about dusk at that time of year. As I moved through the house, I would see him, hunched over the paper, furiously working lead and coloured pencils. He was the only one of us to inherit our mother's ability to draw. Sometimes I would turn from the kitchen and see a twist of golden timber curling from his hands as he sharpened the pencils, the dust of them across the table and the floor. Now and again I took the pan and broom and crept about him, flicking these scraps into the pedal bin. *You'd better clear that away before Mum gets home*, I said, just before six. But he didn't, and she stood by the kitchen bench, her hands on her hips, just as I knew she would. I watched her face as she watched him. But when she looked at me I looked away.

When Dad was alive they had both hit him. When Dad died, I thought it might be better. But it was worse — as if now she had to hit him for the two of them. I waited. My insides shook. He had taken the old white sheet from the linen cupboard, the one that used to be on my bed and which we kept for bandages, and some clean jam jars from below the sink. The sheet was spread out right across the table like a soft white skin, and he was leaning over it, a pencil in one hand and his now completed foolscap drawing in the other. He was dark and fat and intent. *A table is for eating from*, she announced. He didn't even look at her. *I'm making a flag*, he stated, as if that was all anyone needed to know. She stared at his back as she considered this. Her eyes narrowed. *Which flag?* she asked.

Ours, of course. I watched his hand move slowly, steadily, in the top left corner of the sheet. *Not mine*, she said, icily, *and not yours either.*

I was born here, he muttered.

Born, she spat. *What's that? That's just an accident. I was born in Lebanon, that doesn't make me Lebanese.* He said nothing. The TV was loud in the other room.

Clear the table so we can eat, she said.

It's for school, he replied, without looking up. I saw the corner of her eye twitch.

I heard my voice, thin as a thread and quavering, and I hated the sound of it. *Mum, it's his Social Studies project. He's trying really hard to do well.* Slowly she looked away from him and looked at me. I tried to smile. Something in my chest shook. Then she turned on her heel, back to the kitchen and flung open the cupboard doors. I waited a moment and then sidled up to her. *What's for dinner, Mum?* I asked, as she clanged a saucepan onto the electric stove.

Haven't you got some homework to do, too? she snapped.

We ate from our laps, my brother sitting on the floor in front of the TV. *Like a Bedouin,* our mother said. Our sister and I perched like two birds on the edge of the sofa. Mum sat in her usual chair. I liked TV. The best thing about it was hearing what people in families said to one another and imagining you could say things just like that.

We didn't have enough blue paint. He had used all of the coin-sized pats of blue in his paint set and mine just on the Union Jack and even that wasn't finished. So, by Saturday afternoon he was desperate. We found some stubs of blue chalk in a tin on the laundry window sill and we crushed them up with a little water. But he was right, it was poor. We took the sheet outside — him on one side and me on the other, like fire fighters about to catch someone falling

— and laid it on the bare sun-lit concrete of the back verandah. *There's nothing we can do about it,* I said. *If you wanted blue you should have started with blue cloth.* And I warned our sister not to laugh, but I admit it was difficult.

When Mum came home she frowned a minute at his downcast face and then said, *What are you crying for? It's a very good colour. In the middle of summer the sky in this country is just like that. Everything wilts and shrivels up under this sun. People, plants, even the sky almost fades away. See? Look at me,* and she held out her arms to show him. *Your arms aren't faded, they're brown,* he muttered. *Well, that's right,* she replied. *And that's why the Aborigines are black.* And she stroked his hair once before she left the room.

On Sunday he rolled up the flag and tied it in four places with string. And the next morning he carried it to school, balanced in front of him on his open palms. He looked silly, like a priest. I followed him slowly up the hill, his school bag in one hand and mine in the other.

It was a long morning. Maybe it was the particular light that day or something to do with watching my brother walking ahead of me, and then sitting there at my desk seeing him over and over carrying his precious flag everywhere I looked. I don't know what it was that made me do it, but something did.

At lunchtime I went looking for him. I walked right along the wide wooden verandah, past his classroom and peeped in. It was empty, as I knew it would be. It was the walls I was looking at. They were covered in flags. The same flag and, yet, not the same. They were beautiful, all done on paper in neat bright textas with all the right bits in their proper places. Some had used dark blue crepe paper for the background or tin foil for the stars. My brother's wasn't up there and part of me was glad and part was sad. I looked at his desk and there it was, neatly folded into a manageable square, and that made me feel even sadder.

I went behind the building to the oval and walked all around its edge, looking for him. There were a lot of boys playing footy and yelling one another's names, and there were girls in groups or twos under trees, but I couldn't find him. After school I saw him walking home ahead of me, so I ran to catch up. *Did you put your flag up?* I eventually asked. He shook his head. *The old bat said it was much too big and can I get my mother to cut it down to size and what would happen if everybody wanted to take up so much space, how would we get on then.*

What did you say?

I said I don't think my Mum can sew.

What did she say?

She said, 'Ask your nanna or aunties.'

Oh. What did you tell her?

He didn't answer, so we walked the rest of the way in silence.

But that night, over dinner, he said, *Mum, why don't we have any nannas or aunties?* and she didn't say anything either and our sister, sitting opposite me, became very still. For ages I watched Mum carefully cut and lift her food to her mouth with her knife and fork. Then, when we were finished, she got up and, without looking at anyone, cleared the dishes from the table.

The first time I met another Armenian, a proper one like my mother, was also that year. I was twelve years old. The house was near the city and I remember my mother parked her car on the street and that the street was hilly. There was no front lawn. The exterior of the house looked plain and was neatly swept and close to the road. Inside the gate, the narrow strip of land that ran across the front of the house was carefully laid with grey cement pavers. Each paver was clean and straight, with a good inch of dark sand between it and its neighbour on every side. On either side of the door were two large planters filled with brightly coloured flowers. The house was quiet. We pressed the doorbell.

My brother and sister and I were ushered into a room to the left of a corridor and sat at a table with milk and cakes. The children of the family were ushered in after us and took their seats opposite. We were introduced and left alone. I heard the adults open the door of a nearby room and then their voices were swallowed as they closed it behind them. We ate in silence.

Occasionally, I looked up from my plate. There was a boy a little older than me, about my sister's age, and he kept looking at her and sometimes at me. He ate steadily and with a serious expression and when he looked up from his food his expression remained the same. My cheeks felt hot. I played with my cake, breaking off small pieces and popping them into my mouth when his gaze was elsewhere. When he'd finished he took an extra cake from the plate in the centre of the table and left without saying a word.

There was a window behind the heads of the two remaining proper Armenian children. Outside, the light was blindingly white. Against it, their heads were haloed, as if we were sharing cakes with angels. My brother banged his feet against the legs of his chair. It sounded huge in the room. My brother and the little boy eyed each other. An adult came in, a woman I didn't know. She said something I didn't understand. Her son slid from his chair. To my brother she said, *Do you like to play cars? Go with him. He has cars.* And my brother followed the woman and the little boy out of the room.

I looked at the little girl: her hair was dark brown and wavy, and strands spun away from her head and sparked against the white light of the window. Looking at her made my eyes squint, and her eyes were huge and round and very dark and she stared at me. She had propped her elbows on the table and rested her face on the backs of her hands and she stared at me with crumbs on her face. I wanted to tell her that — You have crumbs on your face — but, as I thought of it, I suddenly had no idea whether she would understand me. What was that language the woman had spoken? Did any of the children know English? I thought of asking my sister. Her head was leaning heavily in her right hand, her right arm was slumped across the table, and she was picking up every crumb of cake from her plate with the wet tip of her left index finger. I nudged her. She elbowed me back, quick and sharp, and caught me below the shoulder. I looked back at the girl. If she could speak English, she would understand my question. A crumb fell from her cheek. I wasn't sure if she was smiling at me. If she was, she did it without her face moving at all.

The following year, in the Easter holiday, we packed the car and drove. Mum said some other Armenians were having a party on Sunday. *Why?* I said. *To celebrate,* Mum replied. *Why do you think?* I didn't know but, as we very rarely went either on long drives or to parties, I simply nodded and looked out the window.

Mid-morning, the sun rose above the tree line on our left. It hung white and infinite above us a while. Then suddenly it was dropping — gold, orange, red as an eye — behind the tree line to our right and, I guess, into the sea. I thought about that — how everything seems to rotate around everything else. Moon, Earth, Sun, all those big circles. And then, looking out the window I thought that, if you imagine this country a huge circle of an island, the way a child would draw it, round as a clock, and if you drive around its edge, always travelling straight ahead, the comfort is you will always and finally come back to where you began. Because we were travelling anticlockwise, I realised the ocean was always beside us on our right. I couldn't see it, the roadsides being thick and mysterious with the luminous white trunks of karri — but there is comfort in knowing that, at any time, you can turn right and soon find yourself face to face with the sea. Later, when we travelled home, speeding along clockwise, speeding along like time, our destination became our point of departure, a mirrored image: the sore eye of the sun closing, at last, in the sea always on our left. But for us, driving to Albany and back that Easter, there was no sea view.

All day the road passed through farmland and forests and little towns with one garage and one shop. Each shop had multicoloured plastic fly strips hung across the door, and tins of SPC peaches, packets of Gillette razor blades and jars of International Roast instant coffee on the shelves. The garages sold LPG and ice and bait and, sometimes, frozen sausages for those, like us, who were inexperienced and hadn't packed an esky, believing instead that whatever we needed would be available wherever we went. If it were the esky, itself, that was missing, you could get those too, most places — or, at least the white polystyrene variety that squeaked each time it was touched. I felt ashamed of this esky; I could feel it in the boot behind me even as we sped along, squeaking away, with its thin twine handle. It was an emergency esky, an extra one, or the kind I knew men took fishing. When we pulled up in a picnic bay for lunch, there were Australian families with large metal eskies with sturdy metal handles. Their picnic tables were littered with cans of beer and lemonade and half a dozen colourful aluminium cups, and cooked sausages and cold chicken and a Tupperware container full of a lettuce, tomato and white onion salad.

Mum spread a small white tablecloth on our picnic table and opened a container of falafel and a tub of hummus, unwrapped some flat bread. I sat in the car. She yelled. Everyone looked. I lay down. She opened the door, pulled me out by the ear. *Eat.* So the four of us ate, in silence, listening to the kids at the other tables and all the other cars droning by.

I knew that, if I had asked her, she would have bought a proper esky. I also knew that, if I had asked her for cold chicken and lemonade she would have bought that, too, and she and my brother would have struggled, smiling, to lift it into the car. I knew that. And somehow that made it worse.

How long till we get there? my brother asked.

How do I know? Ask your sister, my mother replied, her hands gripping the steering wheel. Our sister sat in the front with the map.

How long till we get there? he repeated.

I don't know. You know I can't read the map while we're moving.

Mum, can we stop? he asked.

No.

Don't be pathetic, our sister mumbled.

Mu-um.

Be quiet. I'm driving. Do you want me to have an accident and for us all to be killed?

I stared out the window, as far into the distance as I could possibly see.

It was at Bridgetown that things changed. The towns thinned. Now there were long uninhabited stretches between settlements, and instead of fence posts and mailboxes on stumps and green paddocks dotted with white and black cows, it was miles of trees that pressed up against us on either side, along the edges of the road. When this happened, I lost sight of the late afternoon sun altogether. For a while, it flickered brilliantly across us in the gaps between trees, everything inside the car and the road ahead flashing gold between deep, cool patches of shade. Then the road drifted east and it was behind us. And then it was gone, and the sky — the little we could see of it when we found ourselves, for a moment, on a hill or rounding a bend which revealed an elbow of land where the forest thinned — turned from pink to mauve to grey in the long dimming of dusk, and Mum flicked on the headlights.

She hated night driving, even in the city where everything was always lit. Out there, the dark must have taken on the full shape of her fear. The forest leaned towards us, formed a tunnel and it was her job to guide us through. She strained forward. The headlights bounced off tree trunks and low canopies that hung over the road. She slowed down. Occasionally, we encountered another car rushing towards us on the winding, narrow road and she'd slow down even more. I shifted our brother's sleeping head on my lap.

Mum, you can do sixty miles an hour here, you know, I said.

Don't be ridiculous, how can I go fast here?

That's the speed limit.

Oh, for goodness sake, how would you know?

I saw the signs.

Signs! How come you saw the signs and I didn't? On this road? It's too narrow and windy and there aren't even any street lights here. How can I go fast out here? I'll lose control and tumble over the edge and roll over and over and crash into a tree, and no-one will come to find us for hours and by then we'd all be dead. There probably isn't a hospital here, even if they did find us, so what's the use?

Yes there is, Mum, our sister reassured. *There's a hospital here.*

Where, out here?

In Albany.

Oh, yes, and how do you know?

I just know. Everybody knows.

Everybody? Who is everybody? Do you think the Queen of England knows? Do you think the people in this country know anything at all? People know nothing in this place, and where are they all anyway?

Some people live here.

How many people? Just a handful of people live here. Do you think the government is going to spend millions and millions of dollars on a handful of people?

There's always the Flying Doctor, I offered.

Don't be ridiculous. The Flying Doctor? How long do you think that would take? God knows where they'd have to come from. In a little plane. I know what it's like in a little plane. Flying at night, out here in the bush, they'd probably crash into a tree themselves. Even if they made it, by some miracle, by the time they got to us it would be too late.

We drove the rest of the road from Walpole through Denmark without speaking, apart from my mother's muttered exclamations at each tight bend and the decline of each hill. I stared out the window again. I wanted to see something, something small and mysterious, something secret that I could keep to myself. I waited for the strange red lights of a startled animal's eyes to appear on the edge of the road, for the sudden blur of its body as it leapt or scurried away. But, if there were animals nearby, I didn't see them. So, I closed my eyes. I wished I was asleep with my head on someone's lap, and their hand stroking my head the way I sometimes stroked my sleeping brother's.

When at last we entered Albany, we saw nothing of it but its wide straight main street and its reassuring public lighting which spread away below us so we knew we were on a hill. I leaned forward and peered at the lights from between the front seats. Mum's elbows and shoulders sagged as she drove even more slowly. When we pulled into the car park and opened the doors, she stayed in the car, hands on the wheel. Even our brother, who woke incoherently, struggled out. Mum just sat, staring ahead, looking into the wall of the Travellers' Inn Motel, as if she was paralysed, while we all stood, suddenly shy, in the motel foyer.

In the morning, the shape of the town became clearer, the way it all fell away into the sea. Even if I turned my back on the ocean, which was difficult in Albany but which anyone might like to do now and again, I could still hear or smell it. So it struck me that day down there that there was no getting away from it. When I turned myself to look at the ocean, there was so much of it. There seemed to be less land here and much more water and the horizon seemed further away than it did in Perth. And was it the colour of the water or the way it moved, in those huge rolling swells, that made it seem that way? All day it was the size of things that astonished me. The ocean made the town seem tiny, and it wasn't. And that made me feel even tinier, a leaf, and just as inconsequential. Maybe it was just that we were on the edge of things, kind of like I felt years later in Canada, except that here we were on the opposite edge, the south coast of a southern continent, with nothing but ocean between us and Antarctica, instead of hundreds and hundreds of miles of ice that links you, somehow, from Canada through its cold teeth to the Arctic. It's as if, that Easter in Albany and then years later in Vancouver, I was as far from the centre of the world as I was likely to get, if the world does have a centre the way any sphere must have. At those times, I was in places where it was impossible not to know how far from the centre of the world you were because everything about the land and the sea and the wind there told you so, told you that you had turned your back on something, walked away from it — or driven or flown, of course, but in the end it's the same thing. You were near the edge. There was nothing ahead, nothing hospitable, nothing but — sooner or later — the white, hard permanence of ice. You were near the ends of the world and the ends of the world are as far from one another as they can possibly be yet resembled each other closely in every way that mattered. You were standing there, looking right into the hearts of these places, places so cold that, if you ventured into them, your fingers and toes would freeze, your breath would freeze in your lungs, your eyes would freeze. And you would lie down and all the heat from your body, all the momentum of your blood, everything that's whizzed around in you for years, would slow. And your organs — kidneys, heart, brain — would shut down, as if your life is a wheel and you're lying there on the ice by the side of a road so far from civilisation that no-one will reach you, and your wheel is spinning slower and slower, all that energy transferring itself into the ice.

Maybe that meant the way you feel about things in these places is different. Maybe that's why I thought about all this and why things happened there. And maybe all of that explains why, thinking about that Easter in Albany and that summer in Vancouver now, all these years later, I have this idea that they are somehow the same and that makes me think that the world must have a mirror in it somewhere, but one of those funfair mirrors that never gives a true reflection. You know it's you because it has to be, you're the one standing there in front of it, looking in, but what you see is not really you. No-one would say for sure it was you, but you know it can't be anyone else. This mirror in the world must be hidden, though, and maybe the way it is hidden is really very simple and very smart. Maybe it is so big that we can't actually see it. Sometimes you've got to move right back from really huge things before you can see what they are. You've got to be able to see the whole of things. While you're standing close, you can only see parts, and which part you see depends on where you are standing. And if there are a whole lot of you standing close to it in different parts, everyone has a different idea about what it is you're all seeing. Maybe we haven't been able to stand back far enough to see the whole thing yet, so how can we have any idea at all about the mirror? We just keep squinting at these distorted shapes, that must be us and yet are somehow not us, and wondering who these other people could be and how they can walk around in the world like that, looking like us.

It's no wonder I haven't been back there since. There's only so much of this kind of thought you can take, even when you are young and prone to it. And there's only so much of this kind of horizon you can take, too, with its undeniable truth of your being, bound wherever you look by a deep, thick band of unpredictable sea. If I am honest with you, though, it's probably the thing that happened there which is the real reason I haven't returned. Sometimes you just get caught up in events, as if they are a net submerged and come adrift from somewhere, from someone fishing far out to sea, who doesn't know you and who you're never going to meet, and you dive in for a blissful swim and suddenly your hands or feet are caught and no matter what you do you can't get back to the surface to breathe.

We spent that day looking around the town the way tourists do, drifting into interesting shops, sitting down somewhere for cool drinks. We went for a drive along a bit of the coast, which was dramatic everywhere we looked. At one point, the three of us ran down to a beach. The sand was cool and coarse, much more so than at home, and the wind was relentless onshore. As we approached the sea, I became afraid of it and stopped. You could just see how it could snatch you. I lifted the hem of my long skirt and put my bare feet in the water's very edge. Even there the foam tugged me. I didn't say anything, of course, but when my brother began to take off his jumper and shirt and say he would swim in his underwear, I yelled at him and ran all the way back to the car to tell Mum who had, as always, been watching and had stepped out of her driver's seat and was trudging down the dune, waving her arms. Her mouth was moving but the wind took away all her words. Still, he knew what that meant and, when I reached Mum and turned back to look at the beach, he had sat down in the sand, with his clothes over his head, and was flinging angry handfuls of it into the wind. You could see his hands burst open like stars and all the sand hurtle from them and fly back past him towards us.

I remember feeling that I would have preferred to spend the afternoon by myself, just walking and looking at people and their houses, peering in their windows as I passed, or sitting in the main street, flirting with any passing boys. But my brother likes museums and so we stopped there when we saw the sign along the road back to town because he had curled up in a furious ball in the back seat and we thought it might make him happy. I sighed out the window but had to admit, as we pulled up before it, that the building was attractive. It was old, one of the first buildings in the town, and somebody important had once lived there. It had fallen into disrepair, the woman there said, but the town had banded together to raise money for its restoration and now, of course, there was the ongoing maintenance which, as she was sure we could appreciate, was considerable. *You can't have history for nothing,* she smiled. *History is expensive but we simply must preserve it.* Mum nodded gravely. She had that look on her face which we knew meant she was going to say something about Armenia. I studied the floor. *History should be compulsory in school. A society without history is no society,* she stated as she opened her purse to make the donation.

Later — some years later — we would talk about the statue without ever naming it. Years after that, we would refer to it by the subject's last name and speak it only if compelled or if we wanted to make a dramatic point, and always speak it in the particular tone reserved for that name, the same tone our mother used. Sometimes we would ask one another if we remembered that visit, as if we were checking that it had really happened. At the time, we said nothing. We stood about it, the four of us, looking at his face, his hands, re-reading the plaque. After a few minutes I looked at my fingers, my shoes. My brother moved away to look at something else. I glanced at my mother. She was staring past the statue into the middle distance. She looked like someone had hit her. Her mouth had fallen. Her eyes were glazed with tears. Between her and me, my sister stood with her arms folded across her chest. Without looking at anyone, she said, *Can we go now?*

On Sunday night, the supper table was long and draped in white cloth and, at the appropriate time, numerous adults scurried back and forth, carrying platters and bowls and napkins and plates. Mum helped, and so did my sister, but I never know when to move forward in those situations. People look so distracted and harassed. I opened my mouth a couple of times to ask someone if I could help, but they rushed past before I could stammer anything. I picked up some forks that I watched slide off a passing stack of round white plates, and which bounced and spun on brown closely patterned lino. I could hear a woman's voice, *That means a surprise!* and I stood up smiling, looking about, but whoever it was had turned their back. And so I walked, with my fists full of forks, in the direction of the kitchen. *You look dangerous, like Lucifer. Doesn't she look like the Devil?* my mother asked anyone listening as she passed me. *Tch tch, no,* a voice answered. I slid the forks into the sink and pushed them around the hot soapy water with one finger, lifting it out shiny and pink every few seconds and shaking it in the cool air. *I didn't mean she is the Devil, far from it,* my mother's voice approached from behind. *She's a good girl, always has been. Very quiet, very polite.* I turned on the cold water tap and held my finger under the stream.

You're lucky. My daughter turned thirteen and changed into a witch.

My mother placed her hand gently on the woman's arm and the two were silent a moment, staring into one another's face. Then, in a low voice, she offered, *But that's terrible. Is there somewhere you can take her?*

I rinsed the forks one by one under the tap and placed them carefully, upside down and in rows along the draining board, curved steel on rippled steel. I liked the way they looked — a bit like an upturned hull, or like the bleached backbone of something on sand. Beside me there was a laugh and a flurry of white, and, *Don't tell me — architect.*

Pardon? I replied, looking at her. White dress, white skin, brandishing a white teatowel. She scooped up a handful of forks and smiled at me. She had a big white smile, too, with a gap between her front teeth.

Architect. You want to be an architect. You know, they make plans.

No. I mean yes, I know what architects do. I just don't want to be one.

What, you don't have any plans? she teased.

No, I said, looking at her. I had never seen so much black curly hair.

Pity, she grinned. *You're a natural.*

Later, when we were cracking the eggs and I didn't know what to do and she did everything right, I asked her, *Are you Armenian?*

Sure, aren't you?

I'm half-Armenian.

What do you mean? she laughed.

My mother's Armenian.

That means you're Armenian. There's no such thing as half Armenian. And she smashed my egg with hers, expertly, and squealed in triumph and said, *I love this game, don't you?* And then she was gone, running, looking for someone else's egg to crack.

It was like that silly joke people play where they pretend to crack an egg on the top of your head and, for a few moments, you believe that its contents really are running, thick and raw, in your hair. I gasped and waited for the mess and then she ran, and there was no mess, just the sharp and brittle shards of shell in the palm of my hand. I looked around. Everywhere people were busy with eggs. Children were peeling them or adults were collecting them in washed and ironed handkerchiefs spread out in the centre of their table like bright new blankets. I looked for my mother. I hated eggs.

She was sitting at a table with two other women. I heard her speaking as I approached. *How can you live here, in this place, with that, that statue of Ataturk there?* The women shrugged and looked away and one of them waved her hand. My brother sat beside her, his mouth full of white and yellow. I tried not to look. I held out my hand. The room smelled of egg. *What kind of place is this?* she continued. *What kind of place makes a statue of a man who murdered one and a half million people, my family, your family, and puts it in a museum and makes a sign that says what a great man he was? What kind of country is this that I have come to?*

I know, I know, but what can we do? a woman replied. *It is so far in the past, it is perhaps best not to speak, Lucine.*

If you don't want to speak then someone should write, my mother said. *Someone should write and tell them the truth.*

Speak, write, what's the difference, another woman said. *This is a different country, a different kind of country. Do you think they care? No-one here cares about the truth.*

Mum, I said, still holding out my hand. She looked at me. Her face was crumpled a little, like a sheet on a bed. She looked at me. *Someone should write,* she said, and she took the egg and looked at it. *Don't you want this?* she said. *They're good for you. When I was a girl I ate raw eggs for breakfast or sometimes when I was hungry and waiting for my mother to come home in the evening. She would walk slowly up the hill when the sun was setting and I would wait until I saw her coming then run down the hill to meet her. I'd put a hole in one end and suck it all out.* And she lifted her slightly crumpled face and brought her open hand with the egg in its palm closer to her mouth and pursed her lips and made a small sucking sound. Then she smiled at me. For a moment she looked like she was sending a kiss.

The thing I liked most about Rose that night was her skin. There was a lot of it and, when you looked closely, it appeared as if someone had touched her lightly a hundred times with fingers made of orange dust. She reminded me of a cocker spaniel a neighbour once had that never stopped wagging its tail. Nobody else had spoken to me that night, so I followed Rose back to the supper table to watch her replace the forks, filled my plate alongside her and then followed her and her friends to the verandah overlooking King George Sound where we all stood about and ate and they talked and laughed about people they knew at school.

I guess if she was the cocker spaniel then I was some skinny mongrel, happy to attach myself to the owner of the first friendly word. So I stood near her but a step apart, out of the circle of chattering friends. My sister was already standing out there when we got there, talking with a couple of boys, shivering because she had refused to wear a coat, Mum going crazy. *I'm not taking you to a party to catch pneumonia and die like my brother Hovsep did. My poor mother. It was the last straw for her.* I glanced at her and she glanced at me but then she just kept talking, angling her face from me in that way she has that means she wouldn't see you.

It was windy and cold and you could hear the swell rumbling far below. I listened to Rose and her friends a while, looking at my plate or feet, wiggling my toes. I studied their shoes. I wondered what kind of people they were. I already knew you could tell a lot about people from their shoes. The boys wore lace-up sandshoes or slim brown leather boots and the girls wore cork-soled platforms with their cold blue toes peeping out. I felt superior because I wore four-inch wooden platforms with worked black leather tops. When I walked it was like dragging two planks about. But I wore them because they gave me height and they gave me sound. They made me as tall as most of those boys and I could see further when I wore them. The horizon was a little more distant, yes, but I knew that also meant what was beyond the horizon was closer — if not to my body, then to my imagination. And when I walked in them the timber soles banged along the floor like a pair of drums, and people would listen for a moment as I approached. I liked that.

Even if my mouth had no words, those shoes spoke. But they didn't help me when I was standing still. I rested on one leg and then shifted my weight to the other. I wanted to go, but there was nowhere to go to. After a while, I turned my body away enough that I could gaze past them all into the darkness beyond the railing to my right, towards the sound of the sea.

When someone mentioned the gap I thought they meant Rose and her teeth and I felt my face flinch. They didn't, of course — no-one laughed or gasped — but it took me a few moments to work that out. They meant that place I had heard of, a dangerous place where the Southern Ocean swell rolls and smashes against cliffs, a place my mother refused to take us. There were two cars. My sister made sure she was in the other one. Rose got in the front with the driver and another girl and I got squeezed in the back beside two boys. The one closest to me had brown shaggy hair and smelled of beer when he said anything and like Brut 33 when he didn't. I kept my face turned towards the window, as usual, trying to look out, but all I could see was rain and the boy kept laughing and jiggling about and made me push myself further into the lining of the car door. I wanted to jump out. I wanted to say we are going to get wet. I wanted my sister. I wondered what our mother would think.

We were going fast. The driver started swinging the steering wheel, swerving back and forth across the slippery road. I held on to the seat in front of me. I could see the tail lights of the other car, the one with my sister in it, swim red and wet up ahead like two sad eyes across the windscreen. It was like not being able to get away from someone's stricken face. It made me feel sick. Rose would laugh and then yell, *Cut it out, shithead*, and then laugh again and then yell in a language I didn't understand. I wound down my window. The rain came in. The boy next to me said, *What the hell are you doin', I'm gettin wet*. So I wound the window up.

It was still raining when we got there. The car park was deserted except for us and the other car. We pulled up alongside it. I looked past the two boys, trying to see into it, but I couldn't. All I could see in there was a fierce orange glow. I opened the door and a blast of freezing rain blew in from the sea. The boy beside me said, *What the fuck, what's wrong with you? Shut the fuckin' door.*

Be nice, Alex, Rose said, without turning her head, *she's from Perth. It doesn't rain much there.*

Someone laughed and the boy on the other side of Alex leapt out and slammed the door. Alex slid himself away from me. I watched the boy hunch in the rain. He wrenched open the other car's back passenger door and squeezed in. I could hear my sister; she was laughing. I saw his pale hand reach back and shut the door behind him. *Where's he going?* I asked. *Don't worry,* the driver said, pushing a tape into the cassette player, *he'll be back in a minute,* and he pressed play. I knew it in seconds. Pink Floyd's 'Dark Side of the Moon'. I knew it because my sister played it in her room. Sometimes I'd sneak in when she was out and look at her albums, turning the covers over and over in my hands. Looking at that album was the first time I thought about physics, I mean really thought about it, about rainbows and what they were, and about how things look simple and ordinary when they aren't. One afternoon I tried to explain it to my mother, about how light seems like it's nothing but white, but is really seven separate colours all together and how light wouldn't be the way we know it if all its colours weren't there and how you need to see the light through something called a prism to see what it really is, to see every part that makes it. She blinked at me. *A prison?*

No, Mum, prism.

What's prism? So I ran into my sister's room and grabbed the Pink Floyd album. She was cutting something out of a magazine and yelled at me. There was paper all over her floor. *Mum wants it,* I said and ran out. *Like this,* I said to Mum, holding the album out to her.

I thought that's called triangle.

It is, but triangles are flat, on paper or on the ground. You know, two dimensional. And I pressed my hands flat on the table in front of her. *This,* I said, pointing at the picture on the album, *looks like a triangle but it must be a triangular prism because the light's refracted. A triangular prism has, um, depth, it has faces. Each face is the shape of a triangle,* I said, making my hands into a pair of its faces, and then another pair, *but it's three dimensional, like this.*

She frowned at my hands. *You mean like the pyramids,* she said quietly.

Yes, exactly like the pyramids, I exclaimed.

Oh, well I know about the pyramids. I've climbed them and I was terrified and ran all the way down. Many servicemen died during the war trying to climb the pyramids. They slipped and fell to their deaths. She frowned at the picture. *Light doesn't go through the pyramids.*

It would if they were made of glass, I said.

She didn't say anything for a while, and then she looked at me and shook her head. *What about rainbows? There's no glass in the sky.*

No, but there's water in the sky and water does the same thing. It refracts light, too, and that's why we only get rainbows after it's rained, because there's water left in the sky.

You mean clouds.

Yes, I said.

So you are telling me that clouds are like glass.

Um ... I dunno, I s'pose I am.

She was quiet a while, looking at the picture. She turned the album over and back and over again. *Why have they put it upside down on the back?*

I don't know.

She shrugged and handed it back to me. *I see,* she said and got up from the table.

For a while after that, whenever I was with her and saw a rainbow, I'd say, *Look, Mum. Refraction.* And she'd say, *Oh, isn't it beautiful, that thing.* And she would smile at me. And she was right. It was so much more beautiful after we had talked than it ever was before.

Hey, said Rose, turning around to look at me, *do you know where we are?*

I shook my head. Alex said something like, *We're in djinn land,* in a squeaky voice and the driver growled something to him in that language again.

When it stops raining we'll walk down there, Rose said to me, gesturing somewhere ahead. I squinted to see what was in front of us but I couldn't. Someone said, *It'll be slippery* and then the other back door burst open and the rain boy jumped in, clutching his belly. Alex moved closer to me and rain boy slammed his door and then shook his long wet hair. He smelled like a wet dog. *Shit, man,* Alex mumbled, *There's loonies on every side.*

Did ya get it? the driver asked, peering in his rear view mirror. Rain boy pulled something out from under his jumper and the quiet girl, the one who'd said nothing, sitting between Rose and the driver, held a lighter out to him. Its metallic body shone dully silver when he flicked it open and the flame spurted gold in the dark car.

For a couple of minutes I worried about what I was going to do, but I needn't have. Alex didn't offer it to me and no-one else seemed to notice. The fat white joint went round and round and I wound down my window an inch. No-one noticed that, either. Even so, when I opened the door to step out of the car after the others I felt unsteady. It was dark. No lights, no moon. And it was still raining lightly. I stood up. The car park was awash. I could hear the puddles sloshing around the base of my platform soles. It was like I was standing on my own pair of rafts. The ocean was roaring. The wind rushed down my collar and up my skirt. I shivered. The others were already ahead, walking away, stumbling, laughing. Already I could barely see them. *Wait,* I shouted, but shouted it into the wind from the sea, the sea that was all around us all the time, and it stole my voice away.

The track dropped away from the car park and then split in two across the low scrub. I staggered through the soft wet sand to the fork and looked left and right, once, twice. I couldn't see them. I closed my eyes and listened. I could hear nothing but the sea. I turned my head this way and that, searching for something, the slightest clue. The rain, when it came, was so cold it stung.

Back in the car, I wound the windows down a bit to clear the air. At least it was sheltered in there and I dried my face and hair with a towel I found on the floor. Then I folded it up and used it as a pillow.

I opened my eyes. There was a boy near the car, looking at me. I sat up. *Where did you go?* I asked, winding the window down a bit more.

He smiled. *Not far. Just over there.*

I couldn't see you guys, so I came back. It started to rain again.

I know.

I looked behind him. *Where are the others?*

He glanced over his shoulder. *Oh, around.*

Are they coming back soon?

He shook his head. *I don't think so.*

I nodded slowly and looked at him. He was dripping wet. He was young — not as young as me but not as old as the others, either. He was wearing shorts and a t-shirt. His feet were bare. I didn't remember him. Maybe he was in the other car. I thought about the verandah, the shoes. Who was there? I looked again at his bare feet. Then I slid my hand up to the door lock and pressed it. It made such a loud click I thought he might hear it, so I said, *The other car's probably open. Why don't you get in it? You must be cold.* I smiled. There were three other door locks.

I am, he said, looking at me, *but I can't find my towel. Do you know where it is?*

Your towel? I said, touching my makeshift pillow on the seat beside me. I leaned forward, feeling around in the dark at my feet, and I pushed the towel onto the floor. *Um, no,* I said, loudly, *I don't think it's here. What colour is it?*

I looked up. He wasn't there. Maybe he had heard the sound of this lock and was at one of the still unlocked doors. I looked around. No, he wasn't. My hand flew to open the lock. I froze. Maybe he was still there, alongside the car, crouching, waiting for me to get out to see where he'd gone or to try to find the others. I snapped down the remaining door locks. Then I sat still and I listened — hard. What am I listening for? I thought. What would I hear? What sound would a hiding man make? Would his heart be pounding as loudly as mine? Do I really think I'd hear his breathing? Perhaps he'd gone to the other car, after all. I looked over at it. I hadn't heard anything, no car door slam. It was very dark but it seemed utterly empty. But perhaps he was lying down? Why would he lie down, he was soaking. Maybe he just went back to the others. I shivered. I was suddenly cold. It doesn't matter, I told myself. Wherever he is, he can't get in. No-one can get in. I'm safe. I'm safe and I just have to wait.

Suddenly there was a voice beside me. I opened my eyes. There was a hand reaching in. The window. I had forgotten to close it. The hand was small and white and it groped along the sill. It fumbled with the door lock.

Bloody hell, it's freezing out here. Let us in.

Okay, hang on. It was Rose. Her voice, her hand, her beautiful skin. *Who locked it anyway?* She pulled the door open and stared at me. *What are you doing here?*

Hurry up. Open the bloody doors, someone said.

So I did.

The driver started the motor and put the heater on, and they all sat, rubbing their arms and legs.

Man, Alex said, *did you feel that ground shake?*

It was amazing, said Rose, turning around in her seat to see me. *You should have come.*

I tried, I said. *I tried but you disappeared.*

Did you hear that swell? It cracked like a bastard.

You should have yelled. I would have come back for you, she said.

I did.

Well, sorry.

Yeah, we know. You shat yourself, said rain boy, grinning at me from the other side of Alex's jiggling head.

Why would I do that? I said, weakly.

Well, you don't want to be caught out here on your own, you know. All kinds of things happen out here.

Shut up, idiot, said the driver, quietly.

Fuck, shrieked Alex. *Man, I thought we were dead for sure with that one.*

I said shut up. The driver spun around.

Yeah, said Rose. *Be nice you guys.*

Well, shit. She doesn't know anything, said rain boy, jerking his thumb at me.

No, growled the driver, *but the rest of us do, and she's my girlfriend and this is my car. So unless you wanna walk home, I suggest you shut your fat trap, okay?*

Yeah, okay.

Wow, man, this is freaking me out, moaned Alex, slowly

shaking his head.

I frowned out the window and took a deep breath. *I saw someone.* There was a silence.

Oh, yeah, said Rose. *Who?*

I dunno, some guy. He wanted his towel.

Whadya mean?

He was wet.

We're all wet. It's raining.

I know but —

But what?

Rose, the driver said.

But what? she repeated.

I dunno, I dunno, I said. *I don't know who he was. He was wet, he was in board shorts, he said he was cold and he couldn't find his towel. Is he in the other car? Because if he is, there's a towel in the back he can use. I should've given it to him, but — I didn't.*

Told ya she shat herself, mumbled rain boy, turning his face to his window.

The driver hissed, *Oh, man, you're really fucking asking for it, you know?*

There was another silence. Then the quiet girl said, *What did he look like?*

Um, he was young. He had, um, short dark hair.

She turned to her boyfriend, the driver. *I wanna get out.*

No.

Let's go, said Rose, and the driver put the car in gear and blasted the horn. The wheels spun as we reversed, stopped, then moved ahead slowly down the potholed track that led back to the road, our headlights bouncing over the scrub on each side. I looked behind. The other car was turning around, its headlamps sweeping a wide arc like a lighthouse and us sailing away, out to sea, away from whatever danger it signalled, from whatever lay submerged.

We turned back onto the deserted road in silence. I wanted to know what was going on, what it was I didn't know, and what it was I'd done anyway. But there are some kinds of silence that are so heavy in the air that nothing you can say will shift them. I knew that. I knew when to shut up. I was good at it. In my family, you learned those things along with speech. I just missed the cue. Maybe it was because of the smoke, because I was dizzy. Maybe it was because I didn't know, until then, that other people lived like us, had secrets like us. Not that I knew, at that time, what our secrets were. I just knew they were there, huge and awful. You might wonder, as I did for some years afterward, why this didn't draw us together somehow in that car that night. But no-one likes to be a mirror. Or worse, just a sheet of glass — transparent, invisible, like you're not even there. Someone who sees into you quickly, who sees through you, sees themself reflected in you, turns you into a freak or a ghost, is a dangerous thing. Someone like that makes you feel small and dirty and ashamed.

I didn't understand any of that as we began the half-hour drive back to the town. I just knew something I had done, things I had said, had caused all of this. If I'd gone with them wherever they had gone, if I hadn't stayed by myself, nothing like this would have happened.

After a very long time, I said, *I didn't mean to make everyone angry.*

No-one said anything for a while and then Rose replied, *It's not your fault. Look,* she said, turning towards me, *nothing ever happens here. Sometimes hai fall, that's all. They fall in love, they fall pregnant or they fall off cliffs. But that's all, no matter what anyone says. They fall.*

You should have let me out, the girl said to Rose.

What for?

He's my brother. I wanted to see him.

You can't see him, he's dead.

What are you talking about? She saw him.

No, she didn't.

She saw him, and I didn't. Because you wouldn't let me out.

Rose looked at me. *What was his name?*

I dunno, I stammered.

There, she said, turning back to the girl. *Could have been anyone.*

Yeah, said Alex, *Rose's right. Stacks of people go out there. It's one of the most popular places around to top yourself.*

Shut up, snapped Rose.

Shut up, just shut up, screamed the girl.

So nobody said anything more on the long slow drive back, with the driver hunched over the steering wheel and squinting out the windscreen down along the narrow tunnel of light that guided us, and the car behind travelling way back and just as slowly. The only thing that happened was that, somewhere along the way, Rose pushed the cassette back in and pressed play. I wished she hadn't.

When we got back I expected Mum to scream at us the way that girl had screamed and I hung back as the others went in, thinking that if she started yelling at my sister I wouldn't go in at all and would just wait outside until the three of them came out and we drove back to the motel. But all I heard was a loud and foreign music. And then all I saw was my mother dancing in a circle with a dozen men and all the other women still sitting on their plastic chairs, watching. She looked so beautiful. Her sleek black hair gleamed under the lights and her red dress swirled around her knees as she turned, her arms raised above her head like she was reaching for God. The men smiled and clapped their hands or clicked their fingers in time and, looking at them all, I couldn't help it. I started to cry.

Dead centre

One summer, towards the end of high school, I drive into the wheatbelt with my best friend and her mother. After climbing through the forested hills, the land stretches into endless flat plains of yellow wheat stubble. I doze in the silence and the heat. We arrive for lunch. My friend's married sister's house is old and stone and has a large kitchen with a small red laminex table and four chairs dead centre. Adjacent is an equally large lounge room with a single brown sofa and a square orange plastic coffee table. There are incongruous sliding glass doors leading outside. The light out there is so white I can't look at it.

Word has got around and boys have turned up to take us swimming. I can see their cars through the sliding glass doors. The station wagon is sky blue and shining. I sit on the brown sofa, talking to one of the boys. The others leave. Inside the house is cool and quiet. He strokes my arm as he talks to me. I know what this is. I smile back at him. He flicks through the record collection, puts one on. Of course, it is Pink Floyd. I must have told him.

When he slides his hand under my long cheesecloth skirt,

I let him. I think, *Oh well.* It's awkward on the sofa; I don't know where to put my limbs. While it's happening I wish it wasn't, but I don't say anything. It's over quickly. His face is close, smiling. I try to smile back even though it hurt. I say, *I guess I should have shaved my legs.*

No. He shakes his head, runs a hand along my calf. *I love your hairy legs. Don't ever shave them. I love how hairy you are everywhere.* He smiles again and I feel my cheeks burn. He sits up, dresses himself. I find my knickers, step back into them. Then I sit, my long skirt smoothed over my legs. I feel how different my body is where I sit on it. I try to look outside but it stings my eyes. The orange coffee table glares at me; its plastic top is all scratched up.

His hands are in my hair, lifting it from my shoulders, letting it fall. *You have such amazing, thick hair. How long have you been growing it?* I shrug, *Not long.*

Wow, he smiles, lifting it again. Is he ever unhappy? *Where are you from?*

I look at him. *Perth,* I say.

The next day my friend and I are in the back seat of a car with him. Three other boys sit along the front seat. I'm wearing a bikini and my long skirt. The vinyl seat sticks to my back. We turn off the bitumen and roll slowly onto a dirt track. To the left, a dusty stand of sheoaks straggle along the bank of a creek. Up ahead, a young thin Aboriginal woman in a stop-sign red long-sleeved shirt moves off the track, her head bowed. As we pass her there's a silence. Then one of the boys in the front grins at the driver, *Don't know our way around there, do we mate,* and jerks his thumb back towards the creek. *Nah,* the driver grins back. *Never been down there.* They all laugh so I laugh too, and turn. My back peels away from the seat. I look out the rear window. All I can see is the dust we leave behind.

Now I know anything can become ordinary. As banal as cloth, as well worn as my sheet, its texture and scent deeply familiar.

I am the only one I have ever known like me. You say: *half-Armenian.* I say: *Mum, please, which half?* Which of my limbs lies at night in the west of Asia? At night, in my bed, wrapped in the ordinary knowledge of my sheet, Mum, which half of me dreams a story, dreams a million different stories, dreams all of them the same? Sleep in my bed, your head touching mine, and I will take you to them. In the morning I wake with my head full of tears. Tell me which half of my heart has always been broken. And which half, Mum, which half, please, can walk away?

* * *

The flatness of maps is a gorgeous illusion. The smooth, crucial lines of latitude and longitude save countless lives and make possible all manner of journey: trade and pleasure; exploration, invasion and escape. The country I write in owes itself to tens of thousands of years of journeys. And what is a migrant without maps? We carry them in our heads; daily, we negotiate our ways into the world and our ways home.

In the world in our heads, we forget that we really cling

to a sphere that spins and that, when we walk across a sphere, even one as huge and spinning as Earth, we expect to end up somewhere else entirely but eventually arrive at our starting point. The more determined our step, the straighter our line, the sooner we will reach it — and there they will be, as large as life: our foot and finger prints, a piece of hair, our DNA.

In Turkey there are bodies at the bottoms of lakes. The flesh has long been eaten by fish but the bones are there. Some of the bones belong to me. The bones of my beloved ones quiet and still beneath the waters of lakes where people swim and the boys of villages along the shores have thrown in lines and caught some fish and, proud and smiling, carried them home. Hauled those big fat fish back home where their mothers have smiled and baked them and fed the whole family.

One day I enter my son's room. His window is quite high; it overlooks our neighbour's roof. I enter for a reason, but now I have forgotten it. I am facing the window. Something yellow flashes by. It is the girl, the girl again. I stop. I stand still. I am holding something. It is something soft. It is fabric, folded, brought in from the sun. Beyond the window, the entire world is terracotta. And, above it, unbelievably blue. It is summer, of course. It is always summer. I see it again, the movement of that yellow thing. I see again its particular curve, its particular arc through space, and I think that girl again, with the yellow hair, is skipping around my house. I apply the laws of physics — velocity, trajectory. Nothing else will explain it, that small bright movement. I listen for her voice because, I recall, as I entered with my hands full of soft warm things still scented with heat, I thought I heard it. I wasn't listening but I thought I heard it. Now, straining to hear, there is nothing. Just a car passing, the shouts of children from the primary school, a dog, a crow, the drone of a plane. I take a step towards the window and look down through it. The girl's head was small because, I decide, when she passed she was young. When she passed she was smiling. I saw her only for a moment, but you can tell when someone's smiling. There is light in them. Besides, I had seen her before from other windows, from windows that made much more sense, windows through which one could see the earth, not just rooves and sky where girls skipping by must be ten feet tall or angels flying.

That night I wake up, breathless with a sudden knowledge. In my dream, which feels like memory, I am with a woman and her family of children, newly arrived. I am teaching them English. They have glossy black hair. Because it is always summer, I am conscious of my skin. There is too much of it. I am conscious that their limbs are covered. I am conscious of my face because I wear lipstick. They have large smiles. One of them reaches her fingers to my hair and says, *You have a bit yellow, your hair. Yes,* I say, *it is the sun.* Not one of them believes me.

My Yugoslav neighbours are keeping their blinds closed. I hear shouting at night and weeping in the day. I think about knocking on their door; I think *this is no way to face the turn of a century let alone a millennium.* I think that is what I will say to them, and hold up to them a bottle of something red.

They might let me in. I think about phoning the advertised number to volunteer my services to the Kosovar refugees, that handful who come to stay for a while in the navy barracks at Fremantle. But my services as what? Writer? Sympathiser? I dial the number. The switchboard is jammed by nurses, child carers, tailors, solicitors. What on earth would I say to the assessor? *I know their heart and, despite all they'll be told, I want them to hear me say I know it will never get any better, that every day for the rest of their lives they will think of it, wake to it and breathe it; every night they will dream of it.* I want to say this thing I have never uttered, that my mother and I have never said. And it is, I think, very important that we don't. The flatness of maps is what our lives are built upon.

So I don't knock and I don't phone. I listen to my neighbours shout and weep; I watch every broadcast, listen to every bulletin, scrutinise every tone of voice and every look on every face, and I cry, too. I feel like someone has peeled off my skin. At last, I think. At last.

I receive a letter from Elisabeth. I am pleased. As always, I examine the stamps because French stamps don't change, and I smile with the pleasure of being affirmed. That small thing.

Elisabeth and her mother lived in a converted dairy in a village so small it had no phones, and I slept on their floor for a while. Elisabeth told me she grew up in Paris, where her parents had settled some years before, after leaving Kosovo, a place I'd never heard of. They are Muslims. I am surprised. She can see it and she presses me. *You don't look*

Muslim, I say. She laughs then, and I feel my face flush. After that, I feel uncomfortable; I think of home more often. I don't think of a particular place, or even much of particular people, but am aware of a vague, unshakable tug elsewhere. I start planning my escape. This feeling bothers me because Elisabeth and her mother are only ever polite. I watch them more closely, looking for a reason.

Elisabeth's mother was making a name for herself as a puppeteer. She was striking, bohemian, and told me stories about taking her shows overseas, about whom she met and what they created, and she threw up her hands and said how she and the Americans dismayed one another because she refused to include violence in her work and they were horrified that her puppets simulated what she called the making love. She would hold up her hands to represent her puppets when she spoke and, during this story, she wound them together, rubbing the long white inside of one forearm against the other to show the sex.

Once or twice I wandered about and in every room, on every floor of their home — in the large, light attic, in the warren of first floor rooms, and even at the back of the muddy sheds that formed the ground floor level — were scenery flats, wheeled puppet theatres, ladened costume racks, piles of fabrics of every colour and weight. One day I came upon a room full of wardrobes with mirrored doors, and cardboard boxes which, when open, revealed scores of collapsed and strung up puppets, their limbs twisted and their eyes dull and staring. At night, on my mattress on their kitchen floor (which offered the only adequate space), I would pull my sleeping bag over my head and try not to think about them.

That summer in France was cold and rainy. Every day I wore boots, my only pair of long pants and my spray jacket. At night I slept in them. Breathing into my sleeping bag, I would fall into a sleep filled with all kinds of bodies. After a few days I became self-conscious about raising my arms when others were near; after a week, I could smell myself no matter what I did. There was a deep bath in the bathroom and, they told me, hot water if they lit the boiler. But I couldn't do it; for some reason I couldn't remove my clothes and stand pale and naked; I couldn't see my body that way, so vulnerable.

Elisabeth writes to me, a short note.

Have you heard? All my mother's family is there. Or, at least, they used to be there. Now we don't know where they are. No-one has heard from them. Have you seen the pictures? What will become of Pristina? My mother tries all day long, day after day, to phone her brother, her mother, but she cannot reach them. She drives into the town. She sits in the cafe. Every half an hour she crosses the road to the public phone. When it's dark she drives home again. For weeks she has done nothing else. I don't know what I should do.

On the last evening with Elisabeth and her mother, something unexpected happened. Well, two things actually, but they are really both the same thing, the way things sometimes break — neatly, when you drop them, so that when you press the pieces together you can hardly see where they have fallen apart. And you wonder, if you keep quiet, whether anyone will notice, if the way the thing is broken will be a secret you can keep.

It happened like this. Suddenly, in the middle of the usual evening banter over a glass of wine — the dinner dishes pushed aside on the table, Elisabeth watching, me watching, her mother talking — I remembered a face. It was something she said — I don't remember now what — a word, perhaps, that opened something. I don't know much, but I do know that there are occasions when a word is all it takes to change everything. So much is context that it can be an ordinary word, particularly said, that rolls away the stone. One moment you are in a landscape utterly familiar, and the next the very earth itself changes shape. Suddenly, there was this face, staring at me as if he knew me. For a moment I had no idea who it was. This was a distinctive face, its combinations uncommon — not strictly beautiful, not the way you might imagine, but arresting. It was the expression in his eyes — so intense, so unwavering; I could hardly bear to look. How long I was engaged in this, I have no idea, time and space being what they are. One shifting, altering the other. Perhaps it was less than a minute, perhaps more than five. I don't know. But, in that time, two things happened: I remembered who he was; and they noticed. They noticed, of course, because I was no longer watching. I had stepped out of my role, become something else. I was no longer laughing or nodding. There was no longer an audience. It could have been that I had disappeared. I could have slipped into the darkness at the back of the house and stepped out. I neither saw nor heard them. Nor did I move or speak. Nor am I certain they spoke to me, although I imagine that they did, as anyone would, calling my name, trying to bring me back. If I could be recovered quickly, then maybe the show could go on at least. Not as before — life and theatre are never that convincing — but on, nonetheless. It had been such fun. No-one wants their fun to end. Not suddenly. Not out of their control, in the middle of a story, when they least expect it. So, whatever they said, whatever they did, it made no difference. I saw his face, I remembered his name, I recalled his story, and then I came back.

I apologised, of course. That's what you do when you act like that, when you don't answer people, when you make them concerned. And they were concerned. I could see it on their faces. I apologised, and I told them that I had just recalled a story, a story I had completely forgotten, about a boy I knew named Smelly Dragon. And then, for the first time in the ten days we spent together, and without even an invitation, without suggesting Elisabeth's mother complete her new tale, forgetting all about being a guest and that I hadn't washed, I began animatedly — with voice and face, arms and hands, just like Elisabeth's mother — to tell them the story of Smelly Dragon, who lived in a cave and flew off a cliff.

Smelly Dragon wasn't his real name; I realise now that we never knew his real name. He appeared on the roll as 'Dragi, Milos'. I know this because sometimes, when I was asked to deliver the roll to the office, I would sneak a look at it because I so much liked the copperplate script in blue ink and the columns of identical ticks. I thought it the most ordered, the most beautiful thing, and I wanted so much to write like that.

'Dragi, Milos'. I had never heard of a name like his. Decades later it occurred to me, if occurred is the right word, that his family name was probably Dragisovich, or something like it. It took a long time for this knowledge to form. I was never aware of its arrival, as if someone had entered my house when I wasn't there and slipped a new book onto the bookshelf. That's all. They'd left no other clue that they'd been. So, when I came home I had no idea things had changed. And I came and went and came and went for goodness knows how long before one day, looking for another book, I saw the new one, in exactly its correct place, as if it had always been there. And I picked it up and turned it over and thought, *Where did this come from? How long have I had it?*

And so it was with Smelly Dragon, whose real name, I imagine, was Milos Dragisovich but who, even in the adult world, the official world, was 'Dragi, Milos'. Now, where I grew up no-one can have a name without it being shortened, and a name like Milos offered the irresistible possibility of Milo because everyone knew what Milo was and, in the far inland suburbs in the '60s, no-one had ever heard of a Milos. So, 'Dragi, Milos' became Dragi Milo, became Daggy Milo became Daggy Smilo, then Daggy Smello, Smelly Dag, Smelly Dragon.

Only slightly less astonishing than his name was his hair. Smelly Dragon was the first — and, for many years, the only — person I had ever seen with thick and very blond hair on his head and thick, black eyebrows. Somehow, this combination frightened me. Smelly Dragon frightened me. Not because he swore or teased like all the other boys except the minister's son. I don't ever remember even hearing him speak, although I'm certain he must have. No, he frightened me because he smiled. That's how his name went from Milo to Smilo, because he smiled all the time, and no-one does that, no matter how happy they are.

Smelly Dragon must have been in the year above or below me because I only ever saw him going home in the school bus. The bus was often noisy, with everyone talking — except Smelly, of course. And sometimes except me. I was too busy watching him. In order to do that, I always sat behind him. Not directly behind, of course. That would have been too risky. But behind, back a few rows so that I wouldn't have to see his face, that blond hair and black hair, and his smile. He always sat near the front, never near the back. He hardly ever turned around, which suited me, and most of the time kept his face to the window, which was also a relief.

At Smelly Dragon's stop, which wasn't far, everyone at the back of the bus would yell, *See ya, Smelly*, and laugh. It would be a huge chorus. He wouldn't ever look around at anyone as he stood and made his way off the bus, no matter how loud it was. But when he was out on the footpath and beginning to walk and the bus started to move and kids were hanging out the windows, waving and shouting *See ya, Smelly Dragon*, he would glance up at them with that big smile stuck on his face. He had white teeth and brown skin — olive, my friends' mothers called it, always glancing at me. I had no idea what Smelly Dragon's skin had to do with me, or why they looked at me when they said it. Was I supposed to know something about skins? Did they think I should make some remark like adults do to one another when they're together? In the summer, Smelly's skin went very dark. Although he would wander around at lunch time with his shirt off like all the other boys, he never came to class with red shoulders, and his nose never peeled. He just turned darker and darker, and his hair turned whiter, as white as his teeth became against such skin. Every summer he turned into something I had never seen anywhere else. So that, in the second half of summer when we had all returned to school and sat through afternoon after shimmering hot afternoon and he glanced up at those kids hanging out of the school bus windows with that fierce white smile, and he walked straight ahead, looked straight ahead with that fierce white smile, along that footpath as the bus pulled away from him, he scared me even more than at other times of the year.

Like so many of the others, I would turn my head to watch him, hoping to see where he went, hoping maybe to see his mother. Other people's mothers held a grim fascination, but Smelly Dragon's mother became an unshiftable presence, like a ghost. Something you know you are one day going to see, and probably when you least expect it. But the bus always moved too soon, and all I ever saw was him walking on the footpath with his weird looking face.

Rumour had it that he lived in a cave. I wasn't certain there were any caves in our suburb, but it was possible. There were hills, and there was plenty of rock. There was more rock and stone than anything else. Our school had no lawn at all. Even the oval, where the girls played softball and the boys kicked footballs, had more stones than grass. If you slipped on it running for a base you'd spend the rest of the day picking bits of gravel from your knees. So, the idea of caves couldn't be dismissed. Sometimes, when we were out for Sunday drives, I would see bits of the hills that looked white with shadowy holes at the base. That could be a cave, I thought. The holes looked pretty small, much smaller than our house. Smaller, even, than a room. How could a family live in there? Once I asked Dad what they were and he said they were quarries where they cut blocks of limestone from the earth. So I asked what limestone was and he said it's the stuff at the bottom part of our house. It seemed possible then that caves existed because, I deduced, if you put together all the limestone from the bottom part of our house there would be quite a lot and wherever you cut it from it would be a pretty big hole, bigger than a room, maybe bigger than two rooms, and that would probably be big enough.

My friend thought it was possible, too. Her parents had said that people like Smelly used to live in caves where they came from, so they didn't mind. They liked it that way, she said, because it made them feel at home. Put them in a proper house and they wouldn't know what to do. The mother would cry all day and the father would drink and the kids would get belted. I agreed with her that nobody would want that, and we came to the conclusion that the reason Smelly Dragon smiled all the time was that he really was happy because they lived in a cave just like they wanted to and, because they did, his father didn't drink and belt him. And, said my friend, it's probably because he can't speak good Australian, as well. People who can't speak good Australian think that, if they smile a lot, other people will like them and be nice to them and want to come to play at their house. But who would want to go to play with a kid who lived in a cave? We decided it was hopeless. No-one would. And no-one would be allowed to, either. If they insisted on living in a cave, it was their own fault that they never had any friends.

After my friend explained the cave to me, things made a bit more sense. Suddenly, his name was perfect: Smelly Dragon. Dragons, we knew, lived in caves, and they had big teeth and strange-looking heads. True, they were green, but they were also unlike anything else we had ever seen. Dragons were different and they were fierce and nobody's friend, and it struck me that we must have somehow known about the cave all along and, rather than make up a name, we had uncovered for him his real name, the name he should have always had.

I am tempted to say I should have known better, sitting in Elisabeth's kitchen, hardly pausing for breath. When one is far from home, one sometimes does things one shouldn't; adrift, one can lose judgement. Someone like that is likely to grasp at anything offered, anything at all that floats by — reeds, mud, an upturned hull, even a dead body — anything that may offer anchor. If a whale had passed, I would have gladly been swallowed. She said something and some other space opened and, before I knew it, I had dug in my fingers as if my life depended on it.

It is also true that some tell stories much better than do

others. And remember I was young and had spent ten whole days in stories. Night after night I had heard things I would never have imagined, things I would never do in places I would never visit. And, although I couldn't have known that then, somehow I knew my life had a much smaller shape. Yet day after day, I had thought about these stories. They filled me to bursting. The real story unfolding in the world — Elisabeth, her mother and me in this house — and the different story in my head — the one I was hearing — ran parallel. I could see them both at any given moment, as if one eye only was trained on each, each eye just lens, each lens a camera. If I wished, I could shift from one to the other, but much of the daylight hours in those ten days found the stories superimposed, as if the brain is merely editor and whoever we are inside the brain wants to hold on to everything. Strangely — or perhaps not — in those ten days, once I fell into sleep, I didn't dream. Or, at least, I had no memory of dreams. Perhaps I was doing my dreaming in the day, alongside my living. Perhaps that's what her stories did, gave me a different kind of dream, or a different way, or perhaps they gave me dreams that weren't my own. And perhaps that is why I did what I did, opening my mouth like that about Smelly Dragon and his cave, thinking that a story is a story and nothing more than that, that you can just give them to whomever you meet, swap them like you'd swap any other thing. Perhaps I didn't realise that a person can't take another's dreams and exchange them for stories, no matter how much fun it is, no matter how far from home they are. I should have known that, or she should have, or Elisabeth. But I didn't. And there I was, halfway through, about to go on and tell how one summer morning, about a year after I finished primary school, Smelly Dragon slid out of his cave, clambered up the quarry face and threw himself off, flapping his arms, so the other kids said, because dragons can fly. And about to say the only other dragon I knew anything about was Puff, the magic one, and only then because we sang it at school; and how I liked to sing, but not that song, because every time we had to sing it, someone would giggle. And how if Smelly had been there we would have looked at him, but he was there anyway, in our heads; and how that song always made me feel, and that it's hard to sing when your throat is like that, although I could sing it now if they wanted me to because they probably don't know the song in France. There I was, about to say all these things when I looked at them.

It was not that I wasn't accustomed to being looked at. It was just that I was used to particular kinds of gaze, although at the time, if you had asked me about this, I would have struggled. I was used to gazes of suspicion, disapproval, scrutiny. These I could identify. I knew the face of quiet amusement. I knew smugness, too, and disbelief. I'm not sure what it was I had expected when I looked at them. I imagine now that I assumed they would take up the role of audience with the same ease I had, that a simple swap would occur. And that maybe Elisabeth's role would continue unchanged, that simply her point of focus would alter the trajectory of her gaze, that her quiet delight would be trained upon her mother's face because her mother would be captured, nodding and smiling her encouragement to me, perhaps even more highly delighted because she could see she had taught me well, so easily had I taken the stage. Whatever it was I had expected, this was not what I saw. What I saw, in the first instance, were two faces turned to me when there should have been only one. And then, in the next instant, I saw those faces were stone.

It was as if they were someone else, not Elisabeth and her mother at all. While I knew, or at least I know now, that it is impossible for people to turn into other people, this is precisely how it appeared. Suddenly, I was not sure where I was or where I had been. Everything in the room looked new and unfamiliar. The room shone with light, and the rims of all the dishes glinted. Even the surfaces of the salad leaves were glossy and their stalks and edges brilliant. It was as if it had rained, as if the cool wet summer had come indoors, and everything was now drying, jewel-like in the sun. Only there was no sun. Above the table there was a pendant light and around the table were the three of us, Elisabeth on one side of me and, directly across from me, her mother. And, for a while, nobody said a word.

Happiness is not the same as the simple absence of tears, but I suspect it is not much more. Just what it is I cannot say for I have not yet encountered it in any sustained way. It may not exist, of course. It may be that happiness is the name we give something else, that the name and the state don't quite align and that this misalignment is rarely seen for what it is. Instead, we believe that happiness is somewhere else, waiting for us, if only we were better sleuths. Or better, anyway. So we try harder, look more closely, examine everything. The world is full of clues. We may not know just what and where our happiness is but we know what it is not.

Like so many other things, it is easier to see in the appearance of its nemesis, in the way that, tucked in their beds between the lamp and wall, children turn their hands into an unfamiliar shape that throws its shadow. And their body becomes something else — now rabbit, now dingo, now swan.

Just what shape I had made in the room that night, I could not tell. I didn't recognise its shadow, the shadow of the creature I had made with my arms and my hands, the shadow that fell upon their faces and turned them to stone. What is it that turns skin to stone? What had I called up with my face and my limbs, and my breath and my words? If I had been more a child, or less of one, would I have known it?

Stones don't speak, no matter how we wish for it. Nor do they feel. My son tells me, *No, not so. There is life in stones.* I want to believe him. How many times have I held a stone in my palm and stroked it, examined it, closed my eyes, waited for … for what? Truth? A story? What kind of life is there in stone? I have collected them, lined them up on windowsills, carried them, forgotten, in my bag. I have brought them home from journeys in my hand or pocket, as if having them here will then keep part of me there, where I found them. And then I have thrown them away. Yes, stone is ancient. And, yes, it endures. But that's not enough. And what, in that, is particular to stone?

All these thoughts occurred much later, of course, along with many others. At the time, I simply looked away from Smelly Dragon and the bus and the roll and my school friends, and looked at them — Elisabeth and her mother, the Kosovars in France who don't look like Muslims — and at the evidence of our meal, the bones, the shining leaves. I saw what the light above our heads made of us, the curls of shadow beneath the eyes and mouth, the dark caves of nostrils. And I said quietly, looking away, *Forgive me*, and, pincering a leaf of baby spinach between my index and middle finger, popped it whole into my mouth.

It was imperative I have something to do. I chewed it slowly, as if it was a meditation, swallowed and looked up. I'm not sure what I'd hoped for — possibly to see them smiling at me, as they had always done when we sat here in the long evening. Nor was I sure of what I had done. What kind of shadow turns a human face to stone? And what thing in the world can make such a shadow?

As it was, Elisabeth stood and began gathering dishes. And so I stood, too, reaching for our water glasses, my hands trembling a little, so that the glasses rattled together and a clear high note rang from them. Elisabeth and I washed the dishes, exchanging only the words necessary to the task. When we turned away from the sink, her mother had gone. Despite hardly speaking at all, I hadn't heard her leave. My ears had been filled with the sounds of things below water and how they squeaked when my fingers rubbed on them as I lifted them, one by one.

On her way to bed, Elisabeth took hold of my arm and said, *Don't worry. Tomorrow will be better*, and I looked at her face, so much like that of her mother's, and I wanted to kiss it. I wanted to do something — something strong and bold and magic — but magic needs a much, much greater mind, so I nodded and smiled and turned away. It's like the shadow puppets: you have to recognise what creature it is before the shape of the hands makes sense. Back then, all I knew was that Elisabeth was wrong, and things wouldn't ever again be as they had. And I knew, too, that it was because of me, and because Smelly Dragon's face had appeared like that, and because I had to open my mouth when someone else was speaking, as if I had a right.

I think I lay for half the night with the whole story of Smelly Dragon playing in one side of my head and Elisabeth and her mother playing in the other, as if each of my eyes was in a different place. My eyes played the same things over and over until my forehead hurt. I must have slept because when I woke it was with a gasp and watching Smelly's flailing arms as he flew, dark-skinned with his white hair shining like a halo against the face of the limestone cliff.

When I recovered my breath, I did as I have told you. I crept downstairs and walked away. It was raining. And, if I had to walk all the way to Paris, then I would. For, as you have seen, the room had glowed and everything had been revealed — although it was years before I had any idea what everything was, any idea at all.

* * *

When I left Elisabeth and her mother asleep in their converted dairy in their tiny village that summer, it was because I had to. Without quite knowing how, I had somehow driven myself out. The prospect of staying, with all its reproach and awkwardness, loomed larger for me than the prospect of walking north, alone and in the rain, all the way to Paris, arriving with one address and high school French. I believed that walking would separate me from my unease, for there is something about walking that can do this, and I knew it because I had walked before. Odd things happen when you walk from place to place. People driving their cars stop, whether you ask them to or not. At least, they did then, when all this happened. And I imagine that a certain kind of person anywhere would still stop upon seeing a young woman alone on a country road. This can be difficult enough even when the weather's fine and, when you lean in through the car window, the two of you speak the same tongue. Some people just can't take no for an answer. They seem bewildered that you choose to travel in this way, so slowly, expending so much personal energy. Some change their mind as soon as they see your face suddenly too close — as if the idea, like so many, was good only at a distance. I can't imagine myself capable of frightening anyone, although how I appeared on that road between the tiny village and the next town — so early in the morning and so bedraggled — I also can't envisage.

I sat at that cafe, the very one of which Elisabeth writes. I know this because it is a small town, not as small as the village, it is true, but there was only one cafe. It is also true that towns grow. But there are places where they seem to grow more slowly or hardly at all. Or where growth occurs in other ways. There are whole peoples who make do with their history and its inconvenience — in the way that Elisabeth and her mother have remained for thirty years in the one hundred and fifty year old, abandoned, rodent-infested, sagging timber dairy. When I walked into that town, there was also only one public telephone, and it was, indeed, directly opposite the cafe.

I hesitated on the footpath. Where did she sit, that mother, Elisabeth's mother? Quiet Elisabeth with her intelligent eyes, who never reproached me for my rudeness, who stood beside me at the sink, who held my arm. Elisabeth with the cool pale cheek I should have kissed and whom, instead, I humoured and then left alone. Where did she sit, that dark-haired mother, that storyteller? If I were her, at which table, inside or out, and facing which direction? If I were her, I might watch the public telephone as if it were a magician's cabinet in which something could materialise. But I'm not.

I turned my back to the street, sitting alongside the doorway, under the narrow eave. I turned my back to the street, hunching myself over the table so that the morning sun, slanting in against the cafe's thick stone walls, would warm my shoulders, spine, the back of my skull, as one might turn one's bones before a fire. I ordered hot chocolate because I knew it came in a cup the size of a cereal bowl and I could hold it between my cold hands, close to my face so that the steam warmed my skin.

Resolve is important, but homelessness is much more powerful. I thought about finding a bus shelter, a train compartment, a flat in Paris with heating, a small balcony, its own bathroom. I even thought with some longing about Elisabeth's kitchen, the view from that window over the valley, all the black and white cows every day in the rain. I thought about navigating my way along the narrow passages, through room after room of resting theatre, rooms that made me listen with my ears and skin, as if all the players had heard my step outside the door and just shut up. Like a game of statues. And it occurred to me there, sipping at my hot chocolate, that I had never seen just where Elisabeth and her mother disappeared to at the finish of our nights, just which narrow lane they took or where they slept, that everything we did together took place in that cramped living and kitchen space with its bright lights and that, late at night, they would wander off stage and disappear.

I tried to remember all I had heard before I came here, all the images I had gathered, all the reasons I had come, that I had gone and done this thing that worried everyone because I was a girl and all alone. In my backpack, I told myself, was an old postcard, a black and white photograph of a man alone on a Parisian bridge at night. He is thin. Of course, he is wearing a fedora. He also wears a buttoned winter coat. His collar is turned up; his hands are deep in his pockets. His leading leg and coat hem blur, for he is caught mid-step. Around him, the street lamps burn. He is on his way. He is determined. And he is utterly alone.

That's me, I thought. *That has always been me. Even though I am not French. Even though I am not a man. Even though I have not yet been.*

Because I am older now, I know that it is often at the most unexpected moments that things occur. I also know that, if I had been facing into the sun, I would have seen him. I might have seen only his silhouette as he approached, the shadow he threw me, but I would have had a little warning. And, if I had had that, it would have been different when he spoke — less shock and more guardedness. We both would have seen what was about to happen.

As it was, his voice — materialising behind me as he approached as if from my most secret thoughts — made me leap in my seat. And, when I span, flinching, to see what had so crept up on me, I saw against the sun a face, itself quite taken aback at the violence of my response.

Mademoiselle, pardon me. I had no intention of —

What do you want?

Please, mademoiselle, sit down. Perhaps I can, er ...

Thank you, but I am fine. I would be grateful if you would leave me alone, please.

But your coffee —

There is no need for you to be concerned. And I turned my back on him and sat, hot chocolate dripping from the table into my lap. Never mind, I reminded myself, such stains can be removed more easily than other things.

Real life is not like a movie, no matter how much we wish it to be. The trickiest thing about happiness is that the experience doesn't fit our expectation and so we call it something else. The trickiest thing about ghosts and their shadows is, therefore, self-evident.

He hovered behind me. I could say I felt him there, but that would be untrue. Rather, I heard him, muttering. I heard his step, and heard him open the cafe door. I thought about fleeing, but to where? I was wet, cold, stained by chocolate. There were no buses or trains. I had no car. If I started out on foot, he could easily find me. Better that he gives up, disappears, goes wherever he has to go. Yes, better he leaves first, that I remain and he thinks I might sit all day, in the main street, in full view.

And then I heard voices and the door swung open again and the proprietor was upon me, taking the cup from my hands, her own arm around my shoulder, guiding me from my seat, all the while clicking her tongue and exclaiming, *You poor little cabbage, come inside where it's warm.* And over her shoulder to the man behind me, *What has happened to this country that a pretty girl, and a visitor, can be left in such a state?* And so he opened the door and I was taken in.

I have always been a foreigner. I guard this closely. I regard it, too, holding it at arm's length. I imagine that, if one belongs, foreignness in others may appear as disguise. When you live it, it is not like that all. There is no mask. But now, as then, I am accustomed to no other scrutiny. Language aside, if one has always been a foreigner, crossing one country is little different to crossing another. I say 'language aside' as if this were possible. You and I both know it is not. Without language you and I have nothing to say. Without this language, this colonising language of which my mother, with the years, grows more and more suspicious, there is no story because there is no country. The country we remember is not the country we tour. But the country we tour is not the real country either.

So, the story I am telling you could be doubly false. No, let's face it, it is doubly false. Although, I assure you, it appears as true, as I write, as any other thing. It is as true as the proprietor's plump arm was true, her firm grip, her clean tub, her bathroom door that locked. It is as true as the pink voluminous nightgown she gave me while she laundered all my clothes.

Sometimes I wonder what would have happened if I had

just kept walking or given in and accepted one of the lifts I was offered and found myself dropped on the other side of town. Or if the local mechanic's son hadn't crept up behind me or if he had taken me at my initial word and walked into the street instead of the cafe. Over dinner that evening, my clothes and me all washed and dried, he said he was home from university for the summer. My mouth twitched into a smile. I closed it around my spoon.

It is incorrect? he asked.

No, it's just — well, calling this summer seems funny to me.

He frowned a little, stirring his vegetables with his fork. *Summer. That is the correct word?*

Yes. It's the weather that's wrong. Where I come from summer is hot, not like this, and I waved my hand towards the outside.

Sometimes it is hot here, too.

Really?

Yes.

Mmm.

But this year, pfff, and he raised his chin in that particular French manner and I laughed despite myself. I leaned across the table to him feeling, for a moment, capable of anything.

Look, I said, *we are talking about the weather.*

Yes, he smiled broadly.

No, I smiled back, shaking my head. *That's not good.*

Not good?

No.

He looked away. His earnestness disarmed me. I hadn't met anyone who seemed to be as unsure in the world as I was, and all the ease that flooded me just seconds before vanished in this recognition. I looked into my plate, desperate for a sign to will it back, but all that I saw was an apology. But an apology for what? What was it I had done? He filled his mouth with potato and chewed it slowly. Then he looked at me and said, *I don't understand.* And I shrugged and said, *Neither do I.*

It was so hard not to like him. He had noticed the smile I tried to hide when he said 'summer'.

The story one desires is never the story one tells. I used to think that ability was fixed in the way one might have dark or light-coloured eyes. I can see now, at this point in the tale, just how naive I have been. There are things in the world — holes, caves — that, once you've stumbled upon, you just have to look in. And once you've seen what's inside — a snake, perhaps, flicking its tongue or the fine translucent parchment of its skin, or the white dry skeleton of some other creature — that's it. There's no going back. You've seen it. You. There, all alone. You might not tell anyone what you have discovered but it's there inside you as surely as it's in that hole.

The story I desire is a story of grand passion and betrayal. In this version, I am in Paris. I am feverish with love. You can see where this is leading. It is a well known story. Such things could happen to all of us. Not in Paris, perhaps, but does that matter? Does Paris assist or undermine us? In the story I desire, the liaison is brief and brilliant. For the rest of my life it glitters when I think of it, long after I cease to be able to walk or to see. It lasts a week before we dress and stumble, weak-kneed, into the street to meet his friends and find ourselves face to face in a basement restaurant, my lover beside me and his best friend opposite me. Beside him, his lover, staring hard at me with her older and exquisite face.

In truth, there was none of this. No week of fever, although if I had shifted the weight of any element there might have been. In truth I didn't suffer the illness of love. I suffered only the brief hot burn of three days of friendship. There was no longing; I didn't find him beautiful. When we walked in the churchyard, we did just that. When we went out to dinner it was, indeed, to eat. If he ever reached for my hand it was only to steady himself. If I ever leaned on him it was with the weakness of laughter.

But some things are true. We were in Paris. He drove us there the following day, the day after we walked behind the church and he showed me the oldest graves — babies' graves and women's graves, and the graves, too, of many young men — and I could hear nothing but the light rain on trees and feel nothing but how suddenly alone we were.

What did they die of? I asked. And he paused beside me and said nothing for a long moment and when his answer came it was almost a sigh: *Disease. Birth.*

And I thought of death and birth in the same moment, and this felled me for I was young and had never seen that these two had the same face.

All around were headstones broken down by too much time, their inscriptions partly obscured by lichen or obliterated by weather or an occasional malicious act. I read what I could and I thought, *Things don't stop; they never do. One thing just becomes another. Mother, child. Child, earth. Earth, stone. Stone into words. And then the words disappear, go back to the earth. And where do the stories come from then, when there are no more mothers to tell them? And where do the children come from then, when there are no more mothers and no more young men?*

And I knelt in the rain and scratched with my nails at the lichen. Another letter, another word. And then he was beside me, his hand on my arm. *What are you doing?* he said. *It's alive. It takes a long time to grow.*

On the drive to Paris, I spent a long time picking at the matter beneath my nails. And when we sat at the restaurant table that night, the four of us, and I listened to the men talk and laugh in the way only old friends do, and I heard what I heard, I hid my hands, laying down my cutlery and closing my fists as much as I could, as if — in those thin dark lines — lived all the shame in the world.

Of the story I desire, one other thing is true. Those three days with him, that brief hot burn, gleams like a scar, a new and shiny skin. I am not yet too old. I walk; I see. But the older I become, the more it glitters, that gap, that blink with him in another country between one departure and the next.

I am remiss, I know. I have not named him. This is my fault; my memory deserts me in particular ways. Decades on, I will remember the shape of a person's hands, but not their name. All this while, writing this, I have hoped his name will suddenly be restored. This is foolish, I know. Why should it be restored after so many years banished? No doubt, it has long since taken up some other residence, crossed over into another tale or slipped off the edge of stories altogether. If it ever returns, it will return when it chooses, possibly when it least suits me, long after this is written and when it no longer matters. I could have simply renamed him, but names are never simple.

I didn't find him beautiful, but he needs a beautiful name. I didn't find him beautiful, but there were many things I had not yet found.

The girlfriend's cigarette was thin and dark, too, and she lifted her chin to blow her smoke in a blue jet above our heads. I couldn't take my eyes off this. Her small pointed chin, her tiny nose, her long bony fingers around the stem of her glass. Each of her nails was symmetrically filed and painted a frosted pink. While my friend and his friend leaned across to one another and then back in their chairs, laughing, I kept one eye on her. This, I thought, must be what is meant by elegance.

When she caught my gaze and smiled coolly, I felt my cheeks burn, but she remained unmoved. Against the black of her shirt, her neck and wrists emerged like three white mysteries. When she placed her hand, palm up, beneath her lover's, I saw her veins blue and clear under her skin. She was like water, another element altogether, and I wondered if I could grow gills to swim untouched in the world, like her.

Suddenly, she spoke to me. *Where are you from?*

I swallowed. *Australia.*

Oh.

We met on a pavement, my friend said. *She was wet to the skin.*

The man opposite eyed me. I smiled weakly. *Really?* he said.

She had walked for hours in the rain. She had made an escape.

Were you being held against your wishes? the woman asked.

No, I replied.

Perhaps, then, it was yourself you were escaping? said her boyfriend.

Perhaps, I smiled.

Or Australia? she asked. They laughed. *Ah,* the boyfriend said, *that is always the most difficult,* and they laughed again. *I am from here,* she said. *But he,* and she stroked his arm, *is from Turkey.*

It was a narrow table. It was a small room. I tried to conjure a map of the world in the space between us, but there wasn't enough air. Where was I sitting? How far had I come? How far from his face was mine? I looked and looked, but nothing appeared: no maps to guide, no locks, no keys. Sometimes will is not enough.

He was speaking. I tried to listen. His French was good and slow, international. This suited me. He was saying, *We are a modern country now. We've worked hard.* I looked away. The hairs on the back of his wrist were dark and soft; his hand rested easy on the surface between us. The palm was broad and the fingers tapered like church candles to five clean nails. She was saying, *The people were very friendly, very hospitable, everywhere I went.* Beside me, my friend's voice: *Yes, I have heard others say so.* I couldn't look at him again, so I tried to remember his face, to bring it into being somewhere I could look — the plate, the tablecloth, my closed fist. There must have been something I had not seen: eyes, perhaps, some proportion of the mouth, his name —

yes, his name, the name that meant nothing to me, the one I couldn't recognise and which I have forgotten now, along with so many others.

Maps are thin, transparent. They are much thinner than skin, as thin as air. But, like skin, we must carry them with us. Waxy and supple, they fold themselves into us. Maps are illusions, intricate, capricious. They unfold from us quick as longing. We hold them up to read them and see nothing.

He was saying, *Kemal Ataturk was the father of modern Turkey. Before him, there was chaos. Because of him, we have great prosperity.*

This entered my ear and travelled. I felt my ribs vibrate the way earth does underfoot. Beside me again, my friend asked: *Didn't you say your mother was from the Middle East? Yes,* I said, raising my head, at last, to look at the man. *She is Armenian.*

In the story I desire, I am a warrior. I rise slowly before him and I say, *You see, you didn't kill us all,* and his mouth gapes. He is a hooked fish. He cannot look away from me. His jaw works. His eyes bulge. As I watch, his own words fill his mouth and suffocate him.

In the story I desire, I bid the others goodnight and walk away. I walk across Paris. No-one speaks to me. I walk and walk without growing tired. Some time, very late, I find myself on a bridge. Behind is a bend in the river. Ahead, lights from the shore tremble and slide on the glassy surface. The river is alive with rain. Beneath me, all that water swings away, swift and forever.

In the story I desire, he fights for his life — the way my grandfather did. But, in truth, I am no warrior — this, I'm sure, you know by now. And, because we had nowhere else to go, my friend and I slept that night on his friend's living room floor. And all night I thought of him beside his girlfriend in the next room. What were they doing in there? I strained to listen, but heard nothing from them. Surely they spoke. Why then, they must be whispering. And, if so, for what reason? What is he telling her? His version of the truth, the official Turkish version? Of how the Armenians plotted against them, an uprising that had to be put down? What is she asking him? How many Armenians died? I could hear his voice: *Not so many. They always like to exaggerate, those people.* What did they do while they said these things? Or are they the kind who do not speak, but make love without a word?

I felt his presence beside me as if it was his body, and not my friend's, that slept nearby, back discreetly turned; as if it were his soft snore against the rumble of traffic, as if it were he who mumbled and turned in dreams. And all night, wherever I looked, I saw his face as it appeared across the table when, at last, I had raised my head to look at him.

I placed my hands on my ribs, one on each side of me. First above my breast, then below. I know this place well. This is where I had been shown to breathe as I sing, one hand on each side, feeling the breath enter and exit beneath the broad muscles of the diaphragm. My belly rose and fell. I waited for something. A tremor perhaps, a movement like the one I had felt beneath his voice. I pressed my fingers lightly along the curve of these bones, my lowest ribs. There should be evidence, some surge, some small change, something I could measure, that I could point to. See, doctor, here. I am ill. This is the place where words had lodged, in Paris. Here, in this irregularity, in this pebble or this unfamiliar ridge. I waited, but beneath my hands my blood and breath shifted in and out as they'd always done. I closed my eyes. Beneath my lids, they were hot and gritty. My face burned. I saw his wrist, his smooth palm, his clean nails.

Touch me, doctor, I am ill. Under my ribs is a world I know little of. I have organs here, and here and here. I know this, for I have read in books that this is how each of us is made. I know this, for sometimes I feel them. I can give them their names. I can tell you their broad function. I speak such a rudimentary language. But you, what can you tell me? Books will tell me that under my bones lives everything that makes me: this particular piece and this. But, doctor, enlighten me. How does one piece connect to another? What is the structure in me that allows this? What is the texture of every piece, and how do we hold ourselves together? For everything about us seems either too soft or too brittle. We are the strangest of architectures. No earthquake is required, no biblical flood. Sit alone and time itself will undo us all, as will the simple fist of just one other person. And a fistful of words? A mere fistful of words and I am anonymous and burning, doctor, searching my own belly with my fingers like a faith healer, my own nails like knives. A fistful of words and I am lost and sleepless, my hands slipping eagerly through my own entrails. And for what? Slice me open and what would spill could belong anyone.

Tonight my belly feels cold and vast like an ocean. My

hands are hot. They settle on its surface like two small creatures. I am feeling my way. I am all at sea. I dive through my surface. All this is mine. It is all in place. It is self-contained and self-referential. No-one else can claim this. It feeds me, carries me, makes me who I am. It should steam, but it doesn't. It should be busy, but it isn't. It is cool and still. It is completely unfamiliar.

I heard of a man who suffered a sudden and terrible pain. For one day and one night he endured it before he was taken to a hospital. There, the doctors studied his measurements and located the site of a blockage where something in his blood had lodged, and had stopped that very force, that blood, from entering his belly. By then, it was too late. He had what they called dead gut, and there was no turning back. The damage was massive. There was nothing they could do but wait as each part of him that fed him, carried him, made him, turned itself away from him and closed down. And whoever he thought he had always been disappeared. It was quick. *And all this time there I was thinking,* he mused in his bed when he once broke the surface of the morphia, *that whatever I was existed only in my head.*

In Paris at dawn I did what I've always done. I packed my belongings and crept down the stairs. I have always adored old buildings but that morning the age of this one chilled me. That morning its being medieval meant only that all that must have happened in it was too large and impossible to imagine. This thought alone made me want to run. I felt my way down. Its corridors were wide and dim, even in daylight. The yellow floorboards had worn slick and treacherous with age. The stairwell was smooth, cold stone, and unlit. I crept further down, from the idiotic grin of one silent floor to the next, and I began to see vertically. For, on each floor, the building's layout was identical: each front door placed precisely as in the floor above; the single toilet for each floor in precisely the same place; everything was stacked and mirrored, as it is in one of those dreams in which what we try to get away from just keeps reappearing.

I visited the toilet two floors below, as far as possible from those I'd left. It was dark when I shut the door. The building was under a protection order, so no electric lights. I tried not to think about the column of plumbing above my head. I hesitated before I turned the lock, and pondered the greater danger — a human lurking in the hall or a structural collapse? Just how long can such a construction live? To what would I cling if all this ancient engineering came undone around me? The stairs wound further down, cold and dark, and finally delivered me into a small entrance hall behind the double green doors to the street. A dozen large, wheeled bins were lined up inside that hall, crowding around the foot of the stairs, so that the stench of rotting rubbish was a first and last impression as one came and went.

Dawn is always cold, even in summer. And this French summer dawn made me shiver as I stepped into it. The street, the world, was grey, mauve, edged in silver — as if the moon, and not the sun, was lighting it. White shutters made every shopfront window blind. Above them, the occasional window was open, the edge of a long pale curtain sometimes visible, wrapped as a leg or the edge of a dress might wrap itself around something solid at the end of a night. Seeing it made we want to weep. Someone was in each of these rooms, perhaps — strangers asleep, vulnerable and unafraid. I had no idea where I was going.

Jingled, invisible

As a girl, Lucine had wept and begged, but Hovsanna was unmoved. *Languages are bracelets around your wrist,* she said. And so Lucine wrestled with English, which proved much more slippery an opponent than the others. She could understand it, read and write it. But speak it? Why? This language demanded a different kind of mouth, some unnaturalness of the lower jaw, a chamber to be made of the tongue. *Lucine, Lucine,* her teacher shook her head. *I fear you will never speak English.* But Lucine shared neither this fear nor any other, except the most biblical and, therefore, respectable. She trembled at the thought of the trees of Eden, laced with serpents who speak. She imagined they spoke English, these serpents, because of the strange shape of their tongues and how they could separate their jaw to swallow their prey whole. Yes, they would have spoken English beautifully, Lucine might have thought. Once, in the hall of the monastery on top of Mount Carmel, she had seen a stuffed serpent upon the wall, stretching from one end of the hall to the other. Was this, she had wondered later, trembling in her bed, Eden's speaking snake?

And so, my mother wore several priceless bracelets. As she entered a room they jingled, invisible at her wrist, as if a bell had been rung. There is language in everything: in the way we move and in our faces, too. Even my lover says, *Your mother must have been extraordinarily beautiful; she is still a very good looking woman.*

I wear three thin silver bracelets, neither priceless nor invisible, given to me by my sister. She gave me four but one broke. When it broke, I was distressed because I wore them for the four of us, my mother, my brother, my sister and me. I never asked why she gave me four — that is simply what I made of them. I thought about having it soldered when it broke, but it would always be weak and it could break again and fall from me when I was unaware, in the street or in the sea, and I would lose it forever. So, it lies in two pieces in a small satin-lined box in my drawer.

They are soft Thai silver, finely etched, bought in another continent, in a market my sister talked about once but to which I've never been. Now I wear just three — one each for my brother, sister, mother. I am the one who thinks this way, who makes much more of everything, who sets up the world in particular ways and stakes everything. The others would laugh at me if they knew. If one of us must break, it must not be them; it can only be me.

Mother, you have made your own fate; you have no need to make fates from bangles, no need to keep safe some broken gift. But how can I be expected to have read the signs? It was, I now knew, his name that should have alerted me. It should have jingled as I heard it, jingled like your bracelets, like a bunch of keys.

I walked and walked and tried to unpick everything. The streets were full of women wearing jewellery — a pair of drop pearl earrings, an antique cluster ruby ring, a gold bracelet full of charms, many gold wedding bands and small simple crucifixes. I listened to them speak. I thought about keys. I imagined their names. I thought about going home. I wondered where that would be.

My mother was named by the ghost of her sister, Lucia. She had returned to Hovsanna in a dream, weeks before Hovsanna knew she was pregnant, and she had touched the tip of her finger to her mother's belly. And she had smiled at her mother and said one word: *Lucine*. Hovsanna awoke with her heart breaking open. She turned on her side and wept. And, in this way, my mother followed her name into the world, and filled the space her sister's ghost had made for her.

The world is full of moments like that. The ghost of my aunt Lucia, my mother's dead sister, had touched the edge of something, the very edge, of something both living and not yet quite alive, that irresistible point at which one element dissolves, unbecomes itself. At that table in Paris, there were many points like this: the rim of his glass, the prongs of my fork, the sharp corners of our chairs. And high on the wall to my right, behind all the other diners, the grey curtains' frayed hem. And behind those curtains — beyond the row of high milky windows in this basement where I'd heard what I'd heard and those words had lodged — I imagined all the feet of Paris were walking by, the sharp edge of their heels clicking past us in the rain.

I walked and walked and Paris changed to streets and

streets of golden, summer morning light, and joggers and dog-walkers and delivery vans and trucks washing the pavements down, great piles of litter swishing away into street drains. And then, as is always the case in that city, I found myself beside the thick and grey-green Seine.

It was a quiet river, much narrower and more polite than those I was used to. I couldn't see into it at all and I sat beside it, staring across its flat dull surface, understanding for the first time why people might throw themselves into rivers, just to see if they're really alive. The earthen bank beneath a row of trees I couldn't name was cold through my trousers. I leaned back against my pack and looked up into the dark green underside of those trees. There were birds up there — small, dull birds with short, shrill calls like little screams. They were hopping about in a way that made no sense to me. I could see no pattern, nor could I tell which one of them was the interloper. Their cries and their bodies seemed a tangle of distress. I closed my eyes. Through the earth, I could feel the rumble of growing traffic on the road somewhere behind me.

When I opened my eyes, the darkness above me was much less dark. The birds were gone. I blinked into the light and sat up, then gasped. My friend lay curled beside me, his cheek resting on the inside of his arm, his knees drawn up towards his chest, his face still and grave and his serious blue eyes steady upon me. For those few moments, I couldn't speak. It was impossible, like seeing a ghost. He smiled at my astonished face. *I thought you were going to walk all the way home.*

What do you mean? I managed to stammer.

Australia. And then, in response to my blankness, *Your home.*

I could hear him but I wasn't listening. I was five years old. I had missed the school bus that took me home, to the end of our long gravel street. I ran and ran but the bus didn't see me. The bus began to drive away. I watched it move slowly, away from me, down the long hill. I made a strange noise, a howling noise, as I walked. I watched the bus go down the hill. It was green. I walked after it but I suddenly knew that I was small and slow. It was green and large but it was shrinking, shrinking. I was wearing my blue dress. I vomited. The bus disappeared; it turned and disappeared. I knew it turned. I knew that, but where did it go then? I tried to remember. Inside my head I was on the bus. I was on the bus and the bus turned left. It turned left and then it went. It went along a road. The road became white. The grass and trees and houses became white. It was like I was looking at the sun. The whole world was white, was a big empty page and I was walking into it. I tried to remember the way to get home but I couldn't. There was nothing in my head. In my head was white and blinding. The houses I passed were flat and blank. I was making a noise. My legs and arms stuck out of my blue dress; they were small and brown, like wood. I walked. I walked to nothing. It was flat and white. It was the sun.

He was holding my hand. *Are you all right?*

I, I fell asleep.

I know. I'm sorry, I didn't mean to frighten you. And he stroked the back of my hand with his thumb. I watched it. It was shaped like a spoon. I wanted to suck it.

You didn't.

Later, as I waited for him, sipping coffee at a grubby pavement table outside the narrow shopfront of the cafe La Mimosa, I was overcome by a moment of both gratitude and déjà vu which caught me, breathless, like an invisible and paralysing sea. These moments are all the more strange when one is in another country and I was gripped by its wave, lifted up so that I lost my feet, turned upside down by it and deprived of air until it passed me. God, oh God, I thought. I was damp with sweat. My hand shook and I spilled the coffee. It ran across the table, a Rorschach blot I couldn't read, though I tried hard, staring at the peculiar shape of it, my heart bashing inside my chest. I set down the cup and lifted my hair from my neck with two hands. A light breeze cooled my burning skin.

I looked up. I desperately wanted nonchalance; I was in Paris. There, beyond a roof top, was the Cathedrale Notre Dame, like a handful of fingers turned up for begging and, beyond that, a hazy sky. Later, this would be remembered as an opportunity I didn't see, just as I didn't see the Turkish man's name or, all those years before, a way to get home. At the time though, I thought only that I felt sick — weak, shaky, as if I'd been given a terrible fright, sitting there in Paris on a mild summer morning, as if the world had quaked and I was the only one who felt the tremor, waiting for a man who had just kissed me on the bank of the Seine, the man whose thumb I had wanted for a moment to suck, but whose tongue I had taken into my mouth instead, my lips opening — perhaps too easily, too quickly? What did he think? — against his.

He had gone back to get his car. He would be gone a while. I had said not here, not here and pulled away, sat up, patted down my hair, glanced around. *There's no-one nearby,* he said, his voice hoarse, fervent. *I know, but ...,* I had replied, not looking at him. *You don't want me,* he asked, although it wasn't a question, his voice flat now, angry. *It's not that,* I lied, although was it a lie? My body wanted him, I could feel myself, warm, engorged, slightly open. Yes, my body wanted him, right there, on the bank of the Seine, in the shade of that unfamiliar tree, in the middle of the frantic city. And so I said, *It's not. It's ... ,* and gestured quickly with my open hands, stretched them out to show him where we were, the time of day. My eyes stung with tears. Why couldn't he see? This wasn't my country, my language. I had no home to go to, nowhere to wash and change, no bed to lie on quietly and alone and remember it, no friend to say, *No, are you mad? Tell me you didn't.* What would happen to me if I hadn't sat up, if people on the ferries passing by were squinting, *Look there, do you see them?* Shrugging their shoulders and turning away, *It's summer.*

I knew what was at stake, but it was too late. Everything had changed, already, by the time I looked at his thumb, even by the time I woke up. I had fallen asleep beneath a tree like a silly girl in a story, as if there had been an enchantment and with birds shrill and nervous in the branches above me, warning me, warning as if they knew it. It was summer, but what excuse was that? Everything was upside down. In Perth it was winter. People wore scarves and had their fires on. As for love, it could have been, and that was the worst of it. It could have been.

He caught one of my gesturing, open hands in his, pressed some money into my palm and closed my fist over it. *For coffee, over there.* He cocked his head. *I will bring the car. Wait for me.*

I have money, I said, an edge in my voice despite myself.

Take it, he said, his eyes bright, his face flushed, like a man falling ill.

I was to wait. I understood. We were on the edge of something. I understood completely. I can't plead ignorance. I knew what would happen when he returned with his car. That car I had travelled in, along the quiet roads to the outskirts of Paris, comfortable and laughing, gazing out into green. Greener than I'd ever seen, or ever been able to even imagine, thinking this must be what it is like to be happy. Dozing and waking to us whizzing down the ring roads, the buildings close together, close to us, his hands tight on the wheel. I had watched his face — his eyes a little wide and darting, his jaw clenched — and I think I knew then.

And I knew as he reached across and unlocked the door, as I sat, as he indicated left and pulled out into the traffic, turning his head once to glance over his shoulder. I knew as we drove, but still I asked, *Where are we going?* Staring out the passenger window, thinking: there is the red and white striped wrapper from the sweets we ate. That dirt on the floor is the dirt from my shoes. There is the small blue pillow I leaned my head on to sleep. But this space feels like someone else's space now, as if something in it has changed its shape, thrown off its disguise.

I know somewhere, he replied and reached with his right hand for me, resting it on my knee. And I looked at it, its dusting of fine black hairs, its spoon of thumb, looked at my own hand lifting from my lap, taking his, guiding it along my thigh. So that, hours later, when I stood beside him at the door to his sister's flat, it was already too late. It had always been too late.

She smiled widely and threw her arms around him, exclaiming, *Why didn't you let me know you were coming?* He introduced me as she ushered him in, smiling over her shoulder at me and calling out to the rest of the apartment that he was here, slipping between French and something else. She was wearing blue and later, when he fucked me again in his nephew's room, given up by the boy with a shrug and a sidelong glance, I thought of the billowing long-sleeved sheen of that blue, her loose blue trousers, the gleaming copper pots of Turkish coffee, the twirl of steam from gold rimmed bowls, handle-less and small as egg cups, her long brown fingers holding cardamom seeds, the sigh of them falling, her gold rings; the broad earthen tiles of the livingroom floor, two red silk rugs, the aqua and yellow mosaic in the courtyard wall behind the deep green fish pond, the slowly circling orange carp; her husband's thick black curly hair, the thick black curl of his eyebrows, eyelashes, the hairs of his arms; his big square hands, his lopsided white smile, its one gold tooth; how he sat back in his chair, talking with his brother-in-law while I perched, watching, as she fetched and poured and cleared away, until I excused myself to join her in the kitchen, where she asked about Australia, about where I lived and my family and where I went to school, as we washed and dried and wiped everything clean; and where she said at last, *And your family, they don't mind you taking a lover who is an Arab?* and where I looked at her not looking at me and smiled and said, *An Arab?* and where she said, *At least you're both Christian. In Lebanon it is difficult to be Christian. Is it difficult to be Arab in Australia?* to which I said nothing until she suggested we rejoin the men, to which I smiled again and said, *Thank you. You have a lovely home.*

It was only when I was on his nephew's bed and he was inside me that I thought of all these things. I closed my eyes and held on to his skin and saw everything. I saw I was expanding, that all of his body was moving in me, and that everything we had said to one another and all the places we'd been were there — the rain, the spilled chocolate, the deep clean bath and dinner plates, the graveyard with its long wet grass, the open windows of his car and the road flashing by, the wind in my face, its loudness, my sleep, the name of his friend and his girlfriend's long white neck, and *Turkey is such a beautiful country*, the stone stairwell, the walk through Paris, standing on a bridge at night, and Turkey, such a beautiful country, the river black and unstoppable beneath me and I should have known, I should have known and perhaps I did, perhaps I did and Turkey, and his hand closing mine around the money in my palm, such a beautiful country, my knee as he hooked it, the brick wall warm and sharp against my back that morning, the sun too bright in my face and his head just light I squint against and words as he came that I didn't understand and I did.

I saw the way they laughed together at the restaurant, he and his Turkish friend. I knew that, although *the Christian Arab is a different kind of Arab* (and I knew this because my mother had always told me), *Arabs and Turks are all the same people,* because she had told me that, too. And I knew then, on his nephew's bed, that in a fortnight I'd take the Paris–Calais train, just as I'd always planned — and, that, as I board he would kiss my face and the backs of both my hands and say he would see me in London as soon as I wrote. And that I never would.

Opening, closing

Now I know that, if the knife is sharp enough, nothing is as simple as butchery. In the butcher's shop of my childhood, on the butcher's block, spotless and smooth (no smear or fingerprint on the windows or the cabinet glass, and never a fly although the day bakes us flat outside, where they swarm in our eyes and the corners of our mouths and, sometimes, appalled, we breathe them in and, sometimes, where we see men on the TV wearing corks on their hats and wonder where these men live because they're not in the offices or in the cars or on the streets). In here, inside this business, in this suburb of well-ironed clothes and of big smiling mouths, this Dick and Dora country, it is always cool and always quiet — although people talk, butchers being the best at this, and knowing, after a while, everything that has happened: who has died and how, and who has gone to prison or run away, and who's been pregnant and probably to whom when no-one else is supposed to know. Here people talk, but talk quietly. The door opens and closes quietly. It is like entering a church. Everything is ordered; these men at their work, the precise work of knives and cleavers. All the lamb chops lined up and the sausages bundled tight in wide smooth sheets of white butcher's paper. It is impossible not to imagine death, all the squealing and wriggling and where all the blood goes. But there is something sacred here, the respectful way my mother and the other women speak to them, the two men with the bloodied hands who move about softly across a litter of sawdust. That clean blood smell that women know, and the way birth smells, the way it fills a room so that even in hospitals, with beds lined up in rows and privacy just a dark drawn curtain, the sharp blood smell, the clamps, the sharp steel scissors, the needles and their threads, work simply at the opening and closing of our flesh.

I know that, sometime, I will have to write about birds. I do not want to write of them. Three crows flutter down to perch on the boughs of a ghost gum outside this window. Another crow comes daily to steal our hen's eggs. Perhaps it is not another crow; perhaps it is one of these three. How could I tell?

I see this thief, this other crow, flying over our neighbours' houses, a large brown egg wedged in its beak. When, astonished, I tell people what I witness, I am not sure they believe me. Who can blame them? I hardly believe myself. When I tell my lover, he is at first amazed and then delighted being, unlike me, an admirer of crows. He takes the story as if I've handed it to him which, in a way, I have, turns it over like a treasure and says, *I'll use that in a poem.* And I wonder, *Is this what happens to all the things we tell each other?*

When I was born, an owl entered the room. My mother knew nothing of birth. She did not realise she was already in labour, that her dull pain meant my head was already at its work. When my son was being born, my mother met a magpie on my doorstep. *What is it that magpie is trying to say?* thought my mother, and they eyed one another the way the wary and uncertain do. And so my mother read the silent house, the empty yard, while I lay curled on a delivery bed, trying to become a child again, my son's face inching open my resistance to the world.

My mother has more faith than me. She knows birds are messengers, but I am not interested in their language. I have seen hawks hook ducklings from under their mother's wings. I have seen five hens tear an injured hen apart. An eagle has hovered close over my lover's sleeping face. And another has entered my brother's car and, in the following years, driven him to despair.

So, I do not want to write about birds. No-one has ever talked to me about dogs and vultures and the Caspian tigers come down from the mountains, about creatures that grow fat on the dead and the dying. Land creatures, yes, and marine creatures, too: crabs, eels, the white eyeless fish at the bottom of Lake Van. No-one has said this, so where did I discover it? From which eye witness, in which written account, in which dream, during which of my grandfather's visitations did he tell me? There are some things, Mum, like the work of birds, I do not want to write about, even though it is ordinary work. Ordinary work amongst ordinary mess, that mess we are and which we all become.

Perhaps it is simply a matter of scale. Perhaps I have a different kind of eye; perhaps I have the wrong kind. There are those who are able to fly up, way above their country, and look down, seeing everything at once. They have a tremendous eye for pattern; they understand strategy. They are good historians. I am not at all an historian. I fly up only in order to come down somewhere else, take a slow walk through a small town, sit day after day in its market square, watch a child skip in the dust. Ask me about light, yes, or scent, and I will tell you. Ask me to imagine the body of a single baby as it arcs through the air and I will do that, too. The arc of a baby flicked from the point of a bayonet. A baby is soft, its head is soft, its fontanelle. Soft as an apricot. A baby opens easily. A baby flies up easily, too. She is astonished; she sees everything. Nothing escapes her but language. She opens her mouth; she hears someone screaming. Something is not right. She flies up for a long time.

And then she flies down.

Moments before, there had been only her mother — the heat of her body, the beat of her heart, her step. She knew these things. They were all she needed to know, and she knew them well. Moments before, she had been possibility. She had not known her place in the column, nor even that the column existed. If she had not flown up, she would have kept no memory of these events, this long march. All this — the march, the men on horseback, their bayonets and swords, the screaming — mothers, babies, her own sisters — and her mother caught around the throat by the crook of an arm as she ran, her mother's feet swinging, eyes bulging, her sisters laid out on the side of the road, side by side where they had run, their skirts over their heads and their bodies sliding back and away, little by little, under the weight of the men, towards the fields where other men, interrupted in their work, watched a while before turning back to their hoes or their herds of bleating goats — all this would have come to her in some other way, if she had not flown up to see just how many women and children were all along the road behind them and all along the road ahead. If she had not flown up, maybe she would have been collected eventually, bawling and cold, from a field or a road, taken gently to a house by one of the men and given to his wife.

Sometimes a woman would put her young child down and walk on. She could not carry the child any further, not this child. This child has language; this child is heavy. He is old enough to walk, but she knows she will have to carry him. He is hungry; he is tired; he cries all the time. He sucks at her breast. Her breast is for the baby. He cries as he sucks. Whatever she gives him is never enough. Whatever he takes he takes from the baby. The baby cannot walk. The baby cannot eat anything else. The baby cannot beg for food; the baby cannot beg for water. The baby cannot yet hold out her arms and say her name. So she puts this child down and walks on.

One day, my mother put into my hands a photograph of her mother. She did it in the way she does such things — without ceremony, in passing, as if it were a plate. But there was a hesitation in her voice. *I, I found this, I thought you might like to see it*, and she walked on, the light ruffling her clothes and hair. What was it she was unsure of? I can still see my fingers pulling away from the print as if it were so fragile that I shouldn't touch it, as if it would turn to dust.

My instinct was to pull my hands away. But if I dropped it I was sure it would disintegrate. I couldn't breathe. It was as if my mother had left the room, incanted her mother's ghost and quietly ushered her in. I could feel my mouth was open. I made some noises — *oh, oh*. I looked at the size and shape and colour of this materialisation. It was too small, too sepia. I looked into the frame.

My grandmother is sitting. She is fat, like me. She has long plaits. I hear her. *When we get old*, she tells me, *we go like this.* She is sitting outside. She has sad eyes. She has a round face. Her dress is very plain. Her plaits are thick. I see the texture of her hair. It is wiry, like mine. This is a photograph I want to keep. I stare hard at her, right into her eyes. I imagine she can feel me stare at her and that she stares back. *Yes*, she says, *you are my granddaughter. You look so like me. I would know you anywhere.*

I know I will be able to hold this for just a few minutes. I never before knew I looked like anyone.

My mother's hair was black and sleek. When I was young enough she cut my hair short like a boy. I watched other girls. Their hair was blond and glossy and slipped across their backs like seals. They had a different kind of mother. Their mothers drank tea in the day and shandy in the evening and wore shorts and slacks with a low-heeled sandal. My mother would say, *Your friend has such lovely smooth hair; you should make your hair smooth.*

When I was a girl I loved to brush my beautiful mother's long black hair. *Once*, she told me, *I mistook a scorpion for my favourite black velvet ribbon.* She had reached to pick it up from the floor. The ribbon had arched its back beneath her hand.

Nothing about my mother was ever plain. She wore slim red pencil skirts and gold strapless evening dresses. I used to open her wardrobe just to look at her clothes. The cocktail dress with the full chiffon skirt in what my mother called Chinese pink. Later, the yellow and green bold-checked woollen pants suit she bought for me and which I never wore. Wherever we went, men would stare and stare at her. She wore high heels and a white broiderie anglaise frock to the beach. She sat in a deck chair, shading her eyes with her long slim fingers; her olive skin glistened. As she had never learned to swim, she never took her eyes off us.

When I was a girl, she would say on our way to the barber, *my mother wouldn't let me cut my hair. I used to plead with her. I had to wear it in two long plaits and I hated it.* And there she is, in the background of this photo. She wears a light-coloured dress tied behind at the waist, and a pair of slim white patent sandals. She is tall for her age. She is also thin. She must be nine or ten. *As God is my witness*, my grandmother tells me, *I used to be thin too. But not tall. Tall she was given by her father.*

Soon after that, my mother stopped being tall. She left school. She was fourteen. She cried. My grandmother said, *Don't be silly. Dry your eyes. I was married at your age.*

Because everything about my mother was long and graceful and because she never entered the sea or the pool, my mother seemed to me to be a cat. Somehow having a mother as elegant as a cat meant I could go barefoot and braless to skinny dip and op shop. I knew early on there was no possibility of contest. When I brushed her long glossy hair I always thought of black panthers, their yellow eyes like fierce suns.

In the photo, my mother's body is turned away from us and she looks back at the camera over her left shoulder. Even then she had that look, the one she throws back at the world, the one that dares. Already, it seems, she knew she would spend her life being looked at. My mother is seventy-five years old. Men still kiss her hand.

Once, in Paris at 3 am, when I was there for the second time, two young men stopped me as I walked slowly along la Place de la Bastille towards my hotel where I knew my mother and my son slept. I wore stout walking boots with a long winter skirt, purple-rimmed glasses and a thick coat. We had spent the evening in a tiny, brightly lit jazz cellar. Once you squeezed into your seat behind a table, it was difficult to get out. Was this why no-one else danced to the Moroccan band? My brother, wedged in beside the window, looked like he could have jumped out of his skin. Later, one of the young men in la Place de la Bastille gave me a carnation and spoke to me carefully in slurred French, and then he kissed my hand. Perhaps he does that kind of thing often, out on a Saturday night, making inelegant foreigners feel anything really is possible in their city. I imagined, for a moment, that I was as desirable as my mother and, in Paris, maybe even as exotic. I imagined I would keep the carnation, press it between two heavy books, knowing that one day soon I would doubt it ever happened. But I didn't. Two days later, as we left the hotel, I threw it away. I'm not sure why.

When my mother can't see something she knows is there, she speaks sharply in a language I don't understand. She says it means a curse on Satan's horrible face, which she sees instead of what she wants to see.

Hovsanna sees the woman put the child down on the roadside and walk on. The woman has a slow deliberateness; she performs the act without anger or haste or even resignation, her movements as smooth as if she was setting him down in front of his favourite toy. Hovsanna looks at this clearly: what does it mean? It isn't that the question speaks loudly in her heart or ear — it isn't the voice of God. It is more that it passes through her, a fleeting, familiar sensation. She feels it enter her skin like a gust. It is on her, in her, through and then gone, and she wonders simply: what was that which passed across me like a dream?

Later, she will often wish she didn't have eyes. And later, even in Jerusalem, she will often be grateful that sometimes she didn't, that sometimes she had been able to put them out.

No more breath

My mother is turning into someone I don't know. *Oh dear,*
she says, *as soon as I put something down I don't know where
it is. But ask me a question about what happened years ago and
I'll tell you, with clarity.* My mother is slowly forgetting her
English. Will all her other languages, laid down deeper, rise
to her surface? At the end of her life, will I understand her
at all? Will she die further away from me than her mother
was from her? Hovsanna in a Jerusalem hospital, cold and
still, and Lucine, my mother, running all the way from that
loud, cold stillness to their home and back again to bring
Arusiak's photograph and lay it on her mother's chest and
say, *Arusiak's here now, Mama. Arusiak's here,* and, all alone,
laying her own head on her mother's arm and hearing the
sound of no more breath, and running, running all the
empty corridors.

My mother takes four hours to fill in an order form and
make two calculations. She calls me six times that day. I
don't want to lose my mother, so I don't offer to make her
phone calls and send her faxes. I don't want to lose her, so I
listen to her struggle. I recall a visit to some of my mother's

Armenian friends on the other side of this continent, on the rainy coast where things are always green, as they should be. *And their house,* my mother exclaimed over the phone, *it's a cave of treasure.* They are exquisitely polite. The wife gives us drinks and says, *I am not the healthy young woman I once was.* And, smiling, I reply, *Well, there is fortune in growing old.* And she narrows her eyes at me across the room, so far away from her.

On 25 April, the day after Genocide memorial day, I am watching television. The Prime Minister stands at the ANZAC memorial in western Turkey and delivers a poetic and moving speech. My eyes fill with tears, and I moan a little and cover them. In this speech he talks about the heroism of the Turkish soldiers in their defence of their homeland, about the extent of their losses — sixty thousand men. I glance at my son. He raises his eyebrows at me. I lose count of how many times Kemal Ataturk is mentioned as the Father of modern Turkey. I think of my grandmother and grandfather, and all my baby aunts and uncles.

Before I went east, to the other coast, my mother said, *All these years I have wondered why they didn't leave the country when things started to go wrong. They had money.* We looked at each other. She tipped her head quizzically to one side. I waited. *They took their passports,* she sighed. *Yes,* I said, *that was the first thing they did.*

On ANZAC Day I curl over like a mollusc; the ache in my chest draws me in. I feel small and very tired; I feel like I need to wash.

Is it true that if we repeat something often enough and

loud enough it becomes the truth? The Prime Minister quotes Kemal Ataturk: the ANZACS who died and are buried on that western coast are decreed 'sons of Turkey'. My son turns my grandfather's, my mother's, my eyes to me and says, *It is amazing how they can be so friendly after we attacked them.*

I draw up my knees to my chest, lay my head and arms down. My limbs feel weak and useless. My throat hurts. I look at my Australian son with his Armenian face. I think I hear the phone ring but nobody moves. Later, when everyone is asleep, I am wandering, wandering through the house. I see the small red flash. I play the tape. The caller has said nothing, but I hear the breathing. I play it again and then once more, listening hard, as if the way someone breathes can tell us who they are, and then I erase it.

All those dumb and riotous leaves

When I left Vancouver, suddenly, all those years ago, I spent a few days staring out the window as we travelled along the southern edge of the Rockies, which rose stark and black against the sometimes blue, sometimes cloudy summer sky, and then on, into the high flat treeless plains. To be fair, I hadn't let my aunt know I was coming; I was too cowardly. If I gave her time to think, I somehow felt she would decide not to see me. So, I simply turned up, knocked on her door, watched closely her startled face. She asked me in, made tea and sandwiches, like the aunts in novels I'd read. When she asked me to stay I felt something in my chest open and my face warmed with happiness.

She lead the way up the narrow staircase, onto the small landing of the attic room. I had never been in an attic before. It was painted white and the small high window looked out into the street. The bed was clean and soft and warm and, lying there, I felt content at last, as if I had entered my favourite story, the one in which the girl, who has been lonely and afraid for such a long time, finds a safe place and someone kind.

In the morning I was again struck by how much she looked like my mother. It was hard not to stare and this made me shy. When I came to the breakfast table, just before eight, she was already dressed. She wore a bulky red jumper, a knee length dark woollen skirt, and dark, flat, soft leather shoes. Her footsteps were quiet. She poured cream into her porridge and stirred it slowly; she drank her coffee long and black. She barely looked at me and didn't say much. I said I thought I'd go to the zoo. She told me to make sure to rug up warm, just like I had always imagined an aunt should, and then she left for work.

The next day was Saturday and that's when she suggested we take a black cab downtown to shop. The streets were busy with traffic and pedestrians. The wind was cold. I drifted along behind her and stared in the windows: TVs, handbags, new season's coats. At a jeweller's she said, *I just have to go in here.* I followed her, stood just inside, looking about, as she spoke in low tones to the assistant. The shop was brightly lit, glass cabinets glinting with watches and rings. I waited. People looked at me and I grinned at them, my mouth shut tight. I peered at all the wedding bands. I drifted closer to her, strained to pick up the conversation. I wondered if she was buying me anything.

It was on the way home, in another black cab with a storm blowing up across the Bay, that she asked if I knew she was left in an orphanage and I said I did know, and she said she doesn't know what family is because it was too late when her mother came back for her and I nodded as if I understood. And that night at dinner she asked what I thought of Vancouver and I said, *It's pretty*, and she said she couldn't believe the price of a plain leather watch strap and pulled up her sleeve to show it to me.

Next morning she stirred her porridge again and told me calmly it was time for me to go. It had been nice to see me. She was glad I popped in. I packed my bag and came back down the stairs. She held out her hand. I took it. *Thank you*, I said, and I leaned in and kissed her cheek. She drew back a little; her eyes widened. I ran down the front steps and waved from the street, not turning fully but just glancing over my shoulder so she couldn't see my face, and she waved back, disappeared inside the tall timber house and closed the door.

Staring out the window at the Rockies and then on and on over the endless plains, heading east towards the Great Lakes. People in warm red jackets and bright yellow raincoats, and little prairie houses perched utterly alone without a tree or a car, sometimes even without a barn, and Montreal and Ottawa with their lights that made the night sky glow blue-white long before I knew they were there, way beyond the approaching horizon, and then the quiet undulation of low scrubby hills and bodies of water vast and cold and silver as glass. And then Niagara, and couples and families and the noise, the noise, the thundering noise and the vapour rising hundreds of metres that made me cling to the wet metal railing the way, before, people must have clung to trees and rocks and one another. Then bigger hills of New England and broader forests, rises and valleys thick with trees much more polite than the ones I knew, and the colours of the fall I had thought I had imagined in all the books I thought I'd read, all those dumb and riotous leaves that made my head feel as if it was taking on a slightly different shape, while I stitched closed my chest, quietly, staring out the window all the way from Vancouver to Boston, stitched closed that opening in me that had, so suddenly, become a hole when my aunt had spoken.

The muted September light of Boston reminds me now, long after my time there, of the softness of Melbourne — green places, where it rains a lot, and where there is, still, a British settlement architecture: two-storey bluestone with strict faces, doors dead-centre, and wide marble steps between them and the street. I spent the first two nights in the hostel's four-bed dorm with a pair of glowing Norwegian girls and a row of grimy windows that stared past a faded Stars and Stripes flapping from a flagpole screwed into the eaves over a busy grey street. Directly across the street was another grimy building fronted by another waving flag. On the third day I walked across town and caught a bus to the affluent suburbs, where wide avenues rose and fell and rose again, meeting and crossing over each other, on each side flanked by wide green lawns that sloped up to houses with shutters and attics and cars in the driveway.

It wasn't that I didn't have the telephone number. But it had been a spur-of-the-moment thing, and all the way there I had secretly hoped there'd be nobody home. So, when I found the address and stood on the street, looking up at the house and the striking green of the deep, broad, slightly shaggy front lawn, and saw the white station wagon parked near the door, I tried to imagine what I would say — *Hello, I think I'm your cousin, your father Krikor's youngest sister's child, Lucine's daughter.* I stood there, on the road, for a few minutes, trying to imagine, half-hoping someone would see me and step out onto the porch. And then, when they didn't, I walked away.

The third collision

Before I came to this house — and kept this kitchen table, even though it is too big for the room, and planted that lemon tree outside the window — I had no certainty that it is possible to rest. I had a notion that rest existed. I had seen people who seemed to have it in their lives, to be intimate with rest. I had been into their homes. I'm not talking about sleep. Sleep and rest are not the same. Unconsciousness requires only a pill. You know nothing, then you wake. No, often these people were kind to me. Sometimes they weren't, and sometimes I deserved disdain, for I was an inept guest. There were many things I didn't know, things other people seemed so much at ease with, moving into spaces with such grace, as if it were the most natural thing. During a weekend visit, I recall asking my friend's mother if I might use their toilet. And I recall, too, the astonishment on her face as she said, *You make yourself at home, do what you have to do. You don't have to ask permission.* I knew she was being kind — I heard it and felt it. She was wrong, of course, but she couldn't have known. I have always had to ask permission. I knew my place, on the edge of things.

Before I came to this house, I moved more times than I can remember, changing suburbs or schools every year or two, becoming the stranger over and over. I never built a cubby or a secret place. I would leave each back yard as I found it, without a mark upon it to show I had been there. I would open the back doors and stand on the steps, gazing out. The grass grew and then someone mowed it. In summer the light was so hard I had to shield my eyes. I stood on the steps and then I shut the door.

One year my parents bought us a tent like a tepee, and Dad helped us put it up. It was tall and pale. It filled the hot space of the back yard like a huge white sail. Each time I moved along the rear of the house, I would gaze at it through the louvre windows. As the day passed it grew whiter and whiter, blindingly white until it hurt me. At night, lying on my warm white sheet, all the louvre windows open, I could hear it flapping, flapping in the wind, all pale and wild beneath the moon. When sleep came I dreamed hot and fitful dreams. It was windy. I was alone on a beach. I looked up the coast and down the other way. There was no-one. I stepped into my tent and sat by the door. And then, by my will, I left the shore, I left this island, set sail in my tent, sailed fast on the water, heading north. And then, again by an act of will, I flew through air. I took my tent with me, peering out through the open door, my face in the wind, my ears thrumming with the loudness of it all.

When I came to this house I told myself I would never again move. Never.

I was younger then, I was used to change. I had no experience of anything else. I had built nothing. Rest, peace, these were abstract things I had never made.

Some things happen that take a lifetime — or more than that — to understand. Things so large it takes a hundred years to move back far enough from them to begin to see what they are. Sometimes you need to say *stop, just stop*. You're feeling ill. You've known you need to say this for some time. You need to find a place that's safe to stop. It's like you're travelling in a car all the time with someone else driving and you keep waiting for them to pull over so you can rest, get out and see where it is you are, but they never stop. Day night day night, they never stop. And then one day you realise that it doesn't matter how long you wait, you can wait forever, you can die waiting for that person in the front, in the driver's seat, to stop because there's no-one else there. You're the only one in the car. You're alone, you're driving, you've always been driving. You're moving fast, fast, everything is rushing past. If you could take your eyes off the road, you would see that the world alongside you is blurred and unfamiliar, but is still there alongside you. You are cutting through it. But you can't take your eyes off the road. You know that if you do, even for a moment, you will crash. And you know that, at this speed, a crash would be a spectacular thing, a real event. You see it: for an instant you play it, small and slow and superimposed. You see your car touch the edge of the road, lose its grip and catapult. It turns hugely in the air, hits the earth and bounces, bounces. You know what this would mean. Nothing would save you. Inside the car, your limbs smash against door and dashboard. But this is not what kills you. You can live without limbs.

When the car comes to rest, there is a silence. You are still strapped in. Perhaps your body is pressed against the airbag. Perhaps, when someone finally approaches, they are puzzled. You are not what they expected. Perhaps you have some broken limbs, but they look at your face and your chest and there isn't a mark on you. You know this is possible. You know something of anatomy. And you drive for a while remembering this, remembering that our bodies don't need to be in any way breached. As we lose our grip and turn in the air, so does everything that makes us. As we bounce and bounce we take it all with us: heart, brain, each inner organ smashes against the inside of us, against bones and skin, against the slippery, hidden sides of the body, the neat, contained body we present to the world.

You think about this as you drive and drive, afraid to look away from the road for a place to stop. You drive and drive and think and think and then one day you just stop. You stop the car and get out and walk. You walk to a house and you enter it. You close the door. You don't lock the car. You leave the keys in the ignition. Maybe you hope someone will steal it, but no-one ever does. How can they? No-one in their right mind would want a car like that.

When I visit my mother's house, it smells faintly of shit. We sit in her living room. She is curved into a soft lounge chair. Suddenly, in these last weeks, her spine has curled into a tight question mark. Her feet are propped on a stool beside the heater, and covered with a red checked blanket. Outside, it is May again. Winter has come early. The sky is ominous with scudding cloud. I sit beside her on the sofa. Beyond her

I see, in the dull gold light of the late afternoon, the tiny silver spears of a sun shower. The wind blows them crazily.

In here, it is Jerusalem in 1946. She tells me again about the ruby and diamond watch one of her friends stole from her at a party she hosted. Then it is 1959; she tells me every country she has lived in has been dangerous: Palestine, Singapore, Lebanon, Egypt, Ireland. I say, *But Australia's not dangerous and you've been here for forty years.* And she blinks at me.

I wheel her to the toilet, steady her onto the seat, return to flush and straighten her clothes. She refuses to wash her hands. Back in the living room, once she is settled, I say, *What are we going to do?* She grimaces with pain, shifts in the chair, tells me the bones of her pelvis are hurting against her skin. I hear a key turning in the front door lock. Her evening carer, Yvette, has arrived. She blinks at me again, says, *I don't know why this has happened to me.* Then she lifts her hand, palm open and, looking up, waves it at the ceiling, says, *Was I really so bad?*

Yvette smiles at us as she passes through the living room on her way to the kitchen.

It has nothing to do with God, Mum.

What? What do you mean? Who has it got to do with, then?

It's just in your genes.

She shakes her head a little, looks towards Yvette, who has appeared holding a tray. *I must have been very naughty.*

Yvette places the tray on my mother's lap, shrugs and says, *It's possible.* And, for a moment, we all laugh.

Driving home, I can still smell the faint stubborn odour of her excrement. I shower, wash my hair, dump all my clothes in the machine. I turn on the television, gulp two quick glasses of red and, much later, after losing myself in a stream of documentaries, fall asleep. In the night I wake up crying but I can't remember why. There is just a fragment of a song I can't quite catch, and I stumble off to bed.

A song can open space we try hard to keep closed. Perhaps that is why Mum never played the CDs I bought for her on the player we gave her one Christmas: Judy Garland, Frank Sinatra, Ella Fitzgerald, all those songs she used to sing in her soulful, quivering alto. When I look for them, thinking I will put them on the player, they are gone.

Hollow-boned, her muscles wasting, she is becoming as light as a bird. She says she likes what is happening to her hands — the prominent knuckles and translucent skin — but she doesn't like what has become of her breasts: she is as tiny and flat-chested as a girl. When I kiss her goodnight the pale rose-print doona is tucked up under her arms. They stick out from short wide sleeves, and rest like wings, her slender ulnas rising, slow and luminous, to the surface. As she speaks, I watch the skull beneath her face, her clavicles, sternum, two top ribs. Against the rose-pink pillow, her hair is a soft white shock; her eyes are small, round, grey-filmed and bright. She looks at me quizzically.

Once — how long ago was this? — she came home from months at sea with her second husband to find me ill. She had had a dream, she later said, and had woken, bolt upright and distressed. I don't remember where they were — anchored at Durban, cruising the coast of Pakistan — but she insisted. So, her husband arranged a launch and she was gone. I don't remember her arrival very clearly. I remember taking to my bed, now that she was back to look after us, now that I didn't have to try to be her anymore. I remember, too, that I didn't cook for Christmas when she was gone. Instead, I took her car keys and, unlicensed, drove the two of us — my brother and myself — to the sea. We sat on the kerb of the Scarborough Beach car park, eating hamburgers. There weren't many people around. I looked at my brother eating hungrily, and I wanted to cry. If it hadn't been Christmas and the middle of the day; if it hadn't been just the two of us; if it hadn't been so bright and hot, the cars shining.

By the time she arrived in late February, I hadn't eaten for three weeks. Every morning, I caught the bus to work, washed cars in a used-car yard, vacuumed them, painted on the tyre black, then walked to the supermarket, bought meat and vegetables, bread and milk, caught the bus home, cleaned, cooked, washed out my work clothes. I don't remember what my brother did; my sister came and went. I was eighteen years old. And then one day Mum was back, beautiful and laughing, laden with presents. And I went to my bed that night and didn't get up.

The hospital is a series of fragments, a string of short, asymmetrical beads. I wake, sleep, wake; I am in a treatment room, an ambulance, a wheelchair, a bed. It is night, day, night; I wake shaking and cold in sweat-drenched sheets. I am turned right and left. Somehow the bed and I are stripped and re-dressed. White-coated doctors come. Later, one returns alone, pulls a chair close. He is young; he leans towards me like a friend, says, *Your mother said your boyfriend recently broke off your engagement.* I stare at my hands, two dead things in my lap. *How do you feel about that?*

The day she came home, she rang my best friend's mother. And, later, she took gifts to them, had a couple of drinks. The following day, when my friend came to visit me because I was feeling ill, she told me Mum had said that, when she received my letter telling of the broken engagement — the one it had taken hours to write in its carefully casual tone — she had danced about in her husband's quarters and shouted, *I've won! I've won!* I looked at my friend, at her dark hair shining as she laughed. Then I stretched my mouth into a smile and looked at the window, at all the sunlight crashing in.

She brought me silk from China, a ruby from Ceylon, a carved sandalwood box. She showed us photos she had taken from the deck: mist-shrouded peaks; tiny forested islands; flying fish. Her clothes, hair, skin smelled like somewhere else. She padded about in soft shoes decorated with small, hexagonal mirrors; she flashed light on everything she passed.

She had been away, too, when I had met him eighteen months before. It was the first beach weather — sunny, not yet blinding — and I watched him run and dive into the churned-up sea. He was a butcher's apprentice and I liked the way he held up his hands, spread his fingers, said the saws and knives are unforgiving and that he came to the ocean to help them heal. I invited him home for a cold drink and we had sex in her double bed. By the time she returned, I was seeing him every day. I liked the way he looked when he knocked off: sawdust on his socks and boots; the clean smell of blood on his clothes; his spotless, wounded hands. I was out when she arrived that time; it hadn't occurred to me to change the sheets.

Her face was taut with righteous indignation, and I felt my own cheeks burn, couldn't meet her gaze, turned my back on her. I had been careless and now she knew something she had no business to know.

He spoke with a broad accent and a slight impediment, just like his father, and she hated it that he said 'haitch'. I started saying it too. He resented her cold disdain, her assertions that he should stay away and let me study, have a family life. Once, at the end of the week, he brought her five rump steaks that wouldn't keep much longer and that he would normally have given his mother. She eyed the blood-stained parcel. *What's this?* She opened the butcher's paper, stared at the meaty pile. Then she picked it all up and dumped it in the pedal bin, saying, *We only eat the very best cuts.*

At his house, no-one shouted. His sisters, younger than me, caught the bus to and from work and sat in their short pink dressing gowns in the evening, watching American sitcoms. His mother and father still held hands.

All that summer, between high school and university, my sister ignored him, tossing her hair and walking out of the room, her hips swinging. *What's her problem?* he would ask me. And I would shrug because what could I say? If there was a problem she had always had it. But he would watch her, his eyes half-closed and his lips pressed tight, and I'd watch him.

She's right, you know, my sister said, leaning into the

bathroom mirror, mascara wand in hand. *What do you see in him?*

What do you mean?

She shrugged. *You know. The way he looks at me.*

I blinked at her reflected face, at her wide eyes that saw only the brush as she guided it along her lashes in smooth, slow strokes, at the little gold crucifix glittering at her throat on its fine gold chain.

Anyway, she said, shoving the wand back and twisting it shut, *you can tell him I'm not interested.*

When the summer ended and university began, Mum drove me there every morning after dropping my brother at school and my sister at the station. Then she drove herself to her work. In the car, we spoke as little as possible. I stared out the window, kissed her lightly on the cheek, said *Thanks.* I went to lectures in shorts, dressed as if for the beach, and tried to hide my legs by sitting at the back. I made notes on the reading. At home, I shut my bedroom door, turned the radio on low, re-arranged the apples in the blue Chinese bowl by my bed, burned incense, alphabeticised my high school French and Literature books: Bronte, Camus, Golding, Lee. I sat on my bed, opened my file, looked at my notes, closed it again. I looked closely at all the surfaces — bedspread, walls, doorknob, carpet — and opened up the file again, stared a long time at the hieroglyphics on the page.

The ring he gave me was diamond and old-fashioned. When I showed it to Mum she screamed at me. I went to my room, slammed the door. Later, the handle turned and she said, *May I come in?* She sat beside me on the bed, took my hand.

Darling, she said, *you are a clever girl. You're at university, where you belong. You will meet boys there, your own kind.*

I don't want to meet any other boys.

You say that now, but you are young. And when we are young, things change.

I love him, Mum.

Love! You don't know love! You're seventeen years old.

I turned my face away.

I lost my mother when I was seventeen, she said. *I would have done anything not to upset her. I loved my mother.*

I took a breath. And another. Suddenly there was not enough air.

Please, she said. Something in her tone made me turn back. Her eyes were glistening. *Promise me you won't see him anymore.*

I stared at her face. I had only once seen her cry, when our father died. I wanted to say, *Oh, Mama. I love you.* I wanted to say so many things. My mouth opened but no sound came out. I shook my head slowly and looked down at her hand holding mine.

The slap made my head roll to the right and my eyes sting. Both my hands flew to my face, felt the hot welt on my cheek. She was standing now. I looked up at her, my mouth agape. Her teeth were clenched but her words were guttural and clear. *I should have done that years ago,* she said, and walked out.

I didn't know how to tell her I'd dropped out. I'd kiss her on the cheek in the mornings; I'd walk into campus with my bag and my books, so heavy with sadness, knowing I had cut myself off from something I'd always wanted but not really knowing how it had all happened.

One morning I didn't get dressed. She said, *Aren't you going to uni?*

And I said, not looking at her, *No, I've withdrawn.*

What do you mean, withdrawn?

I'm not going anymore.

Her mouth hung open. *When did you do this?*

About three weeks ago.

But I've been driving you there every day.

I know.

What have you been doing? Going to see that boy, I'll bet.

He's at work.

This was his idea.

No.

He's caused this.

I was going to fail.

Because of him.

I went to bed. I stared at the wall. I listened to them leave. I lay very still. The house was achingly silent. The occasional hum of a car passing. I got out of bed and opened my door. When she was here I closed it and opened the window, as if breathing a different stream of air would somehow break the circuit, somehow disconnect me from her anger and disappointment. But even if she didn't walk in, I waited for her to. And sometime or other I would have to step out. As if her anger were nothing. As if it weren't even there.

The following evening, when I next saw her, she said, *What are you doing here?* I wasn't sure what she meant, so I watched her dart between the kitchen and the dining table, dropping cutlery and saucepan lids onto the table and bench top. I looked at my brother, sitting small in an armchair in front of the TV. He was watching her. Then he looked at me with round, solemn eyes and I smiled a bit, looked at the screen. A quiz show. Someone asking questions about sheep.

She said, *Come to the table.*

As we ate, she said, *So. You. Idiot. What are you going to do now? Marry that boy, I suppose, and have babies.*

I stared at the pretty tablecloth she worked hard to buy us, at the food she cooked us. I pushed a forkful into the hole of my mouth and chewed. I couldn't think of a single thing to say, and I knew it wouldn't matter.

On the edge of my vision, I could see the doctor's forearms resting on his knees, his grey twill trousers, his polished black shoes. The hairs on his arms were golden in the morning light. I thought about his question: *How do you feel about that?* This time I would not be careless. I will change the sheets; I will bar the door. *Okay,* I said and shrugged. I did not look at him.

They took out my healthy appendix because they couldn't diagnose me. My mother, visiting before work or sometimes in the evenings, was insistent. Later she would say, *I told them: 'Take it out! Take it out!' And all those doctors, they looked at each other.*

And even later she would nod gravely. *People have died. It's just as well I made them do it.*

She had brought me carnations, wine-red and heady.

When I came to, she was sitting beside me. I looked up at her. Behind her head, the flowers were clots against the clean white wall. When she touched her cool hand to my cheek, and murmured, *It's all right, darling. It's all right now,* I closed my eyes. Then she sang a little song, a quiet, quivering fragment of song, and I thought then that I might live.

Now, at night all these years later, sleeping beside my lover, I am as close to alone as any of us can be. When I entered this room, this house, this dream, I thought I would meet a staircase, conventionally designed, steep but regular, with a railing to steady my hand and wide steps my feet would grasp. I expected to understand. Instead, here I am, gazing up into a joke. Who designed this? It twists away from itself and vanishes into ... what? The room is full of cordial voices. People have gone before me: I waited in the queue behind them and now I see them disappear above me, their legs climbing strongly. People are waiting politely behind me. I pull at the structure, testing it. It is sturdy. It does not budge; it will take my weight. Indeed, it is already holding a number of people. I have no choice. I have to go. But I don't know where to put my feet, my hands. I am not an ape. I am not strong enough for this. This is like climbing a mountain; this is someone's idea of a challenge. This is not what I came here for. My child is behind me. I am blocking his way. I must show him how to do it. No-one else appears afraid. I know my son will follow me. That's what children do. If I step aside, he will step aside too. Where is everyone going? The structure is like an enormous puzzle, strong timbers nailed and bound together crazily. It is a crazy, leaning, vanishing tower. Near the top, the tower is suddenly made of metal — huge cogs, anvils, hubs, anchors welded together, their surfaces slick and treacherous from use. They offer me nothing to hold; I am clinging for my life. My son is at my heel. Someone is smiling, someone who has gone ahead of me and who waits on a white mezzanine. I know that you and I and everyone who comes to this must leap. I know, now, there is no going back. This is the only way to our destination.

* * *

When I came to this house — the one I live in now — my son was smaller and it was bigger. Houses are like that, they shrink and expand the way people do. Now the house is full. It's so full it's jumping. I have to sit on the roof. I feel it quivering beneath me. This is the only place I am alone. When I'm in the house I am never alone. Never. It's this writing, of course, that has caused it all. You just write away, not knowing much, just blithely thinking you are moving towards some resolution. And now, here you are, on the roof because your house is so full of ghosts. My mother is right. There are dangerous things, things you can't change so what's the point, things better left.

From my roof, so much is visible. Garden, street, my rusting fence. My neighbours' yards with their huge terracotta pots and their wrecked cars and children's cubby houses, their washing sparse and limp on their lines. Perched here, I can see the footpath as it passes and where it ends. I can see the park with its trees and anybody walking there.

On my roof, in the evenings, the sky turns every colour. In the south, it burns with light from the top floors of the tallest city buildings. Windows appear and disappear as light is turned on and off in them. Who is in there? Planes blink, blink above our heads as if they can't believe what's happening to them. They blink and circle and rise and leave us. I hear them before and long after I see them. I don't see many stars but, when the moon is full, it sits thick as a belly, ahead of me, in the east, over the roof of the house across the road. When it is new, as it is now, it slips a low northern arc to my left. I see it often from my bathroom window when I'm there before I sleep.

From my roof I know everything that happens. I know, for instance, that the man next door once dug a grave in his back yard. He and a friend. I saw them standing over it, standing close and side by side. It was dusk. They spoke in low voices.

I rang the police. I said, *Can I come in and speak to someone.* The officer said *Sure* in an uncertain voice, and I never did because what does it matter that two men dig a hole in their back yard? I could just hear the policeman's questions, see his sceptical eyes. *Where were you standing?*

On my verandah, then I climbed up onto the roof.

The roof?

Yes.

Why were you on the roof?

I go up there to check.

To check what?

That everything is as it should be, you know, watertight, gutters clean, no cracked tiles and things.

And where were they?
Just on the other side of the fence.
And they didn't see you?
They were busy.
Doing what?
Standing there, by the hole, with shovels, talking.
What did they say?
I couldn't hear them.

Yes, officer, I am a writer. You solve crime; I make things up.

If I come to you, will you tell me about truth — the thing you say you look for as if it were hard and elemental — plunge your hands, rifle deep, pull out your prize. You want to sift truth from lies. You believe the lie will betray itself. You are sure that you will feel it.

You think, if you stare long enough, you will feel it because someone will flinch. Or blink. That's what I used to think, that it was simply a matter of time, that the longer the world stared the more nervous history became. But I was wrong. We have already waited a hundred years. Our eyes are tired, our sight is failing, our vision is burnt by a deep, inconsolable fever. Now we have stared for more than a century; now for more than two; now, ten. Soon it will be another ten. Centuries fly by as we blink, blink as if we cannot believe something.

We were patient, but we were wrong. While we waited, the truth was stolen and made a lie. The play was rewritten, the stage reset, and all the lies became the truth. And here we are, in the wings, still waiting, scrabbling around in the oily soup of this script, feeling for the prize to hold in our fist when we raise it in triumph, when we storm the stage. Look at us. Look at our angry raised fists. Open them. Where are the caves of skulls, the discarded bullets, the burned out boats, the skeletons picked clean? Look at the audience. People are leaving the auditorium. *Wait,* we say, *wait. We have so many stories.* But they turn their backs, throw their programs to the floor. *Impostors,* they spit. *We didn't pay to see this.*

September 10, 2001, the day before the planes and the towers, before the world seemed to change, on the last day of the world blind and smiling at itself, a small article appeared in our morning paper: in *the European quarter* of Istanbul, two Turkish police are killed and other passers-by are injured. A government spokesman says the twenty-five year old suicide bomber was *from a left wing group and had recently been released from prison.* I think a long time about my grandfather. And then I think about my uncles, most of whom were dead before they even grew up. I try to imagine them, but I can't. I think of my brother and my son. I think of a young man strapping explosives to his body, strapping them tight against his ribs. I think about him dressing himself, choosing his shirt. It is summer in Istanbul and he will not need a jacket. Does he wear one anyway, to assist deception? Is that wise? I think of him leaving his home, waving to his mother, walking away from her, cool, as if it were nothing, as if his heart were beating, as always, against his ordinary skin.

I know this: murder and suicide are both about logic. I imagine him walking from his room and into the street. He approaches the police. The detonator is easy in his fingers. He stands behind them as they wait to cross the road. Does he say anything? Do they turn their heads towards him? In that instant, he completes the circuit. He smiles. He completes the circuit. What could be simpler?

On the roof, no-one sees me. Sometimes I have called out to passers-by *Hey! Up here!* And sometimes they've stopped, looked back, looked around. *I'm here!* I've called, and watched as they take a few faltering steps and then walk away. *That's understandable,* I've thought. *After all, who would expect to look for a woman on a roof?* Once or twice, someone has looked up. They've looked up and looked directly at me. For a moment, we've stared directly into one another's eyes. I'm not sure what I expected but I know it wasn't that kind of look, the blank kind, the one they could have used just as easily if I were a boot or a ball. I wasn't expecting that fist of panic in my belly either. That flat curious look on their face and their head turning away. At those times, I've just watched the figures of strangers recede and disappear and thought nothing very much. I didn't think, *Am I really here?* Doubt in the solidness of things had begun a long time before that. But I can see that the doubt began to have language. I can see that now, much later. Not words yet, but a sound. It was then that I could hear it, buzzing softly in my skull. The way you hear the first note of a song gathering itself before you can sing it. Sitting there, on the roof, I began to hear the low hum of myself, like the hum of electricity, as if I was plugged into something and I didn't even know it. I started to think that maybe I was electricity, that was why they didn't see me, that I was something no-one knew was there. And then I thought that, if I went down into the street and walked among everyone as if I were just flesh and blood in a real and ordinary body, like them, maybe people would just hear a low, strange humming. And then, when they got close, very close, I would fly across to them in a bright and powerful arc. They'd know I was there then. There would be no denying me then.

* * *

In Perth, rain in summer means the days build to suffocating humidity, that thunder wakes you in the middle of the night. I skip across the surface of sleep. When I go under, the water is murky and I am flailing, I can't swim. In the mornings I wake, grateful, scattered as a handful of pebbles. In the nights I wake to the rustling of something. Is it outside my house or within? One morning, when he is still there, my son says, *I woke up last night because there were footsteps, just there*, and he points to the foot of his bed by his window. I remember the girl with the yellow hair. I say, *It was me, checking to see if the rain was coming in.* One night, when he is away, I sleep in his bed. For hours I am jerked awake by the softest sound, as if someone is moving across the room in bare feet, or is it their breath, or are they whispering?

I'm making coffee, dropping the cardamom seeds, one by one, into the gleaming copper pot, watching them fall, when he says, *I'm going to Paris.*

They make a clear, light sound — clear and light as a single thought. I hear it as if at a distance. I raise my hand to my face. *What?* I say. The scent of the seeds is strong and pink on my fingers.

Paris, my son says, *I've decided to go to Paris.*

It's a long time before I turn around. When I do, he is no longer there.

Later, I ask why. *You can't speak French,* I say. I hear my voice, strung more tightly than I'd like. He shrugs, smiling, his knife waving at me in the air.

I'll learn, he replies through a mouthful of food. He swallows, and smiles again. His big, confident, Australian smile. I look away to my food. Light is on everything, glistening.

It's not as easy as you think.

You went there.

That's why I can tell you.

Tell me what? To stay here?

I look up at him. He stares at me. I feel my face grow hot.

No, I say slowly. *But you won't find what you're looking for.*

Jesus. He almost growls it. *How do you know what I'm looking for?*

I don't know, of course, how could I? We're not the same, we're not. I put down my cutlery, put my hands in my lap. He continues to eat. My arms shake, my ribs, the long tough muscle of my diaphragm. We're not the same. Don't let him see. I take a breath to speak; I take another. I think I must have a mouth like a fish. Don't let him see. There is too much air in the room. That's what it's like here, in this country. There's too much, too much. It makes me dizzy; I lose my balance. I fall down in the street, stagger against things, hold onto walls, hold myself up. I am holding myself still. How must I look? Pathetic. Small and beaten by the most normal thing, the most predictable thing. The uncontrollable thing. Another breath, another. This is how I measure time. How I keep breathing. How I pick up my fork. How I shrug and say, *You're right.* How we smile.

Acknowledgements

I wish to thank Professor Dennis Haskell for his unfailing support in the writing of a previous version of the manuscript, originally as part of a PhD thesis at the University of Western Australia, which then became this book. Equally, I am indebted to Susan Midalia for her rigorous, sensitive editing. My thanks also to the University of Western Australia, Murdoch University and Edith Cowan University for giving me — in various ways and at various times — the opportunity to complete it.

Many people have been instrumental in the realisation of this work: my husband, Mike Williams, and my sons, Julian and Brendan Polain, who never despaired, even when I did; my brothers, Richard and Gregory Kirk, and my sister-in-law, Liis Kirk, who were always generous; and friends, colleagues and students over the years, particularly Sari Smith, Jan Teagle-Kapetas, Marion Campbell, Morgan Yasbincek, Mal McKimmie, Gail Jones, Nicholas Jose, Brenda Walker, Clinton Bell and Brendan Ritchie.

Thanks also to the Perth Armenian community, particularly to Shoushan Boyajian, and to Krikor and Shogher Jerejian for their support, to Ric Chaney for his wonderful letter from Turkey, to Zaven Stephen for his artistic courage and to Malcolm Traill, of the Albany History Collection, Albany Public Library, for his assistance.

And deepest thanks to my mother, Lucin, who is so greatly missed.

www.ingramcontent.com/pod-product-compliance
Lightning Source LLC
Chambersburg PA
CBHW030633020726
47493CB00006B/1690